THE MIRACLE STRAIN

THE MIRACLE STRAIN

MICHAEL CORDY

BANTAM PRESS

LONDON • NEW YORK • TORONTO • SYDNEY • AUCKLAND

TRANSWORLD PUBLISHERS LTD
61–63 Uxbridge Road, London W5 5SA

TRANSWORLD PUBLISHERS (AUSTRALIA) PTY LTD
15–25 Helles Avenue, Moorebank, NSW 2170

TRANSWORLD PUBLISHERS (NZ) LTD
3 William Pickering Drive, Albany, Auckland

Published 1997 by Bantam Press
a division of Transworld Publishers Ltd

A catalogue record for this book is available
from the British Library.
ISBN 0593 042204 (hardback)
0593 042433 (paperback)

Typeset in 12/14pt Garamond 3 by
Phoenix Typesetting, Ilkley, West Yorkshire.
Printed in Great Britain by
Mackays of Chatham plc, Chatham, Kent.

For Jenny

ACKNOWLEDGEMENTS

GIVING UP A GOOD JOB TO WRITE A FIRST NOVEL, JUST BECAUSE YOU have an idea in your head that won't go away, isn't easy – especially when you haven't a clue what the process entails. I was lucky because I have a wife of unusual courage and belief, who has been a genuine partner throughout the venture. Apart from offering financial and emotional support, Jenny stiffened my resolve to resign and initiated much of the early research, finding relevant magazine articles and key books, such as *Perilous Knowledge* by Tom Wilkie and *The Transformed Cell* by Steven A. Rosenberg MD.

Jenny was also my first reader, editor and story consultant. Together we learnt what did and didn't work. My harshest critic and most fanatical supporter, she was forever giving me ideas on how characters such as the Preacher could be improved, and the plot tightened. I am not being over-dramatic when I say that this book would not have been written without her.

My other major thank-you is to my parents, Betty and John Cordy, who encouraged me from the start, and in particular my mother, who provided invaluable feedback on the novel throughout the process.

For checking and correcting my understanding of genetics, I am grateful to Susan Robinson, who generously gave of her time while studying for her PhD in Biochemical Engineering at University

College London. It goes without saying that any remaining mistakes are mine alone.

I thank my other first readers: Kathryn Leach, Andrew Sutcliffe, Anna Bharier and my brother Robert Cordy for their constructive criticism. My good friends Charlie Trier and Andrew Walker for their support. My excellent agent Patrick Walsh for bringing the manuscript to the attention of the publishers, and Bill Scott-Kerr for his incisive and perceptive editing.

'They are in you and in me; they created us, body and mind; and their preservation is the ultimate rationale of our existence . . . they go by the name of genes.'

RICHARD DAWKINS

'Ah, but a man's reach should exceed his grasp or what's a heaven for.'

ROBERT BROWNING

PROLOGUE

1968. SOUTHERN JORDAN.

WAS IT REALLY TRUE? AFTER TWO THOUSAND YEARS OF WAITING, had the prophecy finally come to pass in his lifetime, during his leadership?

The Sikorsky helicopter passed over Petra, its shadow flitting like an insect over the ancient city carved into cliffs of rock. The magnificent statues and pillars glowed red in the late afternoon light, but Ezekiel De La Croix didn't look down; for once he was oblivious to the breathtaking beauty of the deserted city below him. Keeping his eyes on the horizon ahead, he searched the endless ocean of sand for the place where the helicopter would eventually set down.

One of his two fellow passengers – their dark suits as creased as his own – stirred beside him. Both men slept, exhausted from their journey. They had not rested since travelling to Geneva, where they had interrupted his board meeting at the Brotherhood's bank in order to bring him the news.

The news that would change everything. If it were true.

Checking the Rolex on his wrist, Ezekiel brushed a hand through his thin white hair. From being told what had happened, to chartering the plane to Amman and boarding the Brotherhood's waiting helicopter, it had taken a whole working day to get here, as well as costing thousands more Swiss francs than the scheduled flight. But

11

then money had never been an issue for the Brotherhood, only time; two thousand years of time.

They should be only minutes away now. He nervously twisted the ring of leadership on his finger – a blood-red ruby mounted in a cross of white gold – and reassured himself that he couldn't have come here any sooner.

The rhythmic 'whup-whup' of the rotor blades only served to heighten his tension as the helicopter sped across the sand, leaving the cliffs of Petra far behind. A further ten minutes elapsed before he finally saw what he was looking for: five lone rocks clustered in a defiant fist against the surrounding desert. He sat forward and looked down at the tallest pillar of rock, over forty feet high. Its crooked shape seemed to be beckoning him. A shiver ran down the back of his neck. The power of this place had always moved him, but today it was almost too much to bear.

The five rocks featured on few maps, and then only as a series of contour lines, never a name. Few outside the Brotherhood were aware of their existence, apart from the ancient water finders, the Nabataeans, who thousands of years ago wandered this sandy wilderness. And in more recent centuries, the nomadic Bedouin. But even these princes of the desert avoided the cluster of rocks, eschewing their meagre shade, preferring to move north to Petra. For reasons known only to themselves they felt uneasy going too close to this place they called *Asbaa El-Lah* – the fingers of God.

'Going down!' shouted the pilot above the noise of the rotors.

Ezekiel said nothing, still mesmerized by the rocks looming up below him. Parked beneath the overhang of one, he could make out three dusty Land Rovers. A fan of matting was draped from their rear bumpers to cover their tracks in the sand. Clearly other members were already here.

Ezekiel glanced at the men asleep beside him. In the world outside the Brotherhood one was an eminent American industrialist, the other a prominent Italian politician. Both were members of the six-strong Inner Circle and Ezekiel assumed that the others had already assembled by the Sacred Cavern. He wondered how many more from the Brotherhood had also been drawn here by the rumours. Even their organization's obsession with secrecy couldn't hide this.

As they neared the base of the tallest rock, the noise of the rotors seemed to increase. When the helicopter finally landed Ezekiel De La Croix threw open the door and, with a grace that belied his sixty years, leaped out onto the sun-baked ground. Squinting against the stinging grains of sand, he hurried out from under the rotors. Ahead he could see an opening in the tall rock. A man, dressed in a lightweight suit, stood beneath the cave's archway and Ezekiel immediately recognized him as Brother Michael Urquart, another member of the Inner Circle. Urquart had been a highly successful lawyer, but when Ezekiel looked at his bloated, aged frame he worried whether the Brother, like so many others in the Inner Circle, was now too old and too tired to meet the new challenges ahead.

Ezekiel extended his right hand, taking Brother Michael's in his. 'May he be saved,' Ezekiel said.

The Brother's left hand then clasped his, the two handshakes forming a cross. 'So he may save the righteous,' replied Urquart, completing the ancient greeting.

Their hands parted and Ezekiel demanded, 'Has it changed again?' His eyes dared the man to tell him his gruelling journey had been wasted.

Brother Michael's tired face broke into a smile. 'No, Father Ezekiel, it is still as you were told.'

The tension Ezekiel felt in every muscle only allowed him to return the briefest flicker of a smile. Ignoring the other two Brothers now alighting groggily from the helicopter, he patted Urquart on the shoulder and walked into the cave.

The eroded space was no different to any of the natural caves found in these parts. Some ten feet high, with a width and depth each approaching twenty feet, there were no obvious signs of man's intervention, apart from the torches resting against the walls. But ahead of him in the gloom Ezekiel was relieved to see that the concealed portal in the far wall had been opened; the heavy stone could take ages to lever aside. Walking through the opening Ezekiel De La Croix was greeted by two large gas lamps, which illuminated a mosaic floor and walls carved with the names of all those who had gone before: the thousands of Brothers who had waited in vain for this moment to arrive. In the centre of the chamber were the Great Stairs, a rough hewn spiral staircase that snaked its way two hundred feet down into the rock beneath the sands of Jordan.

Without waiting for the others Ezekiel made his way down the worn steps. He ignored the rope handrail, using the cool surface of the stone walls to steady himself as he made the descent. At the bottom the inky darkness was beaten back by flame torches, flickering in a subterranean breeze blown in from the labyrinth of air tunnels. In this pulsing light the carvings and frescoes on the low ceiling seemed to dance before him.

From here he entered the meandering passageway that led to the Sacred Cavern. Restraining himself from breaking into a run he hurried down the passage, his heels clicking on the smooth rock floor polished by countless feet before him.

Turning the last corner he heard voices and saw about ten men gathered outside the ten-foot-tall ebony doors, carved with heraldic chevrons and crosses, which guarded the cavern. Plainly the news had spread beyond the Inner Circle, and others from the Brotherhood had come to see if the rumours were true. He recognized the last two members of the Inner Circle standing by the arched doors: stout Brother Bernard Trier, nervously stroking his goatee beard, and the tall, gaunt Brother Darius. Darius had seen Ezekiel first and raised his hand to still the group, who immediately turned to their leader and fell silent.

Brushing past the assembled Brothers, Ezekiel exchanged the ritual greeting with Brother Darius.

'May he be saved.'

'So he may save the righteous.'

Their hands parted and before Ezekiel could question him Darius turned to his younger colleague, saying:

'Brother Bernard, you will wait here while I escort the Father inside. Once he has given his decision, and declared the sign genuine, you may open the doors to the others.'

Bernard opened the left door a few inches, its ancient hinges groaning in protest. Ezekiel and Darius stole inside, then the door was shut behind them, the noise of its closing echoing around the space before them.

As always when Ezekiel entered the Sacred Cavern he paused, struck by its simple grandeur: the rough, square pillars supporting the tons of rock above; the tapestries that adorned the chiselled walls; the multitude of torches and candles whose warm light gilded the hewn ceiling of rock with the appearance of beaten gold. But today his eyes moved to one place only, to the altar at the far end of the cavern.

He strode past the pillars to gain a clearer view, into the centre of the mosaic floor. The altar, with its familiar white linen cloth emblazoned with the red cross, was visible now. But his eyes focused in front of it, on the round fissure in the stone floor. The hole, no larger than a man's head, was lined with lead in the shape of a star. A two-foot flame issued from its core.

With hesitant steps Ezekiel De La Croix approached the Sacred Fire that had burned for over two thousand years. Pacing around it four times he eventually acknowledged the truth of what he saw. There could be no more doubt. The flame that had burned orange for almost twenty centuries had changed to white, a blue-white of dazzling brightness not seen since the first Messiah had walked the earth.

The tears came then. He couldn't stop them. His sense of destiny and honour too great. He had always suspected that with the passing of the second millennium the change in the Sacred Flame that heralded *Parousia* – the Second Coming – could occur. But he had never dared hope that the prophecy might come true in his lifetime. Yet now, during his leadership, it had finally come to pass. He only wished his father, and every ancestor and past member of the Brotherhood listed on the walls above, could share this moment with him – the moment to which they had dedicated their lives.

'Father Ezekiel, shall I allow in the others?' asked the hoarse voice of Brother Darius behind him.

Ezekiel turned and saw that the Brother's eyes were also wet with tears. He smiled. 'Yes my friend. Let them see what we have seen.'

Waiting by the altar, he watched the members of the Inner Circle stream into the Sacred Cavern, followed by those Brothers who had been drawn here by rumour alone. He said nothing for a while, allowing them to feast their famished eyes on the flame. When they had seen their fill he raised his arms for silence.

'My brethren, the sign is genuine. The Prophecy of Lazarus has come to pass.' Pausing, he scanned their faces, trying to meet every eye with his. 'The Messiah walks among us once more. Our long wait has ended, and the search can now begin.'

As he watched his jubilant followers, Ezekiel had only one prayer

15

on his lips: that he would live long enough to fulfil the Primary Imperative of the Brotherhood of the Second Coming. Smiling now, he raised his arms high into the air as if reaching for heaven itself.

'May he be saved,' he said, his voice booming out across the cavern.

Every face glowed with excitement as they threw their arms in the air, responding with one voice:

'So he may save the righteous.'

PART I

THE PROPHETS WITHIN

1

MIDNIGHT. 10 DECEMBER 2002. STOCKHOLM, SWEDEN.

IT CONTINUES TO SNOW. AS IT HAS DONE THROUGHOUT THE AWARD ceremony and the celebration banquet that followed. Huge flakes of white fall from the dark sky, appearing suddenly in the powerful lights that illuminate the red brick of the Stadshuset, Stockholm's City Hall. Despite the cold and the snow, a small hardy crowd has gathered by the steps to watch the Royal Couple and the Prizewinners leave.

Hands pushed deep into overcoat pockets, one broad-shouldered figure moves to the front, perhaps hoping for a better view. But as Olivia follows Dr Tom Carter out of the City Hall and into the Swedish night, she doesn't notice this watcher's unusual eyes staring at her husband.

She's too busy checking that her eight-year-old daughter buttons her red coat. 'Put your hat on too, Holly. It's freezing.'

Holly scrunches up her hazel eyes as she buttons her collar. 'It makes me feel dorky.'

'Dorky? That's a new one.' Olivia laughs and puts the Russian-style fur hat over Holly's spiky blond hair. 'Anyway, it's better to feel dorky than cold.'

'You don't look dorky, Holly,' Tom says, turning to his daughter. He crouches down to Holly's level, his blue eyes studying her like she's something in his laboratory. Then he shrugs and smiles. 'Well, perhaps a little.'

Holly giggles then, as he takes her hand and leads her down the steps.

They look good together, thinks Olivia, following behind. Their daughter is beautiful, although Olivia would never dare tell her that. Just getting Holly to forsake her jeans and Nikes and put on a dress for the ceremony had been a major achievement.

Tom turns and laughs at something Holly says, and Olivia sees his intense blue eyes soften. Looking at his tall, gangly frame and the flakes of snow resting in his unruly black hair, she is reminded how handsome he is, especially in the white tie and tails he wears beneath his cashmere coat. Both he and Jasmine deserved the Prize and Olivia feels so proud of them that she barely notices the biting cold.

At that moment Dr Jasmine Washington comes up beside her. The young computer scientist's short, styled afro is hidden beneath the hood of a bright blue cape, which looks almost electric in the spotlights. The dark skin of her elfin face contrasts with the snow, and the whites of her eyes.

Next to her is Jack Nichols, Tom's business partner at GENIUS Biotech Diagnostics. He walks straight up to her husband and pats him on the shoulder, congratulating him again. A few inches shorter than Tom, Jack is still over six foot, and powerful with it. His craggy face, complete with a crescent-shaped scar running from his left nostril to the left side of his mouth, makes him look more like a boxer than the joint head of the world's largest biotech company.

Their group is now almost complete as they make their way to the waiting limousines, their interiors lit up like carriages of old. Olivia is impressed with the size of the crowd gathered at the base of the steps. She suspects that most of them, along with the police, are focused on King Carl XVI Gustaf and Queen Silvia, whose limousine is just leaving. But more than enough flashlights focus on their small group.

'Jazz, where are the others?' asks Olivia. Tom's father and Jasmine's fiancé are also in their party.

Jasmine gestures behind her. 'They're back there talking with the guy who won the Literature prize.'

'So how does it feel being a Nobel Laureate?' Olivia asks, smiling at her old room-mate from Stanford. 'And to think, twelve or so years ago, you were worried about getting a job that would make a difference. Remember?'

Jasmine laughs, her teeth white against her skin. 'Yeah.' She shrugs dismissively, but Olivia can see how thrilled she is. Getting a scholarship to Stanford, followed by a PhD from MIT, were impressive achievements for anyone, let alone a ghetto kid from the Projects of South Central LA. But this – this was something else.

'And now you and Tom have changed the world,' says Olivia. They had as well, according to the head of the Karolinska Institute, the body that awards the Nobel Prize for Medicine and Physiology. The short, silver-haired man had hailed Tom's brainchild, born of his mastery of genetics and Jasmine's genius with protein-based computers, the most significant scientific achievement since Watson and Crick discovered the DNA double helix. One that would save countless lives. Olivia remembers how back in January 1999 Tom and Jasmine had first demonstrated the Genescope's ability to decode every human gene from just a single body cell. In one stroke their invention had made the international Human Genome Project redundant.

Jasmine reaches forward and pats Holly on the back. 'Well, my goddaughter didn't seem too impressed. I saw her yawn twice.'

'Were you yawning in the ceremony, Holly?' asks Tom with a laugh.

Holly gives a sheepish shrug and blows a snowflake off her nose. 'No. Well, a little. It was pretty long wasn't it?'

Tom turns his head and catches Olivia's eye behind him. They smile at each other and he extends his other hand behind his back, towards her. They are now some ten feet from the limousine. Their hands clasp and Tom turns round, leaning towards her like he does when he's about to kiss her.

At that moment the broad-shouldered figure steps out of the crowd in front of them.

Moving closer to Tom, Olivia doesn't see the person at first. Then out of the corner of her eye she sees the crescent-shape scar on Jack Nichols's face twist into a scowl. Why does he look so angry? So frightened?

Then time seems to slow down.

There is a sharp report, and Jack is pushing Tom away from her. Wrenching his hand out of hers, making him fall against Holly.

In that split instant she clearly sees the man in the big-shouldered coat. He's standing in front of her, pointing at where Tom was.

Where she is.

A flash comes from the man's hand and another report cracks the cold night. An enormous force hammers into her chest, pushing the air out of her lungs, throwing her onto the ground. Then another impact hits her, and another, and another, rolling her down the steps like a rag doll. She is more stunned than pained when she tries vainly to get up.

She must help Tom and Holly.

On the steps above her she can see Jasmine standing stock still, her electric blue cape dark with blood.

Olivia hears a scream and sees Holly's big hazel eyes – so like her own – staring at her with horror. She's no longer wearing her hat and Olivia's first thought is that Holly will get cold. Olivia tries to smile. She wants to reassure Holly, but she can't move and the back of her head feels wet and sticky. She suddenly realizes that this is all she can feel.

As her head rolls to one side she locks eyes with her fleeing killer, who is already fading back into the stunned crowd, and is surprised by what she sees.

Where's Tom? she thinks. He'll make everything all right.

She hears him calling her name. He sounds far, far away.

Then, like a forgotten thought, his voice is gone, and she sees and hears no more.

'OLIVIA! OLIVIA! OLIVIA!'

The more Dr Tom Carter screamed his wife's name, the harder he found it to believe what he saw. Crawling down the icy steps, he ignored the one bullet wound in his own leg. In all his years as a surgeon he had never seen so much blood from one person; the snow around Olivia's body was red with it. This couldn't be happening. Not tonight of all nights.

Everything had happened too fast – *was* happening too fast. Seconds ago he had everything. And now . . .

He could barely continue the thought. The world had gone mad. The crowd was shouting and screaming as the police tried to hold it back, forming a circle around his mini hell. Sirens screamed and cameras flashed. Jack was coming towards him, his face ashen white.

Leaning over Olivia, Tom gently brushed strands of blond hair from her face, expecting her open eyes to blink, to smile in recognition. But they just stared back at him. There was something strange about her head. With horrible detachment he realized that the back of her skull was missing.

He bent down and held her to him. 'Why?' he cried, unaware he was shouting his thoughts out loud.

Then a realization, even colder than the night, froze his heart. Jack had pushed him out of the line of fire. The killer had been aiming at *him*, not Olivia.

He should be dead, not her.

22

Guilt, like a dagger, pierced the shock, making him retch. Then through the chaos, he heard a small whimpering sound behind him.

Holly? A panic seized him, just as Jack put a hand on his shoulder.

'Holly?' he shouted, pushing his friend away, twisting round to see his bloodstained daughter being comforted by her godmother. Jasmine's face was pale beneath her dark skin. Reaching for Holly, Tom checked his daughter for injuries, all the time looking into pleading eyes, which begged him to explain what no sane man could. With a relief so fierce it made him gasp, Tom realized she was physically unhurt and squeezed her to his chest.

'It'll be OK,' he said, stroking Holly's face, putting himself between her and Olivia. 'It'll all be OK. I promise you.' He spoke the words as much for his sake as hers, and as the paramedics pushed through the circle of police, all he could hold on to was the fact that at least Holly was unharmed.

At least she was safe.

2

SATURDAY, 21 DECEMBER 2002. BOSTON, MASSACHUSETTS.

WHAT DR JASMINE WASHINGTON COULDN'T FIGURE OUT WAS WHY Tom Carter had done it, particularly so soon after the shooting. Perhaps it had something to do with the tumour the Swedish surgeon had found in Olivia's brain when examining her head wound. Whatever the reason, it made her angry.

The lawns of Mount Ashburn Cemetery were white-grey with frost, the same colour as the winter sky. A watery afternoon sun failed to warm the hundred-or-so people who had gathered in this monochrome landscape to celebrate Olivia's life, and mark her death.

Jasmine Washington stood between her goddaughter and her tall fiancé, Larry Strummer. She was relieved that for once the media were keeping a respectable distance, along with the discreet police presence, some forty yards away. In addition to Olivia's relations, GENIUS colleagues and Tom's peers from the scientific and medical community, Jasmine recognized many of the mourners. The State Governor stood alongside the Swedish Ambassador, come to show his countrymen's horror and sorrow. Next to them were teachers from South Boston Junior School, where Olivia had taught English and Music. Children from her class were there too, the same class Holly

24

attended. Some were crying, but all kept still and silent. Olivia would have been proud of them.

Jasmine felt too angry to cry for the loss of her best friend. She'd already cried more tears in the last eleven days than in all her thirty-three years. Jasmine had still been a sassy scholarship kid from the Projects when she'd first met Olivia at Stanford. Gaining a prestigious Computer Sciences scholarship to one of the top schools hadn't seemed such a big a deal at the time. As a kid her strict Baptist parents had banned her from the streets of South Central LA, so she'd built her first computer when she was eleven and spent most of her formative years prowling the cyberstreets instead. Still, it was ironic how it had been a computer error at Stanford that had roomed her with a blond, artistic WASP from Maine, majoring in English Literature. It still made Jasmine smile how, despite being opposites, they had been drawn to each other from the start.

Jasmine pulled her canary-yellow cashmere coat tighter around her shoulders. It was the brightest colour she could find for the funeral. Her friend would have approved. She watched Tom, Jack and the other pallbearers carrying Olivia's coffin to the grave. She winced with Tom as she saw how he favoured his wounded leg, no doubt welcoming the distraction of the pain. If she'd hated the last eleven days, then he must have been through the worst kind of hell. Even so, she still couldn't help feeling anger at what he'd done since the killing. Or at least what she *thought* he'd done. The evidence she'd seen in the lab this morning wasn't conclusive.

She looked down at her goddaughter, standing silent next to the slender, white-haired figure of her grandfather, Alex Carter. She wondered how the semi-retired Harvard Professor of Theology would explain why Olivia had been gunned down. It had certainly stretched her faith. The Swedish police and now the FBI had a theory that it was some anti-genetics activist trying to kill Tom. But despite having the killer on film, they still had no real idea of who he was or why he'd done it.

At least the psychiatrists had been encouraged by how well Holly was coping. Far from blotting out the horror of seeing her mother shot, she had almost perfect recall. In many ways she was more prepared to face up to what had happened than anybody. Jasmine had even heard the little girl ask Tom on more than one occasion how *he* was coping. It was this courage and the fact that Holly was doing well that made Jasmine so angry with her father.

Her eyes searched Tom's long face as she watched him and the other pallbearers lay Olivia's coffin beside the grave. The more she looked into those blue eyes, the more she saw something other than grief there: fear, or something close to it. Every time Tom looked at his daughter, Jasmine became more and more convinced that what she had found in the lab this morning had been his work.

It had to have something to do with the tumour the Swedish surgeon had found in Olivia's brain, when examining her. A tumour which by all accounts would have killed her, even if the killer's bullets hadn't. Tom's mother had died of a similar cancer about thirty years ago; Jasmine knew that. It hadn't taken a shrink to know that this was one of the main reasons Tom had applied his incredible intellect to curing the disease, not only qualifying as a surgeon at Johns Hopkins two years ahead of his peers, but then completing a PhD in genetics at Harvard with more ease than most graduate high school. Still, just because his mother and wife had similar cancers, it didn't justify running a full gene scan on Holly.

As Tom moved away from the coffin, Jasmine cast her mind back to her third year at Stanford. Over twelve years ago now. She thought she was so smart until she attended that talk given by Tom Carter MD PhD. Tom was in his early thirties then and already a force in genetics – seeing gene therapy as *the* way ahead for curing cancer and inherited disease. At the time, his company GENIUS specialized in gene-therapy trials and the development of genetically engineered proteins, such as recombinant Interleukin 2 and growth hormone. The company was relatively small, but already growing in size and reputation.

Tom's talk at Stanford had been entitled: *The use of computers in decoding the Human Genome.* Jasmine remembered how she had stifled a laugh when this tall, gangly guy with wild hair stood up to speak. But she stopped laughing as soon as he began talking about his vision of a hybrid computer/microscope that could read an individual's entire genome from the copy stored in the DNA of one body cell. The machine he was talking about would be able to decode every single one of a person's hundred thousand genes from one hair follicle. Tom Carter had wanted to do nothing less than decode the software of the human race. At that moment Jasmine had known she had to work with him, and be part of his vision.

Over three years ago they had realized that vision and created the Genescope. But now just the thought that Tom was using it on his perfectly healthy eight-year-old kid made her seethe. Whatever his reasons were, and however brilliant he was, there were times when Tom Carter could be plain stupid.

Tom limped over to them from the coffin, and stood between Alex and Holly. As the priest began to say his words, Tom reached down to take Holly's hand.

Jasmine tried to catch Tom's eye, but he would only look straight ahead at the grave. There was still time, she told herself. Even if he had run the scan, she could still stop him from reading the results.

TOM WAS OBLIVIOUS TO BOTH JASMINE'S STARE AND THE utterances from the priest at the head of the grave. He could think only of Olivia and his guilt.

Meeting Olivia and marrying her had been his greatest and most undeserved piece of good fortune. He had always been clueless with women, regarding them as a charming but confusing distraction from his work. He still couldn't understand how he had managed to attract the few girlfriends he had. All had been intelligent and most beautiful, although he had never pursued any of them. Like some problem child, they had adopted him, convinced that with enough love and affection they could make him their Mr Right. All of them had eventually given up on him.

But with the golden-haired Olivia Jane Mallory it had been different. When the precocious Jasmine Washington had introduced Tom to her room-mate, he had suddenly understood what the poets meant by love at first sight. His reaction had been a clinical definition: sweaty palms, pounding heart, loss of appetite, distraction. He had no problem identifying the symptoms, but the sickness and its cause were less scientific, more metaphysical. In one blinding moment Olivia had become as important to him as a part of his own body. From that point he had pursued her with a passion he hadn't known outside his work. In Paris eight months later, she stunned him by accepting his marriage proposal. He couldn't dance, but that night in Montmartre he forgot that, and they had danced till dawn.

27

Now she was dead. He still couldn't believe it. Only yesterday afternoon he had been in the conservatory of their home in Beacon Hill, her favourite room. He had walked in half expecting to see her reading, or tending her plants. Part of him still thought she would always be in the house; forever in the room next to the one he was in.

He felt Holly's small hand squeeze his, and looked down to see her eyes staring up at him. She was so desperately trying not to cry that if he'd felt less numb he would have cried for her.

He bent down and hugged her, trying to squeeze the pain out of her.

'I miss Mommy, Dad,' she whispered through her sobs. 'I wish the bad man hadn't killed her.'

'So do I, Holly. So do I. But she's safe now, and it's going to be OK,' he soothed in her ear. But he couldn't see how it was ever going to be OK again. He wished he could take Holly's sorrow and feel it himself. His own grief seemed too deep to reach. He felt so numb he couldn't even summon up rage for the person who had done this.

Only guilt breached his defences. When he had thanked Jack for saving his life, both of them had looked away, not meeting each other's eye; both knowing that Jack's reflexes had not only saved him, but also killed Olivia. Tom shifted his weight to his wounded leg, welcoming the pain. One bullet had passed through his leg while the others had ripped into Olivia's body.

The guilt didn't stop there. It revived memories of his mother's death, and how he had been powerless to help her. Then, after learning of Olivia's tumour, a new strain of guilt had infected him. Instinctively he hugged Holly again. Had other slower, more silent bullets already been fired? Bullets that would again miss him, this time finding an even more vulnerable target?

He had to know.

The priest continued to intone the burial service as the coffin was lowered into the ground. It was only then, as he watched the last, weak rays of the sun catch the brass handles of the casket, that Tom realized his wife was really leaving him; that the sun would never shine on Olivia again. Along with the others he and Holly threw earth into the grave and waited patiently for the priest to finish his words.

As the mourners began to move away from the grave and head

towards the cars, he felt the tug on his sleeve. He turned to see Jasmine glaring at him. She was alone, her fiancé Larry already walking off to his car. 'Tom, we need to talk. Now!'

'Can't it wait till we get to the wake?'

'No!'

Tom's father, Alex Carter, was at his side. Stern-faced beneath his mop of white hair, his piercing blue eyes glared out from behind elegant glasses. As always he looked like he was talking to one of his theology students. 'What's the problem?'

'Something I need to talk to Tom about,' said Jasmine, giving Tom a meaningful look. 'Alone!'

Tom suddenly understood. He had been in such a rush this morning he had left his lab workbench a mess, deciding to tidy it up when he returned after the wake to read the results. Jasmine must have been into GENIUS and guessed what he was doing. 'Dad, could you take Holly on to the wake. We'll follow behind you.'

Alex looked incredulous. 'You should be going to the wake with your family,' he said. 'You have to be with Holly.'

Tom raised his hand. 'Dad, please. I can't explain now.' He knelt down to Holly's level and saw her face crumple in disappointment, her eyes red-rimmed. 'Hol, I just want to talk to Jazz about something. You go home with Grampa, and I'll meet you there for the wake. OK?' He hated doing this, but he couldn't talk to Jasmine about this in front of Holly. Hugging his daughter to him, he kissed her cheek. 'We'll be right behind you. OK?'

She gave him a small nod, trying to understand.

'But Tom —' protested Alex.

'Dad, I'll explain *later*,' he said, taking Jasmine by the elbow, walking her swiftly away from the mourners waiting to offer their condolences, following her into one of the waiting limousines.

'When are you going to check the results on Holly's scan?' asked Jasmine, once she'd closed the car door.

Tom said nothing at first. He felt strangely relieved that she had found out. He hated keeping secrets. 'After the wake,' he replied eventually.

'Why did you do it, Tom?'

'I had no choice,' he said. 'I have to know.'

'Bullshit!' Jasmine replied. 'Complete bullshit. The Genescope will tell you stuff you don't want to know – or even need to know. And certainly not right now, Tom.'

TWO MILES NORTH-EAST, BEYOND THE UNIVERSITY SPRAWL OF Harvard, the campus of GENIUS Biotech Diagnostics was quiet. Most of the employees at the GENIUS head office did not work on Saturday, and certainly not in the evening. Indeed, apart from the halogen security lamps that allowed the CCTV cameras to survey the rectangular protein factories on the eastern perimeter, most of the campus was in darkness.

A few lights were visible in the vast pyramid of photo-sensitive glass that dominated the site, and served as the global headquarters of the world's largest genetics company. But not on the two top floors, which housed the commercial departments, the boardroom and most of the directors' offices, including Jack Nichols's. One light could be seen in the laboratories on the two middle levels. The only glow on the ground floor came from the reception atrium and Jasmine Washington's deserted Information Technology department, which continuously processed data from GENIUS subsidiaries around the world. As happened prior to Christmas, the small ward in the Hospital Suite on the ground floor was empty and in darkness.

At the time Tom Carter and Jasmine Washington were attending Olivia's wake there was no human presence on the GENIUS campus, save the two guards in the main gatehouse and the two who manned the CCTV monitors in the atrium of the pyramid.

However, on the second floor of the glass pyramid, in one section of the Mendel Laboratory Suite, a mind was at work. This mind belonged to an entity called DAN, so named by one of its creators from a simple anagram of the acronym for deoxyribonucleic acid: DNA.

In 1990, based on conferences held in the Eighties the most significant scientific undertaking since the Apollo Space Programme was initiated: The Human Genome Project. Its objective was simple: to identify each and every one of the hundred thousand or so genes that form the blueprint of a human being, by decoding the three thousand million letters of genetic programme in mankind's DNA. Initially led by James Watson, the co-discoverer of the structure of DNA, the Human Genome Project spanned the globe, with scientists of all

30

nationalities showing an unprecedented level of co-operation. But by the mid-Nineties, despite making major progress, rival groups began to patent the genes they found, and the vital spirit of co-operation broke down.

In early 1989 Dr Tom Carter had independently developed the concept of an instrument, half computer and half microscope, that could read DNA straight from the chromosomes in a body cell – much the same way as a checkout scanner reads a barcode. He had perfected the theoretical process by early 1990, but needed more computer power than currently existed to make his concept a reality. In that same year while delivering a lecture at Stanford he had met a young computer sciences student obsessed with protein-based processors. That student was Jasmine Washington. Within nine years they had created the Genescope and succeeded where the world's scientists had failed, identifying the location and function of each and every one of the 99,966 genes that specify a human being.

One of these Genescopes now emitted a low grumbling noise as its 'eye' scanned the three thousand million letters in the sentence of DNA it was decoding:

'ATG-AAC-GAT-ACG-CTA-TCA . . .', read the 'eye'.

DAN, like all the Genescopes at GENIUS HQ, and the more advanced GENIUS processing laboratories around the world, was a fourth-generation version. More than adequate for scanning up to fifty samples at one time. However, this evening it was concentrating on one particular body cell.

Small coloured lights, the size of cats' eyes, blinked intermittently on the black sweeping neck that housed the laser-guided electron microscope, or 'smart eye'. They signalled that the high resolution lens was shifting its scrutiny and focus from one magnetized stretch of DNA to another, reading the encoded genes like a multicoloured barcode.

The rumbling sound came from the ovoid black box that formed the body of the swan-like instrument. This contained the Genescope's 'brain': a seventh-generation bio-computer so powerful it was a 'virtual mind', mimicking the neural networks of the human brain. It was literally alive, using a primitive photo-responsive protein, bacteriorhodopsin, which made the logic gates infinitely faster and more robust than microchips. The processing unit could operate a thousand times more quickly than its most advanced electronic rival. As DAN rumbled on, its 'virtual mind' was deciphering the data being sent to it by the 'smart eye' above, translating the genetic programme of one of the organisms that created it. A human.

DAN was one of six in the Genescope facility at the back of the Mendel Suite of laboratories. Along one wall of the facility were eight workstations. Each gleaming white surface was spotless.

Save one.

Here, a spent plastic cartridge lay next to a portable microscope, and a pipette stood discarded by a bath of magnetized fluorescent dye and agarose. Nearby, a battery of small Eppendorf tubes rested alongside a glass beaker of water and a cheek swab of saliva on a glass slide; the debris left from a hastily prepared gene-scan sample.

The prepping process was standard practice. First a sample of genetic material had to be obtained; a hair follicle or cheek swab was adequate. A body cell was then isolated under the microscope before being placed in an eppendorf tube and steeped in a fluorescent magnetized gel. This highlighted the cell's twenty-three pairs of chromosomes, and dyed each of the four nucleotide bases in the DNA a different colour. Finally the dyed cell was sealed in a bio-sterile cartridge and placed in the breast of the brooding, six-foot black swan: the Genescope that even now was awake, alert, concentrating.

'CAT-ACG-TAG-GAC . . .' DAN's 'smart eye' read off the spiral ladder of DNA coiled in the cell's twenty-three pairs of chromosomes, picking off the different colours of the nucleotide bases that formed the rungs; sending the information down its long neck to its brain. DAN's brain continued to check the order of the letters – each one representing a base: cytosine; adenine; guanine; thymine, and read the genes formed by them. DAN constantly referred to its evolving database and neural net to determine the chain of amino acids being coded for by each gene; ascertaining which amino acids were in the chain, as well as how many, and in what order. The 'virtual mind', always learning, could then determine which protein would be created.

Proteins are the building blocks of life. Through them genes instruct every physiological change in an organism, determining which cells form which organs; deciding how cells should divide and die. Through them our genes make hair grow, make stomachs digest food, produce tears and saliva, even decree our natural 'deathday' as surely as our birthday.

DAN, who was now rumbling so ominously at the end of the facility, was reading the genetic inheritance of the human's cell sample in its sterile chamber; identifying every physical characteristic from colour of eyes to shape of nose; highlighting every strength, from intelligence to athleticism; predicting every disease from cystic fibrosis to cancer. The Genescope was checking for any defects outside the normal tolerances. Making sure there were no spelling mistakes that could corrupt this human's sentence of life.

Suddenly the tone of its rumbling changed and the cat's-eye lights on its neck went out one by one, until only the red stand-by light remained. The Genescope had completed its task. It had translated all three thousand million letters of this particular human's genome, checking each and every one of her 99,966 genes.

In a matter of hours the Genescope had decoded the genetic sentence of life that defined the human organism known as Holly Carter, and in so doing had read her death sentence.

TWO HOURS AND THIRTY-SIX MINUTES LATER THE WAKE WAS OVER. Tom Carter had put Holly to bed and now found himself driving Jasmine Washington into the GENIUS campus. The guards in the gatehouse waved him through, just as the headlights of his vintage Mercedes SEL picked up the chrome letters on the black corporate sign:

GENIUS Biotech Diagnostics
Your genes. Your future. Your choice.

Driving up the frosty drive he passed the silhouettes of the protein shed to his right and the small fountain in the centre of the lawns. Ahead of him the pyramid loomed large. Ignoring the underground parking lot, he pulled up by the main door.

'You still want to go through with this, don't you?' said Jasmine beside him. 'Jeez, Tom, for a smart guy, you can be really stupid.'

He turned off the ignition. 'You still don't understand. This isn't

33

something I want to do. Christ, it's the last thing I *want* to do, but I've *got* to do it. You don't have to come with me, Jazz.'

'Yeah, right.' Jasmine gave a weary sigh, getting out of the car and slamming the heavy door behind her. 'I still don't see—'

'I've told you, Jazz. The glioblastoma multiforme they found in Olivia's brain wasn't that different to my mother's astrocytoma.'

'OK, so Olivia had a brain tumour, but she's dead now, and nothing you can do will bring her back.'

Tom shook his head, too tired and numb to argue. Jasmine was brilliant but hated ambiguity. Everything was either black or white, right or wrong, like the binary code that formed the basis of most of her computer language. Even her illogical faith in God was an irrefutable fact as far as she was concerned. Walking to the main glass doors, Tom placed a hand on the DNA sensor and waited for the hiss as the doors identified him and opened.

'At least what happened meant Olivia didn't suffer for long,' Jasmine said behind him, her voice softer now.

Tom nodded at the two guards and walked across the marble floor, past the IT section to the bank of glass-fronted elevators. 'But Jazz, that's the whole point,' he said. 'I don't want to see Holly suffer in the same way my mother did, and Olivia would have done. Don't you see? We now know that those brain cancers have a complex genetic component. I ducked the bullets which killed Olivia. And I've ducked the genes that contributed to my mother's cancer, because of the healthy set I inherited from my father. But Holly might have inherited a defective set of genes from Olivia *and* a bad set from my mother – *via me*. If she has, then I need to know.'

Jasmine fell silent as Tom walked into the elevator and pressed button no. 2. The doors closed and as the elevator soared silently past the mezzanine level to the next floor, he watched the atrium and the guards shrink below him. In the quiet he could hear Jasmine's breathing.

She started to say something, then seemed to think better of it.

'Go on,' said Tom. 'Ask it!'

'OK. What if Holly *has* inherited the defective genes? What can you do about it?'

The elevator door opened and Tom stepped out into the corridor that led to a secure chrome and glass door with the legend *Mendel*

Laboratory Suite. Authorized entry only etched into it. Putting his hand into the DNA sensor, he waited for the door to recognize him.

'I reckon a gene therapy cure's about five years away. I'll make damn sure it's no longer.' he said. 'So if Holly does have a susceptibility and it surfaces in her thirties, like her mother and grandmother, then she should be OK.'

The door hissed open and they both stepped through. Lights flickered on automatically as the sensors detected their presence. The tungsten bulbs gave the impression of natural daylight as they walked past the large cryopreserve bank where live tumour samples were stored at temperatures of -180° Celsius. The empty laboratory looked eerie with nobody sitting at any of the workbenches; a pristine sea of white, chrome and glass. The only sound came from some of the instruments in the centre of the workbenches and the low hum of the air-conditioning system. Tom strained his ears for the growling sound of DAN, but of course he knew it would be silent by now, its task complete. He could see the doorway to the facility at the far right of the main lab and felt his stomach contract. He had run the test countless times before, but never on someone close to him with a suspected lethal defect.

'But what happens if the prediction's earlier, Tom? Before the five years?'

He couldn't answer that. Tom pulled open the door to the Genescope facility, revealing the six towering black swans that seemed to look down on him with malevolent pity. 'Come on!' he said. 'Let's see what DAN has to tell us.'

JASMINE LOVED THE GENESCOPES. THEY WERE HER CHILDREN. IT HAD been this instrument that had transformed GENIUS from a progressive but medium-size biotech company into a world leader.

The Genescope was so advanced when it had been launched just over three years ago that rival companies had paid to use it rather than lag behind trying to create their own. Jack Nichols had used all his marketing and venture-capital skills to ensure that the instruments were quickly licensed around the world through GENIUS-approved laboratories. As Jack liked to say, sending in a tissue sample for gene scanning was now as easy as 'sending in a film to Kodak'. Genescopes had become the gold standard for reading human software, and only last year *Time* magazine had called Tom Carter the Bill Gates of genetics.

The Genescopes' power was so awesome that even Jack was wary of them. On more than one occasion Jasmine had heard him laugh nervously and say: 'No fucking robot's going to tell me *my* sell-by date.' Always out of earshot of clients, of course.

Jasmine had been one of the first to run the test on herself. She hadn't felt particularly scared, but she had been relieved to discover there were no inherited killers waiting in her near future. But now as she followed Tom past the battery of Genescopes she understood Jack's fear; there was something deeply unsettling about a machine that knew more than you, *about* you. And tonight, she was frightened of what one of her children might tell her about Holly.

She took a seat next to DAN at the far end of the facility. She could hear a slight hum coming from the round body. The monitor on the desk next to it was dark.

She looked over at Tom. 'You sure you want to do this?'

He gave her a tight smile and nodded.

'DAN,' she said into the microphone on the black neck. Not everyone liked the name she had coined, but it had stuck and now they all called the Genescopes DAN.

Like eyes opening, the lights on the neck and the three white lights on the ovoid body came on. Then the hum shifted to a rumbling growl.

'Give me vision,' she ordered.

'DAN, I'm here too.' said Tom.

Suddenly the monitor lit up, showing the GENIUS logo of a light bulb encircled by the spiralling coils of DNA. Beneath it was the corporate motto: *Your Genes. Your Future. Your Choice.*

'*Please select menu,*' said DAN in a droning monotone, its memory recognizing the voices of its creators. She had wanted to give DAN a beautifully modulated voice; the technology existed to give the machine any voice they liked. But Tom and Jack had both preferred the unnerving machine to speak in its robotic monotone. Perhaps it helped reassure them that despite the bio-computer's organic construction the powerful Genescope was still just that: a computer.

'Give me the results menu,' said Tom. Jasmine could see his words appear as copy in the top part of the monitor, verifying that they were being received correctly.

'*What is the subject's name?*' requested the polite monotone.

'Holly Carter.' Tom enunciated his daughter's name clearly.

'*Subject found. Please choose between the options highlighted on the screen: Topline Findings. Analysis by Chromosome. Or Detail Gene Search.*'

'Topline findings, please.'

'*Certainly, Tom.*' The P.A.C.T. menu appeared on the screen as DAN talked them both through it. '*You are now in the P.A.C.T. menu. The Profile selection offers you a general description of the subject based on his or her DNA: colour of hair, skin colour, eyes, height etc. The Assets selection highlights top quartile strengths versus standard genome. For example, immunities to disease, intelligence. The Concerns selection shows bottom quartile liabilities or susceptibilities to non-life-threatening diseases. Threats highlights life-threatening defects and is protected against unauthorized access. Please make your selection.*'

Tom ignored the first three categories. 'Give me Threats, DAN.'

'*Personal password please?*'

'Discovery.'

'*Thank you, Tom. To release Threats results I need second authorized password please.*'

Jasmine sighed her reluctance before saying: 'Tree of knowledge.'

'*Thank you, Jasmine. Are you sure you want to go into Threats? Yes or No?*'

A pause.

Jasmine looked closely at her friend. Indecision was in his eyes and she could sense his urge to rush out of there and take Holly as far away as possible from the Genescope and its secrets.

'No!' she heard her own voice cut through the motionless air.

'What?' exclaimed Tom.

The lights on the Genescope blinked and the growl changed pitch for a moment.

Tom turned to her. He looked half angry and half relieved. 'What the hell are you doing?'

'C'mon Tom,' she pleaded. 'Stop this now. It's not too late.'

'*Please confirm response,*' said DAN, its deadpan delivery unfazed.

Another pause. The results just a syllable away. She saw Tom glance uncertainly at her, then back to DAN.

'Yes', said Tom eventually, his voice barely a whisper. 'Show me Threats.'

Jasmine shook her head and studied the image on the screen. DAN's grumble accelerated and then three numbers appeared on the monitor, 9, 10 and 17.

Something was wrong. The very fact that there were numbers on the screen told her that there were dangerous genetic defects in Holly's genome. Each number represented a chromosome on which errors lay.

'*Serious coding errors exist on chromosomes 9, 10 and 17,*' said DAN.

Tom looked pale when he demanded, 'Show me 17 first.'

'*Certainly, Tom.*' The screen changed again and what looked like a multicoloured spiral ladder appeared. This was a graphic representation of the dyed double helix of DNA. The heading 'Chromosome 17' topped the screen. Beside the spiral ladder were two blocks of letters formed into triples; one depicting a stretch of code from Holly's genetic sequence and the other the comparable stretch from the notional 'standard' healthy human genome. A cursor like a spotlight appeared next, moving across the screen before zeroing in on a section of the rungs on the spiral ladder.

'*Defect evident in p53 tumour suppressor gene on chromosome 17. Maternal copy corrupted and paternal copy prone to mutation,*' informed DAN. The screen cursor followed its words pointing at the mismatched base pairs on the rungs of the ladder, then highlighting the incorrect letters of code in the maternal copy of Holly's genome.

CAT-ACG-TAG-GAC, it read, the highlighted defects clearly visible.

'What does the *p53* gene do again?' asked Jasmine anxiously, more familiar with the workings of DAN than its results.

'It helps repair damaged DNA. A mutated *p53* gene is the major precursor of clonal evolution. The process that leads to cancer. But this gene alone doesn't necessarily mean Holly will get the disease. Plenty of genes are involved in this cancer; that's why it's so goddamned hard to cure. To get it definitely she has to have inherited a particular combination of defective genes on both her paternal and maternal chromosomes.'

'So she could still be OK? Yeah?'

Before Tom could answer, the screen shifted to another section of the spiral ladder. This time the heading read: 'Chromosome 9'.

'Cluster of genes vulnerable on chromosome 9. Paternal set corrupted. Maternal set missing. cer6 and cer14 at risk. inf19 and inf27 contain reverse code defect.'

Jasmine didn't need to look at Tom's ashen face to know this was bad. But before she could consider the implications DAN shifted the screen image again. 'Chromosome 10', was the new heading. The Genescope was remorseless in its diagnosis, no tact evident in its toneless revelations.

'Four ras genes on chromosome 10 have gaps in sequence. Mutation inevitable,' droned DAN as if forecasting the weather.

'Jeez!' said Jasmine under her breath.

Tom looked straight ahead and didn't speak for a moment. 'It's worse than I thought,' he said quietly. 'One overall defect is usually harmless. Even aberrations in all three chromosomes can be managed if the individual inherited a healthy set from her other parent. But Holly's got the worst combination of all. Every genetic accident that could have happened has happened.'

Tom turned to Jasmine, his blue eyes more angry than sad.

She just shook her head, and put her hand on his shoulder. There was nothing she could say.

Tom looked back at the impassive black swan. 'So, DAN, you goddamned bastard, what's your prognosis? What's going to happen to her?' She could see Tom was stoking his anger; no doubt preferring it to the alternative. Despair was so useless.

'A 99 per cent probability exists that the combination of genetic defects in genome of subject Holly Carter will eventually lead to glioblastoma multiforme.'

The two words sounded so much less frightening than 'cancer' or 'tumour', more like the Latin name of an exotic rose. But Jasmine wasn't fooled. As Tom had told her, glioblastoma multiforme was the worst kind of astrocytoma. The most virulent form of brain cancer.

She thought of Holly walking so bravely from her mother's graveside, all dressed up in her scarlet coat and black furry hat, and she felt an irrational hatred for DAN then. As if it was somehow responsible for the terrible news.

She turned to Tom who just sat there, his blue eyes blazing with Arctic fire.

'God, I'm sorry, Tom.'

'It's not over yet,' he said with his customary stubbornness. 'There's still one more question to ask it.'

Of course, she thought, the time horizon.

Despite his anger she could see Tom was almost paralysed with fear. It took him some seconds to compose himself. Then she heard him demand in a strong voice: 'DAN, you cold son of a bitch, assuming most optimistic environmental factors, and best available medical treatments, when will clonal evolution commence? And when will Holly's cancer reach its fourth and fatal stage?'

There was a momentary pause and the growl of the Genescope deepened for a few seconds.

When DAN gave its verdict Jasmine listened to its metallic words and shook her head. She was proud of her achievements. But at that moment, as she heard the fortune-teller predict her goddaughter's death, she felt almost ashamed of what she'd helped create.

3

THE SAME DAY. LONDON.

'I AM NEMESIS. MAY MY SWORD OF JUSTICE BE KEEN . . .'

Scrape went the blade across the scalp.

'May my armour of righteousness be unblemished . . .'

Scrape.

'And may my shield of faith be strong.'

The cut-throat razor skimmed through the stubbly growth, parting white foam and leaving a swathe of smooth, hairless scalp in its wake. With every stroke Maria Benariac chanted a line from her three-line mantra.

'I am Nemesis. May my sword of justice be keen,' she repeated as she continued her ritual.

When the skin on her scalp felt smooth once more she wiped the mist from the bathroom mirror to check her handiwork. Her striking, intense eyes – one blue and one brown – stared back at her. They were the only feature the surgeon hadn't been able to alter. Turning her head she noticed the tiny, decade-old scars behind her ears; the last traces from when she had made her once beautiful – too beautiful – face less remarkable.

Maria put the blade beside the sink, next to the tubs of theatrical make-up. Her fingers lingered on the razor for a second, tempted. But

41

as she glanced down at the fresh scars that criss-crossed her right thigh she decided to wait for release.

Turning her naked body, she walked out of the small bathroom into the large single-room apartment that housed everything she owned. Enjoying the feel of the cool polished wood beneath her bare feet, she glanced out of the six-foot picture window. The Thames swirled grey and cold, a hundred feet below her. She walked to the far corner of the warehouse apartment and stood beneath the exercise rings hanging from the high exposed beams.

With a leap she gripped her sinewy fingers around the rings. Well-muscled forearms tensed as they took up the weight of her body, lifting it high off the ground until the waist was level with the hands, and the elbows locked the arms rigid. Then she extended her legs straight out in front, forming a perfect right angle with her naked taut stomach.

'One . . . two . . . three . . .' she counted under her breath, her eyes fixed on the wall ahead of her. She didn't pause to rest for a second, as she performed her exercises.

'. . . Fifteen . . . sixteen . . . seventeen . . .'

With each grooved repetition the only visible signs of effort were the small rivulets of sweat that coursed down her sculptured back, and an almost imperceptible shake of the hands.

'. . . Forty-eight. . . forty-nine . . . fifty.'

Eventually she allowed herself a smile of triumph, and released her grip on the rings. Bracing her legs for the drop, she landed catlike on the polished floor. With barely a pause she walked over to the full-length mirror and appraised the naked body in her view.

She studied her tall physique carefully: the shaven head; the uncommonly broad shoulders; the powerful arms; the minute waist, boyish hips and long tapered legs. There was no vanity in her gaze, only objective evaluation, as if checking the condition of a valued instrument or weapon. This dawn inspection was no different to that carried out every morning and today, as with most days, she was satisfied. At thirty-five years of age there was not an ounce of fat on her body and the muscles were as supple as they were powerful. The only blemishes were the scars: the tiny ones behind her ears, the raised cross-shaped scar on the underside of her right forearm, a cross-hatch of self-inflicted cuts on her right thigh, and the two anchor-shaped scars beneath each nipple. These marked where her once full breasts had been removed, leaving androgynous mounds that no longer hampered movement, or drew unwelcome glances.

After evaluating her body Maria Benariac turned and checked her eyrie. The tall room on the top storey of the old warehouse was a throwback to the late Eighties, when young professionals from the City bought up converted properties in the once unfashionable East End because they were cheap and close to their work. But the room was anything but a yuppie pad. An interior designer might have called the space minimalist, but sparse was a better description.

She walked to the panel of four switches by the window.

Click-click. The first naked hundred-watt light bulb hanging from the ceiling was turned off, then on again.

Click-click. The same with the second light bulb.

Then the third and the fourth.

Once she was satisfied all were in full working order, she continued the next stage of her daily ritual. Walking round the perimeter of the room she turned on each of the six strategically placed spotlights. When all were lit she walked to the middle of the room and studied the angle of their beams, checking that not one corner of the room was in shadow. She adjusted two of the lamps, and when she was finally satisfied that all darkness had been banished she surveyed the rest of her apartment, reassuring herself that everything was in place.

Moving to the single bed in the corner opposite the exercise equipment, she straightened the crucifix on the wall above her, then genuflected in front of it. Given to her by the Father after he had taken her away from the Corsican orphanage, the wooden crucifix was the only decoration on the pristine white walls.

Next, she ran her eyes over the bookcase. There was only one book on the top shelf, the Bible. On the next shelf were six separate modules of cassette tapes and a Sony Walkman. Five of the modules were labelled with the name of a language, whereas the sixth was marked 'Voice Exercises'. The bottom shelf contained an extensive range of reference CD-ROMs. All were in their designated place.

Her gaze shifted to the right, taking in the window, and a simple wooden desk and chair. A laptop computer and telephone sat neatly on the desk, both linked to a separate phone socket in the white wall behind. Also on the desk was a watch and a thin manila folder. On the floor beside it lay a neat stack of similar, more faded folders, at least sixty tall. All had their corners clipped like expired passports. All except for the one at the top. This and the file on the desk were still unmarked and intact. But it was the one on top of the pile that her eyes went to, causing her to sigh.

Next, she did an about-turn and let her eyes quickly scan the recess that housed the modest kitchenette, ignoring the adjacent bathroom door, coming to rest on the main door of the apartment. She visually checked all four locks on the steel door, then walked to the vast oak cupboard beside it.

She opened it, revealing its two distinct roles. The left-hand side acted as a wardrobe. Here men's suits hung neatly from a rail alongside women's dresses. Above them an array of exquisite human-hair wigs – some short, some long. On the floor, six pairs of men's and women's shoes, all the same size, were lined up in regimented rows.

But it was the right-hand side of the cupboard that attracted most of her scrutiny. This was essentially a tool rack, similar to those found on the walls of many a suburban garage. But these tools were not used to perform household DIY tasks, or cultivate gardens.

On the top level three knives hung on specially designed pegs. Like exhibits in a museum they were ordered from left to right in ascending order of size. Although clean and in good condition, the worn handles attested to their frequent use. To the right of this trio was a kukri, the traditional curved knife used by the Gurkha soldiers of Nepal. She caressed each of the knives in turn, thrilling to the keenness of their blades.

Beneath the kukri was a lethal nun-tchaka: two shafts of wood, each a foot long, linked by a chain. The tip of each pale wooden shaft was heavily stained a deep bloody red. A garrotte hung from the same peg like a discarded necktie. On the lower level were three guns; a ceramic Glock 9mm semi-automatic handgun capable of evading metal detectors, a SIG Sauer pistol, and a Heckler Koch sub-machine-gun. At the bottom, lying horizontal in specially designed cradles, were a precision long-range sniper rifle and a pump-action shotgun. Among all these articles were neatly labelled drawers and shelves laden with accessories and ammunition.

Maria ran her hands sensuously over her charges, rubbing away a smear on the barrel of the oily Heckler Koch, and straightening a magazine clip beneath the SIG.

When she was satisfied everything was in order she padded across the wooden floor, back to the bathroom. In here she turned on the shower and stood under the warm, steady flow. She took a bar of coal-tar soap from the dish and scrubbed her skin till it felt raw. She used the same bar to lather her shaved head, blinking away the stinging suds. And as her muscles relaxed she surrendered to her feelings of anger and shame. And again she considered the scientist who had been preying on her mind since Stockholm.

It was ironic that she had made her first-ever mistake with the target she regarded as the most dangerous. All the others were clear-cut demons: the gun dealers, the blaspheming movie producers, the crooked TV evangelists, the bent mob lawyers and drug barons. With them the face of the devil was clear to see and easy to eradicate. But ever since the Father had given her the manila folder containing the details on Dr Tom Carter, she had known he was different. His evil was far more powerful and insidious than any of the others she had dispatched. Society actually regarded his blaspheming genetics as good. It even saw fit to honour him as a saviour. And Maria knew that there could be no worse evil than that which effortlessly masqueraded in the trappings of righteousness.

Maria felt the rage build inside her. She was Nemesis. She did not make mistakes. She had intended the kill to be public on the night of Dr Carter's greatest triumph, to show the world the hollowness of his achievements. It was supposed to be a surgical strike, with her gone long before the atheist's body even hit the ground. Instead his colleague had pushed the target aside, and the wife had taken the bullets.

She rubbed the soap harder into her skin. She should have neutralized his colleague, Jack Nichols. The man had been a hero when he'd been in the FBI. It was Special Agent Jack Nichols who had stopped Happy Sam, the serial killer who cut the mouths out of his 'smiling' victims in order to 'capture their happiness'. She knew all this. She could see that crescent-shaped scar clearly on his face; the same scar that Jack Nichols had received from the killer just before breaking his neck. No, she should definitely have factored in the possibility of the ex-agent helping his friend. That was amateurish. Unforgivable.

Maria turned off the shower, picked a coarse towel from the rail and roughly dried herself. When she had finished she walked naked to the desk and picked up the manila folder. She opened it and glanced at the photograph of the next Righteous Kill.

She reached for the stack of similar files on the floor, all but one with their corners clipped, all but one successfully terminated. She picked up the one intact folder from the top. Opening it she stared at the face of Tom Carter; her only failure. The piercing blue eyes seemed to stare back at her from under his thick thatch of unruly black hair. The strong jaw gave his long face a stubborn cast that made her even more determined to stop him. She desperately wanted to finish what she'd started, but knew it hadn't been sanctioned. Still, she could at least visit Dr Carter and make him realize his punishment had only been postponed – not cancelled. She checked the time on the watch by the phone. She'd have to hurry if she was to catch the Concorde flight.

Reluctantly she put Dr Carter's folder back on the stack. Opening it stirred up all the old anxieties and her fingers began to pick at the fresh, livid scars on her thigh. Her picking became more agitated as she recalled the humiliation when Brother Bernard and the Father had learnt of her failure; Nemesis's *first* failure. And how Brother Bernard had rebuked her.

She turned, walked back to the crucifix and knelt before it. Her quick prayer was a simple one; that after completing next month's Righteous Kill in Manhattan, the Father would give her another chance to finish the scientist.

4

BEACON HILL, BOSTON.

THE NEXT MORNING TOM CARTER WOKE EARLY. HE REACHED across the large bed to Olivia. Only when he felt the cool expanse of unoccupied sheet did he remember his wife was dead. It had been his first waking thought every morning since the shooting, and he wondered if it would continue for ever. He opened bleary eyes and watched the clock glowing on the bedside table. 5:16 a.m. Then the second nightmare pierced his consciousness.

How long was a year anyway? Fifty-two weeks? Three hundred and sixty-five days? Eight thousand seven hundred and sixty hours? However he put it he couldn't make it sound longer than it was, and it wasn't long enough. But according to DAN that was all the time Holly had – at the very most. Without a cure she would be lucky to see one more birthday.

When DAN had told him the time horizon he had almost felt a bizarre sense of relief. The deadline was so close there was really *nothing* he could do. He had every excuse to give in; to concentrate on helping to identify Olivia's killer and ensuring Holly's last few months were as enjoyable and painless as possible. But of course that wasn't his way. He had never been any good at accepting anything passively.

He sat up in bed and shook his head, trying to clear all the jumbled thoughts and fears from his mind. If he was even to begin planning what should or *could* be done to help Holly he would need a fresh perspective. And he could think of only one way to get it. Before he broke the news to his father and Jack he would talk it through with the one person who had always listened to him in times of crisis and doubt.

Tom swung heavy legs out of the bed and wandered into the connecting bathroom. Olivia's array of shampoo and conditioner bottles sat undisturbed on the table by the bath. Like so many things around this home, which Olivia had created, the bottles were another reminder of her presence. But he couldn't yet bear to throw away even the smallest memento of her.

He set the shower to the power setting and blasted himself awake till his skin tingled. Looking down he studied the ugly, purple scar above his right knee. The Swedish doctor had told him how lucky he was that the bullet had passed through his leg, causing only minor muscle damage. But few moments went by when he didn't wish every single bullet that had torn into Olivia's body had torn into his instead.

After showering he towelled himself dry and opened the large wardrobe he had shared with his wife. Olivia's clothes hung emptily from the pegs, her smell still among them. He reached into his side and threw on the first clothes that came to hand and grabbed the long quilted leather jacket lying discarded on the floor from last night.

On the landing he paused outside Holly's room and put his head round the open door. She was curled up in bed, asleep. He crept over to her and kissed her forehead. As he studied her peaceful face, DAN's chilling prophecy seemed a distant – even ridiculous – nightmare. If he wasn't back before Holly awoke, then he was sure Marcy Kelley, the housekeeper who lived in the self-contained apartment on the top floor, would be up by then.

Leaving Holly sleeping he stole down the still-dark staircase and quietly let himself out of the house. He went out the back door, because he knew the police car was parked outside the front drive-way, a few yards down the road. He noticed it had snowed overnight as he climbed into his Mercedes and quietly eased out of the side gate, away from his guardians. He wanted to be alone, and didn't really share Jack's concern that the person who had tried to kill him

48

in Sweden might have followed him to the States. Olivia's killer was probably on the run now and Tom wished the police would concentrate on catching him, rather than wasting time watching over him.

The drive from Beacon Hill through the usually congested sprawl of Boston was eerily quiet. It was not yet six on a Sunday morning and he saw only a handful of moving cars on the fifteen-minute journey, including an anonymous brown sedan that overtook him after the snow-capped bridge.

The watery pink of dawn was just breaking when he arrived at the snow-covered fields of the cemetery. The wrought-iron gates were open and he drove to the top of the plot where he could still see the mound of Olivia's fresh grave under the overnight snow. He parked the Mercedes and blowing into his cold hands scrunched across the snow to where she lay. At the grave he sat in the snow next to Olivia, knees hugged close to his chest, and told her what had happened.

Leaving nothing out he started from the beginning. It was as if Olivia was actually there listening to him, as she had done so often when alive.

'So, what should I do?' he asked aloud. 'Do I accept the inevitable and make the most of the time left to Holly? Or do I risk missing the precious year she does have left trying to find an accelerated cure?'

As he sat there quietly watching the clear, cold fingers of dawn push back the darkness he remembered Olivia's favourite poem and he smiled. He couldn't recall all the lines Dylan Thomas wrote to his dying father, but he remembered enough to know he had Olivia's answer. He would not let Holly go gently into any night. He would rage alongside her, using all his skill and resources to hold back the encroaching darkness.

Jasmine would have told no-one of DAN's verdict and Tom wanted to keep it quiet. He certainly didn't want Holly to know anything yet of her imminent illness. He'd tell Alex and Jack tomorrow, along with whoever else could help and be relied on to keep their counsel. Together they would work out what the best plan of attack should be. After all, if they couldn't save Holly, then nobody could.

It was then, just as the rising sun leaked its angled light on the cemetery, that he saw the fresh footprints in the snow. They led his eyes from the grave, across the wide expanse of white to an anonymous brown sedan parked at the far end of the plot, and the broad-shouldered man standing next to it. The man was only a silhouette against the rising sun, but something about his posture told Tom he was watching him.

Tom stood and looked down at the deep prints, following them back to the grave, and for the first time noticed the small cross-shaped wreath of blood red roses on the snow behind the gravestone. As Olivia would have wanted, he had asked well-wishers to make a donation to their favourite charities rather than present any flowers, so he wondered about the donor. Intrigued he leaned over the gravestone and picked up the wreath. An envelope fell from the red flowers onto the snow in front of him.

With numbed fingers he tore it open, revealing a small card. On the top was a quotation: '*The wages of sin is death. Romans ch. 6, v. 23.*' And beneath it he read the words that chilled him more than the icy cold: 'Your wife paid for your sin this time. But your punishment will come.' It was unsigned.

At last he felt something. All the anger and grief he had been denied since Olivia's death now came bursting to the surface. With blood pounding in his ears he squinted into the rising sun. Ignoring the pain in his thigh he began to run in the direction of the lone silhouette. He pushed his legs through the thick snow as fast as he could, his breath visible in the cold air. But before he had covered twenty yards and been blinded by the sun, he knew that the man had already gone.

THREE DAYS LATER JASMINE WASHINGTON SAT WITH TOM CARTER and Jack Nichols in the GENIUS boardroom at the top of the pyramid, on the floor that housed all the commercial offices, including Jack's. She was shaking her head in disbelief. She had barely come to terms with DAN's prediction on Holly and now this.

'What I don't understand, Tom, is why your police protection didn't try and catch him?' she asked.

'Because the police weren't there,' said Jack, his powerful hands clasped on the black table in front of him. 'Mr Einstein here decided to give them the slip.'

'Jack, spare me the big brother shit. OK?' groaned Tom. 'I had enough of a lecture from your friends down at the Bureau.'

Jack kept his weather-beaten features impassive. Despite the grey peppering his sandy hair, and the scar on his face, he looked good for a fifty-year-old. Jasmine had known Jack for almost as long as she'd known Tom. As well as being the commercial brains behind the company, the FBI man turned MBA was a 'fixer', the pragmatic worrier who bridged Tom's flights of fancy to the real world. Jack had told her once that he saw his role to protect their fragile ideas from the 'men in suits', as he called the investors. Ever since Tom and he had met twelve years ago at a biotech investment conference in Manhattan, theirs had been a marriage of minds.

Although GENIUS was already proving a success, Tom had been looking to raise additional money for his Genescope idea without losing control of the company. Jack, fresh out of Wharton Business School with one successful year under his belt at Drax Venture Capital, was desperate to find a venture to capitalize – ideally one that would change the world. They talked off and on for thirty-nine hours, ignoring everyone else at the conference. And at the end of it Jack had resigned from Drax and joined Tom. Within three weeks he had not only interested six major Wall Street investors in Tom's venture, but by playing off one against the other, he had graciously allowed three of them to put up the necessary hundred and fifty million – on condition that they didn't interfere with the running of the business for at least ten years.

'So what do the FBI think, Tom?' asked Jasmine.

Tom stood up, walked over to the glass outer wall and leaned back against it. Behind him Jasmine could see the skyscrapers of downtown Boston looming in the distance.

'They think it might be the Preacher,' he said.

Her eyes opened wide with shock. 'Jeez,' she whispered. 'Really?'

Jack Nichols stroked the scar on his face like he always did when he was puzzled or surprised. 'Are you sure?' he asked.

'That's what the FBI told me last night,' said Tom. 'I spoke to Karen Tanner down at Federal Plaza and she said the handwriting and the use of the biblical quote are consistent with the Preacher.'

Jack let out a small whistle. 'If Karen reckons it's him, then it probably is.'

Jasmine understood why Jack was impressed. Karen Tanner had

been Jack's rookie partner about fifteen years ago. She had helped him put away Happy Sam, the killer who'd tried to 'capture happiness' by cutting out his victims' mouths. Jack's wife Susan had almost become one of the psycho's victims, before Karen had helped Jack rescue her. He had got badly sliced up in the process. It was then that he had decided to get out, to spend more time with his wife and two sons, and find a different way to make the world a better place.

And now Karen Tanner was saying that a killer, who made Happy Sam look like a little leaguer, was after Tom Carter. Jasmine wouldn't have believed it unless she'd seen the way Olivia had been dispatched.

Like everyone else, she'd read the stories. Jeez, there'd been enough of them. The Preacher was supposed to be some religious nut on a warped crusade to clean up the world. It was common knowledge that his victims were mainly high-profile, lowlife scum; mob lawyers, drug dealers, heads of the major crime families – generally any slime-ball considered beyond the reach of the law.

Jasmine could still remember reading about the Preacher's first victim some thirteen years ago. The crooked Evangelist, Bobby Dooley, had been found bobbing up and down in the Hudson with his throat cut from ear to ear, and the message *'Beware of False Prophets which come to you in sheep's clothing, but inwardly they are ravening wolves. St Matthew ch. 7, v. 15'*, rammed down his gullet in a plastic bag.

When the next bodies were found, all with similar messages attached to their person, the press had gone wild with stories about the guy, calling him the 'Preacher of Death'. But over time interest had waned; the police had got no closer to identifying him, and most of the victims weren't likely to win any Humanitarian of the Year awards. Now, with a worldwide tally of some sixty or so victims, the only media angle was whether the police *really* wanted to catch him. Or whether they let him alone because he 'only killed scum' and therefore made their lives easier.

'But, Tom, why are you a target?' asked Jasmine. 'You're not exactly regarded as a lowlife. Unless the Nobel committee is completely out of touch.'

Tom gave a dry laugh. 'I asked Karen Tanner the same thing last night. Her guess is that he doesn't agree with what I'm doing. Her behavioural sciences people at Quantico think that to a religious freak like him, my genetics probably makes me the lowest form of scum around – only a few rungs up the slime ladder from the great Satan himself. And don't forget. Not all his victims have been conventional scum. Remember Max Heywood, the Supreme Court Justice?'

Jasmine grimaced. She remembered.

Max Heywood's only 'sin' had been to say that the American Constitution was as sacred as anything written in the Bible. The Supreme Court Justice had been found in his chambers with the trademark biblical quote written in his own blood, nailed to his chest: *'Fear God, and keep his commandments: for this is the whole duty of man. Ecclesiastes ch. 12, v. 13.'* He had been garrotted, and his tongue pulled out with pliers.

'But why's he after you now?' asked Jasmine. 'You've been involved in genetics for years.'

'Who knows? One guess is that the publicity about the Nobel Prize pushed him over the edge. Anyway,' said Tom, 'I don't care who the Preacher is. If he killed Olivia I want him put away. Which brings me to the purpose of this meeting. I want to discuss a change in two priorities. The first relates to Holly and the second to helping the FBI catch the Preacher.'

Jack reached for his phone. 'I'll get Paul and Jane in here.'

Tom stopped him. 'No. I want to keep Holly's predicament just between us for the moment.'

Paul Mandelson and Jane Naylor were the last two members of the main board. Jack oversaw all financial and marketing matters, Tom the Research and Development department, and Jasmine Information Technology. Paul, the Operations Director, was in charge of all procurement and production. Jane Naylor was the Human Resources Director.

Jack took his hand off the phone and leaned back in his chair. 'OK. Let's start with Holly. I assume it relates to DAN's prediction.'

Tom nodded. 'Because our policy has always been to concentrate on the more common genetic disorders, we've ignored the rarer more difficult conditions, such as brain cancer. So to have even a hope in hell of helping Holly I'm switching three of the top lab teams onto developing gene therapy protocols to get round the blood-brain barrier and specifically target glioblastoma multiforme. That means some of the more mainstream, profitable projects will be delayed.

There will also be increased funding implications which you should be aware of. But otherwise nothing should change. OK?'

Jack shrugged. 'Sure. Whatever you need. Just give me the breakdowns so the bean counters can open the relevant budget centres and account codes.'

Tom turned to Jasmine. 'Jazz, I've told the FBI about the Gene Genie software, and they're keen to trial it. They have no idea what this mysterious Preacher looks like. Even the film of Olivia's shooting just shows a guy in a big coat, wrapped up against the cold. But they're convinced that sooner or later he'll leave a genetic trace of some kind at one of his crimes. And when he does they want to use Gene Genie to summon up his likeness. I want to help them. How's the latest prototype doing?'

The Gene Genie software was a second-generation add-on to the Genescope software. The current Genescopes could give a good physical description of a person from their DNA: colour of skin, hair and eyes as well as ethnic type, probable height and build. The Gene Genie software went one step further. Building on the early Nineties concept of developing computer-generated photo-fits, using input from witnesses, Gene Genie was intended to create a three-dimensional hologram of a subject built up entirely from his or her genes.

Jasmine opened the laptop in front of her and called up the critical path for the project. 'It's almost finished,' she said. 'The latest timetable puts it at being ready for Beta testing in ten weeks.'

Tom frowned. 'If you made it top-dollar priority and threw money at the problem, how soon could you have it finished?'

'A month. Five weeks. Assuming we don't have any major glitches. But it'll cost.'

'It doesn't matter,' Tom said. 'Spend whatever you need to get it operational. But make it four weeks.'

Jack looked at him, no doubt thinking about the millions they would have to spend to bring the project forward a few weeks. 'What's the rush, Tom? We've got a monopoly on the software. And you don't really think this'll help catch Olivia's killer, do you?'

'At least we're doing something.'

Jack looked as if he was about to argue, but then he leaned back in his chair with a shrug. 'OK. OK. But whoever this Preacher guy is, it'll take more than a ghost-making machine to catch him. He's been around for over thirteen years and nobody's come close.' Jack sat forward and looked him in the eye. 'Shit, Tom, the guy's a ghost already.'

5

A MONTH LATER – 2 FEBRUARY 2003. BEACON HILL, BOSTON.

TOM CARTER POURED HIS THIRD CUP OF BLACK COFFEE AND watched the clock ticking away in the quiet of the kitchen. It was 5:58 in the morning; not even Marcy Kelley, their housekeeper, was up yet.

Seven weeks, four days and six hours had now elapsed since Olivia's death – he often wondered when he would stop measuring it so precisely – but still the authorities were no closer to finding her killer. Apart from the Gene Genie software, which was now almost completed, the only glimmer of hope Tom could see was that the FBI were convinced he was still a target. If they were right, then Carter thought there was a chance the bastard could be caught by the agents and police watching over him.

The thought of being stalked by such a killer was frightening, but any concern for his own life was overshadowed by his fear for Holly's. Moment by moment he was aware of the even more implacable killer stalking his daughter. Today, after weeks of work he would know whether one of his team's key experiments had been successful, and whether he had at least a hope in hell of finding a cure in time.

He stood, picked up his crumpled jacket from the back of his chair and left the kitchen. Walking across the large Chinese rug that covered much of the hall, he made his way to the oak staircase. At the top of the stairs he straightened his injured leg and rubbed the area just above his knee. He would need an operation to cure his limp completely, but it was hardly a priority. He gently pushed open Holly's door, preparing to tiptoe inside without disturbing her, when he was surprised by a bright desk lamp shining directly at the door.

'Hi, Dad,' said Holly, her spiky blond hair bent with sleep. She sat at her desk in a baggy green *WHAT ARE YOU STARING AT?* T-shirt, tapping away at her computer.

Tom blinked away the dazzle and ruffled her hair. 'What are you doing up so early?'

'Couldn't sleep. So I thought I'd have one more go on The Wrath of Zarg.'

He smiled and sat on her bed, next to the desk. It was rare to catch her awake this early. Holly was usually woken by the cheery 'rise and shine' of Marcy Kelley's booming brogue just before eight, in time for breakfast and the ride to school with her friends.

He turned to the screen and watched the warrior queen Holly was controlling. The ridiculously muscular figure was standing beneath a ceiling that seemed to be raining fiery bricks down on her head. A dragon was approaching from her left and a huge troll-like animal from the right.

'Looks like you're in trouble.'

Holly laughed. 'Piece of cake.'

'Oh yeah? How are you going to avoid being roasted by the bricks without the dragon eating you, or the troll crushing you?'

'Like this.' Holly immediately pressed a couple of keys and the warrior queen on the screen bent down and picked up a rock from the ground, revealing a small blue bottle. Another few taps on the keyboard and the character picked up the blue bottle and drank it. Suddenly she was glowing, immune to the falling hot bricks. And in no time she was using her sword to dice the dragon, kebab the troll and move on to the next level.

'Magic potion,' Holly explained with a wise-guy grin. 'Makes you invulnerable. Works every time. You just need to know where to look.'

He looked at his daughter, oblivious to her impending disease.

'Magic potion huh. I'm impressed.' He wished it was as easy for him.

The screen changed and a new level came up.

'Level six,' Holly exclaimed triumphantly. 'Awesome.'

Tom was glad Holly liked the new computer. It had been a Christmas gift from Olivia and him. Jasmine had helped choose the model, and it was about the only fun Holly had enjoyed over an otherwise doom-laden Christmas. Sure, Alex and other relations had stayed over, and Jazz and all their friends had been heroically considerate, but nothing could distract them from the void of Olivia's absence. All in all the whole festive season was right up there with a week's vacation in hell.

He glanced around Holly's room. On one wall a *Jurassic Park 3* poster vied with a lifesize picture of The Internet Troopers. A soccer ball sat on the middle shelf above the desk, next to a large photo of Olivia laughing in the garden. He quickly shifted his gaze to the collection of CD-ROM computer games and GI Joe action figures. He smiled inwardly when he considered how there wasn't one doll, cute Peanuts poster or doe-eyed Disney character in sight. From when she was tiny it had been obvious that Holly wasn't a Barbie Doll kind of girl. So much for genetics, he thought.

Suddenly he imagined this room empty. The fear came so quickly and unannounced that he needed a second to compose himself. He took a deep breath and reassured himself that the CAT and PET brain scans they had taken together had shown no sign of Holly's tumour yet. Again he told himself that there *was* enough time to find her a cure. He would find the time.

'Dad?'

He turned to Holly, who was studying his feet. 'Yes?'

'You ready for work already?'

'Of course. Why?'

'Your socks don't match.'

He looked down and saw she was right. He was wearing one blue and one brown sock. 'They're not meant to match,' he said. 'They're a special pair.'

Holly just raised an eyebrow. 'Yeah, right.'

Tom stood up and kissed her on the cheek. 'No really, Hol. I can prove it.'

Holly narrowed her eyes, 'How?'

He couldn't resist a grin as he moved to the door. 'Because I've got another pair just like them.'

He heard her groan, 'Daaad,' but Tom managed to get out the door before the pillow reached him.

BY SIX-THIRTY TOM WAS DRIVING THROUGH THE GATES OF THE GENIUS campus, his discreet police tail not far behind. He normally liked to be at his desk before six-fifteen, but seeing Holly awake had been a welcome break to his routine.

He drove the Mercedes into the underground parking garage and noticed it was virtually empty. He smiled when he saw the lone bright green BMW convertible parked in the first available spot. He had a running joke with Jazz to see who could be in earliest and who-ever won invariably took the prime spot to prove the point. Occasionally Jack Nichols would get in at some stupid time and park his car there, just to tell them he could be up with the best of them, but most days it was between them. Usually he won. But not today.

He got out of the car and walked to the stairs that led to the atrium. Before the shooting he would have run up them, but now he only walked. He refused to take the elevator out of principle.

It was quiet save for the hollow click-clack of his heels on marble. To his left through tinted glass walls he could see Jasmine wandering around the main computer room. Leading to her from the atrium was a door of black opaque glass marked: *Information Technology Section – Authorized Access Only*. The IT section, along with the central atrium and the Hospital Suite, occupied the ground floor of the GENIUS pyramid.

He returned her wave and walked to the middle of the atrium. Here, reaching up to the apex of the pyramid was a thirty-foot-tall multicoloured hologram of the DNA spiral, rotating on a circular holo-pad. As he often did, Tom disobeyed the sign beside it and stepped directly into the three-dimensional image. He looked up through the spiral staircase rotating around him and marvelled at the multicoloured rungs of nitrogen bases. Standing inside the double helix that carried the code of all life never failed to inspire him. This to him was the real information superhighway, along whose route most secrets that mattered could be unravelled. Shaking his head in fresh wonder he stepped off the holo-pad and headed for the Hospital Suite to the west of the atrium.

Pushing open the door he found himself in the small cheerfully decorated waiting-room with its adjoining rest-rooms. Ahead were a pair of swinging doors that led to the experimental gene-therapy ward and the fully equipped operating room beyond. Approved by the National Cancer Institute at the National Institutes of Health in Bethesda, Maryland, the ward had ten beds. Fully funded by GENIUS, it was staffed with four doctors and ten nurses, one for each bed. Two of the doctors were on sabbatical from the NIH; both were charged with ensuring the cross-fertilization of ideas and best practice – plus of course checking that GENIUS obtained the necessary Federal Drug Administration and NIH approvals for all experimental treatments on their human guinea-pigs. He valued the NIH doctors' presence and hid nothing from them. Well, almost nothing. He hadn't shown them the IGOR DNA database yet. He was sure that despite his motives, the National Institutes of Health wouldn't approve of that.

Tom opened the door and smiled at the sunny room that greeted him; yellow walls, curtains of cornflower-blue; house-plants; pine beds in semi-private cubicles. All added to the impression that this wasn't a ward at all, but a large bedroom. However that wasn't what made the place so special, or Tom so proud.

The ward was unusual because patients could only qualify for a bed here if they met one stringent criterion: they had to have less than three months to live. People came here when chemotherapy, radio-therapy and all other treatments had failed. This was literally their last resort. It was where they came to have their genes reprogrammed.

Tom had initiated the ward to ensure that his scientists in the labs upstairs saw the direct application of their work, and never forgot that medical research was meaningless if it didn't help save human lives. Many of the terminally ill patients still died, but a significant few had missed their stop and kept on living. Back in early 1999 the first accredited cystic fibrosis cure through gene therapy had happened in this room, as had the first recorded successful gene-therapy trial for Huntington's Chorea a year later. This modest ward had seen more than fifty people's lives saved in the last nine years, plus countless more throughout the world as a result of what was tested here.

Only six beds were being used at the moment. Five of the patients were asleep but he wasn't surprised to see that Hank Polanski was sitting up talking to the Ward Sister, Beth Lawrence. Today was a big day for the young twenty-three-year-old farmer from North Carolina. The FDA had finally approved their new treatment and this morning Hank Polanski was to be injected with the HIV retrovirus that causes AIDS.

The patients were mainly treated by the other doctors, simply because of his laboratory commitments. But Tom still couldn't help regarding each and every one of them as his own personal responsibility.

Nurse Lawrence, a tall prim-looking woman with a surprisingly open smile, was busy fitting an intravenous drip into Hank's arm. When she looked up she greeted Tom warmly. 'Good morning, Dr Carter.'

'Morning Beth, Morning Hank. How are you feeling today?'

Hank turned his pale face to him and gave a defiant grin. 'I'm still here Doc.' When he spoke he did so with a breathless wheeze.

'You ready for the treatment?'

Hank nodded nervously. He was a volunteer for the experimental gene therapy, but Tom knew he had no choice. Hank had lung cancer and would die without radical treatment. This involved inserting genes into Hank's tumour cells, genes that would tell the immune system to kill the tumour. Cancer cells are cells that have rebelled against their strict genetic orders, and are growing out of control. To put down this revolt Tom had to make sure he killed *all*, or virtually all, of the tumour cells. To do that he needed a vehicle to get the killer genes into the rebel cells without harming the good ones. That was where the HIV retrovirus came in.

Retroviruses could enter a body cell, incorporating its own genetic instructions into the cell's healthy DNA. Like cruise missiles, retroviruses could be reprogrammed in the laboratory, their harmful code turned off and good genes inserted. By neutering the genes in the HIV retrovirus that attacked the human immune system, and putting in special therapeutic genes, the killer that caused AIDS could be tamed to cure lung cancer. Tom and his team had proved they'd made the retrovirus harmless. It had been successfully loaded with genes to target and kill cancerous lung

61

cells. All that remained was to test the genetically engineered retrovirus in a human.

'What are the risks again?' asked Hank, trying not to look frightened.

Tom put his hand on Hank's shoulder and rested it there. As always he was careful to be completely honest.

'One risk is that the retrovirus goes AWOL and invades a healthy cell, and then inserts the genes into the wrong part of your genetic sequence.'

'What would that do?'

'It could give the healthy cells cancer too. But the odds of that happening are very, very small.'

'Could I catch AIDS?'

'No, we've tested the retroviral vehicle – or vector as we call it – over the last three years, and we've proved that it's harmless. That's why the FDA sanctioned it. Frankly, Hank, the only real risk to you is that it might not work. He felt the bony shoulder shrug beneath his hand.

'So I ain't got zip to lose, then?' asked Hank.

Tom paused for a second and looked into Hank's eyes. He remembered him first coming here three weeks ago, the once fit, outdoor man already so weak he could barely walk. 'I ain't good at being sick,' he'd explained then. 'So kill me or cure me. But just get me the hell outta here.' The man had been willing to try anything as long as he could get out of his bed and the hospital.

'Let me be completely straight with you, Hank,' said Tom. 'The chances of this treatment failing are high, perhaps eighty-five per cent. But the odds of it making you worse are minimal. And the chances of you surviving without it are zero. So you have a choice. One, you do nothing and let the disease take its course. Or, two, you do this and have a fifteen per cent chance of being cured.'

Hank frowned as if thinking, then wheezed, 'Fifteen per cent?'

Tom kept his face impassive. 'At best.'

Hank smiled, a big grin that lit up his thin face, and made him look almost well. 'I've had worse odds.'

Tom returned his smile. 'So have I. I've seen people with far less chance than that walk out of here. So don't give up on me just yet.' It would take many weeks, months, even years before the results were conclusive. But Tom didn't care how long it took, if he could only keep death's greedy hands off this young man for a while longer. He turned to the nurse who was hanging a drip bag on the stand by the bed. In the bag was the first batch of red retroviral serum that had been cloned in the upstairs lab.

He said, 'Right Beth, we'll wait for Hank's mother to arrive. She said she'd be here at seven. Then could you get one of the NIH doctors to check what we're doing. I suggest Karl Lambert. When you've done that come and get me and we'll start the first intravenous drip. OK?'

When Beth nodded, Tom could see the excitement in her eyes. He felt quietly confident about curing Hank. He only wished he felt as confident about the infinitely more complex cancer threatening his daughter. Bob and Nora had said they'd be ready to check the retrovirus they'd developed to combat glioblastoma multiforme at nine o' clock. He checked his watch; only two more hours to go.

ACROSS THE GROUND FLOOR OF THE PYRAMID JASMINE Washington was spending the first half-hour checking around her domain. Soon, the keenest of her staff would start arriving, and she liked to have some time alone with her machines.

She walked through the Experimental Genescope facility. This facility was similar to the one upstairs where Holly's genome had been read. Except here there were only four Genescopes, and all were upgraded experimental models. The two on the right were holo-models equipped with the prototype Gene Genie software. Jasmine was confident they would be up and running within the next few days.

Again she felt the conflicting emotions stir within her. Four days ago she and Larry had taken Holly to the classic Disney cartoon movie, *The Lion King*, and as always they had laughed and teased each other, but Jasmine had been unable to stop thinking about DAN's verdict. She was proud of the Genescope's ability to predict disease, especially when it could be prevented or cured. But if all the invention could do was predict misery without offering any solace, then it didn't seem so very clever.

She sighed and walked through the Genescope facility, passing the main IT office suite on her right, with its silent workstations and terminals. She opened the chrome and glass door in front to reveal a large dazzling chamber. This room was the heart of her IT department, and the information heart of GENIUS worldwide.

It was in this cool, all-white space, referred to simply as the White Room, that Jasmine liked to walk and think. Kept at a constant 55° it contained four enormous boxes that hummed away in the centre. Two of the four large boxes housed 'Big Mother', the large protein-based ultra-computer that was linked to all the Genescopes in existence. This mother brain knew at any one time what scans were being conducted by its 'brood', anywhere around the world. And it was 'Big Mother' that allowed the existence of the database that resided in the other two boxes, the Individual Genome Ordered Repository – IGOR.

The ethical guidelines on gene scanning were rigorous. Genomes could only be tested if patients were accompanied by their doctor, or had professional counselling. Strict matching checks were used to ensure that an individual couldn't have his genome scanned without his knowledge. The other major guideline was that all scans should be kept strictly confidential. The life and health insurance companies had frequently tried to challenge this, claiming that if an individual discovered that he or she had an imminent incurable disease, he or she could take out extremely high insurance coverage at standard premiums. The law however was adamant that the privacy of the individual was paramount. And this was why Jazz and Carter were so keen to keep the database secret. IGOR was strictly illegal.

The Individual Genome Ordered Repository had been Tom's idea. He had asked Jasmine to tell 'Big Mother' to pull off one in five of all gene scans conducted by the licensed GENIUS processing labs around the world and store them in a database, along with the names, addresses, family and medical records of the individuals concerned. There were now over one hundred million people on IGOR and GENIUS knew more about them than they did themselves.

Tom's motives were far from sinister; he wanted to use the database at a macro level to validate much of his genetic work – checking trends of actual medical illness in families versus genetic markers for the illness. IGOR had helped validate much of the work that led to the cure for schizophrenia and had given vital clues to treating other genetic diseases. However, despite this worthy intention, Jasmine had no doubt that if any of the individuals or relevant authorities learnt of the database they would be horrified and GENIUS's credibility would be seriously compromised. But Tom had judged that the benefits outweighed any potential threat to the particular individuals and to his company. So he had taken the risk.

After walking round her domain Jasmine returned to her computer and began her daily cyber-patrol. She clicked on the computer. With a processing speed of 100 terrahertz, 600 gigs of disk space and 200 gigs of RAM it was easily powerful enough to cruise the fast lane of the congested information superhighway. The computer monitor flashed into life and a virtual reality head, the spitting image of Jazz, appeared. The afro hair and fine-featured dark face almost matched her own reflection in the screen. The image greeted her with *'Salutations Razor Buzz. Where are you going today?'* Even the synthesized voice sounded like her own. She rarely used it any more, but the Razor Buzz tag was a throwback to her youth in LA, when she had been an irresponsible net head with a sharp attitude and a haircut to match. If her strict Baptist parents thought they were keeping her out of trouble by banning her from the streets and allowing her to kick up her heels on the information superhighway, then they were mistaken. She had chosen the anonymous user ID of Razor Buzz, because a lot of what she did in those days wasn't strictly legit. Still, legit or not, back then she was something of a legend.

She spoke into the microphone. 'Today, I'm on patrol.'

'I need the code before you can go on the road,' said the talking head.

Jazz smiled. The password she'd chosen this week still gave her an adolescent kick. It was the name of a job that harked back to the bad old rebellious days before she went legit and won scholarships and Nobel prizes; to when she could hack into everything and anything. This job wasn't 'Accountant', or 'Doctor', or even 'GENIUS Information Technology Director'. No, this job was cool, seriously cool.

'Cybercop,' she typed, enjoying playing the ultimate poacher turned gamekeeper.

The head on the screen suddenly donned a helmet, did a double flip and saluted her. *'Special Agent Razor you are now free to roam the infobahn. Take care out there in cyberspace.'*

She reached across the ordered desk for her can of Diet Coke, and considered her destination. Most days she would try and break into one of GENIUS's technical or financial systems. She employed two other guys to try and breach these protected databases, highlighting weaknesses and suggesting better protective measures. Both guys were good, but she still liked to check for herself how good her defences really were. Today she would try to hack into their most sensitive and best protected database – IGOR.

She ignored the Worldwide Web, because none of the GENIUS systems were visible there. Instead she tapped out the number of 'Big Mother', intending to hack into the live connection used by all the Genescopes to feed data into the mother brain, and then into IGOR. Almost instantly the front end screen appeared demanding a password. She punched in yesterday's – she had purposely not looked at today's.

Access denied flashed up on screen.

Good. The password had been changed. The data was secure from her.

Or should be.

She'd have to find another way in. She pressed the keys on the board in front of her, trying to get round the front end title screen, which gave no information about what IGOR contained. She would still not be in the system once she'd done this, because she had designed IGOR to have two levels of security, one to prevent prowlers browsing the front end menu and one to stop them from accessing the data – but at least it would be a start. She tried the easy tricks first, the ones known to all high-school cyberpunks. First she tried to find it by interrogating the programme behind it.

No joy. All the simple breaches were closed.

Good. So far.

She moved on to the next approach, using the base computer language to reprogram the password commands. This was more difficult and took years of experience. If you put in the wrong program code you could damage all your other software.

She did it without thinking. It took her a little over four seconds to try this technique. But then Razor Buzz was a supremo, a cyber-lord.

Nothing. No breach. Her team had covered off this angle.

Excellent.

Now to the final approach. This entailed writing her own program to tell the program that ran the password system what to do. Like creating higher orders for the system to obey. This took Razor a little longer. This was clever.

Then her eyes saw the message flashing on the bottom right of the screen.

Program already resident . . . Program already resident . . . Program already resident . . .

This had never happened before. 'Shit,' she said aloud, both impressed and nervous.

The screen changed and she realized she was entering the first stage of IGOR – only one final password defence away from the data.

But she hadn't finished her own higher language program. She must have got in on the coat-tails of *someone else*.

Someone else must have opened the door using the same program she was writing and inadvertently let her in. Ignoring the perspiration on her brow she rode the intruder's slipstream, checking how far they'd penetrated. Whoever it was, they had infiltrated the first-stage defences and appeared to be browsing the front end menus – just window shopping, seeing what IGOR contained.

Her hand hovered over the hot key that would catapult both the intruder and herself out of the database.

But she didn't press it yet. She would only press it if the intruder looked as if he was doing the impossible: breaking through the impregnable second stage of defences and accessing any of the highly confidential data stored there. Before that happened she wanted to find out who the intruder was. The automatic PREDATOR tracer would start immediately if the intruder managed to get beyond the second stage – assuming they could. But she wanted the trace to start now.

She addressed the receiver on her computer, 'I need you to start a trace. Activate PREDATOR.'

A small Help icon opened on the top right of the screen containing her computer-generated head, still wearing the cop helmet.

The head asked, *'Stealth mode or alarm mode?'*

'Stealth. Don't want to frighten our visitor off yet.'

Another small icon opened up on the top left of her screen. Above it was a clock ticking down from sixty seconds, the time it took to effect a complete trace. At the bottom of the icon was a row of nine flashing numbers. The numbers were changing at a frantic speed, searching for the right combination. Suddenly the left number locked in place, leaving only eight flashing. Then the second locked. Once all nine were locked Jasmine would be able to trace the intruder's origin.

25. . .24. . .23 ticked the icon on the top left of the screen.

The sixth number locked into place. Only three to go.

Then the intruder suddenly logged off, his cyber trail vaporized. Gone.

'Shit,' she muttered to herself, just as one of her staff walked into her office.

Jasmine checked the six numbers on screen, to see if they gave any clue to the origin of the intruder. But all she could be sure of from the codes was that it came from outside the US; between South-East Europe and India. The Middle East or North Africa would be her best guess. But who from that part of the world would bother to hack into the superficially boring IGOR?

The tall blonde woman held up a bulb from the new holo-projector. 'Morning Jazz, you OK?'

She looked up and smiled at her technical manager. 'Yeah, Debbie, thanks.'

'Can I show you something?'

'Sure. Will it take long?'

'About half an hour. I just need to talk you through the final mods to Gene Genie. We reckon we've cracked the holo-image.'

'Including face definition?'

Debbie grinned. 'Come and judge for yourself.'

'Great! Just give me five minutes and I'll be with you.'

Despite her worries Jasmine was excited about the new Gene-Imaging software. As for IGOR, she reassured herself that at least the actual database hadn't been breached, only its general purpose discovered. She was convinced that the final defences were secure, but she would still tell Tom. He would want to know that for the first time since its creation someone was showing an unhealthy interest in the anonymous IGOR.

6

LATER THAT MORNING. GENIUS ANIMAL LABORATORY, BOSTON.

'SO, NORA, HOW'S IT GOING?' ASKED TOM, OPENING THE SWING-doors from the corridor linking the main laboratories of the Mendel Suite with the animal laboratory, or 'Mouse House' as it was known. Immediately after Hank Polanski had received his first infusion of genes with no initial side-effects, he had hurried here, desperate to know the results of the experiment that could determine Holly's future.

Nora Lutz looked up from inputting data into her laptop, her natural frown softening in greeting. In her late forties, Nora was small and round, with brown hair cut into a short bob. Large tortoiseshell glasses gave her the appearance of an owl. She was a dedicated lab technician and Tom knew that despite her grumpy demeanour she loved her job here – if only because it got her out of the house. A spinster, she lived in Charlestown with her demanding invalid mother and five cats. Leaning back in her chair, Nora pulled up the sleeves of her white coat and gestured to the eight empty cages behind her.

'Just finished,' she said. 'All forty-eight mice have now been dissected and their met count checked.'

Tom nodded. He didn't like using animals for experiments, and many of the *in vitro* experimental protocols he'd developed had done away with the need. But at times, particularly in the field of gene therapy, it was unavoidable.

In this experiment all the mice had been infected with astrocytoma cancer cells. Half had then been injected with a genetically engineered retrovirus designed to kill brain cancer cells, whereas the other half had been treated with nothing more than a simple saline solution. Their brains had then been dissected to count the amount and size of tumours or metastases. If the mice treated with the retrovirus had less tumours than the control group injected with salt water, then the experiment had worked. And it was vital that it did work. Otherwise the already tissue-thin chances of finding a cure for Holly in time would dissolve into nothing.

'Any feel for the results yet?'

Nora gave him a 'you should know better' look and shook her head. 'Can't tell you that until Bob comes back with the envelope.' Bob Cooke was Nora's boss.

None of the three teams working on the new brain-cancer project had been told about Holly yet. Tom had done this for a number of reasons. The more people who knew of Holly's predicament, the greater the risk she might learn of it herself. He couldn't allow that to happen. When and if it was appropriate to tell the teams he would, but for now all they needed to know was that the project was top priority.

So far only this team of Nora Lutz and Bob Cooke had come close to developing the complex retroviral vector required to get past the blood-brain barrier protecting the brain. Their progress in a little over five weeks had been exceptional, but as Tom glanced at the spreadsheet on Nora's laptop screen he felt more nervous than excited about the results. The spreadsheet showed the tag numbers of each mouse in the left-hand column, the number of their tumours – alarmingly high as far as Tom could make out – in the column next to it, and the size of these tumours alongside that. One column remained blank: the one that indicated which treatment each mouse had received. Only Bob Cooke had this information.

Years ago Tom had learned the importance of not allowing personal bias to influence results, and had made it obligatory that all GENIUS experiments were conducted 'blind'. He knew how tempting it was for even the most scrupulous scientist to 'find' the results he was hoping for. So Bob Cooke had administered the original injections to the mice, recording on computer disk which coded mice had received the genetically engineered virus treatment and which had received the salt water. Bob had then kept this information sealed in a brown envelope and had been excluded from counting the metastases.

'Where is Bob now?' asked Tom.

'In the Mendel. Shall I get him?'

'No, I'll go. You finish up the figures.'

Tom walked out of the Mouse House, down the small corridor and through the sliding glass doors of the main laboratory suite. He scanned the expanse of white, glass and chrome and saw Bob Cooke immediately. The man's whole appearance and body language set him apart from almost everyone else in the laboratory. The other scientists were stooped over their lab benches, but the loose-limbed Californian with his blond hair and tan was lying back in his chair, holding a microscope slide up to the light. He looked more like a surfer checking out the next wave than a scientist. His broad smile and easy manner made some people underestimate him. In many ways the young man's irreverence reminded Tom of himself.

He could already see the brown envelope on Bob's desk and had to quell the sudden impulse to run and grab it.

Bob saw him and smiled. In one fluid movement he seemed simultaneously to put down the slide, pick up the brown envelope and stand up. 'Looking for this?'

Back in the animal laboratory Carter found himself searching Nora's face for any more clues, now that she'd had more time to look over the data. If the results were clear-cut then the disk wasn't necessary. If all the mice had the same number of large tumours then the experiment had obviously failed, and if half the mice were completely clear of tumours then it had almost certainly worked. But Nora's owlish face gave nothing away.

Bob knitted his eyebrows in a mock frown. 'The nominations for best picture are . . .', before ripping the envelope open and handing her the disk.

Nora gave her Californian boss a weary smile, inserted the disk in her computer and ran the software program. The spreadsheet immediately began importing the information. Tom could see the

71

blank slots in the right-hand column filling up with 'yes' or 'no' to denote which particular mouse had received the retrovirus treatment.

Come on, he thought, let there be a difference between the groups. But before Tom could even finish his silent plea the screen shifted to conclusions, and Nora's disappointed voice told him the worst.

'There's nothing between them,' said the lab technician abruptly. 'Nothing statistically significant anyway.'

'Shit!' He couldn't believe it. The results were even worse than he'd feared. The gene therapy had had no effect at all.

'What went wrong?' asked Nora.

Tom frowned and crossed his arms, drumming the fingers of his right hand on his left arm. 'Perhaps the virus didn't get to the tumour cells? Perhaps the blood-brain barrier stopped it?'

'But the virus was modified to get round that,' said Bob, his voice unusually flat.

'Yeah well, perhaps they didn't work. Or the virus may have got to its target, but the genes either didn't express themselves properly in the cells, or didn't produce enough proteins to make a difference. Either way we'll have to analyse the tumour cells to be sure. But the bottom line is that this time the bastard hasn't worked.'

The door opened to his right, and Jasmine walked in. Her usually sunny face was pensive.

She said, 'Tom, can I have a word? It's pretty important.'

What she wanted to say was obviously not for general broadcast, so he excused himself to Bob and Nora and followed Jasmine out into the small corridor.

'Sorry,' said Jasmine, 'but I've got some bad news.'

He had to laugh. 'Great! Well, you've come to the right place. Let's see if your bad news can beat ours.'

'I caught someone trying to get into IGOR.'

Tom groaned. This was all he needed. 'Did they get in?'

'No, but I reckon they know what it contains – in principle.'

'Who was it? Do you know where they came from?'

Jasmine shook her head. 'Nope. That's the weird thing. It wasn't one of the key Triad regions. The signal didn't come from either Europe, the Far East, or the US.'

'You sure?'

'Positive.'

'Can you find out any more?'

'Not really, no. I've told Jack but he can't understand it either. All the big insurance companies and rival biotech companies who might want to sniff round our databases are all in the Triad. It doesn't make sense.'

Tom rubbed his temples. He didn't even want to think of the implications of this data getting into the hands of insurance companies, or the press, or . . . 'How about the authorities?'

Jasmine shook her head. 'No. This was three hours ago. If it was them, then they'd already be breathing down our necks.'

'So who do you reckon it *might* be?'

'Don't know. Might just be a lone hacker fooling around. But it doesn't feel like that. I got the distinct impression that whoever it was knew exactly what they were looking for. Anyway, I've battened down the hatches, and I'll keep a closer watch on it.'

'What happens if they try again?'

'They won't get in. That isn't the issue. The issue is whatever else they might do now they know what we have. Anyway, there is some good news. The "Gene Genie" software is looking great.'

Tom smiled at that. 'Excellent. Well done, the moment you're happy it's glitch-free let Karen Tanner at the Bureau know.'

'What about your bad news? The experiment didn't work out?'

He led Jasmine back to the animal lab and gestured to Nora's laptop. 'Have a look for yourself.'

Nora made way as Jasmine moved to the screen.

'It bombed,' said Bob Cooke.

Tom watched silently, as Jasmine scrolled down the screen, studying the base data.

'What's this?' she said suddenly, pointing to a zero in the tumour count column.

He bent to take a closer look.

Nora peered at where Jasmine's fingertip met the screen. 'Mouse C370 had no mets. It was completely clear,' the lab technician sounded puzzled.

'Is that significant?' asked Jasmine.

Bob Cooke shrugged. 'Perhaps the original cancer cells didn't take.'

Nora's frown deepened further. 'No, I remember C370, because it definitely had metastases, but they were necrotic.' She looked at Jasmine. 'Dead.'

'A fluke?' asked Bob, turning to Tom.

'Some fluke,' said Jasmine pointing at the 'No' in the right-hand column. 'This mouse was in the control group. It only received a syringe of salt water. Yet it managed to cure itself.'

Nora flashed Tom a quizzical look. 'Spontaneous remission?'

A flicker of excitement cut through Tom's gloom. He'd never experienced complete spontaneous remission firsthand before, either in the laboratory or on the ward. It was extremely rare, well documented but rare. No-one understood or had ever satisfactorily explained how for no apparent reason some people's immune system suddenly decided to rid themselves of cancer. Medical proof abounded of these untreated cures, but no medical explanation.

He turned to Bob Cooke. 'Did you by any chance take a DNA reading before the experiment?'

''Fraid not. It's not part of the protocol. Why do you ask?'

Tom wasn't exactly sure, but he felt an idea begin to form in his head. 'Perhaps we can find a clue why this particular mouse got well. If we could compare its pre-cancer cells with its cancer cells and its "cured" post-cancer cells we might be able to identify the sequence of genetic code that was responsible for the natural remission. So far we've spent all our time trying to impose a theoretical, "test tube" solution. Why don't we instead look at the rare solution that already exists in nature, and try to replicate it?' He looked for feedback from the team and could see Bob and Nora nodding thoughtfully.

Jasmine looked at Tom for a moment, a small frown creasing her smooth forehead. 'But how can you be sure the answer's even scientific?'

'What else could explain it? Faith? Mind over matter? Come on Jazz.'

'Why not?' said Jasmine. 'Many unexplained cures are attributed to faith. When I was a kid, the only holiday my parents ever took to Europe was to Lourdes with my sick Aunt Angela.'

Nora nodded. 'I took my mom to Lourdes two years ago. She felt a lot better for a time.'

'So did my aunt,' said Jasmine. 'Some of the most famous and comprehensively documented cures happened there.' Jasmine began counting cases off on her fingers. 'There was a Rose Martin in April 1947, who had complete remission of uterine cancer. There was Vittorio Michelli in 1962 whose thigh tumour vanished over days after bathing in the holy water. And Klaus Kunst who drank the water in '66 and cured his kidney cancer.'

Tom smiled. Only Jazz could have a mind like a computer and still allow the existence of God. 'I thought Baptists didn't believe in all that Lourdes stuff. I thought that was for Catholics.'

'No way. When you need a miracle, you go where the action is.'

'Well one thing's for sure,' interrupted Bob, pointing at the zero tumour count on the screen. 'If it was faith, then mouse C370 must have been one helluva believer.'

They all laughed at this, but the idea growing in Tom's head wouldn't go away. 'All I'm saying is that something must have changed in that mouse's genetic make-up. And whether you want to call it science, nature or something else, it must be worth trying to understand how we could replicate it.' He paused and looked each of them in the eye. 'Just bear with me for a second, OK?' We're all pretty sure we know *how* this spontaneous remission works, but we don't know why. Basically cancer cells are the body's own cells turned traitor, so the immune system leaves them alone. But what happens in spontaneous remission is that for some reason the body's immune system suddenly recognizes that these cancer cells don't belong to it; that they are foreign and non-self? The immune system then nukes the tumours and they melt away. Right?'

He waited whilst the others, including Jasmine, shrugged their agreement.

'Now for this to occur, something has to happen to the genetic code of those bad cells, to alert the antibodies of the immune system that they are foreign. That's basically what we were trying to do in this experiment. We tried to use an engineered retrovirus to change the tumour cells' DNA in such a way as to attract the attention of the body's immune system.'

'So?'

'So what if there was a *natural* retrovirus that killed tumours?'

'What!' exclaimed Bob.

Tom put up his hands to calm him down. 'Look, a retrovirus works by invading a body cell and then changing the DNA to its own.

75

That's how it reproduces and that's why it's so dangerous. It scrambles our natural genetic code and spreads through the body. Look at how effective HIV is at doing this. Now imagine if there was an extremely rare retrovirus that didn't scramble DNA, but reassembled it. *Repaired* it?'

'One that occurred in nature?' asked Nora, her eyes wide behind her owlish glasses.

'Yes. One that could insert a gene that killed off cancer cells, or repaired damaged cells. Think about it, many genes repair DNA; we know that. And many genes instruct cells to die; we know that too. So if the right genes were inserted into the right cells, order could be restored.'

'Is that possible?' asked Jasmine quietly. 'Could a *naturally* occurring retrovirus do that?'

Bob shrugged. 'I guess so. It's just that no-one's ever asked if *positive* retroviruses could exist in nature before. But that means diddly squat. Look at micro-organisms. We always saw fungi and bacteria as harmful stuff to control and protect ourselves from, because they could infect us. Then Fleming discovered penicillin, which is from a natural mould that *countered* infection, killed off gangrene and syphilis, and saved countless lives.'

'Precisely,' said Tom. 'And all I'm saying is, let's check it out.'

'I agree, Tom. But how?' asked Nora.

Tom paused, as he tried to think through the best approach. Then to his surprise Jasmine answered the question for him.

'We'd need to use DAN to analyse the DNA of someone who'd experienced spontaneous remission,' she said. 'We could run a check on the subject's genetic material taken before they had cancer, during their cancer and then after remission. See what happened to their DNA over time.' Tom could see an excited gleam in Jazz's eye, as if she'd suddenly remembered something. The computer scientist walked to the PC in the far corner of the room; unlike Nora's stand-alone laptop this was on-line, plugged into the Internet. 'But you say these subjects are rare,' Jasmine said as if talking to herself.

'Yeah, and we'd need a *live* patient,' prompted Tom, watching Jasmine turn on the computer and enter the Global Medical News bulletin board on the Worldwide Web.

'I'm sure I saw something on the Medical Watch service a couple of days ago. I was browsing and saw a name I recognized.' Jasmine turned to Carter. 'Jean Luc Petit?'

Tom nodded. Jean Luc Petit, the French cancer specialist, had visited GENIUS on more than one occasion to see the first Genescopes in action, and to check out the ward. 'Yeah, I know him well. He's a good man. Runs an oncology department in Paris. What about him?'

Jasmine used her mouse to select an icon on screen. 'Well, he'd put something out on the "Interesting Facts" bulletin board of Medical Watch.'

Tom was intrigued. 'He's got someone on his ward who's experienced spontaneous remission? A live patient?'

Jasmine clicked another icon and pressed two more keys. The screen changed, showing a page of French text. 'Here it is. I knew I'd seen it.'

Tom bent forward, grateful for his months of exchange study at the Pasteur Institute in Paris. But what he read was so surprising he decided to check it with the English translation that appeared at the bottom of the screen.

'Well?' demanded Bob behind him. 'Has this French doc got one on his ward?'

'No, Dr Jean Luc Petit hasn't got one,' said Jasmine, her elfin features creased into an enormous grin. 'He's got *two*.'

Bob and Nora both stared at Jasmine in disbelief.

'Finding one's pretty amazing,' said Bob, pushing both hands through his blond hair, 'but the odds of two, especially on the same ward . . .' He trailed off at a loss for words.

'They couldn't have caught the cure from someone and passed it onto each other, could they?' asked Nora.

Tom shrugged, too stunned to speak for a moment, still trying to absorb the possible implications. 'Jazz,' he managed eventually, 'can you answer one more question for me, before you log off?'

Jasmine's grin broadened even further as her fingers tapped on the keys. 'Let me guess, Tom,' she said, as the screen changed, bringing up the Air France booking service. 'You want to know the next flight to Paris?'

7

CAVE OF THE SACRED LIGHT, SOUTHERN JORDAN.

TO KILL HIM, OR TO WORK WITH HIM? THAT WAS THE QUESTION.

On the other side of the world from Carter, beneath the five rocks of *Asbaa El-Lah*, Ezekiel De La Croix rubbed his tired eyes and felt the once snug ruby ring of leadership slip on his ancient, gnarled fingers. This dilemma had sharper horns than the Devil himself. If he chose the wrong path now he was certain to jeopardize the primary goal of the Brotherhood of the Second Coming.

Behind him in the Cave of the Sacred Light, the Sacred Flame still burned blue-white, as it had done for the last three and a half decades. But for how much longer? He dreaded the day when either the flame reverted, or he died – before finding the New Messiah. His frail shoulders shuddered when he considered that he was already in his tenth decade. Time was not on his side.

From his seat at the head of the vast oak table he watched the five men who sat arguing around it. Each wore a dark suit, white shirt and blood-red tie. A ceremonial sash of white satin bearing a crimson cross was draped over their shoulders. The heads of the three regions sat at the far end. Brother Haddad with his hooded eyes headed up the Holy Lands, the most ancient and prestigious territory of the Brotherhood; covering the Middle East and the Levant. Opposite him was the tall, silver-haired Brother Luciano who ran the second most important region of Christendom, which included Europe. Next to him sat the most junior of the regional heads, the sallow-skinned Brother Olazabal, who controlled the New World. All three were over seventy years of age and like most senior members of the Brotherhood were linked by distant blood lines to the early disciples of their founder Lazarus. Each held positions of substance in the outside world, and as members of the Inner Circle were powerful men within the Brotherhood. But they deferred to the two men who sat on either side of Ezekiel, who in turn deferred to him.

Ezekiel turned to the Brother sitting on his left. Now in his seventies, Brother Bernard Trier was the only other member of the Inner Circle still alive from that fateful day when the Sacred Flame had changed. The stout brother with the goatee beard and now wispy grey hair had once been a senior officer in the German Army. But ever since he had been promoted to the Champion of the Brotherhood's Secondary Imperative, he had become the only member of the Inner Circle to relinquish all commitments outside the Brotherhood. The Secondary Imperative with its rigorous demands on protecting the organization's security, gathering intelligence on those targeted for the Righteous Kills, as well as running the two operatives who carried out the Kills, was a full-time role. Even the more senior Brother Helix Kirkham, who as Champion of the Primary Imperative was charged with achieving the Brotherhood's main goal of finding the New Messiah, still maintained his Physics Professorship at Oxford. And Ezekiel himself found time outside leading the Brotherhood to oversee their considerable international banking interests.

Typically, during this monthly assembly in the Sacred Cavern, Brother Bernard and Brother Helix were arguing. It was understandable that they should fight. After all, five years ago Helix had succeeded Brother Darius as Champion of the Primary Imperative, and Ezekiel knew Bernard resented his influence. At fifty, Helix Kirkham was not only twenty years younger than Brother Bernard, he was also the youngest ever Champion of the Primary Imperative.

This tall bald man with the round wire-rimmed glasses represented the new blood the Brotherhood so sorely needed. Helix had been educated at the top universities, steeped in the science and technology of the age, equipped to guide the ancient Brotherhood through the modern maze of today's world. Ezekiel had selected him to inject new thinking and ideas into their search.

But surely this idea that was causing such disagreement now was too much? Too radical? And what frightened Ezekiel was that it could only be considered because Nemesis had so uncharacteristically failed in Stockholm over six weeks ago.

Bernard looked to him in exasperation before turning back to Helix, who seemed out of place in the cavern as he fiddled with his laptop computer and modem link.

'Brother Helix,' said Bernard, 'you can't seriously expect us to suspend the Righteous Cleansings for this . . .' he pointed at the laptop, 'this fantasy of yours.'

'It's not a fantasy,' replied Helix calmly. 'It could help us find the New Messiah.'

'But how do you know it will work?' asked Brother Luciano, running an agitated hand through silver hair.

A shrug. 'I don't. But it has to be better than the old ways. I was fifteen when the flame changed. And ever since then the network of Brothers has been searching the world for the New Messiah. But with what success?'

Brother Haddad blinked his hooded eyes. 'We are still looking.'

'But what have we *found?*'

A pause.

'Exactly! Over the last three decades we have sent out our best eyes and ears to investigate all those who claim to have visions, or perform miraculous feats. But although we have a short list of possible candidates who fit the ancient signs, not one of them tallies perfectly. We and the Brothers before us waited two thousand years for the flame to change and signal that the Messiah had come again, each of us hoping that the honour of searching for him would fall on *our* shoulders, in *our* time. Well, that honour has fallen on us. The New Messiah has been walking among us now for over three decades, and we *still* haven't found him.'

Bernard Trier pulled at his goatee in frustration. 'But Brother Helix, the man you expect to help us in our search is on our list of Righteous Kills. Dr Carter is an enemy, not an ally.' The stout Brother's tone became more controlled, but no less menacing. 'Brother Helix, we all bow to your technical wizardry. And I'm sure that one day it will add considerable value to our organization. But this is not the day. Perhaps I should remind you of the words and purpose of the Secondary Imperative.'

Before Ezekiel could stop him, Brother Bernard allowed himself a portentous clearing of the throat and pompously recited the ancient pledge.

'*To engage in the practice of Righteous Cleansing in order to purge the world of those who undermine the values, aims and beliefs of the Brotherhood of the Second Coming, and threaten the righteous salvation of mankind.* The dangerous scientist is close to the top of our list of kills. Through his genetic meddling he believes man will soon know enough to make our Lord redundant. He is playing God. That was why all of us – including you, Brother Helix – sanctioned the Stockholm purge. The only issue for me is *when* we complete the kill, and whether I use Nemesis again or give the job to Gomorrah.'

Helix nodded slowly, and his eyes smiled behind the thick glass of his round spectacles. As ever Ezekiel was impressed by the younger Brother's refusal to be intimidated by the aggressive Bernard.

'Thank you for reminding us of your important role, Brother Bernard,' said Helix without any trace of irony. 'However I'm sure that *I* don't need to remind *you* that the Primary Imperative of finding the Messiah takes precedence over any other – especially if it jeopardizes our search.'

Ezekiel was unhappy about so radical a swing from 'cleansing' Dr Carter to working with him. But he was equally reluctant to rush into killing the scientist before he fully understood how he might be useful.

'Brother Helix,' Ezekiel said before Bernard could reply, 'you say you need the scientist's technology to find a match for the genes. But why do you need *him?*'

'For two reasons,' replied Helix. 'First of all, we can't conduct the gene scan through the normal channels. Ethical guidelines are so strict in all the GENIUS processing labs throughout the world that questions are bound to be asked. The only way to get round the rigorous checks is to get Dr Carter himself to sanction the scan. Secondly, when it comes to finding the match, we will need his help to get into the IGOR database.'

'Can't we just pay to use the database?' asked Brother Luciano.

'No. As I've already explained, IGOR isn't a public service. In fact the contents of the database are supposed to be secret. I only stumbled across it when I was researching the scientist and his company for Brother Bernard. And since then I've only managed to hack into the front end screen to see what it contained.'

'Brother Helix,' interrupted Ezekiel, 'why don't you just *hack* into the database itself and look for a match that way?'

'Because it's too well protected. Just finding out what it contained was difficult enough. The system architect, a Dr Washington, is one of the best in her field. She's made IGOR virtually impregnable.'

'So you need Dr Carter's help to conduct the initial scan, and get you into this . . . IGOR?' concluded Ezekiel, frustrated with all the jargon and acronyms.

Helix nodded.

'But why should the scientist help us?' scoffed Bernard. 'How could we control him?'

Helix shrugged. 'I don't know yet. But at least if he's alive there's a chance of finding a way.' Helix took off his glasses and rubbed the lenses, then turned to him. 'Father Ezekiel, surely you must understand how important Dr Carter could be to the Primary Imperative? It would be unforgivable to preside over the white flame and *not* find the Messiah, and madness to rely only on our Watchers. Surely we must try everything to find the chosen one, whatever that entails?'

'But equally, Father,' Brother Bernard Trier quickly countered, 'we must also consider the implications of not only allowing the Secondary Imperative to slide, but of actually co-operating with one of the kills.'

Ezekiel kept his face impassive, refusing to decide immediately. Helix was right of course; he couldn't bear to think of them failing to locate the chosen one. But he also had some sympathy with Bernard. The idea of working with the dangerous blasphemer they were dedicated to cleansing made him uneasy.

In the middle of the vast table were platters of food and demijohns of aromatic wine. Ezekiel reached over and poured the spiced red wine into six pewter goblets and passed them round. The others took this as the signal to eat and drink while he thought through his decision. The older men helped themselves from the laden platters of stuffed vine leaves, figs and meat laid out before them. But Helix fingered his computer and glared impatiently at the altar behind Ezekiel; the candles and torches that illuminated the cavern reflected in his thick lenses.

Ezekiel admired the younger man's passion. But he was also painfully aware that the Brotherhood had not been in existence for over two thousand years for him to risk everything on one impetuous plan.

He looked over his shoulder, past the Sacred Flame and the altar, to the sealed stone door of the Vault of Remembrance – and thought of what lay hidden behind it. He suddenly felt weighed down by the two-thousand-year-old responsibility that rested on his old shoulders; when he thought of Lazarus, the founder of the Brotherhood, addressing the first followers in this place. He considered how on the night of the Crucifixion Lazarus had dreamed of a flame burning in the bowels of the earth, beneath a hand of rock marooned in the desert wilderness. With no map Lazarus had led his followers here, where they had chipped and carved their way through the natural caves and fissures to the flame. He had gathered them in this secret place where they could plot and prepare for Christ's return, ensuring that Golgotha would never be repeated. Then Lazarus had told them of the prophecy that had come to him in his dream:

The next Messiah would be unaware of his calling, and for the righteous to guarantee their salvation they would have to find and anoint him. There would be no star of Bethlehem to guide them, only this Sacred Fire burning deep in the earth. When this flame turned to white then the New Messiah would be abroad in the world. But he had to be found and anointed in the white fire before it reverted to orange, before the Final Judgement was visited upon mankind. Since only they had access to the Sacred Flame, this responsibility rested on the Brotherhood of the Second Coming. The salvation of mankind depended on them.

Ezekiel envied Lazarus's absolute faith. When Jesus Christ brought you back from the dead, then surely there could be no doubt in your heart that the man was divine, worthy of complete devotion.

He shook his head in awe. For the first millennium the Brothers had spread their covert influence across the Holy Lands, recruiting Christians and Messianic Jews alike to their ranks. All united behind the Primary Imperative of finding the New Messiah.

83

As Ezekiel watched the Brothers eat their fill, he reflected on the Secondary Imperative. During the Crusades of the twelfth century the Knights Templars had left Europe for the Holy Lands, determined to wrest Jerusalem from the Saracens, and had become involved in the Brotherhood. These warriors spread the sect's influence throughout Christendom when they returned to the great courts of Europe. But they also influenced the then Inner Circle to embrace a more aggressive policy to complement the Primary Imperative. They believed that instead of just watching and waiting for the saviour to arrive, the Brotherhood should dedicate themselves to purging the unrighteous while they did so.

The Secondary Imperative was thus born, but only those on the Inner Circle, and the two Righteous Cleansers, forever known only as Nemesis and Gomorrah, were told of its existence. The growing number of Brothers covertly seeded in various positions of influence throughout the world were only ever aware of the Primary Imperative.

The Secondary Imperative had inevitably caused problems in the past, but not in the way killing Dr Carter could. Ezekiel knew that it had never happened before; that the subject of a Righteous Kill for the Secondary Imperative also held a possible key to achieving the Primary. But then the flame had not burned white before either.

He felt Brother Helix tap him respectfully on the arm. 'Father Ezekiel, what is your decision?'

Ezekiel frowned. Dr Carter was a threat and every day his power was growing. He had to be stopped.

'Until I am convinced that Dr Carter would be willing to help us, then I can only make one decision: to kill him.'

'But if he could be persuaded?' probed Helix. 'Would you then postpone the kill?'

'Possibly,' Ezekiel turned to Brother Bernard. 'When is the earliest you could safely cleanse the scientist?'

'Well, there's additional security around him now, but it's superficial. Gomorrah will be too busy, but after completing her kill in Manhattan Nemesis should be available to complete the kill inside two weeks.'

Ezekiel thought for a moment, then turned back to his Champion of the Primary Imperative. 'Brother Helix, we will delay for a further two weeks. You therefore have one month to convince me we can safely and effectively work with Dr Carter. But after that time I will personally call up Nemesis and sanction the kill. Is that clear?'

Helix smiled at a frowning Bernard, and closed his laptop with a triumphant click. 'Perfectly clear, Father Ezekiel, perfectly clear.'

8

MANHATTAN.

THE STRIKING MAN WITH LONG HAIR AND SKY-BLUE EYES WAS whistling 'Frère Jaques' as he walked down Fifth Avenue. The pale afternoon sunlight caught the white-blond of his hair, so it seemed to halo his head and broad shoulders. The man's angelic air was further enhanced by his black, almost priestlike garb. Only the blood-red roses that peeked out of the tote bag in his right hand, and the tightness of his black leather trousers, hinted at a more earthly passion. As he whistled he wore a serene smile of utter contentment on his fine-featured face.

Passers-by noticed him, but they had no way of knowing that the object of their admiration was not a man at all, but a woman. They certainly had no idea that this woman was on her way to perform a righteous execution.

Maria Benariac blinked, momentarily hiding her coloured contact lenses and tried to stop the maddening need to scratch her scalp. She usually wore specially designed wigs, but she had needed to 'borrow' this one. She was acutely aware that others who shared her vocation preferred the faceless 'grey' look, staying as inconspicuous and un-noticed as possible. That worked well for some jobs and usually she hated unwelcome attention. But on other occasions she liked to use her surgically smoothed face and body as a canvas upon which to paint a strong misleading image that witnesses would later remember. This was one such occasion. Plus, today her very appearance should help her gain access to her prey.

Maria could see Sly Fontana's apartment block now. Overlooking the park. Very impressive. According to Brother Bernard's manila folder Fontana used this apartment as his east coast residence, coming here whenever he needed to escape from LA, or spend time with Babe, the high-class male model-cum-prostitute he was addicted to. Maria didn't find it ironic that Sly Fontana, notorious as a producer of hard-core hetero porn movies, should be gay. She knew from her own personal research that Sly Fontana was into every kind of sexual perversion. The winner of eight Hot D'Or porn awards at Cannes, Fontana controlled a huge share of the international sex film industry. However, his real passion was for snuff movies: videos showing victims, usually women, performing sex, before being sadistically murdered at the moment of climax. To prove their deaths were 'real' the victims' throats were cut on camera; always in close-up and often so severely that they were practically beheaded. Maria had seen one of these films. It was a grainy, scratchy copy many generations removed from the master tape, but the content had been clearly visible and it was still worth thousands of dollars.

The copy had belonged to Babe, and Maria had seen it last night when she'd visited his well-appointed apartment in Greenwich Village. His address was in Brother Bernard's manila folder, and it had been simple to break in and 'interview' him. A knife and six minutes was all she'd needed to convince the body-builder to tell her everything about Fontana, and arrange a meeting with him today. After breaking the worthless Babe's neck she had rifled through his wardrobe, selecting the all-black ensemble Fontana liked his favourite companion to wear.

Scalping Babe's head had been more difficult than she'd thought, like trying to peel an orange in one, without breaking the rind. But eventually after much effort she had succeeded. She had left it to dry overnight, and this morning had used talc and adhesive strips to apply the scalp to her shaven head. The effect was good but it itched like crazy.

She took the Ray-Bans out of the black leather tote bag and put them on. She was only yards away from the uptown apartment tower now. The familiar feeling of excitement and righteous anticipation rolled like warm, delicious syrup in her belly.

The doorman was standing beneath the entrance awning. He looked huge in his uniform, but he posed no threat. He immediately turned away when she approached in her blond, black-clad disguise, just as Babe had said he would. Babe had explained that the doormen knew all the whores, male and female, who serviced the tower's well-heeled residents. Without exception the doormen knew when not to notice people coming into the block. Maria allowed herself a thin smile at the irony of Sly Fontana slipping the protective doorman money to grant his killer access to his home.

With barely a glance towards the doorman Maria strolled confidently into the gloomy marbled lobby and headed straight for the elevators. Once inside she checked her watch. 14:52. Fontana was expecting Babe at exactly 15:00. Plenty of time.

On the seventh floor she got out and walked to the stairwell where she waited. It was dark here, pitch black, and as always it made her uncomfortable. Taking a deep breath she reminded herself that the darkness was only temporary. To her right she saw a timed switch glowing like a beacon. She pressed it and the sudden light chased away her demons. She looked into her leather tote bag and pulled out a pair of condom-thin surgical gloves. Expertly she rolled them onto her hands, then returned to the contents of the bag. First she checked the video camera; no incriminating tape of course, but it would suffice. At the bottom of the bag, beside the camera, lay her trusty kukri. She foraged around under the red roses for the remaining three smaller objects: a roll of strong, highly adhesive duct tape, a garrotte and a black fountain pen. She put the first two in the side pockets of her jacket. The pen looked quite normal until she opened the top revealing its unusually long nib – not far short of a hypodermic needle. She blew down the nib, confirming it was clear, then replaced the cap and put the pen back in the tote bag. Everything was ready.

She felt the righteous thrill fill her chest. She was the avenging angel, the scourge of God. On this day the vile tide of Evil would be stanched momentarily, one of its many hydra heads severed.

She opened the door onto the seventh floor and looked down the corridor. She could clearly see the dark wooden door at the end of the corridor with its brass number 70 prominently displayed. Behind that door Sly Fontana should be alone, expecting three knocks and a pile of red roses on the doormat; Babe's trademark greeting. How touching, thought Maria, without a trace of a smile touching her lips.

The pulse alarm on her wristwatch vibrated silently against her skin. She looked down. 14:59. It was time.

She walked down the lush-carpeted corridor, placed the pile of roses on the floor outside apartment 70, then flattened herself against the wall to the left of the doorway. Her right hand played with the garrotte in her pocket as if it were a string of worry beads. And once she had controlled her breathing she rested her knuckles against the door.

Knock. Knock. Knock.

Movement. The shuffling of feet moving towards the door.

She heard a bolt being pulled, and a chain lifted. Then a key being turned. Followed by yet another key. Security-conscious, thought Maria with grim humour. She listened to the door opening, sensed a subtle shift in air temperature. It was warm in the apartment. She heard an intake of breath and then an excited chuckle as a man stooped to pick up the roses.

Adjusting her shades and lowering her head so Babe's long blond hair fell over her face, Maria stepped out in front of Sly Fontana, the crotch of her tight leather trousers inches from his head. Even though Fontana was bending over, she could see that the porn producer was a short man, less than five seven. He had thin, straggly black hair and a flabby body that even his outsize silk shirt couldn't disguise.

She watched him slowly straighten, holding the roses. He looked up at her with hungry, beady eyes, trying to see her face beneath the hair. It reminded her of a time back in the orphanage, a time she'd rather forget.

'Hiya Babe,' Fontana said excitedly, his hand unconsciously rubbing his crotch. 'God, I'm glad you're here. I've been set to explode ever since we talked on the phone.' He backed into the apartment, beckoning her to follow.

Maria, whose hands were busy preparing the garrotte behind her back, kicked the tote in front of her and walked into the apartment, allowing the door to close behind her. Fontana glanced down at the bag by her feet and licked his lips. 'You've brought some toys for us to play with?'

'You could thay that,' answered Maria, doing a passable imitation of Babe's lisp.

But perhaps the imitation wasn't good enough, or the hair was no longer covering her face, because Fontana suddenly looked at her more closely. 'Have you grown or something?' he asked.

Maria stepped forward and smiled, bringing her hands round to the front as if to embrace him. 'Not really. I've been this height for years.'

Fontana was frowning now, the lust in his eyes replaced by suspicion and fear. He realized something was wrong. But Maria didn't care; it was already too late, she was inside. Even as she watched his lips start to form an outraged 'Who the hell are you?' Maria brought the garrotte around his neck, squeezing off his question with the practised skill of a surgeon. Fontana immediately dropped the roses, gasping and twitching like a landed fish as he clawed at the cheese wire digging into his neck.

Why did they always do that? Maria wondered, looking into his bulging terrified eyes. No-one ever did the sensible thing, and focused on her fingers, breaking each one in turn, until she had to let go. They always went for the wire that was already cutting through their neck. It was so foolish; so futile.

Maria quickly scanned the open-plan apartment, until her eyes settled on the pale leather chairs and the all important TV in the living-room area. Pulling Fontana like a whimpering dog on a leash she led him past an ostentatious pink marble fireplace, and pushed him into a chair directly facing the magnificent television screen. Large and as black as polished jet, the TV was a fitting altar for her task.

She released the garrotte, but before Fontana even had time to catch his breath she took a small pink marble egg from the nest of similar *objects d'art* on the coffee table beside her, and pushed it into his mouth. Then she pulled the roll of duct tape out of her pocket, tore off a strip and sealed his lips with it. Without a pause she wrapped the tape around his body and the chair. Finally she taped his eyelids open so only his darting, panicky eyeballs could move. She reached into the tote for the video camera. She could now take her time preparing for the performance.

It took her a moment or two to fathom all the controls on the smooth, apparently buttonless TV once she'd located the flush sliding panels. After connecting the necessary cables she placed the camera on top of the TV, and pointed the lens at the gagged man. Then she reached for the remote controls and activated both machines. The picture flickered for a second, until the large screen was filled with the top part of Sly Fontana's forehead. The definition was good and Maria could see each drop of sweat forming below his receding hairline.

'You look nervous, Sly,' she said. 'I'd have thought you'd be used to auditions by now.' She adjusted the camera and zoom lens, until the screen showed Fontana from the waist up in perfect focus. Dark circles of sweat radiated out from the underarms of his pale cream silk shirt as his frantic eyes pleaded with her. His every muscle seemed to be straining against the reinforced tape. She smiled and pulled off her wig. Sly Fontana's eyes bulged further, taking in her shaven appearance, and then almost came out of their sockets when she reached into the tote bag and pulled out the unsheathed kukri.

'Right,' she said, walking round to stand behind him, her left hand holding the camera remote and the right hand the curved dagger. 'Let the show begin.'

She bent down so her face was alongside his, both clearly visible on the screen. She put her mouth close to his ear and saw wax and hair, then she whispered with the intimacy of a lover, 'I've seen some of your more specialized work, and although I can't hope to match it, I would like you to think of this as a kind of homage. Remember the Bible. All they that take the sword shall perish with the sword.' With the remote she zoomed the lens onto his neck until the whole screen was virtually filled with his sweaty Adam's apple bobbing nervously up and down. Then she looped her right arm around his neck and placed the edge of the dagger to his throat. On the screen the flawless silver of its keen, curved blade contrasted with his LA tan. She felt Sly try to turn away, but the tape and her arm locked his head in place.

As she slowly pushed the razor-sharp edge of the kukri into his flesh she directed the camera lens away from the neck and onto his eyes, until only his eyeballs filled the screen. Sly desperately tried to close his eyelids, and look away from the screen, but the duct tape held them open. And as her right hand slowly drew the blade across his throat, severing muscle and tissue, Sly Fontana had to stare into the windows of his own soul: the terrified star and audience of his own snuff movie. Those trembling eyeballs were forced to witness their own agony and death, to see the perfect moment that Maria always looked for; the flicker of dilating pupils that marked the departure of a damned soul to another place, where judgement would be stern and punishment eternal.

Just before her blade reached the jugular she pulled back from the already copious flow of blood and hissed into his ear, 'You will die now, and be damned for ever.' Satisfied that the man knew his sins had caught up with him she pulled the blade across the rest of his throat. She watched, along with Sly, as the blood from his ruptured jugular sprayed the screen, then after a second or two the giant pupils flickered and went blank.

Maria released a small involuntary sigh. The kill had been executed. She should leave now. She was Nemesis, the professional avenger who had performed another perfect kill. But she couldn't go. Not yet.

She had to sign her work, to prove that she'd performed the act. She reached into the tote bag and pulled out the fountain pen, unscrewing the cap to reveal the custom-made extra-long nib. Then she approached the corpse, and after locating the jugular in Sly's neck wound plunged the long nib into the artery, filling the pen's reservoir with blood.

When she had enough she withdrew the nib and proceeded to write on the dry area on the back of his pale cream shirt collar.

All they that take the sword shall perish with the sword. St Matthew ch. 26, v. 52

Afterwards she replaced the cap on the pen and put it back in the tote bag with the rest of her equipment. Then she fixed Babe's blond locks back on her head, picked up the roses lying on the floor of the hallway and threw them into the kitchen trash can. She thought nothing of the small pain as one of the thorns ruptured the rubber glove, and pierced the soft flesh of her right thumb. And as she sucked it clean, she barely registered the metallic, salty taste on her tongue.

Finally she checked that the hallway corridor was clear, and quietly left the apartment, closing the door behind her.

No mistakes this time. The perfect kill.

DAMASCUS.

EZEKIEL DE LA CROIX WALKED PAST THE ORANGE TREES IN HIS garden to the olive grove that sloped down to the perimeter of his land. He stopped and looked out at the Damascus skyline two miles to the south. The air was chill, but the late afternoon light cast a warm golden glow on the twisted olive trees and distant city. He had spent his life travelling the world but the large old house behind him had always been his home, as it had for six generations before him. It saddened him that he had no child to inherit it. He loved this place, especially at this time of day. It reminded him of the walks he used to take with his wife when she was alive. When they would talk, and soothe away each other's problems.

A sudden searing pain in his stomach made him reach for the small metal box in his pocket, and take out a white tablet. He swallowed it, letting the antacid work on his ulcer. As the pain softened he thought of Brother Helix's plan. Last night, after returning from the meeting of the Inner Circle, Ezekiel had endured his recurring nightmare again. And as always in the dream he had not only failed to save the New Messiah, but had helped crucify him too. It brought home the dread he felt of failing in his life's mission, making him consider Helix's proposal more seriously. He was only too aware that as each day passed without finding the Messiah, the balance of risk moved in favour of adopting the younger Brother's daring plan. Assuming of course that Helix could convince the blaspheming scientist to work with them.

He turned and began to walk back up the hill to the large house. What if Helix did get Dr Carter to co-operate with them? Would he, as Leader of the Brotherhood of the Second Coming, really enter into an unholy alliance with the atheist?

He was wrestling with the implications of this when he saw his manservant beckoning from the arched courtyard of the house. Ezekiel waved in acknowledgement as David's tall figure began walking towards him across the manicured lawns. He held something in his hand, and when Ezekiel scrunched up his eyes he could see it was a phone.

'Who is it, David?'

'She would only give her name as Nemesis.'

He took the phone and sighed. The message would be digitally encoded. Still, he didn't encourage Maria to call him direct, especially at home. Putting the phone to his ear he said, 'Nemesis, what is it?'

Her voice was contrite. 'Father, I had to call you. You haven't contacted me since Stockholm. I needed to explain my mistake. To tell you that it won't happen again, and that I want to correct it.'

'You should talk with Brother Bernard, not me. If you want to explain or apologize to anybody, it should be to him.'

'But Father, I need to know if *you* forgive me for Stockholm.'

He shook his head in exasperation. Maria had always been like this, ever since he'd found her twenty years ago. She could at once be the vulnerable child craving a parent's love, and the most ruthless operative their training camp had ever produced. He didn't blame her for Stockholm, not really. It was her first and only mistake. 'Nemesis, Stockholm is over. It happened and now we must all move on.'

'Do you forgive me, then?'

He could hear the anxiety in her voice. He allowed himself a small smile, remembering her in the Corsican orphanage, so damaged and so desperate to belong. He'd been tempted then to think of her as the child his wife could never give him. And even now he had to admit that he had an affection for her. 'Yes, Maria, my child. I forgive you. Now, what—'

'Can I finish the scientist, then?'

He hesitated. 'Wait, you have other priorities. The Manhattan—'

'That's done. I've successfully completed the Manhattan kill. I deserve another chance with Dr Carter.'

Ezekiel chose his words carefully now. He knew how passionately Maria took her responsibilities.

'Nemesis, you don't decide who is to be cleansed. You are an excellent operative, but as I've already said, your role is to carry out the kills given you by Brother Bernard.'

'But—'

'Nemesis!' His voice was firmer now. He hadn't even decided what to do about Dr Carter yet. 'When and if the scientist is to be cleansed we will tell you, assuming of course Bernard chooses you to conduct it.'

'But, what do you mean, if? What has changed? If Dr Carter was a kill two months ago, then surely he still is. And if I don't complete the deed, who will? . . . Gomorrah?'

'Nemesis, listen to me!' As he lost patience, his stomach ulcer began to hurt again. Usually he supported giving Maria a free rein. It helped keep her motivated, and even her obsessive need to leave messages on her over-elaborate kills had done the Brotherhood no harm. But perhaps Bernard was right; perhaps he did give her too much leeway. 'Nemesis, you should deal with the Champion of the Secondary Imperative, not me. And remember! You *take* orders from him. You do not *give* them. Is that clear?'

'Yes, but . . .'

'*Is that clear?*'

Her voice sounded subdued, but cold. 'Yes, Father.'

'Good!' He hung up. Ezekiel was seeing Brother Bernard Trier tomorrow and would tell him of this conversation. It was important that the Champion of the Secondary Imperative stopped Maria from dwelling on her failure in Stockholm before it affected the rest of her work.

He walked back to the house, watching the sun set to his right. And as he thought of Maria and Dr Carter, he reached for another white tablet. He was too old for this. He was ninety-six. Was it right that the salvation of mankind should rest on his decrepit shoulders?

Anybody else would be relaxing now in the sunset years of their life.

Or dead.

He gave a tired shrug, and for a fleeting moment welcomed the rest that death promised. But even as he stepped onto the terracotta tiles of the courtyard, his nightmare intruded on his consciousness, kindling afresh the fire in his heart. He knew that he could never die in peace. Not until the prophecy had been fulfilled. Not until the New Messiah had been found, and anointed in the Sacred Flame.

9

L'HÔPITAL DE MÉDECINE, TROISIÈME ARRONDISSEMENT, PARIS.

JEAN LUC PETIT WAS AS FULL OF ENERGY AS TOM CARTER remembered him. Despite Tom's superior height his limp meant he had to lengthen his stride just to keep up with the Frenchman, as they raced down the corridors of L'Hôpital de Médecine.

Tom still felt dazed, and it had nothing to do with the eight-hour flight from Logan Airport to Charles de Gaulle. When the mouse experiment had failed so disastrously he'd resigned himself to beginning again, even though he knew there was no hope of developing a genetically engineered solution in time. Then, almost immediately the idea of searching for the viral root of spontaneous remissions had come to him. And if that wasn't enough, minutes later Jasmine had found not only one, but two rare cases of the phenomenon – on the *same* ward. If he'd been a religious man Tom might have even been tempted to call it divine intervention.

'Jean Luc. *Plus lentement, plus lentement*. You walk too fast,' said Tom, slightly out of breath.

Tom watched the French doctor turn his head, his dark, comically sad eyes brimming with remorse, his splendid nose pointing at him. The man gave a shrug, sidestepped two nurses without missing a pace and apologized. 'I am very sorry. I don't know how to go more slowly without stopping.'

Jean Luc was slightly built but carried himself with the relaxed stoop of a much taller man. His short legs moved like pistons as he clattered down the fluorescent-lit corridors, throwing out the occasional *'Bonjour'* and *'Ça va'* to those caught in his wake. The French doctor carried two files under his left arm as he led Tom to the François Mitterand Oncology ward, where the so-called 'miracles' had happened.

'Jean Luc, are you sure you've got no idea at all why they got better?'

The Frenchman's shoulders shrugged, his face turned and the dark hangdog eyes smiled. 'Perhaps it's a miracle. Like everyone says.'

'But there must be a reason,' Tom insisted as he avoided a porter wheeling a patient down the corridor on a gurney. 'Something that explains what happened. Something we can learn from. Surely? What have your tests shown?'

'You can see for yourself later, but nothing really. Nothing to explain *why* their bodies cured themselves. Only that they did.' Jean Luc's smile broadened, wrinkling his impressive nose. 'My friend, why must science always explain everything? It is so rare that something *good* happens that we cannot understand. Perhaps we should just be grateful. *Non?*'

Dr Petit barely broke his stride when he came to the closed swing-doors of the Oncology Ward, and pushed them open. The room was surprisingly cheerful, with a similar bright blue and yellow colour scheme to the ward back at GENIUS. Carter wasn't sure if it was copied, but it had definitely been redecorated since Jean Luc had last visited him in Boston. There were two rows of ten beds, each with enough space between them to offer a modicum of privacy. Some had curtains pulled around them.

Still moving at full speed Dr Petit scanned the beds, his nose pointing like some targeting device. Then he spotted his objective. *'Ah bon.* We shall visit Mademoiselle Dubois first.'

As he followed the doctor through the ward Tom was struck by the atmosphere of the place. There was a palpable buzz coming from the patients and staff. He'd never experienced anything like it in a mainstream hospital before. Cancer wards were usually hushed, reflective places, populated by people trying to come to terms with their life and the possible end of it. But this ward was charged with more expectancy than reflection. And the bed they were heading for was surrounded by flowers. Not formal wreaths, but riotous blooms that confidently shouted 'get well soon'. Tom could tell that this was the bed of someone who would be leaving. Out of the front door. On her own two feet.

When Dr Petit introduced Tom to Valerie Dubois, the first thing he noticed about her was the calm in her violet eyes. They radiated a self-assured, almost arrogant serenity. Those eyes had witnessed what few mortals had. They had stared death in the eye and seen it blink. Tom could tell just from looking at her that she was well. She was slender to the point of thin, and a cap covered her hairless scalp, but there was nothing frail about her. The skin over her high cheekbones had none of the chalky pallor associated with disease. Instead it had the subtle blush of the convalescent, the pink that heralded the dawn of a new lease of life.

Dr Petit beamed and patted her proudly on the shoulder. 'Valerie is a twenty-five-year-old law student studying at the Sorbonne. So I'm glad she's better, otherwise she might have sued.' He laughed and his shoulders moved with every chuckle.

Valerie seemed pleased to have him here, as if his wonder at her condition reinforced the fact that she was indeed better. Tom guessed it made a change from before, when every doctor she saw only gave her bad news.

Dr Petit opened one of his two folders. 'She had primary tumours in her stomach and kidneys. And secondary metastases all over her body, including two on the meninges of the brain.' He handed Tom two X-rays.

Tom held them up to the light. The shadowy tumours in the stomach and the kidneys on the chart in his left hand were clearly visible. And the small but distinct shadows on the brain were unmistakable on the other chart. This woman had cancer all right: rampant terminal cancer that was well into the final stage of clonal evolution.

But not any more.

'We were just about to start her on immunotherapy with gene-modified cells,' continued Dr Petit, 'when she told us her headaches had stopped and that the metastases she could feel on her side were shrinking.' His intelligent dark eyes looked down at Valerie, who smiled back at him.

'Valerie, how sudden was it?' asked Tom. 'The decrease in your tumours.'

'It was noticeable in a day. At first I thought I must be imagining it. Hoping it. But then by the evening I decided to tell Dr Petit.' Valerie shrugged, her eyes radiating confidence. 'Also I felt better. I just *knew* I was getting better.'

He nodded as he looked into her assured eyes. What was that over-used Nietsche quote? 'That which does not destroy us makes us stronger.' He understood what the philosopher really meant then, and felt a rush of envy. This woman would never be frightened of death again.

'How long ago did this happen?'

Dr Petit checked his file. 'Today's Tuesday. Valerie alerted us on Thursday evening. And by last thing on Sunday we had seen this much improvement.' He handed over two more X-rays.

Tom took them and again held them up to the light. The difference was remarkable. They could almost be the charts of a different patient. The large tumours in the stomach and kidneys had shrunk to just a smudge and the brain looked clear. No tumours at all.

'We also conducted exploratory surgery to check,' explained the French doctor. 'The pathologist confirmed from the tumour samples that they were now necrotic. The tumour tissue was dead, killed by the body's antibodies.'

Tom looked at the two sets of X-rays side by side. 'And there's no clue at all how, or why?'

'Nothing. Except the DNA analysis we got from GENIUS Paris.'

'You've already done DNA analysis?' he asked with a mixture of excitement and disappointment. 'And you found nothing?'

'*Au contraire.*' Dr Petit pointed across the ward at another bed similarly bedecked with flowers. 'We used the GENIUS Processing Laboratory in Paris to scan the blood of both the patients, Valerie here and Monsieur Corbasson over there. The gene scan showed that their blood prior to the remission carried the genetic defects that led to their disease. But after the remission their genome was changed, altered . . .'

'The genetic sequence in their genome had corrected itself? Their *whole* genome? Not just the affected cells?'

'*Mais bien sur*,' said the Frenchman. 'But we don't know how. The only link between the two is that they share the same blood type and could have received blood transfusions from the same batch. But we don't have any samples left of the batch used.'

'They received the same blood transfusion, but nothing else? No other links?' asked Tom.

Dr Petit shook his head. '*Rien.*'

'Were any other patients treated with the same batch?'

'Not cancer patients. No. It was a rare type. AB.' Jean Luc's doleful eyes sparkled again. 'Come! Let us meet with the second miracle patient. *A bientôt*, Valerie.'

Tom thanked Valerie and said goodbye. And by the time he turned to follow Dr Petit, the Frenchman was already standing across the ward by the other bed, beckoning him with quick impatient gestures.

The second miracle patient was Guillaume Corbasson, a forty-five-year-old farmer from near Toulouse. Tom shook the man's hand and greeted him in French.

Dr Petit took a photograph from the second file under his arm and explained, 'Monsieur Corbasson had a major sarcoma on his thigh, and a number of secondary metastases throughout his body.' He showed the photo to Tom, who studied the hugely distended lump on the man's right thigh. A tumour the size of a grapefruit, it threatened to break through the skin.

Tom asked, 'When was this taken?'

'One week ago exactly. It had doubled in size in almost eight weeks. So we were getting desperate to control it.' Dr Petit looked up from his file. 'Again we were just about to put him on gene therapy, when it began to decline.'

'At about the same time as Valerie Dubois's condition began to improve?'

'Within a day or so.' replied Dr Petit. The French doctor asked his patient if they could see his leg.

'*Mais bien sur*,' declared Guillaume, eagerly pulling back the covers to show the proof of his victory.

Tom reached down and ran his hands over the man's thigh. It was virtually flat. If he pressed hard he could still feel a small ball of hard tissue, but it was tiny, a pea compared to the photograph.

'Incredible!'

'*Oui. Incroyable*!' agreed the patient with a gleeful grin that revealed two missing teeth.

Tom smiled back, then turned to the doctor. 'How about the secondaries?'

'All are necrotic, completely dead. Now I suggest we go back to my office where we can talk further.'

Tom thanked Corbasson and followed the doctor out of the ward. As they walked he continued to bombard the French doctor with questions.

'Jean Luc, this can't just be coincidence. You have two terminally ill patients, months away from death, then all of a sudden they're both cured. And the only link, apart from being on the same ward with the same doctor, is that they have the same rare blood type, which means they may have shared a similar batch of donor blood. Perhaps there was something in the blood transfusions?'

'Like what?' Dr Petit asked.

Tom shook his head in frustration and said, 'A new virus perhaps. A rare positive one that carried a corrective genetic sequence in it. It could happen, Jean Luc.'

Dr Petit sighed and rolled his dark doleful eyes. 'Yes, it *could* happen. But the odds are long, are they not? Both patients have been thoroughly screened for viral infections and nothing's been found. And don't forget that all the blood samples undergo numerous heat treatments to kill all known viral agents.'

'Yes, but only *known* viral agents.'

'But there was no evidence of *any* virus in either Valerie Dubois's or Guillaume Corbasson's bloodstream. Nor any change agent either.' Dr Petit stopped outside his office and then walked in. He gestured for Tom to take a seat and walked to the coffee machine where he poured two cups.

Tom took the coffee offered by his host. 'But there was a change,' he insisted. 'That's evidence that something happened. Something changed. Perhaps there was something in the genetic make-up of the blood they received that modified their own DNA? An instruction that cancelled their own badly spelt programme and replaced it with the correct code in the donor's blood?'

'Perhaps,' admitted Dr Petit, taking his seat and a drink of his coffee. His dark eyes looked at Tom over the rim of his steaming cup. 'Look, I want to find the reason as much as you do, obviously, because then we could perhaps replicate the effect. But we can't find the reason. As you know the blood transfusion came from a compound batch of numerous anonymous individuals. And because we don't have any remaining samples of the particular batch, we can't analyse the blood. Of course you're welcome to analyse the cured patients' blood, and look at all the gene scans. But that will tell you nothing. It would be like using a spent match to re-create fire. The catalyst has gone. But anyway, Tom, if this miracle strain of yours does exist, why haven't we all caught the virus?'

Tom frowned. This was the one question he had been avoiding asking himself, because he couldn't think of a convincing enough answer. Most contagious viruses didn't spread throughout the whole human population because they burnt themselves out, killing their hosts before they could pass it on. But a miracle strain like the one he was pinning his hopes on would actually extend its host's life. So assuming the positive virus had been around for even a few decades, then logic would dictate that most of the world population should have caught it by now. 'I don't know, Jean Luc,' he admitted after a short pause. 'But everything has a cause and an effect.'

'OK. Then could your miracle strain be chemical instead of viral?'

'Chemical? What do you mean? Like pheromones?'

Jean Luc performed yet another shrug. '*Oui*. Why not? If insects can secrete chemicals, then why can't we?'

Tom nodded cautiously, aware he was clutching at straws now. Still, it was true that some insects did secrete pheromones to arouse potential mates, and it had long been believed that humans secreted similar chemicals through their sweat and blood. He knew for example that when two or more women lived in the same house together the timing of their menstrual cycles would coincide over time. No-one yet knew exactly how this happened, but it was suspected to be due to some chemical stimulus passed between them. A chemical rather than viral agent for the healing gift would also explain its rarity. A healer might possess rare genes in his DNA which allowed him to secrete healing chemicals through touch, or bodily fluids, without passing on, or 'spreading', the ability.

'Still sounds a bit thin, doesn't it?' he said.

'Perhaps the cures weren't scientific at all, but God's will,' replied Jean Luc with a smile. 'Tom, if you were a fellow-Christian you might understand. Christmas has just passed and Easter is not far away. Perhaps God simply had mercy on two unfortunates? Decided to meddle in nature to commemorate the birth, death and resurrection of His son?'

Tom gave a wry smile and immediately thought of Jasmine. He envied her and Jean Luc's faith. Whenever they didn't understand anything they just had to say, 'Oh it must be God moving in one of His mysterious ways again.' No more questions, no more doubts, no more headaches. Too difficult to work out? Then it must be put down to God. Easy.

'So Jean Luc,' he asked with a weary sigh, 'help me to understand. How would your God have gone about saving them?'

Jean Luc smiled and his dark compassionate eyes searched Tom's face. It was plain that the French doctor was unsure how serious he was being. 'Well, God can do anything. He is omnipotent, you know.' The Frenchman spread his hands wide in an expansive gesture and shot Tom a mischievous grin. 'Perhaps He just decreed that they both got better. Or perhaps He did as you say. He tampered with the blood . . .' Suddenly the Frenchman chuckled at something he'd just thought of. 'Yes, Tom, perhaps He changed the blood transfusion into the blood of Jesus. It will be Easter soon, so it would be right that His son's blood should again save mankind. *Non?*'

Jean Luc Petit laughed again, an easy innocent laugh that clearly gloried in the happy salvation of his two patients.

But Tom didn't join him.

Jean Luc suddenly stopped and looked upset, as if he'd caused offence. 'I'm only joking my friend. I'm a doctor not a philosopher and I still don't know.'

Tom didn't respond because his mind was elsewhere, making a connection between two apparently unrelated thoughts: the notion of a healing virus or pheromone and something else Jean Luc had said. When brought together they formed the germ of a preposterous idea. He tried to remember that article he'd read in a magazine a few weeks back. Where was the place again? Somewhere in Sardinia? He'd ring

Dad. Alex would know. And he'd ask him to brief him on the rest of the topic too.

He turned to the concerned doctor. 'Jean Luc?'

'*Oui, mon ami.*'

Tom rose from his chair and patted his friend on the shoulder. 'Thanks for everything, but could I please ask you two more favours?'

'Anything.'

'First of all, can I use a private phone?'

'*Mais bien sur.*'

'And can your secretary get my return flight diverted to Sardinia?'

'Sardinia?' Jean Luc gave him a bemused smile, as he rose to lead Tom to the next office. 'Certainly, Tom. Is anything wrong?'

'No, Jean Luc,' he said, trying to get his mind round his far-fetched idea. 'Nothing's wrong. Nothing's wrong at all.'

10

GENIUS HEADQUARTERS, INFORMATION TECHNOLOGY SECTION, BOSTON.

JASMINE WASHINGTON WATCHED SPECIAL AGENT KAREN TANNER'S face and waited for her reaction. She wasn't disappointed when it came. The auburn-haired FBI agent's green eyes opened wide and an involuntary 'Jeez!' issued from her parted lips. 'How the hell did you do that?'

Jasmine shared a conspiratorial smile with Debbie, her tall blonde assistant. The Gene-Imaging software was virtually glitch-free, and the definition on the hologram was excellent. Even the technophobic Jack Nichols looked impressed.

All four of them stood in the Genescope facility, next to Jasmine's office in the IT Section. Since Tom had dashed off to Paris three days before she had been working around the clock with Debbie and her team to perfect the software. And it was just as well, because earlier today Jack Nichols, still fuming about Tom's unescorted jaunt around Europe, had been telephoned by an excited Karen Tanner. There had been another murder in Manhattan with all the Preacher's trademarks, but this time the killer had apparently left something behind that might identify him.

'So, how does it work?' asked Karen Tanner again, staring at the lifesize hologram of her head as it floated above the holo-pad next to the farthest Genescope.

Jasmine studied the 3-D image for a moment longer before answering. It was a pity Tom hadn't returned from Paris, or Sardinia, or wherever he was now. He hadn't yet seen a totally glitch-free demonstration of the technology, and this was perfect. The hologram was so lifelike it was spooky; even the auburn hair and green eyes were identical. If anything, it looked slightly younger than the real-life original, but that could be modified just by entering more accurate environmental inputs.

'It works by reading your genes and calculating your appearance,' Jasmine said eventually. 'When you came in this morning I took a hair from the shoulder of your jacket. I had to check it still had the root attached, but then the rest was easy.'

Karen reached out and put her hand through the ghostly head. 'It looks just like me. It's incredible. Can you only do the head?'

'No, we can do the whole body. But we decided to protect your modesty in front of Jack here.'

Karen gave her a puzzled look.

'Clothes don't have genes,' explained Debbie, grinning from ear to ear.

Jack gave the crescent-shaped scar on his face a pensive stroke. 'What a shame, Karen. You and I have been through some scrapes together, but I've never seen you "au naturel" before. I've often wondered about it though.'

'Well you can keep on wondering, Jack,' laughed Karen. 'Unless of course you want to show me yours first.'

Turning back to Jasmine, Karen nodded towards the hologram. 'So you got that from the DNA in my hair root?'

'Yup. The Genescope has always been able to tell physical characteristics from a person's genotype, but this new software takes it one stage further. It builds up a three-dimensional computer-generated picture of an individual from their genes, and then converts it into a hologram.' She pointed to the suspended head. 'We only used your hair to show you how accurate it is.'

'I'm convinced. But how about the suspect's DNA? I can't wait to get a look at the bastard.'

Jasmine turned back to the Genescope and punched four keys on the adjacent keyboard. This prototype had no voice commands yet, but that would come. In time she would even be able to make the holograms talk back. She pressed one final tab and the lifesize head of Karen Tanner vanished into thin air.

Jasmine turned back to the screen above the keyboard. Karen's colleagues in forensics had found fresh blood on the thorns of a rose in the murder victim's kitchen trash; the same roses witnesses had seen in the blond suspect's tote bag. 'OK, we've done the analysis on the blood sample found at Fontana's apartment.'

The FBI agent nodded, her green eyes expectant. 'And?'

Jasmine watched Debbie check the holo-lamps, then give her a thumbs-up sign. 'Well, what do you want? Just the Preacher's head or his whole body?'

Karen smiled. 'Give me the works.'

'OK, time to summon up the Genie.'

Jasmine pushed the enter key.

The rumble from the Genescope changed to the crackling sound of static, then the holo-lamps around the circular holo-pad lit up, and a ghostly figure appeared before them. The apparition conjured up from the Preacher's genes gradually became more solid in appearance as the four coloured holo-lamps – one magenta, one cyan, one yellow, and one white – merged to create the necessary variety of hues, painting in the higher levels of definition fed to them by the Genescope's bio-computer.

This 'painting' happened from the feet up, line by line, and within seconds the figure was complete. It was perfectly lifelike, except there was one thing wrong with it. It was a woman.

Jasmine turned to the stunned FBI agent, staring open-mouthed at the hologram and said, 'I thought the Preacher was a man?'

Karen nodded vacantly. 'So did I.'

'She's beautiful,' said Jack.

And she was. Her hair was a rich coppery chestnut and her tall, athletic figure with its full breasts and long shapely legs was stunning. However it was the large eyes that were most striking; their catlike shape was remarkable enough, but it was their unusual colour, the left one blue, the right one brown that really made her stand out.

'She should be a man,' said Karen Tanner. 'We know the Preacher killed a male prostitute called Babe and took his place to get close to

107

Fontana. But when we questioned the doorman he described a blond *man*. Christ, only the height matches his description.'

'Are you sure the blood came from the Preacher?' asked Jack. 'Perhaps you've got a copycat killer.'

'No way. The blood was fresh and it wasn't Fontana's, so it must have been the killer's. But the murderer didn't only leave the Preacher's biblical message, which everybody knows about; he used his pen too.'

'Pen?' asked Jasmine.

'Yeah, the Preacher almost always writes his message in the victim's blood, using a special nib to aspirate blood from one of the arteries – usually the femoral. But in this case he – or she – used the victim's severed jugular. The writing matches that found on other homicides too. No, this was definitely the work of the Preacher.'

'So, now you know the Preacher's a woman who's good at disguises,' concluded Jack.

'*Really* good at disguises,' muttered the FBI agent, taking a computer-generated sketch out of her pocket. 'This blond guy was seen by a ton of people approaching the apartment. Despite the obvious disguise we've got what we think is a pretty good idea of his facial structure. But the nose, chin, cheekbones are all wrong. Even the guy's eyes were a different colour.' She pointed to the hologram. 'And look at those breasts. You can't hide a chest like that even with strapping. This is one good-looking woman, and believe me, some of the witnesses I interviewed were the kind of guys who would notice a looker. Yet they all *swear* they saw a *man*.'

Jasmine shrugged. 'People do change the way they look. All the Gene Genie can do is replicate a person's appearance from the genes they were born with on the basis of a lifestyle "norm" that takes into account average diet and exercise. It can't factor in cosmetic or surgical changes later in life.'

Karen Tanner grimaced in frustration. It was obvious that the agent had been expecting a major breakthrough, and this wasn't it.

'At least you now know she's female,' said Jack. 'Surely that must put a whole new angle on the case. I bet you'll turn up new leads when you review the Preacher's past homicides in the light of this. And you know roughly what she looks like now.'

Karen turned and flashed her green eyes at him. 'Do I, Jack? Christ, for all I know she could look like Marilyn Monroe or Arnold Schwarzenegger by now.'

CITTAVECCHIA, SARDINIA.

IN FACT MARIA BENARIAC RESEMBLED NEITHER AS SHE STUDIED THE man coming out of the small white church of Cittavecchia in Sardinia. Dr Carter seemed to be smiling and despite his slight limp moved with fast purposeful steps across the sunlit street. In his right hand he held a case, and in his left something small, which she couldn't recognize. It looked like a glass tube.

She adjusted her compact Olympus auto-zoom and leaned back in the hired Fiat, watching him approach a similar white car, parked three spaces away.

Click. Click. She took two pictures, the camera's quiet auto-wind motor purred in her ear.

Dr Carter had been in the church in Cittavecchia for almost two hours, speaking with the priests. She couldn't understand it. He was an atheist. What business could he have here?

After her unsatisfactory phone call to the Father when he had been so evasive about the Brotherhood's plans for Dr Carter, she had determined to shadow the scientist. It seemed to her that for some reason the Inner Circle lacked the courage or the will to finish what it had started, and she hated the idea that his evil might go unpunished.

It hadn't been hard to track him down to Sardinia. A call to GENIUS had told her where he was in Paris, then a concerned call to the Paris hospital had soon elicited the scientist's travel arrangements from there. At first she had tried to convince herself that she didn't need to follow him here. But she knew her reluctance stemmed from the fact that Corsica, with all its memories, was only a short boat trip away.

Click. Click. Two more snaps. If the camera was a gun, she mused, the scientist would be dead. If only.

She watched him open the door to his hired car, stoop his tall frame and climb into the driver's seat. When he was comfortable she saw him put his case on the dashboard, open it and then after one last glance at the glass tube put it in the case.

She heard the car's engine stutter into life, and watched as he pulled out from his space and turned towards the airport. For a second she considered following him, but stopped herself. She had the plane timetable and there was plenty of time before the next flight back to the Italian mainland, and then Boston.

With one last glance at Dr Carter's receding car she left her own vehicle, making sure her dress didn't catch on the car door, and walked to the church. Inside she addressed the first priest she saw in Italian, explaining that she was looking for her brother-in-law – a tall American man with a limp. He and another priest listened to this well-dressed woman with her sophisticated Rome accent, and respectfully informed her that her brother-in-law had just left for the airport, but that she shouldn't worry because he had found what he came for.

Before she could even ask what that was, they led her to the statue of the Madonna at the back of the church. Still not understanding what the scientist had taken she explicitly asked the priests to tell her. Their answer made her leave the church both baffled and outraged.

It was only when she was driving back to the airport that the thought came to her.

She always made a point of studying the motives and practices of those she cleansed. It added to the righteousness of the kill to know what the targets did and why. After all, she wanted to satisfy herself that their deaths were necessary before she killed them. Dr Carter had been no exception. She had read up on genetics when first receiving his folder. Although she had only gained a superficial understanding of what the science could and could not do, it had been enough to convince her that Dr Carter was playing God.

Now, as she tried to fathom why an atheist had chosen to visit a small church in Sardinia, she couldn't rid herself of the terrible notion forming in her head. If the thought was correct, then the scientist was even more dangerous than she feared.

But she wouldn't act yet. She would gather more evidence, and confirm the facts. Only then would she tell Brother Bernard and the Father.

Despite her outrage, she smiled. At least, if her suspicions were proven correct, then the Father and Bernard would have no choice.

They would be forced to let her finish what she had started in Stockholm.

BACK BAY, BOSTON.

JASMINE WASHINGTON HAD NEVER SEEN SO MANY GUNS IN HER LIFE, and they frightened her.

'Larry, what the hell are you doing with these in the apartment?'

'Relax, will you? They're fakes.' Larry smiled and put the brown box on the floor of the spacious lounge.

'Fakes?'

'Yeah, fakes. Props. They're samples for the thriller we're making in LA. I only had the consultant send them here because I'm seeing the director first thing on Monday. She wanted to see the kind of weapons the hero and villain might use.'

Jasmine hated guns, and it wasn't just because of what had happened to Olivia. Throughout her childhood in South Central LA guns had been a daily feature, as had the shootings and schoolyard murders that went with them.

She said, 'Just keep them out of sight.'

Larry raised his hands in a placating gesture. 'Come on Jazz, you won't see 'em again. But perhaps you should at least consider looking at one of them. Just to see how they work.'

She shook her head. She remembered her elder brother saying the same thing back in the 'hood, when she was almost ten. Just before he'd been killed by a random drive-by shooting and her parents had banned her from going out on the streets alone. 'Put them away, Larry. OK?'

Larry bent and pushed the box behind the couch. His voice was apologetic. 'They're gone. OK. I'm sorry.' He walked over to her and took her in his arms. He was a tall, athletically built man with a sensitive face. But it was his strong arms that Jasmine loved most. She prided herself on her fearless independence, but there were times when it was reassuring to surrender all that hard-won independence for a moment, and retreat into those arms. Olivia's death and Holly's disease had made her realize how very fragile everything was. Her recent exposure to the Preacher's exploits hadn't exactly restored her faith in humanity. So Larry's protective embrace felt particularly comforting right now. She knew it was irrational, but she believed that nothing truly bad could happen while he held her. Offering no resistance, she allowed him to guide her gently onto the couch as he kissed her mouth.

Unusually, she had got back from work early tonight and despite the guns package, was delighted to find Larry at home. They hadn't seen much of each other recently. He had spent half the week in Los Angeles preparing to shoot his new movie there, and she'd been working all hours getting the Gene Genie software to work. It was bliss to be at home by six-thirty on a Friday night with the whole evening and weekend to themselves.

She snuggled closer to Larry as she felt his arms tighten round her and his sweet breath warm the back of her neck. Inevitably it was when his hand slipped inside her silk blouse and began to caress her left breast that the phone rang.

And rang.

And rang.

'Shit,' she said under her breath.

'Relax! Let it be,' he murmured behind her, his fingers now undoing her bra, and moving to cup her other breast. 'The answer machine will get it.'

She sighed, and surrendered to the warm feelings coursing through her body. She murmured, 'You should stay away from home more often.'

The phone kept ringing.

'Shit,' she said again.

Larry continued to stroke her breasts, then began to move down her stomach, making those warm feelings heat up in her belly – and lower.

He whispered urgently in her ear. 'The answer machine will kick in soon. Don't worry about it.'

But she did worry about it, and the answer machine wasn't kicking in. Ever since she'd almost ignored that scholarship call from Stanford, she'd been unable to leave a phone ringing. Convinced that each call could be the next *big one*, the one she ignored at her peril.

She disentangled herself from Larry and moved to the phone. 'Must have turned the machine off.'

'Well, turn it on again.'

112

But she couldn't. She had to pick the phone up now that she was standing over it.

She spoke into the mouthpiece, 'Jasmine Washington.'

She recognized the voice instantly. He sounded more excited than usual. 'Jazz, it's Tom.'

'Hi, where are you?'

'Back home.'

'How was Paris?'

'Very interesting.'

'What about Sardinia?' She glanced over at Larry, who was frowning at her and gesturing for her to wind the call up quickly. She wanted to get back to him but was curious about Tom's trip. 'Jean Luc called me three days ago to ask if *I* knew why you'd dashed off there. Why did you, Tom? Was it to do with the spontaneous remissions?'

There was a pause. 'Kind of.' Then Tom said the words she'd heard so often before, the words that usually made her completely revise her understanding of what was or wasn't possible. 'I've had an idea.'

She braced herself. 'Yes?'

'It's a long shot, but I think I may have found a way to help Holly.'

'Really? How?'

There was almost a pleading quality to Tom's voice when he replied, 'That's what I wanted to talk to you about. Are you doing anything now? Can you come over? It's important, Jazz. Alex and Jack will be here too.'

'Come over *now?*' She flashed a questioning look to Larry, who angrily shook his head.

'Only if you can make it of course . . .' she heard Tom say quickly.

Larry looked like thunder, daring her to defy him and go. So she smiled at him as sweetly as she knew how, then put the phone closer to her mouth. 'Sure, Tom, I'll be there in a moment.'

11

BEACON HILL, BOSTON.

IT WAS ALMOST EIGHT BY THE TIME JASMINE PARKED HER BMW convertible outside Tom's house in Beacon Hill, having taken a few minutes to calm Larry down, promising to make it up to him when she returned.

Alex's Saab and Jack's vintage E Type were already there when she arrived, and she wondered again what Tom's idea might be. He had said it was only 'kind of' related to the spontaneous remissions he'd gone to investigate in Paris. But she'd learnt from personal experience that whenever Tom Carter said 'kind of' it usually meant 'not at all'.

When the Carter's housekeeper Marcy Kelley opened the front door, she directed Jasmine to the kitchen. Jasmine walked across the large hall and since there was no sign of Holly, guessed she must be in bed. At the closed door of the kitchen she halted. Jack's angry voice was audible through the oak.

'Tom, there's somebody out there trying to fucking kill you. Christ, just before you left, the Preacher sliced up some sleaze in Manhattan.'

'I know, you've told me enough times already,' she heard Tom reply. She could hear the strained patience in his voice.

'Well, you can't just fly off where you like without telling people where you're going. You have a police escort for a reason, dammit. And what the hell were you doing in Europe anyway?'

'If you'll just calm down, Mother Hen, I'll tell you.'

Jasmine opened the door and paused in the doorway, loath to get involved in their argument. The three of them, Tom, Jack and Alex, were gathered around the old pine table at the far end of the large kitchen. Tom sat at the head, his hair even more wild than usual. He held what looked like a small glass phial in his right hand. On his left sat his father, Alex. The semi-retired Harvard Professor of Theology was as composed as ever, pouring steaming coffee into four cups. A manila folder and a pile of books lay in front of him. Jack Nichols stood opposite in what looked like jogging sweats. Tom had obviously called him away from his Friday night wind-down as well. Jack was frowning, and she could imagine his wife and two kids giving him as much grief about deserting them as Larry had given her. The atmosphere in the kitchen was as thick with tension as it was with the aroma of strong coffee. She'd rarely seen this tight-knit partnership so volatile.

Tom looked to her and smiled with what looked like relief as much as anything else. 'Jazz, thanks for coming.' He waved his hand towards the chairs. 'Grab a seat.'

As she sat down, Alex smiled, creasing eyes almost as blue as his son's, and pushed one of the coffee cups across the table to her. 'Hello, Jasmine. I think you've missed most of the fireworks.'

'Story of my life, Alex,' she replied with a grin, glancing at the pile of books in front of him. Their titles surprised her. If they were related to Tom's idea then it clearly went beyond normal gene therapy.

Jack gave her a wry grin, and took a seat himself. 'Hi Jazz, I reckon we'll all need to sit down when we hear what Tom's got to tell us. After all, it's got to be big. The stupid bastard risked his neck to get it.'

'It is big, Jack,' said Tom, raising the phial in his hand. 'If I'm right, then this small glass tube could contain the cure for all genetic diseases – perhaps others too.'

'How can you say that, Tom?' scoffed Jack, his arms folded across his chest. He was clearly still pissed off with his partner. 'You disappear to Sardinia, giving no explanation to any of us . . .' Jack glanced at Alex. 'Most of us anyway. Then you come back

115

here and tell us you've found a miracle cure. Give me a break!'

'I'm being serious.'

'What's so special about what's in the phial, Tom?' asked Jasmine.

'It's blood and if it's genuine, then it could contain healing genes.'

She sat forward. 'How come? Whose genes are they? Somebody with your positive virus?'

'Kind of. If it's genuine.'

'Did it cause the two spontaneous remissions in Paris?'

Tom shook his head. 'I doubt it.'

'So, whose blood is it?' Jack asked. Jasmine could see his eyes narrow as he tried to work out where Tom was going with this. She certainly had no idea.

Tom said nothing. He just looked at them, a weird gleam in his blue eyes.

'Must be somebody interesting,' she said slowly.

'Goddamned interesting,' agreed Jack. Jasmine could see he was intrigued now, despite himself. 'Who?' he asked again.

Tom smiled at them both and shook the phial. 'What if I said this contained the DNA of a man who died some two thousand years ago? A man who was a tradesman; a carpenter, to be exact. A carpenter from Nazareth.'

Jasmine froze, her mouth wide open in shock. And she could see Jack wasn't immune either.

She heard him mutter, 'Jesus Christ . . .' under his breath.

'Exactly,' said Tom, putting the phial on the table in front of a silent Alex. 'Makes you think, doesn't it?'

THE STUNNED SILENCE SEEMED TO LAST MINUTES.

'But it isn't genuine, is it?' said Jack eventually, reaching for the phial, watching the brown-red liquid move around the glass. 'This can't be two-thousand-year-old blood.'

Alex sat forward and said, 'You're right. It's not. It comes from the weeping statue of the Madonna in Cittavecchia in Sardinia. The locals claim that the statue weeps blood – the blood of Christ. Back in '95 they tried to get the Vatican to declare it a miracle officially. But they never did. The blood is human all right, male too. But tests at the time proved that it matched one of the villagers'. Even so, the statue still weeps blood and the tourists keep on coming. You may have seen an article on it in the papers a few weeks ago.'

'So it's just a hoax?' asked Jasmine, surprised at how relieved she felt.

'Yes,' said Tom, 'but it got you wondering, didn't it? What if it really was *His* blood? What could it contain?' Tom turned to Jack. 'And before you both dismiss it, let Alex talk you through the research.'

'Hang on, Tom,' said Jasmine. 'Just give me a second to understand this.' She regarded Alex and Tom Carter closely for a long moment. The semi-retired Harvard Theology Professor and genetic scientist both looked unfazed by the outrageous idea. She glanced at the books in front of Alex. *The Dead Sea Scrolls and the Christian Myth* was tooled in gold leaf on the spine of the top leather-bound tome. Beneath that in a torn dust jacket a thicker volume: *The Nag Hammadi Texts in English*. And the other three books had similar titles: *Edgar J. Goodspeed: A Life of Jesus*; *The Apocryphal New Testament*; *The Agrapha of Jesus*.

She looked up at Alex, as an undefined unease began to uncoil in her belly. 'You guys are serious, aren't you?'

Alex shrugged and gave a small smile. 'Sure Jazz. Why not?' he said, as if Tom's bombshell was no big deal. This was typical of Tom and his father, thought Jasmine. Both of them thrived on new ideas; the more wacky and uncomfortable the better.

She was a little different. Although proudly open-minded, she needed time to accept weird notions, particularly ones that challenged what she believed in. When she glanced at the frowning Jack, arms folded defensively across his chest, she could see that his pragmatism was being sorely tested too. On a scale of normal to strange she reckoned this idea went way beyond Orville Wright saying to his brother, 'Hey, Wilbur, let's try and get this thing to fly.'

She cleared her throat. 'Let me just make sure I've understood this.' She paused for a moment, not quite sure how to express it without sounding foolish. 'You want to find a sample of Jesus Christ's remains; some genetic material which contains his DNA. You then want to run this through the Genescope to analyse his genes and unlock any healing powers he might have had. And you want to use those powers to help Holly. Is that broadly correct?'

A calm nod from Tom. 'Broadly, yes. In a roundabout way Jean Luc Petit gave me the idea.' Jasmine listened as Tom briefly outlined what had happened in Paris. He concluded, 'So instead of a virus, Jean Luc suggested that chemicals might be the genetic agent of change between humans – like pheromones with insects. So a person with the right rare genes could heal others through the secretion of certain chemicals.'

Jack put his coffee down and frowned. 'But why *Christ?*'

'Because we don't have time to search for people who may have these healing genes – if they even exist. A chance remark by Jean Luc made me focus instead on the one person with the best documented record of healing. And that of course is Jesus of Nazareth.'

Jack shook his head. 'But, Tom, you're a goddamned *atheist*. You don't even believe in Christ.'

'That's the whole point, Jack. I'm perfectly prepared to believe the man existed.' Tom patted the pile of books in front of Alex. 'I've seen enough evidence of that. I'm even prepared to believe he had certain abilities. What I don't buy into is that he was the so-called Son of God. If he could do what the scriptures say, then as far as I'm concerned his ability must lie in his genetic make-up. Jack, just imagine what we might find there: smart genes that can repair DNA; codes for proteins with undiscovered healing properties. Whether the man got these endowments from God or the lottery of nature, his genes may hold the key to correcting all our genetic flaws.'

It was now that Jasmine's initial unease began to take shape. Tom Carter, the man she admired above most men, seemed to be suggesting something alarmingly close to blasphemy. She thought of her Baptist parents back in LA; the strict values they had drummed into her and the faith they had passed on to her. The familiar guilt weighed down on her now, like a priest's heavy hand on her shoulder. She wasn't strictly religious any more and certainly wouldn't call herself devout, but she did have faith. God might move in ways so mysterious she couldn't fathom them at times, but in her mind He existed all right. And this plan of Tom's made her feel uncomfortable. It was just too ambitious, even by his standards.

Jack on the other hand seemed to be warming to the idea. 'Tom,' he asked, 'do you seriously believe you're going to find special genes in his DNA?'

Tom shrugged. 'I don't know, but there can only be three options. One, the guy was a fraud; two, he had divine powers; or three, he was a genetic rarity, blessed – or cursed, depending how you see it – with supernatural abilities. Naturally I don't believe in option two.'

'What if it's option one?' asked Jack.

'Then it won't work of course. But because I can't see any other way of helping Holly in time I'm willing to take that gamble. The patients in Paris who experienced spontaneous remission had their genomes changed by just a few code letters; just enough to kill their cancers. We don't know how or why this happened, but I guess the change agent for their DNA came from outside their bodies, probably via the blood transfusion they both received. I don't know what form that catalyst took. It might have been a virus or a chemical secretion, or something else. But the fact remains that their DNA *did* change, so a catalyst must exist. And I can't think of a better place to look for it than the DNA of Jesus Christ.'

Jack frowned, stroking his scar in thought. 'OK, you're the genius and if you think you can get some gene corrector, or clever proteins from the DNA of Christ, who am I to argue? But however feasible your idea might be, it's entirely academic if you can't answer one simple question.' Jack reached across the table, picked up the phial of fake blood and laid it in the palm of his right hand. 'How the hell are you going to find a *genuine* sample of his DNA? The man's been dead over two thousand years. Where are you going to find what's left of him, if anything still is?'

Jasmine watched Jack sit back, arms folded, studying Tom and Alex. His whole posture seemed to say, 'OK now let me hear some facts; some evidence.' She and Jack both instinctively looked to Tom, but it was his father who leant forward to reply.

Alex put on his glasses and quietly opened the folder in front of him. He looked up at Jack and gave him a small smile. 'Is that all you want to know?' He seemed disappointed as he flicked through the bulk of the papers in the folder. 'Not the documented evidence of Christ's healing powers? Not the debate about whether he was even crucified, or whether his so called "signs" were just political symbols? You don't want to know about the historical evidence from the Dead Sea Scrolls and the Nag Hammadi texts? Or see a list of his miracles? Or examine the fact that he features in the Koran as well as the Bible because even the Muslims thought he had powers?'

A pause as Alex looked into Jack's eyes. 'You just want to know where we need to look?'

'That'll do to start with,' said Jack gruffly.

Alex shrugged and turned to the back of the folder. He pulled out three pages covered in immaculate handwritten script. Not for Alexander Carter the soulless convenience of a word processor. Alex passed the sheets over to Jack, who leant forward to take them. Jasmine had to admit that despite her reluctance she was intrigued. Still saying nothing, she sat up and looked at the papers laid out before Jack.

They were lists. Three lists. One in green ink, one in black ink and one in red. Each list had four columns headed: Source. Location. Background. Authenticity. In the 'Authenticity' column each entry had been given one, two or three stars. She scanned the entries. Some words jumped out at her . . . *Turin Shroud . . . Weeping Statue . . . Stigmata . . . Foreskin of Christ . . . Santiago de Compostela . . . Lanciano Eucharist . . . Relic of Christ.*

'Why *three* lists?' asked Jack.

'I've been a bit lateral in my interpretation of possible sources of Christ's genetic material. The red list is the straightforward inventory of sites around the world claiming to have relics of Christ. You know? Churches, cathedrals and the like that claim to have either his blood, or his foreskin, or some other part of his body.'

'His foreskin?'

'Yes, it was a common relic in the Middle Ages. At one time about five churches around medieval Europe claimed to have it. Anyway the green list contains all known phenomena where what is apparently "Christ's blood" has been seen. For example the Weeping Statue of the Madonna at Cittavecchia in Sardinia, where Tom got that fake sample. There are other examples which may be worth looking at. Such as at the bleeding Oleograph in Mirebeau in France. The crucifix of Maria Horta in Portugal . . .'

Alex checked himself, as if realizing he was getting carried away. 'Anyway, they're all on the list.' He pointed to the third sheet. 'The one in black ink is a list of all registered stigmata. People who apparently bear the crucifixion wounds of Christ. You know? Unexplained wounds in the hands, feet and side. I just thought it might be worth running some of the blood from their "wounds" through the Genescope.'

Jasmine could see Jack nodding as he went through the list. Alex's notes were neat, thorough, scholarly. Even credible. Jack was plainly hooked and she had to admit she was interested too. Alex knew his stuff, but it was the old man's understated excitement that was so infectious. He was letting Jack sell the idea to himself.

'What about the stars in the right-hand column?' asked Jack. 'Three for promising, one for a long shot?'

'Exactly.'

'Not many three stars,' Jack said, flicking the pages over. 'In fact, they're almost all *one* stars.'

Alex gave a wry smile. 'I didn't say it would be easy. And given the time I'd only bother with the three stars. The others are undoubtedly fakes. I only listed them to show how many places claim to have these kinds of relics.'

'Which do you reckon are the most promising of the few three stars then? You've given the Lanciano Eucharist a good write-up for containing an authentic sample of Christ's blood. And the bleeding Oleograph in Mirebeau.'

Alex reached across the table, squinted behind his glasses and directed Jack to a couple of other entries. 'The shrine of the Holy Blood in Jerusalem looks good. Relatively. And it's worth checking out the hair sample in Santiago de Compostela in Spain. The circumcised foreskin kept in Calcata *was* very promising – but that was stolen some years ago. I wouldn't bother with most of the other phenomena or relics.'

Jack read them. 'What about the Turin Shroud? I thought that was a dead cert?'

'Tom needs biological remains. Not fabric.'

Jack nodded. 'Uh huh. How about the stigmata?'

Alex shrugged. 'Anybody's guess. But the Michelle Pickard woman in Paris and Roberto Zuccato in Turin seem the most authentic. The rest are pretty dubious. Of the total items on all three lists I would say that at least five or six are realistically worth examining.'

Jack seemed to become further wrapped up in the list as he quizzed the erudite Alex on the different items. But Jasmine felt more and more confused. On the one hand she remembered reading about some of the entries in *Time* magazine, which made the idea suddenly seem less fanciful, even possible. And on the other hand she couldn't stop herself thinking that the whole notion was blasphemous. She had always squared her Christian beliefs with her work on genetics by telling herself she was saving lives, and therefore the sin of letting people die had to be greater than any charge of tampering with God's work. God, after all, had seen fit to give mankind the intelligence to learn the secrets of its own existence. But this was different, wasn't it?

Jack, oblivious to her disquiet, was clearly more concerned with the practical considerations. 'OK, Tom, so maybe, just maybe you get lucky. You find an authentic sample, but surely after two thousand years it'll be in no state for you to do anything with it?'

Tom shook his head. 'That shouldn't be a problem. In the mid-Nineties scientists were analysing the DNA of Egyptian pharaohs over three thousand years old. That's over a thousand years earlier. There's even been successful DNA analysis done on the five-thousand-year-old remains of indigenous Indians in South America. As long as the sample's been kept dry it should be OK. Basically, if we can find the DNA, we should be able to use it.'

Tom seemed so confident, so sure that this was the right thing to do for Holly, that for the first time Jasmine could recall, she found herself avoiding his eye. Even so, the scientist in her forced her to consider the implications of her friend's proposal. What if they could analyse the genes of the man responsible for the greatest religion the world has ever known? A performer of miracles believed by many to be the Son of God, God made flesh? What would they find in the DNA of that flesh?

She felt the hairs rise on the back of her neck. Yes, this was definitely different than normal genetics. This wasn't just playing with the genes of man; this was far more ambitious – and dangerous. This was playing with the genes of God.

Tom turned to look at her, and she heard the concern in his voice when he said: 'Jazz, you've been pretty quiet. How do you feel about all this?'

She still wasn't sure how she felt. Except deeply uncomfortable. 'I just don't like it. It doesn't feel right,' she said quickly. The words came out wrong and sounded unreasonable. But Tom just nodded, indicating he was listening.

She went on, 'You don't understand what you're saying. You won't find what you're looking for in Christ's genes. You can't just dissect what made him divine and examine it under a microscope. Christ's power came from God. It was spiritual, *not* physical. By even trying to find his DNA you're saying that Christ wasn't resurrected and didn't ascend into heaven. You're assuming he was just a normal man whose bones are lying around somewhere. That goes against everything I've been taught to believe.'

Tom shook his head and ran a hand through his hair. 'You think I'm trying to attack Christianity but I'm not. I need your help too much to mock what you regard as important.' He turned to Jack then, who nodded his head thoughtfully. 'I need *all* of your help. Without it I've got no chance.'

Tom looked back to Jasmine, and she saw him smile, but his honest eyes seemed to bore right into her. She was glad he hadn't used the blackmail card of curing Holly. She would do anything to help her goddaughter. Almost.

She heard Alex clear his throat then run a hand through his still thick white hair. The old man looked pensive, as if trying to solve a problem. 'It doesn't have to be at odds with your beliefs, Jasmine,' he said gently.

Her fingers absentmindedly played with the handle of her coffee cup. 'Why not?'

The old man stood and began to pace around the kitchen, hands clasped behind his back, as if he was giving one of theology lectures. 'First of all. The resurrection and the ascension are central to your religion. Without them there is no Christianity, right?'

She nodded.

Alex gestured to the papers on the table. 'But if you look at the lists you will see not one mention of a physical part of Jesus that would cast doubt on the resurrection and the ascension. All the samples cited could have come from his body before death: hair, blood and even the famous circumcised foreskin. In fact I could find no records or claims for relics which deny this central tenet of Christianity. Even the ossiaries found in Jerusalem in 1996, the ones that were claimed to contain Christ's bones, were empty. So even if we wanted to threaten your faith we could find nothing to do so.'

Jasmine gave a noncommittal shrug, and waited for Alex to continue.

'You also believe Christ is God incarnate, right? The Son of God made flesh?'

'Yes, I do.'

'But there's nothing in your religion which tells you how your God passed on his powers to his Son, is there?'

A wary frown. 'Not really, no.'

'So God could have passed his strength down spiritually, or – and this is what we don't know – Christ may have *literally* been God incarnate, God made flesh. So that as well as communing with his Father through prayer he could, just possibly, have been given something in his genes which gave him his powers – a touch of the divine if you like.' The old man paused and looked at her while his right hand fiddled with the fob watch in his waistcoat pocket. 'Is that possible, Jazz?'

'It's possible but—'

'But wouldn't you like to find out?'

As always Alex had made her think. The scientist in her challenged the Christian, and posed the great question: *What if it were possible to find divine genes in Jesus' DNA?*

Alex reclaimed his seat and leaned back, relaxed. He said, 'You could well be right about Jesus getting his power through purely spiritual means. But if you're not and his divinity, as you call it, is in his genes, you still won't have compromised your beliefs. Either way your faith is safe.' The old man sat forward then, the blue eyes sparkling with youthful enthusiasm. 'But just imagine for a moment that we could isolate what made him special and use it to help mankind. Not just Holly, but everyone. How could your God be against that? Isn't that what he put his Son on the world to do in the first place? Who knows? It might even be what he intended.'

Jasmine turned from Alex and looked again at Tom. She saw a man who didn't share her faith, but believed in her values. A man more 'Christian' than most she'd met along the way. And then she thought of her goddaughter, a brave, bright kid who deserved every chance.

When she met Tom's blue eyes she knew there was only one choice she could make.

'I think you're wrong,' she said. 'And I don't think you'll find what you're looking for.' Jasmine turned to look at them all gathered around the table, at Jack and Alex and Carter. They were her friends, almost family. She shrugged. 'I'll need to sleep on it before I give a final decision, but if everyone else is committed then you may as well count me in for now.'

She tried to match the others' smiles, but deep down inside her she couldn't quell a small dissenting voice that refused to stay quiet.

TOM CARTER FELT BOTH GRATEFUL AND RELIEVED AS HE REGARDED the others around the table. Just getting this crazy idea off his chest with the people he trusted most had been a release. Over the last few days the idea had been echoing around in his head. And his mood had fluctuated from great confidence that the idea would work, to horror that he was even considering it. As always his father had helped, not just in researching the subject, but playing the role Olivia had always done; asking him questions and helping to order his jumbled thoughts. In the end they had boiled it down to three ifs and a then:
If they could find a sample of Christ's DNA and
If they could find unique genes in his DNA which had healing properties and
If they could exploit these unique genes or their coded proteins
Then they might cure Holly and who knew who else.

It sounded so simple.

But it had been vitally important to get the others on side. Jack as ever had been more concerned with the practical issues, but Tom had misjudged Jasmine badly. He had foolishly thought that being a Christian she would applaud his desire to turn to Jesus for salvation. He'd immediately realized how wrong he was when he'd seen her face. Luckily Alex had been able to show her that his plan didn't have to undermine her beliefs.

'Right,' he said, 'as Jack's already identified, the first task is going to be finding the DNA. Because unless we can do this the whole idea is just that: an idea. I'll try and get blood samples from the stigmata sufferers.'

He turned to Jasmine. 'Jazz, could you section off one of the upgraded Genescopes and fit it with all the latest software? It will also need to be calibrated to handle old and possibly corrupted DNA.

Can you also check IGOR to see if any of the current subjects have a record of faith healing in their files? And if so, whether they possess any unusual genes. It's a long shot, but it's worth a try.'

'OK. But why do you want to "section off" one of the Genescopes?'

'I want this to be kept secret even within the company, and only involve trusted personnel as and when we have to. So we'll need to cordon off part of the Mendel Suite. The individual Genescope you prepare will need to go in the cordoned-off area.'

'How much space will you need?' asked Jack with a frown.

'Not much. About a fifth of the second floor. We could use the back section; the Crick lab and conference room. That should be enough.'

'Won't that disrupt the other projects?'

'We should be able to handle it. And I really do think this should be kept discreet. I particularly don't want any of our NIH colleagues getting wind of this. We haven't got time to gain ethical approvals.'

Jack frowned again. 'I suppose so. Christ, if Jazz feels uneasy about this project, then just imagine how they could feel. Plus I don't think our shareholders will necessarily understand either. We'll need a cover story.'

Tom had already thought of this. 'We could advance the project under the guise of something to do with that evil gene project. You know? That ridiculous thing the President's been trying to get us to help him on.'

'You mean the Criminal Gene Project?' offered Jasmine. 'The one we've been steering clear of?'

'Yeah, that's the one. If people start to pry, then we could say we had a change of heart and now believe there might be genes that account for good and criminal behaviour. And that this is a feasibility study to attempt to answer that question.' Tom paused and then stressed, 'But this is a cover story we only use if we have to – which we shouldn't.'

Jack nodded. 'OK, I'll arrange the cordoning-off. And you'll need account codes for funding. What else do you want me to do?'

Tom hesitated. This was going to be the difficult one. 'I need your advice on the four or five samples we want from Alex's list.' He reached across the table and pulled the papers to him, scanning them for the relevant entries. 'The Lanciano Eucharist, the remains at

Santiago de Compostela, the bleeding Oleograph at Mirebeau, the shrine of the Holy Blood in Jerusalem.'

'What kind of advice?'

'The "how to get hold of them" kind.'

Comprehension dawned on Jack's rugged features. 'So I take it then, that you don't plan on asking permission?'

'Not enough time. And there's no guarantee we'd get it if we did. We only need a scraping. No one will miss what we take.'

'So you want me to recommend people who can help *liberate* these relics?'

'Yes.'

A great buccaneering grin suddenly creased Jack's whole face. Just as Tom had hoped, the ex-FBI man relished the idea of using his old contacts.

'When do you want everything?'

'As soon as possible. It's now the middle of February, so let's say the end of March at the latest.' Tom looked around the table. 'OK?' He felt like King Arthur as each in turn nodded, knights of the round table preparing to embark on their search for the Holy Grail.

Jack reached across to the manila folder in front of Alex, Tom's Merlin, and slid the folder closer to him. 'Project Cana?' Jack said, reading the title on the front. 'Is that what we're to call this among ourselves?'

Tom looked to his father. 'It's Alex's idea. I don't see why not.'

Jack nodded and pushed the folder back. 'OK. But why Cana, Alex?'

'I bet I can guess that,' replied Jasmine before Alex could respond. 'The wedding at Cana was where the water was turned into wine.'

Jack shrugged. 'I know that, but so what?'

'It was Christ's *first* miracle,' Jasmine explained. 'The first of many.'

PART II

PROJECT CANA

12

THREE WEEKS LATER. PARIS.

MARIA BENARIAC SIPPED HER COFFEE IN THE SMOKY CAFÉ ON THE Rue de Castiglione. She glanced at the clock above the bar, where the obese *patron* was trying his luck with an ageing blonde. It was almost two in the afternoon. Maria had been watching the clinic across the rain-soaked street for almost three hours now, but still no-one had arrived to explain why Dr Carter had rented the small surgery.

Since Dr Carter's trip to Sardinia three weeks ago Maria had kept a close eye on him, despite what Brother Bernard had said. It was maddening; when she had last contacted the Champion of the Secondary Imperative to check what his plans were for the scientist, she had been told in no uncertain terms to stay away from him. When she'd asked why Dr Carter was being ignored, he had warned her about becoming obsessed with the man.

Obsessed? She wasn't obsessed, just concerned. Which was just as well, since Bernard Trier didn't seem to care. Her role in the organization was to perform the Righteous Cleansings; that is what she had been trained for. So, if the scientist was deemed a prime candidate for cleansing in Stockholm, why wasn't he any more? What had changed?

Who was Brother Bernard to tell her who she should or shouldn't stay away from? Just the memory of his officious voice telling her she was only an 'operative' was enough to provoke her. It was as if she wasn't a member of the Brotherhood; just hired help to be bossed around. She took a deep breath and reminded herself that when she confirmed her suspicions about Dr Carter, then the Father and Brother Bernard would be forced to listen.

She had tailed Dr Carter easily. His discreet police protection amounted to little more than a patrol car keeping an occasional eye on his house, and following him to and from work. But outside the USA he was on his own, apart from Jack Nichols who had been by his side some of the time. She had already tracked Dr Carter to Turin, Frankfurt and now Paris.

'*Encore de café?*' The obese *patron* was suddenly standing over her with a flask of coffee. She looked up and caught him leering at her. The lust in his small beady eyes reminded her of Sly Fontana. It brought back the older memories along with a cold clammy panic. She immediately wished she'd come disguised as a man, and gave him her coldest glare.

'*Non merci.*'

Something in her look must have reached him. He stopped leering, gave a diffident, almost nervous shake of his head and walked off.

The large black car stopped across the street and the driver got out and opened the far side rear door. Maria ignored the car at first, still disturbed by the memories the barman had raked up. Then she saw the door to the clinic open and the tall figure of Dr Carter step out into the rain. He was holding an umbrella and an envelope. Maria remembered that he had also held an envelope when he had met the man at the clinic in Turin. Afterwards the man had left with the same envelope clutched in his hands. Was it payment? If so, what for?

Maria sat forward in her chair and peered out of the window. She saw Dr Carter approach the car and lean forward with the umbrella, as if to offer assistance and cover to the passenger. When he stood again and stepped back from the car, Maria saw a small, elderly woman leaning on his arm. Then he turned and walked towards the clinic door with the old woman hobbling beside him, as if her feet were giving her great pain. Maria felt a tightness in her chest as she realized that her suspicions were indeed confirmed. She raised her miniature Olympus camera and looked through the zoom lens, studying the woman's hands.

Click-whirr. Click-whirr. Click-whirr.

She shot off three frames of film, the automatic motor barely troubling the quiet of the café.

Yes, she thought, just like the man in Turin, the old woman's hands were covered in thick bandages.

TOM OFFERED THE BENT OLD WOMAN A COFFEE BEFORE USHERING her into the small private surgery he'd rented from a local doctor friend of Jean Luc. It looked remarkably similar, if slightly more elegant, to the small white rooms he had rented in all the other European towns he'd visited over the last three weeks. A sink, a leather couch, a hard-backed chair, a medicine cabinet and a white steel table were the only furniture. This particular facility also had a mini-lab in the back.

In his heart he realized that what he was doing stretched the limits of science. There was only the slimmest scientific basis behind Cana; the wildest of hypotheses. But he was in need of a miracle, and as Jasmine had said about going to Lourdes, you had to go where the action was.

He sat Michelle Pickard down on the brown leather couch.

'How long have you had the wounds?' he asked in his stumbling French, as he started to undo the bandages on her hands.

'Seven years. They first appeared when I was sixty-five. When my husband died.'

'Do you have them all the time?'

'No, just on Friday to Sunday. They heal on Monday. And from Tuesday to Friday afternoon the wounds disappear.'

Tom nodded. The pattern was typical of some of the other stigmata he'd seen, but this didn't particularly encourage or discourage him. He was only too aware that he was sailing on uncharted seas here, and was determined to keep his natural scepticism in check and just examine the facts before him. He gently took off the last layer of dressings on her hands. The marks were visible on both the palms and the backs of her hands. As usual the blood was fresh and there was no sign of infection or inflammation. But the wounds were deeper and larger than any he'd seen before.

He then revealed the wounds on Michelle Pickard's feet and found them in a similar state, open and glistening with fresh blood. The same with the wound on the woman's side. He winced as he studied the lesions.

'Are they very painful?'

The old woman's small, smiling eyes watched him closely. 'It's good. My pain is my comfort.'

There was no answer to that. He took a swab from deep within each of her five wounds and placed each swab in its own labelled, sealed glass tube. Then he took a sample of Michelle Pickard's blood from the vein in her arm. He placed this sample in a sixth tube. After asking the old lady some final questions he re-dressed her wounds. Then when Tom was done he thanked her, made sure the old woman took the envelope containing the payment and walked her back to the car.

Michelle Pickard seemed disappointed that it had been so quick, as if she wanted to tell him more about her stigmata. But Tom was tired and had heard all the stories before. For now he just wanted the samples. Samples told their own story. All the other stigmata he'd checked so far had yielded nothing of any real interest. Two were obvious fakes, driven by some warped desire for attention and profit to mutilate themselves. The others, including Roberto Zuccato in Turin, merely had blood that was genetically unremarkable. Michelle Pickard looked more genuine than most, but it was the samples that counted. They couldn't lie.

After seeing the old woman off, he walked back to the small mini-lab behind the surgery. He began to pack up the samples, keen to move on. He hadn't seen Holly for over a week, and wouldn't see her until after he met Jack in Italy tomorrow. Alex was looking after Holly, and she was used to him being away, but he still missed her. *What the hell am I doing here?* he asked himself again. And as always he came up with the only reply he could: trying to give Holly a chance.

He looked in his samples bag and reviewed the stigmata samples he had collected over the last few weeks. Almost all the holding compartments were full so he decided to run a preliminary screen on the six samples of Michelle Pickard's blood. He would then take only the vaguely interesting swabs with him to Italy and then Boston.

Using the microscope in the small laboratory he first tested the blood sample from the old lady's left hand, then the sample from the vein in her arm; the only one not to have come from her wounds. His first thought when he looked at the second blood slide was that he must have made an error. He checked the sample tubes again to make sure he hadn't been looking at the wrong blood. But there had been no mistake.

He frowned and he felt a tremor of excitement. 'How strange,' he heard himself saying. 'How very strange.'

THE ADRIATIC COAST OF ITALY.

THE NEXT NIGHT AS TOM CARTER STOOD ON THE DECK OF A forty-foot fishing boat off Italy's Adriatic coast, he still hadn't worked out the mystery of Michelle Pickard's wounds. He'd told Jack about it two hours earlier when they'd boarded the boat at Pescara. 'It's got to be a scam', had been the ex-FBI man's first reaction before calling up some 'friends' to check her out.

The boat lurched and Tom's aching stomach lurched with it. The enigma of Michelle Pickard suddenly seemed very unimportant. He groaned and bent his legs, trying to roll with the swell of the waves as the crew attempted to anchor the large fishing boat as close as possible to the shore. The trip from Pescara had been relatively short, but he wasn't a good traveller, particularly by sea.

He stood next to Jack Nichols, who to Tom's annoyance seemed unperturbed by the motion of the boat. The night was clear and surprisingly mild for early March. Tom could make out the beach ahead, glowing in the moonlight; a pale sliver of silver. As he scanned the shoreline for the two men, the sound and movement of the waves made his empty stomach contract.

He felt Jack Nichols' hand on his shoulder, and heard his friend ask with a chuckle, 'You OK? You look pretty green.'

'I feel goddamned green,' he scowled. Still, at least it took his mind off his nerves. The two men Jack was meant to redezvous with were already late.

Jack had arranged for the two men, contacts of old, known simply as Dutch and Irish, to visit the selected sites on Alex's list and liberate the necessary items. Even though Tom had given the professional thieves the correct equipment, with instructions on how to store the samples, everything had been done at arm's length with every link back to GENIUS covered up. But since tonight was the final job – the two men should have visited the church at Lanciano by now – he had decided to join Jack to pick up all the samples collected by the two thieves over the last few weeks. It was a risk but he'd told himself it was necessary to ensure the samples got back safely. He also had to admit that at the time it had sounded exciting. But now, even though Jack was clearly enjoying being out in the field again, Tom wished he'd gone straight home to Holly.

'Not again,' he muttered, as he felt another cramp in his gut. He leaned over the side and dry-retched before gulping in the cool, salty air.

Jack passed him the infrared binoculars. 'Have a look through these. It'll take your mind off the boat.'

Tom groaned, put the binoculars to his eyes and scanned the beach. Through the lenses the scene appeared to be illuminated by green light. Everything looked clearer and he could now make out a small rubber dinghy on the sand, but there was still no sign of Irish and Dutch.

Wait! What was that?

He could have sworn he saw a reflection of moonlight on metal or glass coming from the right of the beach, by the cliff. Fingers of ice walked down his spine. Were they being watched?

Then he saw the two figures running down the left of the beach towards the dinghy. He patted Jack on the arm. 'They're here.' The taller man, Dutch, threw a bag into the boat and helped Irish drag the dinghy into the lapping waves. Both men then jumped in and began rowing out towards the fishing boat. Tom panned the binoculars back to the right of the beach, by the rocks. Nothing. He must have imagined whatever he thought he saw there in the eerie green light.

Within a minute the two men arrived at the side of the boat and Tom and Jack helped haul them aboard.

'Any problems?' Jack asked.

Dutch smiled, revealing strong white teeth. 'No, it was as quiet as a church.'

Irish delved into the large bag on the deck beside his partner. He pulled out an aluminium case and a dog-eared list. 'I think you'll find it's all there. Labelled and ordered as you wanted.'

Tom checked the list. Every one of the five entries had been crossed off, and when he opened the refrigerated case a crack and peeked inside, he saw that all five slots had been filled with labelled glass phials. He closed the case, clutching it tightly to him. 'Well done. You got all of them.'

Dutch nodded. 'Yeah. We had some trouble with the Santiago sample in Spain. Some smartass had put the blood in a container, which was designed to destroy the contents if it was forced open.'

'What happened?' asked Jack.

'Don't worry! Irish found a way.'

'And the Lanciano sample tonight?' asked Tom. This was the one he was most interested in. The blood in the Lanciano Eucharist had already undergone carbon-dating by Oxford scientists over a decade ago and the results had been particularly promising.

'Like I said. Easy. No security at all. And don't worry – in every case no-one'll know anything's been taken.'

Jack took an envelope out of his coat pocket and handed it to Dutch. 'Untraceable yen.'

'Thanks, Mr Nichols. Just like old times. Pleasure doing business with you.'

Carter watched Dutch take the money and put it in his bag without counting it.

Jack helped them up. 'We'll drop you off at Pescara as agreed. Then you're on your own.'

When the two men had gone below deck, Tom opened the aluminium case again, and studied the row of five neatly laid-out phials. Each one was labelled with a date and an address. The last phial bore the legend: *Eucharist of Lanciano, Italy, 6 March 2003*. Ignoring the others he took this out of the case and held it up to the moonlight. The rusty powder inside seemed to glow like crushed rubies.

'Is that the one?' asked Jack as the crew weighed anchor.

Tom felt a shiver, which had nothing to do with the cold night breeze blowing over the Adriatic, and as he felt the boat move towards Pescara, he realized that his seasickness was gone.

He turned to Jack and whispered, 'According to tests conducted at Oxford, this blood is two thousand years old, male and human.' He paused and smiled. 'Certainly narrows down the odds, doesn't it?'

*   *   *

CLICK. . .WHIRR. CLICK. . .WHIRR.

Maria Benariac stood by the rocks on the darkened beach, holding the night-vision camera as she watched the boat leave the shore. Her body felt stiff from the cold, but inside she was burning with a blend of anger and righteous vindication.

It was true then, there could be no more doubt about it. Not only had she seen Dr Carter studying the stigmata, but now she had witnessed the two thieves taking the sample from the Lanciano church. And if that wasn't enough she had actually seen Jack Nichols paying for the stolen property, and Carter openly studying it in the full light of the moon.

It was unbelievable. Not only was Dr Carter ignoring her threat, but he was taunting her, pushing his blasphemy into still darker territory. The devil was even willing to sacrifice the sacred relics of Christ on his black altar of genetics. If she'd thought Dr Carter was a threat before, she knew he was now far more than that. Why else would a mortal search for the genes of God? If not to become God himself?

NEXT MORNING. SOUTH BOSTON JUNIOR SCHOOL.

THE FIRST GLIAL CELL REFUSED TO OBEY ITS GENETIC INSTRUCTIONS at 11:09 in the morning of Friday 7 March 2003.

At the time Holly was sitting between her best friends, Jennifer and Megan, in the second row of her French class at the South Boston Junior School. When she eagerly raised her hand to answer Mrs Brennan's question, '*Comment allez-vous*', she was a healthy little girl, only weeks away from her birthday. But seconds later, by the time she had answered, '*Je vais bien, Madame Brennan*' and put her hand down she had cancer, and was only months away from her deathday.

In that split second the glial cell in her brain had turned rogue, and the first mutation of clonal evolution that would lead inexorably to cancer had begun. As simply as a switch being flicked, the healthy little girl had become terminally ill.

*   *   *

EVERY CELL IN THE HUMAN BODY IS STRICTLY CONTROLLED, ITS death, renewal and proliferation all kept in check by the genetic instructions in its DNA. In the split second the *p53* gene was lost in Holly's affected glial cell that strict control broke down and the cell began to divide, producing more cells with corrupted DNA.

There are four stages of clonal evolution and in this first stage Holly's affected cell had begun to obey new faulty instructions. These instructions turn off the brakes in the cell's nucleus so it continues to divide and proliferate indefinitely. The cell seems normal, but by proliferating excessively it clones its own rogue DNA, and creates other rebel cells that in turn crowd out its genetically obedient neighbours. And because the body's antibodies don't recognize these rebel cells as foreign, they are left to multiply unhindered.

The second mutation occurs when the still-normal rebel cells begin to proliferate at an accelerated rate, creating pressure on the surrounding area, and in turn Holly's skull.

The third mutation of clonal evolution sees the cells proliferate still more rapidly with some of the cells undergoing structural change. By the time this occurs a whole cluster of key genes on Holly's chromosome 9 will have been wiped out.

The fourth and fatal mutation usually sees the cells become malignant, cancerous. By now the whole of one copy of chromosome 10 has been lost, and all the genetic instructions contained within it. The cells are now obeying only their own selfish instructions; to survive and to multiply, ignorant of the fact that this will kill their host; that Holly will die.

The ultimate irony is that cancer is about a cell's attempt to become immortal. This selfish search for immortality is what kills the rest of the body. And of course when the body dies, the cancer cells die with it.

However, as Holly sat in class with her friends she knew nothing of this. She was blissfully unaware of the traitor inside, rebelling against her. It could take weeks, or even months before she felt any discomfort. Her father would be the first to learn of her condition when she underwent her next CAT or PET scan. Then the slightest suggestion of a growth would be revealed. Of course, even then Holly might still be none the wiser. When her dad looked more worried than usual on their next outing to the hospital, Holly would just assume that he was in one of his moods.

She wouldn't even begin to guess what her father would then know: that the prophecy the Genescope had made three months earlier had finally come to pass. That the dormant enemy within her body had not only awakened, but had already begun its futile and fatal quest for immortality.

13

THREE DAYS LATER. GENEVA.

THREE DAYS HAD ELAPSED SINCE MARIA BENARIAC HAD SPIED ON
Dr Carter and Jack Nichols off the coast of Italy. She sat in the
splendid foyer of La Cicogne hotel, admiring the gleaming wood and
elegant marble while she waited to be called. She had been to this
discreet Geneva hotel a number of times before. Always to meet with
the Father. She knew that Father Ezekiel De La Croix liked it here
because the guests were always greeted with impeccable courtesy and
understated good taste, but never any questions. He kept a suite here,
which he used when making his regular checks on the Brotherhood's
banking interests in the city.

Maria glanced at the ornate clock standing by the reception desk.
She had been waiting now for almost twenty minutes. Usually the
Father was prompt but then she supposed he had much to decide
today. The photographs and notes she had sent to Brother Bernard
must have given them a lot to think about. She crossed her legs,
smoothed her plain navy skirt, and sipped her mineral water. She was
in no particular hurry.

The sound of footsteps on marble made her turn her head in the
direction of the elevators. She picked up her small attaché case and
stood when she saw the obese form of Brother Bernard approaching.

He was dressed in a severe dark suit. His goatee appeared more unkempt than she remembered, but his thick pouting lips were curled in their familiar sneer.

Dispensing with any greeting he beckoned her with a curt 'Come!' and turned back to the elevators. No words were exchanged on the trip up to the third floor, or the short walk from the elevator along the long wood-panelled corridor to the door marked 'Suite 310'. Maria was tempted to ask him what he had made of the photographs, or what he thought Dr Carter might be doing. But she kept silent. And as for praise for uncovering the scientist's plan, she had long since given up expecting or wanting any from Bernard. Only the Father's approval was worth something.

She followed Bernard into the suite. To her right she saw a large marble bathroom, and to her left a luxurious bedroom. Ahead was a softly lit lounge area with a large cream divan and two matching armchairs. At the end of the divan sat a man. She quickly scanned the rest of the well-appointed room, and when she realized there was no-one else there, didn't even try to hide her disappointment.

'Where is the Father?' she asked.

The tall man on the divan stood. He was thin with round wire-rimmed spectacles, and despite his balding head he looked considerably younger than Bernard. Maria had met Brother Helix Kirkham twice before a few years ago, and she couldn't understand what he was doing here now. He was the Champion of the Primary Imperative and this was a Secondary Imperative issue.

Brother Helix smiled at her and said, 'Operative Nemesis, Father Ezekiel will not be attending the meeting. But he has asked us to pass on his appreciation for your vigilance.' He extended his right hand to her. 'May he be saved.'

She completed the ritual greeting and glanced down at the glass coffee-table in front of Helix, seeing her notes and photographs. 'Weren't my findings important enough?'

Helix smiled at her. 'On the contrary. They were so important that he has been detained putting certain related plans in place.' He gestured to one of the chairs, and reluctantly she sat down.

Brother Bernard sat on the divan next to Helix and asked her, 'Do you have the original photographs and negatives with you as we requested?'

142

She opened her case, took out the plastic file containing all her collected 'evidence' and passed it to him.

She said, 'This should be enough to convince you that the scientist needs to be stopped as soon as possible. I am prepared to act whenever you need me to.'

She watched as Bernard and Helix flicked through her notes and the various photographs. On more than one occasion she caught the two Brothers exchanging a glance, and a discreet nod.

It was Helix who finally looked up and asked, 'What do you think Dr Carter is doing?'

'He's trying to tamper with the DNA of God.'

'What are his motives?' Helix asked the question as if he already knew the answer.

She shrugged. She had given this some thought and had gone back to her books to double-guess his aims. She had even sat behind Dr Carter and Jack Nichols on the flight from Italy, trying to overhear their plans. But all she had gleaned was the name Project Cana. 'I don't know exactly what his motives are. Perhaps he wants to discredit religion by proving Jesus was only mortal? Or perhaps he wants to harness Christ's power in some way?' She paused for a moment and crossed herself. 'Maybe he's trying to clone Jesus?'

Helix shook his head. 'No, that isn't possible yet. Even Dr Carter would find that too difficult. Cloning a human being is decades away.'

She waited then to hear what Helix's thoughts were. It was common knowledge that the relatively young Champion of the Primary Imperative had been steeped in the technology of the age. But the tall Brother volunteered nothing. 'So why do *you* think he's doing it?' she prompted eventually.

Helix broke eye contact with her, and his gaze dropped evasively to the table in front of him. 'I'm not sure. It probably has something to do with isolating Christ's genes. He probably believes that if he can find and exploit these genes he could make a miracle drug; a universal panacea for all ills. Commercially that would make him very rich, even richer than he is now. And more importantly, it would make him supremely powerful.' Helix sighed. 'But that needn't concern you any more.'

She was horrified. 'What do you mean? It needn't concern me?'

Brother Bernard then leaned forward. 'Nemesis, let me explain what we want you to do about Dr Carter; what *I* want you to do about him. Are you listening?'

'Yes, of course.'

'Good. It's very simple.' She noticed the manila envelope in his hands. 'I want you to do nothing. You are to leave him alone, until I tell you otherwise. You have other priorities now. Other Righteous Kills that need your expertise; here in this envelope.'

Maria felt cold, then suddenly hot. 'This is because of Stockholm, isn't it?'

Bernard shook his head. 'No, this has nothing to do with Stockholm. We just have different plans for Dr Carter.'

'What plans? Are you going to use Gomorrah? He has no imagination. He would never have uncovered what the scientist is doing. I should have the—'

'Nemesis!' interrupted Bernard, raising his voice. 'The Righteous Kill on Dr Carter is postponed for the foreseeable future. I have given you your orders. Now carry them out.'

She couldn't believe this. 'Postponed? Why? I demand to speak to the Father. He would—'

It was Helix who cut her off this time, his voice firm but reasonable. 'It is decided, Nemesis. Father Ezekiel sanctioned the decision himself. Please let it alone.'

She saw Bernard glare at Helix, angry that his colleague was trying to calm *his* charge. Then Bernard turned to her, incensed that she had challenged his authority in front of Helix. He said, 'Nemesis, you have been indulged too much already. You are an operative. You take strategic orders from the Inner Circle, *from me*. If you question me again you will be suspended, or even replaced. Gomorrah may not be as inventive as you, but he does exactly what he's told. You are *not* indispensable. Do you understand me?'

Maria ignored him and turned to Helix, who she thought looked mildly embarrassed. 'Brother Helix, are you sure the Father has sanctioned this?'

'You heard what Brother Bernard said.'

'Can you tell me *why* he sanctioned this?'

Helix shrugged and was about to speak, when Bernard stood red-faced and pointed to the door. 'Nemesis, this meeting is closed. You will leave your notes and photographs with us, and then leave.'

144

Maria turned then to the Champion of the Secondary Imperative, and met his eye. She lowered her usual guard and allowed her full contempt for him to show in her icy glare. She only stood to leave when she saw his beady eyes flicker and look away.

She turned to Helix and nodded. 'Brother Helix.'

The tall Brother returned her nod. 'Operative Nemesis.'

Then she walked straight past Bernard and out of the door.

LATER. LONDON.

THAT NIGHT MARIA BENARIAC COULDN'T SLEEP AS SHE LAY NAKED on the single bed in her London apartment. She felt wounded, an animal in pain. She couldn't remember feeling so alone and isolated. Not since Corsica. As always she slept in the light, but tonight, despite the four overhead bulbs and six spotlights bleaching away the darkness, she couldn't banish the shadows in her mind.

Before Dr Carter had escaped her vengeance, Ezekiel had always included her, treated her with respect and love. She had been his favoured one – the chosen one. But now the Father was distancing himself from her, leaving all contact to Brother Bernard, who neither understood nor valued her. It was all Dr Carter's fault and only by destroying him could everything be made right again. She was sure of it. Only then could she once again bathe in the love of the Father; be once again a valued, cherished member of his family.

She reached to the small table beside the bed and felt the cold steel blade with her fingers. Its touch sent a frisson of fear and excitement through her, a frisson that cut through her anxiety and promised release. Her hands closed round the handle.

Her hand took the dagger from the table and held it up above her head. She studied the kukri's curved blade silhouetted against the bright bulb above, and with her other hand ran a thumb over its razor edge. Exerting just enough pressure she sliced into the skin of her thumb, releasing a drop of blood so it fell toward her left eye. She watched the droplet grow bigger and bigger, trying not to blink when the warm blood eventually shattered on her open eye.

Then with a steady hand she moved the blade down her body, to that part where the still-fresh scars had barely healed. Without looking down she laid the crook of the curved blade, sharp edge down, on her right thigh. Slowly she began to rock the blade until the exquisite pain came, the skin broke and the blood began to flow.

IT IS ON THE DAY BEFORE HER FIFTEENTH BIRTHDAY THAT MARIA IS summoned by Mother Clemenza, the Mother Superior who runs the Corsican orphanage near Calvi. The stern matriarch doesn't even bother to hide her dislike for Maria when she shuffles nervously into her study and stands in front of the imposing desk. Mother Clemenza is a fat woman with large pointed glasses that seem to rest on her round puffed-out cheeks. The spectacles give her heavy-lidded eyes an unfortunate, evil slant. To Maria she looks like a huge toad in her voluminous habit, squatting behind her desk waiting for flies to pass by. And when the toad fixes her with a baleful glare and speaks, her pointed pink tongue looks like it might dart out at any moment and strike her.

'Maria, as you know, Father Angelo is here on one of his visits. After doing his rounds he has asked to hear one of the girls read to him in the tower library. Frankly there are many more appropriate girls who I would prefer to represent us to him. But for some reason he expressly asked for you. Now, Maria, this is an honour and it is very important you make a good impression on Father Angelo, so behave. If you don't then I will hear of it – and you know what will happen.'

Maria nods. She is only too aware of the punishments the toad can mete out; she has received most of them in the years since she was abandoned here as a three-day-old baby.

The toad's thin lips curl in an attempt at a smile, but her eyes don't even bother to try. 'Good. Now run along, he is waiting for you.'

As Maria walks up the stone stairs of the central tower that dominates the old orphanage she wonders why Father Angelo has asked for her. As one of the most senior members of the order she obviously knows who Father Angelo is, but he has only seen her once before, on his last visit. And that was only because he spied her working in the laundry-room when he was snooping around – or 'doing his rounds' as Mother Clemenza calls it. So it was only by accident that he even noticed her. Unlike the other girls she's usually kept far too busy to be introduced to important visitors.

Maria's long since given up trying to understand why the nuns hate her, but she knows they do. They are forever singling her out and finding reasons to punish her. She knows it has something to do with the way she looks. Some of the nuns call her the 'Devil's daughter' because of her eyes, and they cut her chestnut hair so short the scalp shows through. 'Don't think being beautiful means you're special,' they've told her from ever since she can remember. Maria doesn't bother to try and understand any more. All she knows is that she hates the way she looks and wishes she was plainer, more anonymous. Then she wouldn't be an embarrassment to the orphanage and she'd have friends.

As Maria approaches the closed wooden door of the small library she again asks herself why Father Angelo has asked for her, and not one of the 'better' girls. But far from feeling honoured she feels her stomach contract with nerves. After all, Father Angelo is so important in the Church he must speak to God personally; even the toad, Mother Clemenza, acts nervously when he's around.

At the library door she raises her hand to knock but hesitates for a moment, wondering what would happen if she just turned round and walked back to the laundry. But she knows she'll be punished; probably put in the dreaded lock-away, so she takes a deep breath and gives the door three timid knocks.

'Enter!' booms a voice from inside.

Her hand trembles a little as she turns the metal catch and opens the heavy door. Father Angelo is alone in the room. He sits on the couch by the window that overlooks the driveway. A large book is perched on his lap. On either side of the couch the walls are lined with shelves, crammed with leather-bound books. She has been in this room countless times before, but standing here alone with him now makes it seem strange and alien.

Father Angelo is a thin man and even when he's sitting down, his robes seem to hang on his gaunt frame. His face is long with a misshapen nose and his eyes are too close together. But to Maria his worst feature is his skin: heavily pockmarked and sallow, it gives him the appearance of being ill. When he smiles at her his teeth are yellow. Maria is frozen to the spot, wanting desperately to turn and run out of there, but then he pats the space next to him on the couch. 'Come, my child. Come and sit next to me. It's Maria, isn't it?'

Clenching her fists so hard she can feel her nails digging into the palms of her hand, she forces herself to walk over to him. 'Yes, Father Angelo.'

She takes her seat as far away from him on the couch as she can, but even from this distance she can smell his breath. It reminds her of the rotten cabbage she empties out of the kitchen bins. He passes the book to her, the Bible. Then he stands up and walks back to the door. She feels herself relax when he moves away from her; just his presence makes her skin crawl. But she tenses again when she sees him throw the bolt on the inside of the door.

'Good,' he says with his yellow-toothed smile. 'Now we won't be disturbed. And I can listen to you read in peace.'

147

He walks back to the couch and sits next to her again, but this time he sits so close his thigh touches hers. She tries to squeeze away from him, but because she is already at the end of the couch she can't move any further. 'What would you like me to read?' she asks, trying to keep her voice steady.

'You choose, my child. But don't sit so far away.' He taps his thigh with his bony right hand. She notices how his nails are beautifully manicured. 'Sit on my lap.'

Her heart is beating so fast now she can hardly breathe. 'Thank you, Father. But I'm comfortable here.'

His hand taps his thigh more insistently. 'Nonsense. Come and sit here.'

She turns and sees his eyes staring at her. There's a hunger in them which scares her. It's more animal than human. His forehead and the area just above his upper lip are shiny, covered with a sheen of perspiration.

Then he smiles at her, and it's the most terrifying thing she's ever seen. With trembling hands she opens the Bible and reads the first thing she sees. 'And then the angel said unto . . .'

His hand rests on the mound of her left breast and squeezes it so hard it hurts. Maria can't believe that Father Angelo is doing this to her. She tries to ignore him, hoping he'll stop. She carries on reading, focusing on the words swimming on the page in front of her.

His other hand is now undoing the buttons of her blouse and burrowing under her bra to touch her other breast. His breathing is ragged, like he's been running hard. She can no longer pretend this isn't happening so she puts the Bible down and tries to pull his hands away. 'Please don't, Father Angelo. Please leave me alone.'

'But it's not my fault, my child. You are so beautiful. You are the temptress, not me.' His dark eyes have a fevered look in them now. 'Be still and you won't be punished.'

She struggles but he suddenly pushes himself on top of her. Despite his slender build he is strong and easily holds her down. She starts to cry out but he pushes his foul-smelling mouth over hers. She almost gags when she feels his tongue on hers. His face is so close she can see every blemish on his pock-marked skin, every blackhead on his deformed nose. Then she feels his right hand rummage under her skirt, pulling down her panties; bony fingers pinching her, probing her. She struggles harder but his full weight is now on her, and with his mouth over hers she finds it difficult to breathe. His fingers are hurting her and then for a merciful second he pulls away. He rearranges his robes and she feels something else pushing insistently between her legs, bigger and more painful. He starts to groan like an animal. She panics but can't move or scream as tears stream down her cheeks.

Then he thrusts into her and white hot pain rips through her whole body. She never knew such pain could exist. It feels like she is being torn in two. Again she wants to cry out, to scream, but she can't even move. She thinks the pain will make her go mad, until gradually her mind retreats in on itself, tries to pretend this isn't happening to her; that she is merely a spectator to this unspeakable act, not the victim.

She's vaguely aware of his thrusts and groans becoming more animated, then he hisses, 'My little evil angel' just as a shudder goes through his body. She feels a wetness between her legs and then he rolls off her. Before she even has time to collect her thoughts, Father Angelo is standing over her, pulling her to her feet, leading her to the toilet next to the library. 'Stop crying and wash yourself, child,' he orders briskly. 'And don't speak of this. This was your sin. You will be punished for this if you tell anyone. This must be our secret.'

On trembling legs Maria walks into the toilet. She looks down and sees two dark drops on the cold linoleum floor, then she pulls up her skirt and sees the blood running down her leg. Numbed and frightened, she uses the towel by the sink to wash herself, before putting her panties back on. She looks in the mirror at her puffy eyes and rinses her face with cold water, trying not to cry any more. She can't believe what has just happened. How could Father Angelo, one of the most senior members of God's Church, have done this? And why her? Was it somehow her fault? As she stares at her face in the mirror she screws up her courage and determines to tell the Mother Superior.

When she comes out of the toilet she sees that Father Angelo has gone, and that the couch betrays no sign of his attack. With painful steps she walks back down the stairs to the Mother Superior's office.

But when she reaches the open door she sees that Father Angelo is already there, engaging Mother Clemenza in conversation. The toad is even laughing.

For a second Maria stands in the doorway, not knowing what to do. What has the priest told Mother Clemenza? Why is she laughing? Then for the first time ever, the stone-faced toad turns and smiles at her, a beaming, benign smile of approval.

'Father Angelo said you read most sweetly. And were excellently behaved. He recommends that you be allowed on the special picnic tomorrow with the other girls.'

The priest turns and winks at her, putting his hand on her head, ruffling her hair.

'Good child,' he says.

Maria can't speak, her throat so tight she can barely breathe. She feels such anger that the tears return.

The toad frowns, 'Don't cry, Maria.'

'But he attacked me,' Maria manages through her sobs of confusion and rage. She pats her crotch through the front of her skirt. 'Mother Superior, Father Angelo hurt me here.'

Silence. The toad turns to Father Angelo, who looks shocked, then turns back to Maria. When the toad stands from behind the desk and waddles towards her the nun's face is expressionless. 'What did you say?'

Maria's shoulders shake from her crying. 'He hurt me here. He attacked me.'

Mother Clemenza extends her right arm towards her and Maria instinctively leans into it, anticipating the embrace, needing this fat old lady to hug her and tell her everything will be all right.

The slap when it comes is so shocking, that although the blow from the toad's hand hits her full on the side of her face, Maria doesn't feel it. She is completely numb.

The toad's face is now as grey as rolling thunder. 'How could you say such a thing about Father Angelo – in front of Father Angelo? Maria, ever since you were a small child we have endured your fanciful stories and lies, but this . . . this is too much. You will apologize to Father Angelo immediately, then you will be punished.'

'But it is true.'

The toad's face is purple now. 'You will apologize immediately, or your punishment will be worse.'

Maria says nothing. Nothing on earth will make her apologize.

Then Father Angelo speaks. He has a pained smile on his face. 'The poor girl is clearly disturbed and needs our help. Perhaps I should see her on my next visit?'

'You are too understanding, Father Angelo. Maria has always been a liar. I fear even you can do nothing to change her ways.'

'We can but try.'

Maria is in shock when she is led down to the old cellars. Surely any moment now one of the nuns escorting her will tell her they believe her, and that Father Angelo is the one who is to be punished. But when she sees the *steel door at the foot of the stairs she knows it's she who is to be put in the lock-away, not him.*

She's lost count of the number of times she's had to endure the lock-away, but the first time was when she was four. That was when according to the nuns she began telling her 'lies'. But they weren't lies, not really, although she isn't sure any more. As the years have gone by, she hasn't lost her fear of being locked in the completely dark and silent room. If anything her terror has increased. Although the punishment only lasts a few hours, the demons unleashed in the dark stay with her long after she's been released.

This time as the door closes on her and Maria hears the key turn in the lock, she knows she will be here all night. She's never been in the lock-away longer than five hours before. Fighting back her panic, she feels her way across the stone floor to the corner where the small camp-bed is. She lies down and curls up into a ball, hugging her knees to her chest, rocking herself from side to side. With wide eyes she searches for any strand of light in the suffocating blackness.

To her surprise her fear is not as great as usual. She is so incensed by the injustice of what has happened that her mind doesn't take its usual dark turns. She welcomes the feelings of anger that surge through her, and even the feelings of hate give her strength and a sense of control. She decides then that God must surely demand the punishment of anyone as evil as Father Angelo, who claims to act in his name. And for the rest of the night she plans the punishment she will mete out on God's behalf.

THE PAIN FROM THE FOURTH LACERATION ON HER THIGH JOLTED Maria out of her reverie. She looked down at the spilt blood on the towels beneath her thigh and smiled. She felt better now. The letting of bad blood had released some of the anxiety and evil feelings pent-up inside her.

She wiped the dagger carefully on one of the rough white towels from the stack beneath her bed, and dabbed the four neat cuts on her thigh with surgical spirit. Even the sting of the alcohol made her feel more focused, more controlled. Sheathing the kukri, she lay back on the bed and calmly recapped on her meeting with Bernard and Helix, and their decision to freeze her out of the Carter kill. Now that she had everything in perspective it was obvious what she should do next.

She would visit the Father and resolve this issue face to face. Then she could put it behind her once and for all.

Yes, she thought, now allowing her eyelids to exclude the comforting light. She would return to the Father and together they would make everything right again. Then, even as Maria imagined how wonderful it would be, she fell into a deep, dream-free sleep.

14

GENIUS HEADQUARTERS, BOSTON.

JASMINE WASN'T AS DISAPPOINTED AS THE OTHERS SITTING AROUND the oval table in the Francis Crick Conference Room, but then, as her mother always used to tell her, disappointment hits hardest when least expected.

In the three weeks since Tom initiated Project Cana, she had done all that was expected of her. Despite her reservations she was satisfied that she could have done no more. The most advanced Genescope had been fully prepped and was now fully operational in the Francis Crick Conference Room, which along with the adjoining laboratory had been sectioned off from the rest of the Mendel Suite. She had also searched through the entire IGOR database for individuals who might have unusual genes or a history of faith healing. A number of names had come up, but only one with a documented history. She had therefore conducted further research on the owner of that name.

Over the last two decades Mr Keith Anderson of Guildford, Surrey, in England had apparently acquired a reputation for easing the symptoms of rheumatoid arthritis. No cures were attributed to him or claimed by him, but there were countless testimonials from doctors and sufferers of how just by laying his hands on inflamed joints he could bring immediate relief. By all accounts he was the genuine article, but there were two problems: one, Jasmine couldn't find

153

anything unusual in his genes; and two, he had died in a car crash the previous June and been cremated. Still, Keith Anderson wasn't the reason Tom and the others were disappointed.

Three days ago Carter and Jack had returned from Europe with their samples, and their mood had been buoyant, even triumphant. 'Don't worry,' Tom had said when Jasmine had told him what she'd found. 'Searching IGOR was a long shot anyway.' Yeah right, thought Jasmine. As if traipsing around the world trying to find physical remains of a two-thousand-year-old corpse was a sure thing.

But now the Genescope analysis of the samples had come through. And Jasmine could see that disappointment had hit Tom hard, evaporating his early euphoria like yesterday's rain.

Jasmine glanced around the conference table. Jack and Alex sat opposite, Bob Cooke and Nora Lutz on each side of her. The blond Californian and the bespectacled lab technician still hadn't been told about Holly, but three days ago they had been given a confidential briefing on Project Cana. Both had proved invaluable in prepping the samples for the Genescope to scan. But now, like everyone else around the table, they were silent, watching Tom pace around the room.

Every third step Tom would look up and glare accusingly at the Genescope towering in the corner, and start to say something. Then he would shake his head and keep pacing.

If Jasmine was honest she had mixed feelings about being unable to find rare genes in any of the samples. Naturally she wanted to help Holly, but when she'd first seen the samples purporting to be remains of Christ she'd felt as if she was involved in some sacrilegious act. She'd dreaded having to come to terms with the possibility of Tom's thesis being proven correct. So for her at least the negative results, although disastrous, were tinged with guilty relief.

Eventually Tom spoke, 'OK. I can buy into the Michelle Pickard blood samples being bogus. Having AB blood in her veins, and a different O-type blood in her wounds was too weird anyway. And now that Jack's uncovered she's running a scam, using blood from that nurse friend of hers, we can ignore her. The other samples and stuff I can also accept. Shit, I have to.' He sighed then and looked again at the Genescope, as if willing DAN to admit it was wrong.

'But are we absolutely sure about the Lanciano sample? Could we have made any mistake *at all*?'

Jasmine shook her head. 'We've run it three times.'

'But, Jazz, the age checked out; the gender tallied. It's got to be genuine. Perhaps DAN missed something?'

Jasmine looked to Bob and Nora. Both just shrugged and shook their heads.

She said, 'I'm sorry Tom, but there's no mistake. The scan was fine. It's the sample. There are simply no remarkable genes in it. Nothing that we haven't already seen on the IGOR database anyway.'

'Then it must be a fake,' said Tom emphatically.

Jasmine squared her shoulders and said what she knew Tom didn't want to hear, 'Unless of course the sample was genuine, but the healing power wasn't in his genes in the first place?'

Tom stuck out his chin, and crossed his arms over his chest. 'No, Jazz. If he had these powers, then wherever he got them from they would be in his genes.'

Jasmine decided not to push it and sat back in her seat, whilst Tom looked stubbornly around the team. He seemed to be challenging each of them to argue with him, but they remained silent. It was obvious to her that they were now a lot less sure about finding and using the genes of Christ than Tom was. Even Alex, who had supplied the lists of where to search, looked ill at ease.

They all seemed to want to accept Project Cana as the madcap idea it was and move on to another approach. But Tom clearly thought there was nothing else to move on to. It was as if he had now invested all his hopes in Cana, and believed that if he couldn't make the project succeed then Holly would die. Once Tom had made this simple connection Jasmine realized he had no option but to condemn the Lanciano sample as a fake.

She felt torn between the need to make him see reason, and the desire to support him in his stubborn, doomed quest – even if she didn't agree with it. 'But what can we do, Tom?' she said. 'What else is there? Name it and I'll do it.'

Tom stared at her for a long moment, his eyes suddenly vulnerable. 'I just need one microscopic body cell that belonged to Jesus Christ. That's all.'

Jack leaned forward then and said with surprising tenderness, 'But

Tom, even if such a sample still exists, where and when are you going to find it?'

Jasmine watched Tom turn to Alex, who just shook his head. Her heart went out to him then. For the first time since she'd know him, her friend looked like he didn't know what to do.

SATURDAY. BEACON HILL, BOSTON.

THE NEXT MORNING BROUGHT ONE OF THOSE PERFECT BLUE-SKY days in March that promise an early summer but herald spring. Tom took little comfort from the beauty of the day. On the contrary it mocked his despair, as if nature were telling him that the fate of one little girl, his little girl, was incidental to the passing of time and the seasons.

The watery sun felt warm through the glass as he sat in the conservatory with Jack. His friend had come around for breakfast and they had finished eating some time ago. Now they were watching Holly outside in the garden making giant bubbles with her two school friends. It was Megan's turn, and she was dipping a huge loop of pink fabric attached to a wand into a bowl of soapy water. He watched as she lifted out the pink loop, whilst at the same time retracting the slide on the wand. This action slowly broadened the opening, so the film of detergent spanning it didn't break. Then she waved the loop like a matador sweeping a cape over a charging bull, and a grotesquely bulbous, multicoloured bubble billowed out behind her. The vast bubble now complete seemed to tremble in the cool morning air for a moment, then rose slowly up into the blue sky above.

He thought again of yesterday's results on Project Cana and that feeling of helplessness returned to his stomach. Ironically when he'd checked on Hank Polanski in the ward that evening, the young man appeared to be making good progress with the HIV-delivered gene therapy. But although this delighted Tom Carter the scientist and doctor, it frustrated Tom Carter the father. If only he could find a similar treatment for Holly; one that offered at least the same 15 per cent chance of a cure.

All last night he had lain in the dark willing Olivia to tell him what to do. But he was on his own. He had re-read all of the literature specific to brain tumours. Apart from the ground-breaking work by Blaese in the mid-Nineties, using pro-drug therapy to slow the advance of glioblastomas, there was still no prospect of a cure for at least five or six years. In effect nothing had changed since DAN had given his verdict three months ago in December, and time was fast running out.

He turned to Jack and said, 'Perhaps I should try and accept the inevitable. And make the best of my time with Holly. It's just that I feel like I'm giving up.'

Jack watched the bubble make its quivering ascent, and released a sigh. 'Tom, the issue isn't whether you're giving up or not. The issue is whether you're doing what's best for Holly, not just what's best for you. If you feel better keeping yourself busy, avoiding having to think of Holly's situation, that's fine. But if it means you hardly ever see her, then that can't be good for either of you.'

Tom nodded slowly. Jack was right, and he was beginning to realize he didn't have much choice anyway. 'Even if the Lanciano sample is a fake, then finding an authentic sample of Christ's DNA – assuming against all the facts one even exists – could take me longer than the trials and experiments our teams are working on anyway.'

Jack turned from the window and looked at him. 'Perhaps now's the time to try and accept what's going to happen as inevitable. And try to come to terms with it.'

'But it's so goddamned *hard*.'

'The thing is, Tom, there's no-one alive who's more passionate about saving Holly, or better equipped than you. And if you can't help her, my friend, then no-one can. As for Project Cana, it's at best an academic exercise if we can't find a sample. So the decision is made for you. All you *can* do now is try to speed up the conventional cures, and make the best of the time that's left.'

Tom watched glumly as a laughing Holly deftly manipulated the loop to create an even larger bubble. He sat silently as Holly and her friends giggled and ran around it. Suddenly Holly turned to the house and ran to the door of the conservatory where she rapped on the glass. 'Dad, Uncle Jack, look! The biggest ever,' she shouted, her eyes bright with excitement.

Tom smiled at her and made a thumbs-up sign. Jack and he both stood and walked to the glass to gain a closer look. Holly waved and then turned to run back to her friends and the bubble, which seemed to hover just out of reach of the jumping girls. In the sunlight its surface acted like a prism, giving the obese structure a ponderous, rainbow beauty. Despite his black mood Tom felt a small but genuine smile crack the patina of his despair. He was so caught up with watching the girls that he didn't notice Marcy Kelley come into the conservatory behind him with the late morning mail. It was only when she left that he turned and saw the pile of envelopes by the yucca plant.

Almost without thinking he strolled over and picked them up. Walking back to watch the girls playing in the garden he idly flicked through the mail. There were two buff envelopes containing bills; a couple of invitations to talk at seminars; a letter from his cousin in Sydney; and a small black envelope bearing his name and address in red ink. This last envelope was sealed in red wax, stamped with a cross.

He turned the envelope over in his hand and looked at Jack. His friend raised an eyebrow but said nothing. Tom broke the seal and opened the envelope, revealing a black card, a plane ticket and two photographs. Photographs of him.

The card was clearly an invitation, which he read with growing shock. When he'd finished he was so incredulous he had to read it through again. And only after the second reading did he allow his mind to consider the implications and possibilities of the words in front of him.

'What is it?' said Jack, seeing his shock. 'You look like you've been hit by a thunderbolt.'

Tom nodded numbly. That was how he felt. Trying to keep his voice steady, he read the invitation out aloud, exactly as it appeared on the card.

Dear Dr Carter
We have photographic evidence of your quest to find a sample of the DNA of Christ, including the theft of certain objects from various churches. You have named this quest Project Cana and your aim no doubt is to unlock the power in our Lord's genes. We are convinced that to date you have been unsuccessful in your search. Our conviction stems from one simple fact: only we have what you seek. Only we have a genuine biological sample of Jesus Christ.

We are also aware of your illegal DNA database, IGOR, but as a gesture of our good faith have no intention of revealing its existence to the authorities. You don't need to know who we are at this stage but I assure you we can help each other. We have a linked but different objective and if you help us to achieve it, then we will give you what you seek.

All you need do is use the enclosed ticket to Tel Aviv Airport, where you will be met at 14.00 hours local time on 13 March, the day after tomorrow. Naturally you must come alone. This proposal is not open to any negotiations and any breach of these instructions will precipitate the end of our relationship. We would also be forced to reconsider our decision not to inform the relevant authorities of both the blatant theft of sacred relics and the existence of IGOR.

In the spirit of the Wedding at Cana, after which you named the project, I hope that we can enter into a marriage of resources that bears fruit for both of us.

'So these are the bastards who've been snooping round IGOR,' said Jack, taking the card from him. 'I don't suppose it's signed?'

Tom shook his head. 'There's no clue at all to who sent it, apart from the seal, which isn't exactly unique.' Tom turned his attention to the photographs: him leaving the small white church in Cittavecchia, and a more grainy one of him and Jack on the boat with Dutch and Irish. He opened up the plane ticket revealing an El Al Business Class voucher to Tel Aviv.

'Obviously you aren't going,' said Jack, studying the wax seal on the envelope.

'I damn well am.'

Jack looked up and frowned. 'But this could be a trap from the Preacher. Think about it, Tom. Maybe she's been watching you since Stockholm, worked out what you're searching for and then rigged this trap.'

'I don't care. It's the chance I've been looking for. If it can help Holly, then I've got to take it.'

'But this chance could get you killed. And making an orphan out of Holly won't help her.'

Tom pointed to the invite in Jack's hands. 'Without a chance like this, she won't be an orphan for long.'

'C'mon, Tom, what if it is the Preacher? What then?'

Tom felt his anger boil, remembering the hologram image of the Preacher he'd seen on his return from Sardinia. 'Frankly I'd welcome it.'

'What?'

'Aside from saving Holly there's only one thing that I think about all the time: catching the witch who killed Olivia and making her pay.'

'OK. OK. But then let's set a trap of our own. You don't have a hope in hell against her by yourself. Karen Tanner knows her job. We could tell her about this and together with the Bureau we could finish her for good.'

Tom thought this through for a second as he watched his daughter laughing with her friends on the lawn. 'But what if it's not the Preacher? What if the offer's genuine? Then I lose the one chance I might have to save her.'

Jack groaned. 'Tom, look at the odds. It must be the Preacher. Let's at least check it out with the FBI.'

Tom turned and looked Jack straight in the eye. 'It's decided, Jack. I don't want them involved. They could jeopardize everything. I'd rather die trying to save Holly, than live to see her die. Particularly if I can avenge Olivia. Don't you see, as far as I'm concerned this is a win-win situation?'

'You're being fucking stupid now.'

'I don't care, Jack. Are you going to help me or what?'

Jack shook his head and released a sigh of resignation. 'I don't suppose I can persuade you to carry a gun. I'd teach you how to use it.'

'No way. If the letter's genuine then a gun could wreck everything.'

Jack groaned and fell silent.

Out of the window Tom saw the bubble burst over the three excited and screaming girls. Despite Jack's reservations he felt a sudden rush of excitement. His despair of only moments ago had gone. He had something to work at and hope for again.

He heard Jack say, 'At least let me keep track of you, so if anything goes wrong I know where to find you.'

'Can you do that without them knowing?'

'No,' said Jack, allowing his face to break into a weary grin. 'But I know a guy who can.'

15

TEL AVIV.

TOM CARTER CHANGED HIS WATCH TO 1:58 P.M. LOCAL TIME AND breathed a sigh of relief as the El Al 747 taxied to a stop on the sun-drenched tarmac of Tel Aviv's Ben Gurion Airport. He was only slightly better at travelling by plane than he was by boat. After slipping away from his police protection he had kissed Holly goodbye at Logan Airport and spent the whole flight in a state of escalating apprehension, none of which had eased his travel-sickness. He was still worried that if he was ill he would throw up the low-frequency tracker Jack had insisted he swallow. Jack had already taken an earlier flight out to brief a 'friend' on setting up a monitoring centre to track Tom wherever his hosts decided to take him.

The intercom crackled into life, *'Thank you for flying El Al and please remember to take all your personal belongings with you when you leave the aircraft. On behalf of Captain David Ury and his crew we hope . . .'*

Tom ignored the announcements as he unbuckled his belt and got ready to leave. His only luggage was a small shoulder bag he carried with him in the cabin. At the plane exit the stewardesses said their practised goodbyes, and he walked via an enclosed walkway into the main terminal building. He felt a nervous prickle on the back of his neck and tried to loosen the already open collar of his white linen shirt. As he reached the tiled floor of the main terminal building a tall man suddenly appeared beside him.

'Dr Carter, welcome. My name is Helix, Helix Kirkham. Would you please step this way.'

The stranger was a well-preserved man of about fifty, balding with thick round glasses and intelligent eyes. He looked more like an academic than a killer.

Helix smiled and extended a slender hand, which was firm when Carter shook it. 'I trust you had an enjoyable flight. If you give us your passport we can ensure you avoid all the tedious immigration procedures.'

He spoke with an English accent but there was a trace of something else, as if he had originally come from elsewhere.

Numbly Tom reached into his cotton jacket for his passport. 'Where are we going?' he asked.

Helix took the passport from his hands and passed it quickly to one of two large men who had appeared behind him. Helix barked out orders in a language Tom didn't understand and the man scurried off in the direction of the other passengers.

Helix turned back to him and smiled. 'You do not need to know where we are going. But don't worry. You won't be there long; just long enough to conduct our business.'

Then before Tom could ask any more questions Helix turned, breezed past two armed airport security guards watching the steps down to the runway and descended onto the tarmac in the direction of a Chinook helicopter.

'Come!' Helix said. 'We will answer all your questions when we get there.'

The third man walked beside Tom as he followed Helix. Neither man was introduced to him, but Tom sensed they were here to ensure he didn't waver and try to leave. The man who had taken his passport was of medium height and featureless. But the man on his right was different. He held himself with an air of importance, and was clearly more than just a guard. He was tall, almost as tall as Tom, and powerful too. His blue-black hair was cropped close to his head, and smoky-green eyes looked out from a fine-featured face. If Tom hadn't known that the Preacher was a woman he would have tagged this man with the smoky-green eyes as a candidate. There was something palpably dangerous about him. Even the name by which Tom heard

163

Helix address him was strangely unsettling. Gomorrah was hardly a normal name.

By the time they reached the helicopter at the far end of the runway the man with his passport had returned. Helix handed it back, then led him, into the Chinook. Once inside he heard the doors clank shut behind him, enclosing him in the womb of the helicopter. He remembered Jack telling him not to go and how he'd ignored all pleas for caution.

He thought of Holly. Last night when he'd said goodbye, she'd somehow sensed this trip was different. She'd actually asked him where he was going and why, something she never usually did. He'd told her that he was going to try and help someone who was ill and she'd understood immediately. To Holly that was what he did. He remembered how once at school Mrs Hoyt, the English teacher, had asked the class to say in one sentence what their parents did for a living. Holly's answer had been a matter of fact: 'My dad stops people from dying.'

As he looked around the gloomy confines of the helicopter, Carter kept telling himself that this was what he was doing now. He had embarked on this trip into the unknown to stop Holly from dying. He was right to ignore Jack's advice because it jeopardized the one chance he had. He simply had no choice, he told himself again. It was no more complicated or sinister than that.

Still, he couldn't help a nervous swallow when he heard the roar of the rotors start up, and a few seconds later felt the aircraft move off the ground. He was committed now, there was no going back. His stomach lurched, and he hoped he wouldn't vomit. He wished that Jack was with him, so he could feed off his physical courage.

Especially when Gomorrah reached towards him.

The man held something in his hand that looked like an electric razor with a series of red blinking lights down one side. Tom sat motionless as the guy scanned his bag, shoes and clothes with the gadget. Tom took a deep breath when he realized he was being checked for tracking devices. He'd only agreed to swallow the tracker because Jack had told him it was 'state of the art'; undetectable. But he needn't have worried. After a few moments the smoky-green eyes relaxed and the guy nodded his satisfaction to Helix.

'I am sorry about these precautions,' said Helix with an apologetic shrug, 'but they are necessary.'

Tom nodded, determined not to show his fear. But just as he began to relax Gomorrah reached into his pocket and pulled out what looked like a blindfold. If he wasn't able to see he was sure he would be ill, and aside from losing the tracking device he hated the idea of showing this weakness to his hosts – or enemies. When Gomorrah asked him in perfect, accentless English to lean forward, Tom considered struggling. But he just gritted his teeth and let the man wrap the greasy-smelling cloth around his head. Think of Holly, he told himself again.

The disorientating move from gloom to complete blackness as the blindfold tightened around his head made him dizzy. And, as if to compensate for the loss of sight, his sense of hearing and smell became more acute, as did his sensitivity to the chopper's every movement. He became keenly aware of the smell of sweat and oil in the helicopter. And now that he was blindfolded his escorts began to talk as if they believed the blindfold also made him deaf, or non-existent.

Their unintelligible, guttural tones cut through the roar of the engines. His chest tightened with panic and nausea brewed in his lurching stomach. He felt as if he was shrouded in a heavy, suffocating blanket. He wanted to rip off the blindfold, pull back the doors of the helicopter and breathe in the air and light outside. But he did none of these things. Instead he cupped his hands over his mouth, filled his lungs with his own exhaled breath and forced himself to think of his glass laboratory of light and limitless space. And to imagine standing on the firm, unmoving ground with Holly. At least you're doing something, he told himself again. This has to be better than doing nothing, just letting it happen.

Just letting it happen.

As he listened to the rhythm of the engine and the whup-whup of the rotating blades, his mind folded in on itself. The engine noise had a rattling tempo at its core that reminded him of a sound from his childhood; the summer of '74; that day, not long after his twelfth birthday.

THE DRAPES ARE DRAWN IN THE BEDROOM. IT IS DARK AND THE *whirring noise of the broken air-conditioner beats out its rattling rhythm.*

The room is empty and he ignores the crisp, white piece of paper resting on the bed, and rushes to the closed door of the en-suite bathroom. He knocks of course, but he's excited and knows that if you twist the handle round twice then the old lock doesn't work. So without waiting for a response he just pushes in.

The steam from the hot bath makes it impossible to see anything at first. Then he hears his mother say in a voice that doesn't sound like her own:

'Shut the door, darling, and leave me alone for a moment.'

'What's wrong, Mom?' Something in her tone makes his excitement disappear, replaced by a tight feeling in his stomach. 'Dad says we should be leaving soon. The movie's going to start.' Then he turns from closing the door and sees what will stay with him for the rest of his life.

Tom knows even then that his mother is ill. The visits to the hospital have told him that much. He's heard the word 'cancer' whispered late at night but it hasn't really registered. And he certainly doesn't know she's been fighting the tumour growing in her brain for months, and that it's already changed her personality and brought untold pain.

As the steam clears he sees his mother lying naked in the full bath. Her face is deathly white and the bathwater is clouded pink. Each of her wrists is lined with grisly crimson cuts.

At first he simply doesn't understand what he is seeing.

'Mommy, you're bleeding. What happened?' he asks in bewildered horror. 'Did you fall? Are you all right?'

'I'm sorry, darling. I didn't want you to see me like this.'

His first instinct is to run out of here and get his dad.

His mother says, 'Tom, darling, I'm fine. Honestly. Don't be frightened. It doesn't hurt at all.'

He moves to the door. 'I'll get Dad.' His throat is too tight with sobs to scream, but something in his mother's voice stops him from opening the door. There is a pleading quality he has never heard before.

'No, don't get Daddy. Not yet.'

'But why not, Mom? Why not?' His lower lip trembles uncontrollably. Gradually the awareness trickles into his young mind that his mom has done this to herself.

'I need to rest, darling. My body's turned against me. But I love you and Daddy so much. You will tell him, won't you? But later. OK?'

He is desperate to leave that room, but his mother's eyes are so pained. If he fetches Dad he will only stop her from going. And although he wants his

Mom to stay more than anything else in the world, it doesn't seem right to make her stay.

'Sit down, darling. Stay with me and show me how clever you are by counting like you used to.'

He has the strange sensation of watching himself from outside his own body. He sees himself walk numbly to the chair by the laundry basket. He moves his mother's neatly laid-out wristwatch, bracelet and necklace, then sits down.

'Count for me like you did when you were small,' he hears her say. 'Prime numbers. As high as you can.' Her eyes look so sad that he hurts inside. He leans forward and kneels by the bath, then gently strokes her forehead just like he remembers her doing whenever he was ill. Despite the steam her skin feels cold and clammy, so he puts both his small hands on her forehead, hoping his own heat will somehow warm her and make her well again. Then he starts to count, just like his mother asked him to, 'One, two, three, five, seven, eleven, thirteen, seventeen, nineteen, twenty-three . . .'

IT WASN'T UNTIL HE REACHED TWO HUNDRED AND SIXTY-NINE – the number he'd got to when she died – that Tom Carter snapped back to the present. The noise of the helicopter engine now sounded nothing like the air-conditioner in his parents' room all those years ago. He had to strain his ears even to hear a faint resemblance.

To this day Tom still didn't know if he should have colluded in his mother's suicide. The guilt remained. His father had tried to convince him that he'd done the right thing. But Tom knew Alex must harbour a bitter regret that his son hadn't alerted him; that he hadn't even said goodbye to the woman he loved so much that he had never married again.

As he'd grown older and wiser Tom had taken only two certainties from the experience. The first was that if a blameless woman like his mother could be smitten by cancer, then a god worth believing in – let alone worshipping – couldn't possibly exist. If any power did indeed preside over the cosmos then it was a cruel, arbitrary Lady Luck masquerading as Mother Nature. And only science offered any chance of shortening the odds.

The second certainty was that the next time someone needed his help he would make sure he was as equipped as possible to give it. Even as an adolescent his heroes had been dressed in white coats wielding scalpels or peering down microscopes fighting disease and saving lives. He had known from the start that he needed to be more than just a doctor or 'people mechanic' to win this war. So he had become a genetic scientist too. And he hadn't dedicated his whole life to this crusade just to stand by now that his own daughter needed him.

The helicopter turbulence jarred his unsettled stomach. It took some minutes to realize that the sudden loss in altitude was the aircraft coming down to land. With a mix of excitement and dread he realized that he had almost arrived at his destination.

As he braced himself for the landing he tried to estimate how much time had elapsed, but in the darkness, deep in his thoughts he had lost all track. It could have been one hour or four. Suddenly there was a sharp increase in engine noise and a final vibration, then he felt the helicopter come to rest.

'We're here,' said Helix to his right.

Relief flooded through him when he heard the door being opened and sensed light through the thick blindfold. Warm, dry air blew into the cabin and swirled around him like a sweet ointment, purging his nausea. He could smell dust and sand and the suggestion of spice. He breathed deep and felt his muscles relax one by one. 'Can I take the blindfold off now?'

'Not yet,' said Helix holding on to his arm and leading him out of the aircraft. 'Soon.'

As Tom blindly negotiated the rickety steps down to the ground his face was struck by countless grains of sand stirred up by the dying rotor blades. The sun warmed the back of his neck and his mouth felt dry as his feet found the uneven sandy ground and he was led away.

When the engine eventually died he was struck by the lack of sound. Apart from the whisper of the dry wind and the occasional exchange among his escorts there was no noise at all. No traffic. No distant voices. Nothing. Only the sound of his own breathing and the shuffle of his blind footsteps on the sand. He felt very alone, but the hot air, sandy ground and the hint of light through the thick blindfold encouraged him.

Almost immediately he felt the sand beneath his feet give way to more solid terrain, and the heat of the sun leave his back. He could sense from the new sound of his footsteps that he was entering a building of some kind. Arms pulled him forward, deeper into the coolness. Then suddenly, they stopped him.

'Steps. Be careful,' commanded Helix's voice to his right.

Gingerly, taking his weight on his good leg, he extended his right foot into space and then lowered it. The next step was so deep down that for a heart-stopping moment he thought he was at the edge of an abyss. Then just as he began to lose his balance his foot finally came to rest on hard stone. He had never encountered stairs so large before. He descended lower and lower, gripping the rope of the handrail to keep from falling.

Suddenly the obvious thought intruded on his consciousness: *If you're still alive, then they must be genuine. They might have what you seek.*

Excitement surged through him then, and as he went deeper and deeper down the huge spiral stairwell his fear melted away, replaced by an almost intolerable sense of anticipation.

When he eventually reached the bottom, his escorts made him stoop and led him briskly along what sounded like a narrow corridor. He banged his head on the low ceiling, and his now hyper-sensitive ears were almost deafened by the concentrated, reverberating sounds of their feet clicking on the hard floor.

Then, like the babble of a rushing river dissipating into a great lake, he heard the clattering echoes of their footsteps soften and deepen as the narrow corridor entered a larger space.

Abruptly he was pulled back, his pace slowed to a gentle walk. To Tom's nose this place smelt like the churches he'd visited in his child-hood; all dry dust and old religion. The smell of incense wasn't overpowering but it was in the air with the pungent smoke of candle wax. However, it was the acoustics of the place that were most remarkable. The hollow silence all around him seemed a palpable living thing. And he found himself treading quietly, to avoid the echo of any loud noise he made being thrown back at his sensitive ears.

Eventually he was pulled to a halt and was beginning to relax when a strong hand suddenly clasped his shoulder. Then he felt the icy caress of steel graze the back of his neck.

16

SOUTHERN JORDAN.

MARIA BENARIAC SMILED AS SHE SHIFTED DOWN A GEAR ON THE rented Range Rover. The vast desert landscape all around her was silent, uncorrupted by any semblance of life. Cruising this ocean of sand in her air-conditioned cocoon, she felt a deep sense of peace. Far in the distance she could just make out the five pillars of rock, rising up from the desert like the upended prows of sinking ships. Ever since that dark night three days ago when she had decided to visit the Father she had felt so positive. She wondered now why she hadn't thought of visiting him earlier.

She had been to the Cave of the Sacred Light a few times before, but never unannounced. However, since today was a scheduled meeting of Ezekiel and his two most senior lieutenants, she knew he would be there. After meeting with him she was sure she could get the decision on Dr Carter reversed.

The sun was high in a sky of cobalt blue, and as the car carried her across the roadless plain she allowed her thoughts to wander. In her mind she was the prodigal daughter returning to the bosom of the Father, and she realized how much she looked forward to seeing him again. She hadn't spoken to Father Ezekiel face to face for almost five months, and couldn't wait to see his expression when he learnt of her surprise visit. Yes, she felt confident he would be happy to see her and that he would endorse her right to complete her task. Had he not always told her that she was a natural Nemesis; that no-one else had her talent and dedication for the Righteous Cleansing? She smiled as she cast her mind back to that first kill, the one that brought her to his attention.

THE FIFTEEN-YEAR-OLD MARIA BENARIAC DOES NOT TAKE THE DECI-sion to kill Father Angelo lightly but it surprises her how soon the ideal opportunity presents itself.

Her decision is triggered by two events. One is the suicide of Sister Delphine, a young novice nun at the orphanage, and the other is the third time Father Angelo rapes her.

After the first rape he insists on giving her 'counselling' sessions whenever he visits the orphanage. The blinkered sycophantic Mother Clemenza makes Maria attend them of course, telling her she should be grateful for all the time and trouble the great man is taking with her development.

Maria tries to hide when he visits the second time, but he seeks her out and during the session rapes her again, only this time even more violently than the first. She thinks of showing her bruises to Mother Clemenza afterwards but knows it will do no good.

The third time he ties her up when she struggles, then makes her perform oral sex on him before sodomizing her. And as he thrusts into her he tells her never to forget she is powerless against him; that she is his slave and should accept it. Afterwards he boasts that she isn't the only one; that he even uses some of the younger nuns for his pleasure.

Ten days later Sister Delphine is found hanging from the beam above her bed. She is four months pregnant and cannot live with her shame. No-one has any idea who the father could be.

Except Maria.

She realizes then that unless she wants to end up the same way she will have to kill Father Angelo. She has no other place to go. And she will have to do it in a way that brings none of the blame back to her. She has had enough of being punished.

When Father Angelo comes to the orphanage two weeks later she feigns complete subservience — a child broken to his will. And when he tells her quietly that he is staying in Calvi that night and has arranged for her to secretly visit his hotel room, she accepts without argument.

He smiles at her new compliance and when he leaves, hands her a key to his hotel and a hundred francs. 'If you leave after midnight and take a taxi into town no-one will be the wiser. Use the side door to the hotel so you aren't seen. I'll make sure you're back here by dawn.'

Maria pockets the money but has no intention of taking a taxi. That afternoon she goes to the kitchen to empty the bins as usual, and leaves with the biggest knife she can find hidden under her skirts. Then she goes to the laundry and takes a set of soiled clothes from the large pile of dirty laundry she's responsible for washing the next morning. Finally she goes to the bicycle shed, takes out Mother Clemenza's bike and hides it in the thick bushes by the main gates.

The rest of the day she busies herself in her chores, trying to distract herself from what she has planned to do. She wishes she had friends to talk to, but the other girls have always regarded her as difficult and she has been branded an outcast. When she eventually goes to bed she lies there trembling with fear and excitement. There is no danger of her falling asleep before the allotted hour.

Father Angelo deserves to die, she's sure of that. He must be stopped before he hurts anybody else, or before he kills her. He wears the clothes of God, but acts like a servant of the Devil. God wants her to kill him. She is God's instrument and will be avenging her Lord as well as herself. What she plans to do is a good and righteous thing.

She waits till thirty-five minutes past midnight before making her move. The whole building is fast asleep when she creeps out of her dormitory wearing the soiled set of clothes, and carrying her clean ones in a plastic bag. It is simple to steal out of the building and take the bike from its hiding-place. The clear night air is cool but she is sweating by the time she arrives near the Marina. She parks the bike down the road from the hotel and covering her face in a scarf walks into the hotel parking lot. Using the key she enters the side door.

His room is on the first floor but she encounters no other guests on the way. She is surprised at how calm she feels now she is here and knows there is no going back. At the door to Father Angelo's room she knocks quietly. His pockmarked face appears almost immediately, his eyes bright with lust. He does a quick look left and right then pulls her into the room and closes the door.

'I'm glad you came, my child,' he says.

She barely has time to take in the well-appointed room before he takes off his robes and stands before her, his penis angry and erect.

Not bothering to undress her he forces her to her knees and with a groan moves her face towards his swollen member. 'Pay homage to me,' he says.

Again she is amazed by how calm she feels. The terror she endured during

172

the rapes has gone. Instead she feels in control, powerful. Looking up at him she opens her mouth and moves towards him. She watches him smile down at her from his lofty position as her right hand feels inside her waistband and pulls out the knife.

She has thought about the blood and the noise and wants to minimize both. So when she does it she does it quickly. Even as her right hand severs his penis, her left hand reaches for the pillow on the bed and pushes it into Father Angelo's face to stifle his screams. But the screams don't come for many seconds. At first his face looks more surprised than pained – as if he can't believe anybody could do this to him.

But then his legs buckle and as he reaches for his crotch she pushes him back on the bed. His eyes stare at her with uncomprehending horror. He tries to struggle and scream now but she jumps on him, pushing the cotton of the pillowcase deeper into his mouth, gagging him. Then she securely ties his hands together with the bed sheets, which are red with blood. Blood is everywhere but far from feeling disgust she feels a rush of heady exhilaration.

Leaving him rocking on the bed in silent, impotent agony, she feels around the blood-slick carpet until she finds what she's looking for. Then she climbs back on the bed and smiles into her tormentor's eyes. 'Tell me,' she demands. 'Was Sister Delphine one of your slaves too? If you answer me honestly I will call the doctor.' She feels giddy with power as she waves his severed penis in front of his horrified eyes. 'You can still save this. Did you rape her too?'

He stares at the deflated, bloody slug nestling in the palm of her hand.

'Tell me! Nod for yes.'

Slowly he nods.

'Good.' She pulls the pillowcase out of his mouth, but as he opens his lips to scream she pushes his severed manhood into his mouth and stuffs the pillow-case back in after it. 'Who's the slave now?' she asks, looking into his protruding eyeballs, hearing him gag and splutter as he fights for breath.

Calmly she watches his death throes, feeling a rush of satisfaction when his pupils flicker for the last time. Satisfied he's dead, she gets off the bed and using the bloody knife blade writes on the still-white part of the bed sheets: An eye for an eye, a tooth for a tooth. Then she takes off her bloody clothes, showers in the bathroom, cleans the knife and puts on her clean set of clothing. She bundles the bloody clothes back in the plastic bag. Maria takes one last look at the carnage, satisfied that justice has been done. Then, not bothering to close Father Angelo's staring eyes, she leaves.

It is only as she walks down the corridor that she sees the silhouette of a man waiting in the shadows by Father Angelo's room. She pulls the scarf tighter round her face and tries to ignore him as she flees from the hotel. But on the ride home she senses she is being followed.

Back at the orphanage she feels safe again. She has replaced the knife and bike, put the blood-soaked clothes deep in the pile of laundry and crept back into bed. She even thinks she may have imagined the man in the shadows. She was only out of her bed for fifty-five minutes. There is no way anyone can know she killed Father Angelo.

But a week later when Mother Clemenza summons her, Maria discovers she was wrong.

The toad has been in a state of shock ever since Sister Delphine committed suicide, and Father Angelo's body was discovered. But that doesn't explain the strange way she acts when Maria enters her study. The toad is warm, almost maternal. Maria can only assume it has something to do with the wizened man with black eyes sitting opposite her in a dark suit. The toad smiles and gestures obsequiously to the small man.

'Hello Maria. You have a visitor.' She says it as though Maria is so popular she has visitors all the time. 'This gentleman wants to talk to you.'

Maria's heart freezes. She can guess what the man wants to talk to her about. But what clue could she have left at the scene to lead him to her? How could this man possibly know she killed Father Angelo?

The toad suddenly stands and walks to the door of the study. 'Well, I'm sure you have lots to talk about. So I'll leave you.'

The man stands out of courtesy and says, 'I would rather not be disturbed.' His voice makes the words sound like an order.

Mother Clemenza wipes her palms on her robes and smiles nervously. 'As you wish.'

Maria is amazed. Mother Clemenza has never vacated her study for anyone before, not even Father Angelo.

When the toad has closed the door behind her the man introduces himself and gestures for her to sit behind the desk.

'But that's the Mother Superior's chair.'

The black eyes wrinkle mischievously. 'I won't tell her if you don't.'

She smiles at him and begins to relax. Perhaps he's come about something else? Then just as she sits down he says the words that make her knees go weak.

'Maria, I know you killed Father Angelo. One of my friends saw you enter and leave his room at the time he was murdered.'

She slumps in the toad's chair and looks down at her feet. There's obviously no point in denying it. 'He was evil. God wanted me to avenge him. He raped me three times and made Sister Delphine kill herself.' She says the words automatically, knowing they won't be believed.

'I know,' she hears him say. 'Father Angelo was indeed an evil man who deserved to die.'

Stunned, she looks up and sees him smiling at her. It is a smile of affection and understanding, the kind a father might give an errant daughter. She is surprised to feel a lump in her throat, and the sting of tears behind her eyes.

'Do you know why you have suffered, Maria?' he asks as if he knows all about her.

Not trusting herself to speak, she just shakes her head.

'Because you are special.'

'Special?'

'Chosen.'

'I don't understand.'

'God has singled you out to serve him. He has given you great gifts: intelligence, beauty and courage. But he's also given you great hardship to test you. Now you have overcome this hardship it is time to prepare you for even greater work. Do you understand?'

Maria looks into his dark eyes and nods slowly. She does understand. Everything suddenly falls into place. She was being tested for greater things. Her God has marked her out and now this man will help guide her to her destiny.

'You have talent and you have passion,' he says, his smile creasing his parchment skin. 'And if you agree, I have arranged to take you away from this place.'

Maria smiles. It is the easiest decision of her life.

JUST REMEMBERING EZEKIEL'S SMILE ENCOURAGED MARIA AS THE car neared the five pillars of rock. Of course at the time she hadn't known that Sister Delphine was the niece of Brother Culas, a senior member of the Brotherhood. Or that the novice nun had written to her uncle explaining everything about Father Angelo before she had killed herself. It had been Maria's predecessor, the last Nemesis, who had been sent by the Brotherhood to do what she had already done, and it was he watching her leave Father Angelo's room. It was also Nemesis, nearing retirement, who had recommended the precocious fifteen-year-old killer as his successor. Ezekiel had then discovered the secrets of her life before making his approach.

From that moment her life had changed. Five years in the training school run by Brother Bernard had followed, where she had been tutored in everything from languages to Righteous Killing, to the lore and history of the Brotherhood. For the first time in her life she felt she belonged to a family and truly believed in what she was doing. She still remembered the pride when after five years she had been taken to the Cave of the Sacred Light for her blooding ceremony. As Ezekiel had pierced her forearm with the ceremonial dagger she had felt no pain. Later that day he had praised her, calling her the most dedicated recruit in living memory.

Two years later she was appointed the new Nemesis. And for the next thirteen years she had enjoyed an incomparable record.

Until Stockholm.

Until Dr Carter.

She tensed her jaw as she quickly reminded herself that she would soon correct that. Ahead she could see a helicopter and two Land Rovers parked by the tallest rock. She drove up to the entrance of the cave. Two men were waiting there, watching her closely as she put a baseball cap on her shaved head. Cutting the engine, she opened the door and stepped out into the furnace-fierce heat. She slammed the door to the Range Rover and walked straight for the two men.

Just as the first man's mouth opened in challenge she extended her right hand. 'May he be saved.'

His face relaxed and he gave a small nod, clasping her hand. Then he extended his other hand to meet her left, both handshakes now forming a cross. 'So he may save the righteous.'

TWO HUNDRED FEET BELOW, TOM CARTER'S FEAR CHANGED TO relief when the knife blade moved from his neck to cut his blindfold. He turned and as his eyes accustomed themselves to the golden light he saw Helix standing beside him, a knife in his hand and a small smile on his lips.

He made an expansive gesture with his right hand, taking in the vast underground chamber in front of him. 'Dr Carter, welcome to the Cave of the Sacred Light. The Sanctuary of the Brotherhood of the Second Coming.'

176

Tom marvelled at the carved, vaulted ceiling high above him, supported on heavy rock pillars as thick as square oak trees. The golden glow came from countless candles burning on a narrow ledge, midway up the thirty-foot-high walls. Their flickering shafts of light danced over the chiselled surface of the red stone ceiling. Further light was supplied by gas lamps and torches placed in metal holders on each of the pillars. The sides of the hall were adorned with ancient-looking tapestries that billowed from iron rails like the sails of small ships. Each tapestry depicted religious scenes which appeared, to Tom, to come alive in the flickering candlelight.

At the far end of the hall was an altar, bedecked in a white cloth decorated with a blood-red cross. His eyes were drawn to the dazzling flame of unnaturally white light directly in front of it. The white flame appeared to issue from a hole in the rock floor, its dazzling light illuminating a large, sealed stone door on the wall behind the altar.

In the centre of the chamber, on the worn mosaic floor, was a mighty table that matched the scale of the cavern. Bowls and platters of food sat on the thick, wood tabletop, which in turn rested on sturdy feet, carved to resemble the clawed talons of an eagle. Around this table were six equally magnificent chairs. All were empty.

Even he could sense the power of this place and it made him feel uncomfortable. It was like a huge mausoleum, containing the sum of man's outdated beliefs.

'Welcome, Dr Carter. We are glad you came.' The man's strong voice took Tom by surprise. He had barely noticed the two figures standing beneath the pillars on the far side of the cavern, so dwarfed were they by their surroundings. The man who had addressed him was especially small, out of scale with the cavern.

'Dr Carter,' said Helix, 'allow me to introduce Father Ezekiel De La Croix, Leader of the Brotherhood of the Second Coming, and Brother Bernard.'

Ezekiel walked towards him. 'I apologize for the manner in which you were brought here. But we have defended our privacy for two thousand years.'

'I understand,' said Tom. 'As long as it means your invitation was genuine and my trip hasn't been wasted.'

'I think I can assure you of that.'

Tom couldn't place the man's accent, a strange blend of the Middle

East and French. And as Ezekiel came closer, Carter noticed that although his mouth was smiling in greeting his dark eyes studied him with intense scrutiny. The wizened man with silk-thin white hair was ancient, and Tom reckoned he couldn't be much taller than five six, almost a foot shorter than he was. Yet his presence was such that Tom knew his own height wouldn't intimidate him.

Ezekiel extended a thin, clawlike hand and on his gnarled finger was a heavy metallic ring crowned with the largest ruby Tom had ever seen. He immediately recognized the cross-shaped mount from the wax seal on the envelope. When he took Ezekiel's hand in his the skin felt scaly and desiccated. The man's face looked no different: tissue-thin parchment over bony features. Tom felt that if he rubbed it hard enough it would come away in his hands, revealing the skeleton beneath. Under the old man's dark suit and sash, Tom could tell Ezekiel's slight frame still exuded a sinewy strength. But the man's real power lay in his black, intelligent eyes. Ageless, they sparkled with an alert cunning. This was not a man to underestimate lightly, or trust too readily.

'You've already met Brother Helix,' said Ezekiel, 'he is a scientist like yourself, Dr Carter. He champions our Primary Imperative and keeps us abreast of developments.' Ezekiel turned to the third man. 'Brother Bernard here heads up our . . .' he paused as if searching for the correct phrase, '. . . security arrangements.'

Carter shook Brother Bernard by the hand. With wispy grey hair and a greying goatee beard he looked older than Helix, probably in his seventies. He was a big man, six foot and fat. His mouth with its fleshy lower lip gave him the petulant look of a cruel schoolboy. Carter disliked him on sight.

'Who are you? And what is the Primary Imperative?' he asked.

Ezekiel flashed another of his mouth-only smiles. 'All in good time, Dr Carter, all in good time.' He gestured to the magnificent table. 'Come, let us discuss our marriage of resources. Our treasures of the past with your technology of the future.'

Before Tom could ask him to explain further, the ancient man turned on surprisingly agile feet and walked with neat, deliberate steps to the table. 'We have food and drink. You must be in need of refreshment after your long journey.'

Tom did feel thirsty and as Brother Helix ushered him to his seat he checked his watch. Almost three hours had elapsed since he'd landed in Tel Aviv. He wondered what time it would be in Boston and calculated that Holly would already be at school.

Ezekiel sat at the head of the table with the altar and dazzling white light behind him. The two Brothers sat on each side of him with Tom next to Helix. He noticed that they just used a fraction of the vast table, and could only guess at how many people it could accommodate; certainly three times the six chairs indicated.

'Please eat,' said the old man, indicating the array of food and drink laid out before him.

The array was how Tom always imagined a medieval banquet. There were large pewter platters of dates, figs, pomegranates and cheese; salvers piled high with lamb, steak and chicken; and bowls of pickles and stuffed vine leaves. Next to the food, earthenware demijohns of water and wine sat beside elaborate goblets from another age. Helix lifted one of the wine demijohns and poured the dark, aromatic ruby liquid into Tom's goblet, whilst Brother Bernard moved the salvers of food closer. Despite his nervousness, the food made Tom realize he hadn't eaten for hours. Jack, the paranoid mother-hen, had warned him not to touch anything. But given the welcome he'd received so far he could hardly see the danger. If these people meant him harm then he was convinced they would have done so by now.

The acoustics of the place seemed to magnify Ezekiel's voice when he spoke again. 'Since we invited you here, I think I should lead. Whilst you refresh yourself I will tell you something about our organization. Then we will discuss the trade.'

Tom nodded as if he had a choice, and put the aromatic wine to his dry lips. The rich, heady liquid tasted oddly refreshing. As he tried to keep his mounting excitement in check, he realized he was beginning to enjoy this bizarre encounter.

EZEKIEL DE LA CROIX STOOD, HIS SMALL FRAME CASTING A GIANT shadow on the nearest pillar, and studied his guest closely before he began. He was glad Dr Carter had accepted their invitation and he couldn't help but be impressed by the man's demeanour. The scientist was so different to the brash iconoclast he had expected. To travel halfway around the world on the chance that complete strangers might have what he sought, demonstrated how much he valued their relic. Ezekiel couldn't believe that his motives were purely commercial. The scientist already had more money than he could ever need. But whatever his reasons were, Dr Carter's manner and dedication encouraged Ezekiel that he would be receptive to their trade.

'Let me start at the beginning,' Ezekiel said. 'Two thousand years ago, Lazarus, the man Christ brought back from the dead, witnessed the horror of Christ's crucifixion and vowed that the corrupt religions must never be allowed to commit the same crime again. The night after Golgotha Lazarus had a dream, in which he saw this ancient cave and the light that burned here. The next day he led his followers to this sacred place; a place that would be forever safe from persecution. The Brotherhood of the Second Coming had one overarching aim: to wait and watch for when the Messiah came again, in order to identify and anoint him in the sacred flame. This simple goal – the so-called Primary Imperative – is what guides us still.'

Ezekiel turned to the white flame. 'That is the sacred light that gives this cavern its name. This is where the first meeting of the Brotherhood's Inner Circle took place and where they worshipped before the altar of the Sacred Fire.'

Ezekiel looked back to Carter, pleased to see he was listening intently. 'In his dream Lazarus saw the flame change from a pure white to orange, when Christ died for our sins. But he was told that when the white flame returned so would the Messiah. The sacred fire has only burned white two times in two thousand years.' He paused and moved over to the fire. 'Once when Jesus of Nazareth walked the earth. And *now. Today.* For the last thirty-five years the New Messiah has been among us, and we must find him.'

Carter gave an uneasy frown. 'How do you *know* your Messiah walks the earth now? Couldn't the flame just be a coincidence? A geological shift, a different gas?'

'We *know*,' said Ezekiel impatiently.

Carter picked at the plate of chicken. 'And how do you intend to find this New Messiah of yours?'

'With *your* help, Dr Carter.'

He walked back to his seat and nodded to Brother Helix.

Taking his cue, Helix adjusted his wire-rimmed glasses and leaned his bald head towards Carter.

'We intend to find our Messiah through your Project Cana,' he said.

'I don't understand.'

'We've been watching you and your team. We know you've been trying to locate a sample of the Lord's DNA.'

Carter said nothing.

Helix put his hands together forming a steeple, and studied his fingernails. 'Searching out the DNA of Christ seems an unusual pastime for an atheist. But perhaps your motives are commercial? Perhaps you believe you can extract some wonder drug from our Lord's genes? Now, that would be valuable; having the sole rights to a medicine that could cure everything.'

Carter still said nothing.

Brother Bernard said, 'But you've had no luck in finding an authentic sample, have you?'

The scientist calmly sipped at his wine. 'No. That's why I'm here.'

Bernard smiled his cruel smile. 'First we would need access to your IGOR DNA database. The one you aren't meant to have.'

'What do you want to access IGOR for?'

Ezekiel was as surprised as the other two brothers by the question. They had assumed that Dr Carter must now know why they needed access to his database of over one hundred million people.

Brother Helix frowned. 'Why, to find a match, of course.'

Ezekiel could see the revelation dawn on Dr Carter's face. It had clearly never occurred to him that someone alive today could possess Christ's divine genes. Carter said nothing for a while. He toyed with his wine goblet and appeared to think through the consequences. Then he frowned and asked Brother Helix, 'Won't this New Messiah of yours know about his abilities by now? Wouldn't he have already come to your attention?'

Helix shook his head. 'Not necessarily. He may be aware of these gifts as a child but then "learn" that he shouldn't be able to do the things he can. He might smother his unusual talent in order to conform. So he isn't seen as different to his friends. His gifts could then lie dormant, perhaps for ever.'

Carter nodded thoughtfully.

'Or,' continued Helix, 'he might be unaware of his genetic ability. Simply not use it. After all, every ability needs to be developed through use and practice.'

Carter shrugged. 'It's possible.'

A small pause and Ezekiel saw the two Brothers dart a quick look in his direction.

He cleared his throat. 'So, Dr Carter, if you had Christ's DNA do you believe you could use your Genescope and IGOR to find us a match for our Messiah?'

There was a slight pause. 'If one exists,' said Carter. 'And it's on the database, then yes. I suppose so.'

Bernard and Helix both flashed Ezekiel a quick triumphant smile. Perhaps this unholy alliance could work.

'Dr Carter, if we give you a genuine sample, then you must deliver your part of the bargain, and invest all your resources in a search for a match. If you don't, then we would be forced to . . . *react*.' Ezekiel met the scientist's eye with his. It was imperative that Carter realized he would be punished if he reneged on their agreement.

Carter smiled. 'Don't worry. I'm as interested in finding a match as you are. However, don't forget one small thing. We need an *authentic* sample. Without that, all this talk of a deal is just that. Talk.'

Ezekiel paused momentarily and looked down at his hands, and the ruby glowing like a hot coal on his gnarled finger. Now was the moment of truth. They'd come this far. 'To the trade then,' he said, getting to his feet once more.

He turned toward the altar. 'Come, Dr Carter. There's something I wish to show you.'

17

THE VAULT OF REMEMBRANCE.

TOM CARTER FOLLOWED EZEKIEL DE LA CROIX TO THE ALTAR. HIS mind raced from what he'd just been told. That they'd discovered IGOR only confirmed what they'd told him on the invitation. But the idea that somebody alive could have the same genes as Christ was so simple, it was brilliant. It opened up a whole new avenue for helping Holly. Once DAN had analysed Christ's genome he could search any DNA database for a match of someone alive who carried the same set of genes.

He watched Ezekiel pass the white flame issuing from a lead-lined hole in the floor, and walk to a sealed door set flush into the stone wall behind the altar. To the left of the door was a waist-high wooden stake jutting out of the rock wall, a noose of rough hemp hanging from the end.

As Tom walked past he casually toyed with the noose in his hand.

'I suggest you don't touch that,' said Ezekiel firmly.

Tom pulled his hand away. 'Why? What is it?'

Ezekiel gave him a strange smile. 'It's what you might call a final precaution. Please leave it.' Then he bent down and pulled another wooden lever concealed in the floor behind the altar.

Tom heard a grating rumble as the sealed door slid to one side. There was just enough space to walk through in single file. Ezekiel pushed through and Tom waited for Helix and Bernard, but they didn't move. Clearly Ezekiel and he were going alone.

The air behind the door smelled different, mustier and much older. The small, featureless space was lit by two electric lamps powered by a small petrol generator. He figured that this tall, shallow room had little oxygen. Then he saw another door in front and immediately realized that they weren't in a room at all, but a buffer area between the large cavern and whatever lay beyond the second door. Sure enough, Ezekiel turned and pulled another lever behind him, closing the door they'd just come through, sealing them in.

Tom watched the ancient Leader of the Brotherhood walk to the second door ahead of them and pull another lever. This door opened with a noise similar to the first, revealing an opening of inky darkness. Ezekiel disappeared into it and Tom heard the click of a switch, and the room was suddenly illuminated by bright light.

'This is our Vault of Remembrance,' announced Ezekiel, without explanation.

Tom's first feeling when he recovered from the dazzle of the lights was disappointment. He hadn't expected to see a treasure of gold and precious stones, but even so, he had expected more than this. The unprepossessing room looked like a cross between a vast janitor's cupboard and a tiny, dusty museum. Long rickety shelves containing boxes, documents and unusual artefacts lined the walls. Five ancient chests rested on the rough-hewn stone floor. And at the far end a rope-ladder dangled from a narrow fissure in the rough ceiling. An almost indiscernible breeze came from the fissure and Tom assumed it would eventually lead all the way to the surface if you had the stamina or the motivation to climb it. Next to the rope-ladder was a recess, no taller than three feet high, carved into the far wall. It was covered by a fabric screen. Nothing in the room *looked* valuable; not at first sight anyway.

Then he walked to one box and peered inside. He saw well-preserved scrolls that must have been hundreds – perhaps thousands – of years old, and ancient books written in languages he would never know. He looked down the shelf and vaguely recognized weapons and other artefacts that had long outlived the civilizations that fashioned them. He stood back and studied the small room with fresh eyes and felt the excitement return. Even with his untrained eye he could tell that the treasures in this time capsule were not just valuable; they were priceless.

Tom was particularly drawn to one scroll resting on the edge of a stone ledge. Something about the faded script on the cracked parchment fascinated him. He leaned closer to study it, but made no move to touch the fragile document. He noticed Ezekiel watching him closely.

'That is the account of Lazarus's dream, written in his own hand,' the old man explained. 'It describes this place and the prophecy of the sacred flame – all recorded from his vision. It also lays down the objectives and laws of the Brotherhood, which have remained virtually unchanged for twenty centuries.'

Tom nodded slowly, trying to take it all in, his eyes scanning the shelves until they alighted on a folded piece of threadbare cloth. It looked soiled and was covered loosely in a protective leather wrap.

Ezekiel, still studying him, asked, 'Do you know what that is?'

He shook his head. But he was sure his father would know. Alex would give an arm to see just one of these treasures.

The old man's voice lowered in deference. 'That is the shroud of our Lord.'

Tom couldn't help it. Despite his atheism a shiver ran through him. 'But I thought that was in Turin.'

A dry, contemptuous laugh. 'That is nothing but a circus hoax, to dupe the gullible and secure their allegiance – and money.'

Tom said nothing. What could he say? For the first time in his life he was seeing what appeared to be evidence of a religion that he'd dismissed most of his life. The historical significance of the artefacts was undeniable, but he still remained unconvinced of their spiritual importance.

Out of the corner of his eye he caught sight of an ancient helmet, complete with nose guard. And next to it, leaning against the wall as casually as a baseball bat in a child's cupboard, was the largest sword Tom had ever seen. Its magnificent polished blade was thick tempered steel, its heavy hilt boldly ornate, and the handle bound in some worn fabric he didn't recognize. At its base, set deep into the metal, was a large ruby stone, twice the size of the one in Ezekiel's ring. The sword looked as weighty as a girder, and he couldn't see how anyone could possibly lift it, let alone wield it in battle.

Ezekiel said with obvious pride, 'That sword and helmet belonged to Sir Antoine De La Croix, a Crusader of the Knights Templar garrisoned at the castle of Krak de Chevaliers in Syria. He became Leader of the Brotherhood almost a thousand years ago. I am descended from his blood line.'

'The sword's remarkable. But how did he use it? It's enormous.'

A dismissive shrug. The voice wistful. 'Men were more disciplined then.'

Tom looked at other scrolls and noticed an impressive tablet of stone. There was script carved into its surface, but he couldn't understand the characters. He shook his head in bewilderment.

'Where did you get all these treasures? And why do you keep them secret from the rest of the world?'

Ezekiel's black eyes drilled into his. 'Our founder and subsequent followers have salvaged, redeemed and handed down these items from generation to generation throughout the last two millennia.' The old head nodded in thought. 'Dr Carter, history is not a science. It is only memory. The selective memory of powerful men. If the powerful choose to forget something in the past, or change it, they can. But you can't argue with evidence. History is like faith; it is dependent on what you believe. But unlike faith, one's view or memory of history can be supported by evidence.' The frail hands swept around the room. 'These items constitute our evidence and help us to keep the faith. So long as these survive, and are kept safe from today's political powermongers who want to kill religion, then we shall always have proof of what we believe. Of what we *know* in our hearts.'

Tom suddenly felt the discomfort of the outsider. He knew Ezekiel must regard him with his atheism and science as one of those powermongers intent upon eroding the relevance of religion; using the promise of the future to wipe out the relevance of the past.

'Do you think that by seeing these pieces of evidence I will believe what you believe?'

A shrug. 'Perhaps.'

'But history *isn't* religion. I believe Kennedy existed and that he was a great man. But I don't *worship* him because of it.'

'Just consider one thought, Dr Carter. If we hadn't believed in the divinity of Christ and sought to validate our faith in him by collecting the objects you see around you. If we had chosen instead to ignore the past and scramble blindly towards a technologically breathtaking, but spiritually bankrupt future. If we had done this, would we still possess the very thing that you seek?'

Tom gave a noncommittal shrug. The Brotherhood's use of souvenirs to justify their faith, and Ezekiel's obvious contempt for mankind's desire to take charge of its own destiny, provoked strong feelings in him, but now was not the time to debate them.

Ezekiel stared at him for a moment, then turned abruptly and said, 'We've talked enough. We should proceed.'

He took a small gold key from around his neck and walked to the recess at the end of the room. He pulled back the fabric curtain to reveal an ornate, gilt cage about three feet tall, with a high gabled roof and latticed walls. The craftsmanship was breathtaking.

Tom watched the ancient man bend slowly, and use the key to unlock the lattice door. He heard the hinges squeak with lack of use as Ezekiel reached slowly inside. The man seemed to take for ever before he eventually straightened. In his hands Ezekiel held what appeared to be a casket of precious metal inlaid with gemstones. Tom strained to get a closer look as Ezekiel opened it, the lid hinging away from him.

Ezekiel looked up at him. 'Our founder, Lazarus, brought these here with the shroud. To serve as a reminder of what happened on the day mankind crucified its saviour.'

Tom stood speechless as Ezekiel walked towards him, holding the open box close to his chest. On the side of the small casket that faced him, Tom could see what appeared to be rubies set in silver, forming a cross. Four emeralds adorned the beaten gold of each corner.

Ezekiel said, 'These have never been allowed out of this vault. Not for two thousand years.'

His black eyes looked into Tom's, and thin sinewy arms extended towards him. The exquisite casket was now only inches away. Tom's precise surgeon's hands were shaking as he took the box and tried to peer over the hinged lid. The objects were nestled, partially concealed in a bed of purple silk. Then he realized what they were; or thought he did. He turned to Ezekiel, and tried to speak.

The black eyes took in his obvious shock, and the ancient head nodded slowly in confirmation. 'If you doubt them, touch them,' the old man whispered.

Tom rested the casket in his left palm, then with delicate fingers carefully picked the two objects out of the concealing silk. Now, lying there on the palm of his right hand, it was obvious to him what they were.

A six-inch rusty nail and a yellowed human tooth.

FROM HER VANTAGE POINT OUTSIDE THE DOORWAY TO THE CAVE of the Sacred Light, Maria Benariac could see that the meeting was coming to a close. The Inner Guards protecting the Brotherhood's sanctuary had allowed her to come down unannounced as long as she stayed outside the cavern and didn't disturb the Father. She had waited for nearly an hour, and was impatient to surprise him.

As she looked round the half-open door, past the pillars, she could see the Father standing with Brother Bernard and Brother Helix. They had a guest with them; she would have to contain her impatience. She craned her head round to try and see who the visitor was, but he was obscured in the shadows cast by the pillars. From where she stood she couldn't make out what their echoing voices were saying but it was clear from their movements and the tone of their conversation that they were preparing to leave.

At that moment Helix leaned toward the guest and extended his hand, and as the visitor moved to shake it Maria caught a glimpse of his tall frame. There was something about his stance that was familiar.

The party began to walk down the large chamber towards her. Standing in the shadows she observed them more closely. Their body language was relaxed and their easy gait spoke of people who had satisfactorily concluded something of importance. Bernard now took his turn to shake the unseen visitor's hand. The handshake seemed sincere. This visitor must be valued by the Brotherhood for the Champion of the Secondary Imperative to treat him with such respect. He had never treated *her* with such deference.

All four men now stopped some thirty yards away and talked, their deep voices merging into an indistinct murmur. The visitor held a small parcel in his left hand but she still couldn't see more of him past the pillars. She watched Bernard stroke his ridiculous goatee beard and saw Helix nod in agreement at something the Father was saying. The Father looked even smaller than usual alongside Helix and the tall visitor.

Suddenly she heard footsteps to her right, and saw a man walk out of the shadows. He had clearly been waiting silently inside the door, perhaps guarding it. The man strolled over to the centre of the cavern to join the others, and as he passed the first large torch she recognized him.

Gomorrah.

What was he doing here? Why had *he* been invited to the Cave of the Sacred Light to oversee this obviously important meeting? Gomorrah was only the second operative. She was the *first*. And yet *he* was here, included, involved, valued.

Resentment burned through her when she saw the Father acknowledge her rival. Then she watched him turn back to shake the guest's hand. Perhaps it was just her imagination fuelled by her shock at seeing Gomorrah here, but something in the Father's firm handshake conveyed a bond that made her feel jealous. This visitor must be powerful indeed. Then at that moment he moved, turning his head into the light.

It was Dr Carter.

She wouldn't, couldn't, believe it. How could the blasphemous scientist be in the Brotherhood's sacred cavern? She shook her head, as if to clear it and regain control. As she'd learned in the training camp; control was everything. Her eyes refused to focus for a moment, but after a few deep breaths all became clear. She hadn't been mistaken. Dr Carter *was* here, and not as a prisoner or enemy, but as an honoured guest. What trick had he played on the Father to make him invite him here and take his hand in friendship?

Bile rose in her throat as the group suddenly began to move again, to the doorway where she waited. She retreated into the shadows behind the door and fought to keep her composure as she saw Gomorrah and Bernard, then the others, pass within feet of her. Dr Carter was so close she could have reached out and touched one of the black hairs on his head. Now she could hear every satisfied word.

'So we are agreed?' she heard Father Ezekiel say, extending his hand in a final farewell.

'Yes,' replied Dr Carter. 'I'll tell you as soon as we've found any unique genes in the samples. And obviously I'll contact you when – and if – we find a match for your Messiah.'

Find a match for your Messiah?

Maria could scarcely believe her ears.

They were working together.

The scientist had convinced the Father to work with him. An alliance, so unholy it took her breath away, had been struck. No wonder she had been warned off the geneticist and frozen out of any plans. The Father, the man who preached uncompromising righteousness, had in desperation been duped into doing a deal with the Devil. She watched Bernard apologetically place a blindfold on Dr Carter and lead him down the narrow corridor towards the Great Stairs. The Father stayed behind with Helix, Gomorrah protectively by their side.

'I hope we're doing the right thing, Brother Helix,' she heard the Father say. 'I still feel uncomfortable about working with him.'

'Don't worry,' she heard Helix say, soothingly. 'You've made the right decision. You'll see.'

This was too much, the Father was being led astray by his own Champion of the Primary Imperative. Maria stepped out of the shadows, taking them all, including Gomorrah, by surprise. She made no attempt to hide the rage in her voice. 'Father, don't listen to him. How can you deal with the atheist?'

Gomorrah tensed, ready to match any move she made.

Ezekiel took a moment to regain his composure, his black eyes angry. 'Nemesis? What are you doing here?'

She gave a bitter laugh. 'I came to convince you to let me finish the scientist. But I can see Brother Helix would rather I shake his hand.'

Ezekiel said, 'These are things you don't understand.'

'Understand? Oh, I understand quite well. You have somehow decided to use Dr Carter's blasphemy to help you in the holy quest. It makes no sense, like using the light of Lucifer to guide you to heaven.'

She could see the Father's jaw muscle clenching as he tried to control his own anger.

'Let me explain something to you,' Helix said. 'Dr Carter's genetics offers us a unique opportunity to find the Messiah. An opportunity we cannot take without his help. We need him alive and on our side until he has found who we seek. That is the only reason the Righteous Kill has been postponed.'

She ignored him and kept looking at the Father. 'But Dr Carter will meddle with the very essence of God. How can you allow that, whatever the ends?'

Ezekiel shook his head. 'Finding the New Messiah is all that matters. Everything else is unimportant. The Primary Imperative goes beyond simply choosing right or wrong. I have to consider the ultimate greater good, even if it means dealing with evil along the way.'

'But good and God are about ideals, not deals. *You* taught me that. The scientist has corrupted you and Brother Helix is letting him—'

'Nemesis,' snapped the Father, losing his temper and patience. 'I don't care what you think. The deal is going ahead. You have nothing more to do with the matter. Now let Gomorrah escort you from here, then return home and calm down. Brother Bernard or I will contact you shortly.' With that the Father and Helix turned on their heels and strode back into the Cavern of the Sacred Light. She had been dismissed.

Incensed, she moved to follow Father Ezekiel but Gomorrah blocked her way. She felt her rage boil over then. She wanted to fight with Gomorrah and hurt him just to vent her frustration. And when two of the Inner Guard approached, she considered fighting them all.

But she knew that would achieve nothing – and there was much to do.

Taking a deep breath she turned away and walked down the corridor to the Great Stairs. Increasing her pace she tried to walk off her anger at the Father's weakness. Until now she had always held him up as a paragon, the perfect blend of kindness and uncompromising righteousness. But the great man was growing old and had allowed Brother Helix to be duped by the scientist. Gradually she regained control of her molten anger, allowing it to cool into granite resolve.

She focused her mind on one single thought, her own primary imperative: *Dr Carter will pay for what he has done. And she, the avenging Nemesis, will extract that payment*. Deep down she was convinced that

191

Father Ezekiel didn't really want this deal to go ahead with Dr Carter. How could he?

And as she mounted the Great Stairs it became increasingly clear. The time for waiting for orders from Brother Bernard and the Father had passed. The time had come to take matters into her own hands.

18

CRICK LABORATORY, BOSTON.

JASMINE WASHINGTON SUPPRESSED A SHIVER AS SHE SAT IN THE Crick Laboratory and watched DAN sequencing the genome. She knew that the Genescope's complex brain didn't understand the significance of what it was doing now. Although its supremely powerful eye could see, it couldn't *recognize* what it was seeing. And although its brilliant mind could read, it couldn't *comprehend* what it was reading. DAN just blindly scanned the genetic letters written in the dyed DNA inserted beneath its 'smart eye'. And its 'virtual mind' thoughtlessly deciphered the program encrypted there, determining which amino acids and eventual proteins were being coded for.

The Genescope didn't care about the identity of the subjects it analysed; it only distinguished between the genes that constituted them. To DAN the whole was not greater than the sum of the parts. On the contrary it believed that the parts made up the whole, and were therefore all that mattered. Unlike Jasmine, the Genescope didn't care that the DNA it was currently analysing might contain the genetic blueprint of a carpenter who lived two thousand years ago; a man known to the world as Jesus Christ.

It was two days since Tom had returned from his trip to Tel Aviv and she was as relieved as anybody that he was safe. But when he'd first shown her the tooth and nail he'd brought back with him she had been unable to show the same unbridled enthusiasm as the others. Although neither sample challenged her belief in Christ's ascension into heaven, just the simple realization that they could be genuine was enough to disturb her. She couldn't shrug off the nagging, deeply unscientific doubt that any secrets they might contain should perhaps remain hidden.

She looked over at Bob Cooke. The Californian was pale beneath his tan and looked unusually tense. His bench, and Nora Lutz's beside him, were littered with pipettes, gels and neat racks of eppendorf tubes full of dyed DNA. 'Not much longer now,' she said.

'Yup,' said Bob with a tight smile. 'Seven minutes. The time it takes to cook a good steak.'

'Tom better hurry,' said Nora, 'Or he'll miss it.'

'Don't worry about him,' said Jasmine. Tom had disappeared an hour ago to check on the patients in the ward, but he knew when he needed to return. 'He'll be here.'

When Tom had convinced her to embrace Project Cana she had done so mainly out of loyalty to him, and concern for Holly. She had never really believed they would find an authentic sample, or if they did that it would contain anything. But now she wasn't so sure. In the last two days she had helped Tom, along with Bob and Nora, prep the so-called Nazareth Samples. She had watched the drill going into what might be an authentic tooth from Jesus Christ's mouth, extracting the DNA from deep within it. And she had personally scraped blood remnants from a nail that might have *actually* nailed Christ to the cross.

She took a deep breath. It was frightening and she felt a little out of control. Soon, very soon, she would know for certain if the Nazareth Samples were genuine, and if they contained the genes of God.

'How's it going?' said Tom, bounding into the room. He was breathless and his blue eyes were bright with excitement. 'Almost there?'

She nodded. 'Yeah, we're close now. A few minutes.'

The door to the lab opened again and Jack walked in, followed by Alex. No-one wanted to miss the moment when DAN revealed what made Christ different from other men.

The Genescope's growl suddenly changed tone. Lights flashed on the black sweeping neck.

'This is it,' she said.

And everyone fell silent.

TOM CARTER HADN'T SLEPT IN ALMOST THREE DAYS BUT HE couldn't imagine feeling more alert than he did now. He still hadn't come down from the adrenalin of his visit to the Brotherhood's vault and all he wanted now was to see DAN's analysis of the samples.

He saw Jasmine stand. 'Before DAN starts there are a few things you guys should know,' she said. 'First of all the Genescope's been configured to give us an overview on both the nail and the tooth sample. The nail results will appear first. But because the sample was so corrupted we'll be lucky to read more than a third of the genome from it. So don't be disappointed. The tooth sample should be much better. The overview for both will be presented on the monitor and presented by DAN on voice box.'

Tom watched the large screen beside the Genescope suddenly flicker into life, displaying the GENIUS logo.

Jasmine added. 'Once we find anything of interest we'll activate the virtual reality headset so we can look at any genes close up in 3D.' The great black swan gave a warning grumble. 'Can we have quiet please. DAN, are you ready?'

Instant hush. Only the shuffling of feet as everyone edged closer to the monitor. In the silence DAN spoke: *Scan complete on Nazareth Nail sample. Results available. Please choose between options highlighted on screen: Topline findings; Analysis by Chromosome; Or Detail Gene Search.*

'Detail Gene Search please, DAN', demanded Jasmine.

The screen suddenly changed, as letters scrolled down too fast to read. From time to time the flow would momentarily freeze, filling the screen with countless letters, formed into triples. Each triple was a codon, specifying a particular amino acid:

ATG AAC GAT ACG CTA TCA AGC TTT TTA AAT CGT AAC GAC
GCT TTA GGG CTT AAT CCA CCA CAT GGC CTG GAT ATG CAC
ATT ACC AAG AGA GGT TCG GAT TGG TTA TGG GCA GTG
TTT GCA GTC TTT GGC TTT ATA TTG CTA TGC TAT GTT GTG
ATG TTC TTC ATT GCG GAG AAC AAG GGC TCC AGA TTG ACT
AGA GCA GTC TTT GGC AAC GAT ACG CTA TCA TTT ATA TTG
CTA GCT CCA TTC TTC GAG TTA TGG GCA GTG TTT GCA GTC

195

TTT ACG TTT TTA AAT CGT GGC GTT GTG ATG TTC GTG ATG
TTC TTC ATT GCG GAG AAC AAG GGC TCC AGA TTG ACT AGA
ACA GTC TTT GGC AAC GAT ACG AAC GAC GCT TTA GGG CTT
AAT CCA CCA CAT GGC CTG GAT ATG AAA GTT AGC AAG TCT
ACA GGT GAA GTT CAA GTC GAA TTT TTT AAC CAC GTC TAC
AGA GGT TCG GAT TGG TTA TGG GCA GTG TTT GCA GTC
TTT GGC TTT ATA TTG CTA TGC TAT GTT GTG ATG TTC TTC
ATT GCG GAG AAC AAG GGC TCC AGA TTG ACT AGA GCA
GTC TTT GGC AAC GAT ACG CTA TCA GTG TTT GCA GTC TTT
TTT ATA TTG CTA GCT CCA TTC TTC GAG CTG GAT ATG CAC
ATT ACC AAG GCG GAG AAC AAG GGC TCC TTG TAC TTT ATC
TGT TGG GGT CTA AGT GAT GGT GGT AAC CGY ATT CAA
CCA GAC GCA GTC TTT GGC AAC GAT ACG CTA TCA TTT ATA
TTG CTA GCT CCA TTC TTC GAG TTA TGG GCA GTG TTT GCA
GTC TTT ACG TTT TTA AAT CGT GGC GTT GTG ATG TTC GTG
ATG TTC TTC ATT GCG GAG AAC AAG GGC TCC AGA TTG ACT
AGA ACA GTC TTT GGC AAC GAT ACG AAC GAC GCT TTA
GGG CTT AAT CCA CCA CAT GGC CTG GAT ATG TCC AGA TTG
ACT AGA ACA GTC TTT GGC AAC GAT ACG AAC GAC GCT TTA
GGG CAT AGA GGT TCG GAT TGG TTA TGG GCA GTG TTT
GCA GTC TTT GGC TTT ATA TTG CTA TGC TAT GTT GTG ATG
TTC TTC ATT GCG GAG AAC AAG GGC TCC AGA TTG ACT AGA
GCA GTC TTT GGC AAC GAT ACG CTA TCA TTT ATA TTG CTA
GCT CCA TTC TTC GAG TTA TGG GCA GTG TTT GCA GTC TTT
ACG TTT TTA AAT CGT GGC GTT GTG ATG TTC GTG ATG TTC
TTC ATT GCG GAG AAC AAG GGC TCC AGA TTG ACT AGA
ACA GTC TTT GCT CCA TTC TTC GAG CTG GAT ATG CAC ATT
ACC AAG GCG GAG AAC AAG GGC TCC TTG TAC TTT ATC TGT
TGG GGT CTA AGT GAT GGT AAC CGY ATT CAA CCA GAC
GCA GTC TTT GGC AAC GAT ACG CTA TCA TTT ATA TTG CTA
GCT CCA TTC TTC GAG TTA TGG GCA GTG TTT GCA GTC TTT
ACG TTT TTA AAT CGT GGC GTT GTG ATG TTC . . .

Whenever the screen froze a number flashed up on the screen, signi-
fying which of the twenty-three pairs of chromosomes the DNA code
related to. Next to it was a percentage figure, denoting how much of
the total genome had been analysed. Then the speed scrolling would

start again until the whole genome had been analysed. The final percentage was 32 per cent.

The screen changed one last time to reveal a chart showing all twenty-three chromosome pairs down the left column and the percentage of readable DNA in each of them down the right.

'*All chromosomes corrupted,*' informed DAN. '*No exceptional genes found in readable sections. More information needed to extrapolate missing segments.*'

'No good?' asked Alex.

'No,' said Tom. 'But since we've only been able to read a third of the sample it doesn't tell us much. DNA is pretty robust stuff but because of the corrosion of the nail and the way the blood cells have decayed over time, major sections of the genetic code are either illegible or destroyed. So all we know for sure is that there are no unusual genes in the third we can read.'

'So what now?'

'We wait for the tooth DNA. It's been protected by the enamel surface so it should be fine. We know from studies of the DNA of Egyptian pharaohs, sometimes a thousand years older than this sample, that genetic material taken from within a tooth or bone is the most robust form of DNA there is.'

As usual, Alex wanted to know more. 'But how do you *know* there's nothing there?'

His father liked words, not dumb numbers, and he wasn't used to being the only boy in class who didn't understand the blackboard. So Tom pulled a printout off the printer next to DAN. 'Look, I'll show you,' he said, spreading out the paper in his hand. 'It's easier to see the raw data on a printout.'

Jack walked over to join them.

Tom held the printout so both could see it. 'This should be clearer.'

'Are these the chromosomes?' asked Alex, putting on his glasses and pointing at the numbered headings.

'Yeah, imagine it's a map of the US, where there are only twenty-three states. The twenty-three pairs of chromosomes are the states, and the genes are like towns or cities within these states. Within the genes, you've got the base letters that are like individual citizens. The order of these letters determines what proteins each gene produces. These proteins maintain and develop your body. Make your hair grow. Digest your food. Repair cuts and so on. This topline data sheet is only concerned with genes, and unusual ones at that. You know? Genes that are outside, or on the extreme edge of, the standard healthy genome.'

He pointed to the 'abnormal genes' box on the printout under the number 20. 'If there's anything unusual here you would see the genes highlighted. But as you can see all the genes in this chromosome are within the bounds of normality. The ones that haven't been corrupted by the corrosion on the nail anyway.' He indicated the top of the sheet. 'If you look here, you can see that for the total genome, the intact bit we were able to scan, there are no really unusual genes. Nothing.'

'So you hope that any unique genes are in the 70 per cent you couldn't scan?' asked Jack.

'Yes.'

Jack turned back to the Genescope where Jasmine and Bob were checking the tooth scan. 'And you reckon the more complete DNA from the tooth will allow us to see that?'

'Maybe.'

Alex pored over the printout. 'How does DAN know where the genes are within all the letters?'

'Only a small percentage of the three thousand million letters of human DNA actually code for functioning genes. The others, particularly the so-called introns, don't appear to do anything at all. Every gene is bracketed by a particular combination of letters called stop-and-start codons. These tell DAN where to look. For example most genes start with the amino acid, methionine – that's ATG. So whenever DAN reads ATG it knows a gene is beginning. TAG on the other hand tells DAN when the gene is finished. So it only bothers to read the letters between these markers, in the so-called Open Reading Frames. It ignores the rest as gibberish.'

'*Scan complete for Nazareth Tooth sample. Results available. Detail Gene Search option selected,*' interrupted DAN, behind him.

'We've got a good read,' said Jasmine, the excitement audible in her voice. 'Virtually perfect.'

Tom turned with the others back to the screen.

'*No genes found outside or on extremes of Standard Human Genome,*' announced DAN abruptly.

'What?' said Tom, stunned. He couldn't believe it.

Jasmine released a huge sigh, but whether it was of dismay or relief, he couldn't tell.

Jack muttered a quiet but distinct 'Shit'.

Bob and Nora stood staring at the screen.

Alex just shook his head and frowned.

Tom checked the topline analysis. The genome scan showed no unusual genes at all. Nothing. It wasn't possible. The most remarkable thing about the tooth genome was that it was too perfect. It was an almost exact fit with the notional Standard Human Genome that everyone was compared against, but was always different from. Christ's genome, if indeed it was his, had only one real abnormality. It was too normal. No defect *at all* was visible in his genetic make-up. But apart from that, nothing.

Then Alex's scholastic tones cut through the awkward silence. 'It's probably a stupid question. But could the genes you're looking for have different stop-and-start codons – ones that DAN doesn't recognize?'

Tom looked at Jasmine and could see she was thinking the same thing. It *was* a stupid question, one that no self-respecting geneticist who knew the first thing about the all-powerful Genescope would ask. Which was exactly why Tom *didn't* dismiss it.

'But how can we find the new stop-and-start codons?' asked Jasmine as if reading his mind.

'We could try homology,' said Bob Cooke. 'But we'd need a different stretch of DNA containing the same genes.'

'Homology?' asked Alex.

'Yeah,' said Tom. 'DAN can search two stretches of DNA and try to find a long sequence of letters that is identical in each. The odds of this sequence being a gene are very high. We then take its first and last letter combinations and Bingo! We've found our new stop-and-start codons.'

'But we do need a second stretch of different DNA that contains one or more of these genes,' reminded Jasmine.

'What about that genome you found on IGOR when you were looking at the genes of faith healers?' asked Tom, desperate to try anything. 'What's his name? The Brit who was cremated last year; the one who could ease rheumatoid arthritis with his hands.'

Jasmine turned to the PC on the workstation next to DAN and punched the keyboard with nimble fingers. 'Anderson, right?'

'Yeah, that's the one. Run an accelerated homology study on him and the Christ genome.'

Jasmine's fingers moved again. 'It's done. I've given DAN all the data and it should give us an answer in the next few minutes.'

It took only four and a half minutes for DAN to announce that both genomes shared an identical sequence of fifty-seven thousand base letters, and that the projected stop-and-start codons were each nine letters long; GCCTGACCG to open the reading frame and TCGAGGTAC to close it. It took Jasmine less than thirty seconds to recalibrate DAN to search the total Christ genome for genes between these new brackets.

There followed a pause of some minutes in which Tom heard no sound, not even a breath from the others.

Then DAN spoke, '*One extra gene found outside the Standard Human Genome on the paternal copy of Chromosome 7.*'

Numbers danced across the screen, and this time Tom's eyes danced with them. He was finally seeing evidence of what he'd only hoped for till now.

DAN made a sound as if clearing his throat and spoke again.

'*One extra gene found outside the Standard Human Genome on the paternal copy of Chromosome 10.*'

Two genes. There were two genes. He couldn't wait to ask DAN what they coded for, but before he could speak the Genescope began to growl, as if trying to think though a particularly difficult problem. And when it spoke again Tom fancied he heard surprise in its metallic monotone.

'*Third gene found in paternal copy of Chromosome 18. No more genes outside the Standard Human Genome.*'

Tom felt a sudden rush of relief and elation, his disappointment forgotten. The owner of the tooth possessed three genes that most, if not all, other humans did not. He looked around him and caught the look on Jasmine's face. The others had similar expressions of silent shock on their faces.

It was Jack who spoke first. 'What do these genes do?' he asked, 'Are they worth getting excited about?'

'Let's find out.' Tom turned to the Genescope and said, 'DAN, please estimate the function of these new genes.'

The Genescope's growl lowered in tone, and the lights on the ovoid body blinked. Then the growl returned to its normal pitch. *'Initial extrapolation of coded amino acids indicate that the gene on Chromosome 7 should code for proteins with DNA and cell repair capability. The gene on Chromosome 10 has a cell control function. The third gene on Chromosome 18 is too complex to give any initial indication of function. These are only estimates based on supplied data. Laboratory confirmation is necessary.'*

Bob Cooke looked at Tom, his eyes wide with the possibilities. 'Incredible. The first gene can make or repair DNA. And the second can control cell growth. Perhaps they're smart genes, one acting as a cell accelerator and the other a brake on proliferation. Together they could check the fluctuations in the rest of the genome.'

'If DAN's extrapolation is correct?' cautioned Jasmine.

'Of course,' said Tom, waving away her concerns. 'We'd need to check the findings in the lab, and we've still got to find out what the third gene does. But if they are smart genes controlling the rest of his DNA, that would explain why Jesus' genome was so healthy. Perhaps they gave him a superior immune system?'

'One he could pass on to others?' chipped in Bob with an excited grin.

Tom smiled. 'Well now, that's the sixty-four thousand dollar question. That's what we need to find out in the lab.' He suddenly thought of Ezekiel. 'Jazz, will we be able to find a match on IGOR with these genes?'

Jasmine shrugged. 'Should be able to. It'll take time to recalibrate the database to the new stop-and-start codons but we already know that Keith Anderson had one of the genes. So sure, if a match exists on IGOR, then we might find a live one eventually with all three.'

Tom walked over to the virtual reality headset protruding from the beak of the Genescope. 'Let's take a closer look at the genes. DAN, give me eye presentation.' He felt the others crowd round him as he donned the headset. But they were soon forgotten as he concentrated on his journey into inner space. First he saw darkness, then the whole cell appeared below and around him. All the chromosomes, like continents of varying shapes, shimmered in their splendid hues. He knew the colours came from the magnetized dyes, but they made the spectacle seem more, not less real.

'Give me Chromosome 7,' he ordered DAN. 'And take me to chromosome level resolution.'

Immediately the scene in front of him shifted down to an even greater spectrum of colours. He was now focused solely on one chromosome and the DNA string of life contained within it. It was beautiful. His eye travelled along the rainbow spiral staircase of the double helix. He watched the magnetized dyes highlight the different nucleotide pairs, making the DNA strands stand out in 3-D. The new gene was stretched out before him, and just the sight made his chest tighten with excitement. This was one strip of the programming responsible for the development of the most famous and influential man who'd ever lived, Jesus Christ. And he, an atheist, was the first man alive to see the genetic 'abnormality' that helped determine his destiny.

'DAN, take me to the other gene on Chromosome 10.' The images around him blurred then reformed. He was now inside the double helix looking along its fluorescent, multicoloured length, travelling down an incandescent boulevard of genes. The nucleotide pairs of the second new gene were all around him along the double helix. He was *inside* one of the genes that made Christ different from other men. He felt a sense of genuine awe. But it was to the randomness of nature that he paid homage for creating this exception to its laws.

However, it was the third gene on Chromosome 18 that really took his breath away. No wonder DAN had called it complex; it was hundreds of thousands of base pairs long, far longer than any he had seen before. He could only guess at what wonders its program coded for. His mind was suddenly filled with questions about how they were going to unlock these genes and harness their powers. Would they behave in the same ways as usual genes? Could he use normal recombinant DNA technology to express the proteins coded by them in lab-controlled bacteria? Could he load them into a virus, and insert them directly into a patient, into Holly? So many questions. But they were *good* questions. Options. He now had material to work with. He could do something at last.

He suddenly realized that he'd been monopolizing the headset and removed it to give someone else a look. As usual his eyes took a moment to adapt to the real world, but he instantly sensed that the others were no longer crowding around the headset. Surprised, he turned and through unfocused eyes noticed they were grouped around someone standing on the other side of DAN. He felt his excitement turn to annoyance. It was understood that nobody apart from the Cana team were allowed into this section of the Mendel Suite. And it was especially important today. Now.

He walked towards the group and was surprised by the hush. Nobody was saying anything; the team just stood in a circle staring at the intruder. Then Tom's recovered eyesight caused him to stare as well; the intruder was standing with his back to him – buck naked.

Jasmine was by her keyboard and Tom watched her silently beckon him closer. She looked like she'd seen a ghost. He turned back to the stranger, now only feet away. Jasmine *had* seen a ghost; that of a Nazarene carpenter who had been dead for two thousand years.

Jasmine tapped out two more commands to the Gene-Imaging software, and the eerily lifelike hologram of Jesus Christ rotated on the holo-pad in front of him.

PART III

THE GENES OF GOD

19

BEACON HILL, BOSTON.

AT 3:12 A.M. ON 1 APRIL, FIFTEEN DAYS AFTER THE NAZARETH GENES had been found, all was quiet in the Carter household. The still darkness in Holly's bedroom was only disturbed by the soft, regular sound of her breathing. Her peaceful face smiled as she dreamed her dreams, oblivious to the malignancy growing inside her.

Twenty-four days had elapsed since the original glial cell in her brain had turned traitor. It had now produced countless clones of itself, all with equally rebellious DNA. Even as Holly slept, the tireless revolution was gathering pace, growing faster than even DAN had predicted. The obedient brain cells could do nothing to quell this uprising. Even the immune system, the body's militia geared up to repel invaders, ignored these mutations of the body's own cells, letting them go about their murderous business unchallenged.

Only two days ago, when her godmother and father had taken her to the *Star Wars VII* movie, Holly had experienced the first headaches, accompanied by a rush of giddiness. But she hadn't told anybody because she was worried her dad would blame the computer, and stop her playing on it. So Holly had simply decided to cut down and only use it a few hours at night, feeling sure the headaches would go away. But of course they wouldn't. They would only get worse.

Even as Holly dreamed of last summer when Mom and Dad had

been together, playing with her on the pink-white sands of Horseshoe Bay in Bermuda, the traitorous cells were already entering the second mutation of clonal evolution. And if the rebels of this genetic war of independence remained unchecked; if they were allowed to pro-liferate indefinitely within the tight confines of Holly's skull, then it wouldn't only be in her dreams that Tom's precious daughter was reunited with her mother.

TOM CARTER WAS STILL UNAWARE OF HOLLY'S CONDITION WHEN HE drove to work the next morning, and he would remain so until her monthly brain scan in a little over a week's time. In the fifteen days since finding the Nazareth genes he had been focusing all his thoughts and energies on unlocking their power. He had barely had time to reflect on the significance of seeing the resurrected holo-image of Jesus Christ, let alone worry if Holly had already succumbed.

The first thing Tom did in the Crick Lab that morning with Bob Cooke was check the Gallenkamp incubators. He pulled four of the transparent circular culture dishes from the top rack and studied them closely. Three of them contained *Streptomyces* bacteria with one of the three Nazareth genes cloned into them. The bacteria were acting as factories, converting the new genetic instructions into their coded proteins. The fourth dish contained the same bacterium with all three genes combined.

'Any change?' asked Bob Cooke beside him.

'No, it's the same as the *E coli*. We don't obviously have the same inclusion bodies, but the pattern's similar. You used the same plas-mids and restriction enzymes for all the dishes?'

'Identical.'

'Well, the *naz 3* gene still refuses to behave. Whatever protein it codes for still isn't folding.'

Bob Cooke took the fourth dish labelled *The Trinity - Streptomyces*, and frowned. 'But we're getting the unknown protein when we put all three genes together.'

'Yeah, but what does it do? The human cell cultures prove that *naz 1* obviously codes for some kind of DNA repair protein, but not a paticularly spectacular one. And the protein from the *naz 2* gene has limited cell control characteristics – but again that's nothing new. What I want to know is what this totally new protein from all three

208

combined is. It doesn't actually appear to do anything.'

Bob picked up his notes from the bench beside him. 'If only we could get the damn *naz 3* gene to work in isolation.'

'Assuming it does, of course,' muttered Tom.

'If it doesn't,' said Bob, 'then it's going to take a helluva long time to unravel what it's doing in the total mix. Perhaps it might be better to try and find a match?'

Tom put the culture dishes down and paced around the lab. This was proving more difficult than he thought. He was sure his strategy was correct. But it looked like he might have to shift the emphasis. It had been obvious from the start that if there was something therapeutic in the Nazareth genes, then the answer lay in the composite protein formed by all three together. The enigmatic *naz 3* gene appeared to be adding an unidentifiable element to the other two, turning their individually unremarkable proteins into something unique and potentially exciting. But unlocking the enormously complex third gene in isolation would take even DAN too long. So his strategy boiled down to focusing on three broad areas.

The first involved farming the protein in the lab. By inserting the three genes into bacteria, the bacterial cells could be turned into mini-factories producing the coded proteins. And after some modifications Tom hoped he could then inject the proteins like a drug.

The second meant inserting all three genes directly into live animals, to see what effect they had on an organism and what proteins were produced *in vivo*.

The third option he'd only formulated as a last resort, in case the first two failed, or took too long. This entailed finding a live person who possessed a fully functioning set of the genes. Tom reckoned he could then analyse the naturally occurring genes *in situ*. And if he still couldn't determine how they worked, then he would try and persuade the individual to realize any healing powers he might possess, and use them to save Holly. This had originally been the least attractive option, but as he considered their progress to date it was fast becoming the front runner.

They had already tested option one endlessly. All the genes had been tried individually and collectively in *E coli*, *Saccharomyces cerevisiae*, *Streptomyces* and even human cell cultures. But always the *naz 3* gene refused to express its protein, and always they got the mysterious composite protein when all three genes – what the irreverent Californian had termed *The Trinity* – were combined. However, each and every time they made it, this laboratory-farmed version of the composite protein appeared to be inert.

Option two had also yielded little so far, although there were other tests to run. To date the Trinity had had no effect on mice, or live tumour cells when inserted by viral vector. To his left in the glass-fronted refrigerated cabinet he could see the rack of beautiful serums his team had developed; all designed to deliver the three genes into an organism's stem cells. But the genes still didn't appear to make any difference when they got there.

Unless these serums came through in later tests it looked like Bob Cooke was right, and they'd have to prioritize option three. They would have to find someone who already possessed a working set of these genes, so they could analyse them *in vivo*, or persuade the individual to heal Holly direct. Tom reached for the phone and dialled Jasmine's extension downstairs in the IT section. She picked up on the second ring.

'Jazz.'

'Hi, it's Tom, how's the search going?'

A pause, 'Not good. A couple of people, and I mean a couple, have got one of the genes; either *naz 1* or *naz 2*. But no-one's got all three. I haven't seen anybody with *naz 3* yet. Big Mother's feeding in more scans all the time, but I've been through most of IGOR's past entries now and we're fast running out of prospects.'

'How many scans is Big Mother picking up?'

'The usual. One in five.'

'Make it five out of five. From now on I want to check on everyone who takes a Genescope scan anywhere in the world.'

'Every single one? What's going on? Has your mysterious Ezekiel been applying pressure?'

'No, we've got three more weeks before he starts getting angsty.' Tom remembered how excited the old man had been when he'd returned the samples and told him they'd found the three genes. Ezekiel had asked when they might have a match but hadn't pushed him to pull the five weeks deadline forward. 'It's my other options that are applying the pressure, Jazz. They're running out. You look like being our best bet now.'

'Thanks, that makes me feel a lot better. But don't get your hopes up. It could take years for a subject who has three of the genes to be scanned and deposited in IGOR – assuming one exists.'

'How about the other eighty per cent of genomes Big Mother wasn't storing on IGOR?'

A sigh. 'They're on a range of private databases around the world. Trying to hack into them is illegal.'

'Only if anyone finds out.'

Jasmine tried to sound shocked, but Tom could hear the excitement in her voice. 'They're *extremely* well protected.'

'You're saying it *can't* be done? Or it would take a *genius* to do it?'

A small laugh. 'Dr Carter, has anyone ever told you that you can be a real sweet-talker when you want to be?'

It was his turn to chuckle. 'No, Dr Washington, I can honestly say they never have.'

Another pause, then, her voice more serious, 'How's my goddaughter? She seemed a bit quiet at the movies.'

'I know, but she says she's fine.'

'When's her next scan?'

'About a week.'

'You really reckon you need a match to help her?'

'We're still trying the other routes, but they're not looking good so far. So, yeah.'

A sigh. 'I'll see what I can do. But promise me one thing, Tom?'

'Name it.'

'Visit me in jail!'

HE WAS PERFECT. HIS BUILD, HEIGHT, EVEN THE SHAPE OF HIS FACE was ideal. He was a loner too. Over the last two weeks Maria Benariac had followed the dark-haired man around most of Boston, and it was clear that he was new to the city and had few friends. On the third day he'd gone to that downtown club where she'd discovered he was bisexual, but that wasn't a problem; he only had casual partners. There appeared to be no-one who would miss him for a week or so. Even his phone was barely used – her phone-tap had told her that much – and when it did ring he never seemed to pick it up, preferring to let the answer machine screen the callers for him.

Apart from the obvious necessary changes he was exactly what she was looking for. Even his sexuality made it easier to justify what she was going to do to him. It made him unrighteous and therefore eminently expendable.

Maria took care when she followed him from the company building. Her research had uncovered that he'd once worked for the New York Police Department and would therefore have some training. She noticed the polythene bag draped over his right shoulder and the cap in his right hand. Obviously his midday interview had gone well.

Excellent.

If he hadn't got the security job then all his other qualifications would have been worthless. But with it he was more than perfect; he was a gift from God.

He climbed into his car, and she followed in hers. She didn't need to shadow him too closely; by now she could guess what he was doing and where he was going. He'd rented an apartment in a block near Harvard. When they passed the GENIUS campus ten minutes later she allowed herself a small tight smile. She could almost taste the satisfaction of killing the scientist. And in a few days she would be able to satisfy that taste for real.

As they neared the man's apartment she parked her hired car a block away, and walked. By the time she reached the main door of the brownstone he was already inside. She tried the door and like yesterday, and the day before, found it open. She entered and checked she was alone, then sauntered over to the two elevators, taking the one that still worked. The rundown building had paint peeling off the walls and was mainly inhabited by students. But it would do fine for a few days. Brother Bernard was no doubt still trying to contact her; he had already left three messages at her London apartment, none of which she'd answered. But Bernard, or whoever he sent looking for her, would never find her here. And when he did it would be too late.

On the third floor she checked her overalls, and the contents of her toolbox, then strolled down the corridor to the man's apartment. Number 30. She stopped and knocked.

Silence. Then a muffled, 'Who is it?' She heard breathing from the other side of the black door and guessed he was looking through the peep-hole.

Holding up her toolbox, she turned to show the orange logo on the back of her overalls. In her deepest blue-collar voice she rasped, 'Power company, sir. Been a few dangerous surges in this building and the one next door. Need to check your meter and wiring. Just a safety measure.'

A pause. 'Have you got any ID?'

This annoyed her. Why were people so suspicious? she thought. What *reason* did a fit, young ex-cop have for not trusting a power company employee? What could he possibly be scared of?

She reached into her overalls and pulled out a typed letter. 'I got a letter from the boss. It's on company paper. That OK?' she pushed the letter under the door. 'Or do you want my card?' She made a big show of opening her toolbox, and scrabbling around inside. Like she'd put it in there somewhere, and was trying to find it.

She made a few frustrated noises as she rummaged. But really she was waiting. And listening.

On the other side of the door she could hear the sound of the letter being unfolded. The guy was still there. He wasn't walking back into his apartment to make a call to the company. That was good.

'Goddamn!' she cussed. 'I know it's here somewhere. Hell, if you like I can come back later, when I've found it?'

A pause. She could almost hear the man's mind working, as she heard the crisp letter being refolded. The last thing this guy wanted was her coming back again. He wanted whatever it was she had to do, over and done with.

Suddenly there was a scrabbling sound, as locks were clicked and chains pulled back. 'Come in,' said the man, opening the door and handing back the letter. He was frowning, still holding his cap. 'How long do you think you'll be?'

'Five, ten minutes. I'll be as fast as I can.' Maria closed the door behind her and followed him to a cupboard by the small kitchen.

The man stood with his back to her and opened the cupboard door. 'The meter and stuff's in here. Help yourself.'

'Thanks.' Maria reached into her toolbox, and pulled out a plastic KMart bag and her Glock semi-automatic, complete with silencer. Before the man could turn she flipped the plastic bag over his head, pressed the gun into his temple and fired twice. Even with the bag there was the inevitable mess, but it was minimized. She bundled the man's body into the bathroom, placed him in the bath and ran the cold water. With ice she could slow the body's decomposition for up to a week, and after that it wouldn't matter.

She turned to the man's discarded cap, wiped two flecks of blood off the black peak, and put it on. It fitted well. She was right, she thought with a smile. He was perfect.

20

THREE NIGHTS LATER. GENIUS HEADQUARTERS, BOSTON.

LIKE ALL SOCIETIES THE CYBERWORLD HAS ITS OWN SUB-CULTURE. Bored, computer-literate kids prowl the cyberstreets seeking kicks and recognition by trying to break into any system they can. These so-called cyberpunks cruise the electronic highway, joy-riding from one net site to the next, trying to convince each other that they are the hottest nethead in cybertown. They all share the same dream; to perform some dangerous, heroic feat; to slay some electronic dragon and graduate from mere cyberpunk to *cyberlord*.

Few succeed. But there have been some true legends. No more so than the nethead who broke into the Treasury's Federal Reserve database, the NASA Satellite guidance system, and the Russian Strategic Nuclear Missile command centre, taking complete control of each one in turn. Fortunately the nethead was benign and on every occasion merely alerted the authorities to the breach and indicated how they could, and indeed should, improve security. Naturally these same authorities tried to trace the hacker and arrest him or her, but because the nethead used a complex route, switching nodes and jumping from network to satellite links and back again, they lost their prey. However the cyberpunk community knew who did it. It was one of their own; the nethead who went by the User ID of Razor Buzz.

That was twelve years ago. And after that the Razor Buzz tag virtually disappeared from the Internet, but the name lived on as one of the greats – a true cyberlord.

Tonight however, Razor Buzz was again riding the information superhighway. The nethead's *alter ego* required the tag's anonymity, and felt the need to feed off the reassurances of past triumphs that the name carried with it. Because tonight the woman who had spent years becoming a highly respected member of the scientific community – a Nobel Prizewinner no less – was again breaking the law.

Dr Jasmine Washington took another sip of her Diet Coke and bit into the slice of pizza, her eyes not moving from the twenty-inch screen in front of her. She had been working in her office on the ground floor of the GENIUS pyramid for fifteen hours now. For once she was glad Larry was out of town. She enjoyed the quiet of the night; it was when her mind worked best.

Apart from the blue glow of the screen, the sharp circle of light from the angle-poise lamp beside her was the only illumination in the small, uncluttered office. Next door, in the all-white temperature-regulated room that formed the heart of the Information Technology Section, Big Mother emitted a gentle, almost soothing hum as a tiny section of its vastly powerful brain busied itself with collecting and collating each and every scan from all the Genescopes in operation around the globe. But apart from the quiet ticking of the clock on top of the screen there were no other sounds. It was past midnight and it seemed to Jasmine as if all the world, save her, was asleep.

She checked the notes beside her. The search of all IGOR historical files had been completed two days ago and no match found, although data was coming in every hour from new Genescope scans not yet captured on IGOR. But now she was looking elsewhere. She had already hacked into many of the easier DNA databases on her list, such as the hospitals and smaller insurance companies around the world. In every database she had inserted her compressed smart file, which contained just the genetic sequence of the Nazareth genes, to search for a topline match. And she had just finished some of the larger more difficult databases including the US, British and French military personnel DNA repositories, all of which were protected by software alarms and PREDATOR Version 2 tracing software. However these barriers hadn't proved too difficult for a cyberlord, and she was pleased she had lost none of her hacking skills. But she was disappointed that after screening almost two hundred million individual genomes she still hadn't come close to a full match.

She stretched her arms above her head and stood up from her chair, then walked with stiff legs to the glass wall of the pyramid. Outside all was inky black, although she could just see the stars peppering the clear sky above, and the thin silver slice that was the moon. Ahead of her across the darkness of the campus came the dull glow of the main gatehouse. She knew there were two guards in there, watching over the place on their CCTV monitors. She had accessed the central video computer and fed a film loop into the camera that watched over her. Now any guard checking her work area would see an empty, static office instead of the GENIUS IT director accessing one illegal database after another.

She walked back to the computer and retook her seat. Seeing Christ's hologram had terrified her, making her feel she had somehow summoned up his spirit against his wishes, like some necromancer of old. She had searched her soul the whole night and the better part of the next day after the Nazareth genes had been found. She hadn't known what to do – whether to tell Tom she wanted out of Cana, or to carry on with what promised to be something miraculous. Eventually, after no small amount of good old-fashioned praying, she'd decided that if these genes could help cure Holly and mankind in general, then she had to follow the project through. And it was up to her to find a match now. Tom and Holly depended on her.

She rechecked her notes on all the databases she intended to visit. She had listed them in ascending order of difficulty and risk. It made sense to try and find a match in the safest way possible, and only to take risks when they were necessary. After all, getting caught and convicted wouldn't help any of them. Even so, Jasmine knew that the richest pickings tended to lie with the larger, better-protected databases. The most impressive of these was a Paris-based system she had nicknamed the 'Black Hole' because although it was vast – containing many millions of genomes – it was also protected by the new Version 3 PREDATOR system. This made it as secure as her own IGOR system, which she regarded as virtually impregnable.

Anyone who went into the 'Black Hole' without the proper authorization or the requisite skill would be sucked in, and not allowed to log off, then the PREDATOR system would lock on to the hacker's signal and quickly trace them. Razor Buzz would have found it irresistible, but the older more experienced Dr Jasmine Washington was more mindful of the real risks. She would consider entering the 'Black Hole' only when and if she had to.

She moved the cursor on the screen to the next system on her list. Everyone even remotely connected with genetics knew of the Human Genome Diversity Database. It contained the fruits of the controversial project of the same name. Set up in the early Nineties as the brainchild of two geneticists, Luigi Luca Cavalli-Sforza at Stanford University and Kenneth Kidd at Yale, the Human Genome Diversity Project was an offshoot of the Human Genome Project. Its intention was to capture and preserve the DNA and potentially rare genes of over five hundred ethnic communities in remote areas of the world. Many, such as the Hadza of Tanzania, the Yukaghir of Siberia and the Onge of the Andaman Islands, were on the verge of extinction.

The controversy arose because Western science was seen to be valuing the DNA of these vanishing peoples more highly than the people themselves. There were many notorious cases of the West, particularly the US government, trying to patent rare genes that promised to combat certain diseases. These attempts were quashed, but if they had been allowed to take their course then all the considerable profits would have gone to the US government and the drug companies, not to the indigenous 'owners' of the genes.

The Genescope had made it possible for the project leaders to lay down guidelines ensuring that all individuals who gave samples were identified, so if any rare gene line was discovered it could be traced back to the original person, family or community. That person, family or community would then benefit from any bounty that might ensue. Once these shared genetic mining rights were agreed the project went ahead more smoothly and all the genomes were stored for reference on the Human Genome Diversity Database.

She clicked on the icon and watched the front end panel flash its request for her password. She recognized the basic architecture of the system immediately; an advanced Kibuki 2000 relational database with bespoke security features. As with all things Japanese, Jazz was impressed by the design of the system. The series of gates protecting access to the database were tightly programmed, well thought through and strewn with a number of cleverly placed software alarms.

But she wasn't fazed. Razor Buzz may not have been as active as in the past, but Dr Jasmine Washington had been keeping up on developments, indeed shaping them. In her experience well-designed Japanese systems always had one tragic flaw. The very beauty and clarity of their design tended to be their Achilles heel.

Her hand instinctively reached across and took a slice of cold pizza, and as she chewed she thought. When finished, she absentmindedly wiped her lips with the back of her hand, and started tapping on the keyboard. One by one she undid each invisible stitch of programming the original designer had used to sew up the database. Each time, as she disabled one security gate after another her guesses were proven right. That was the problem with this system. It was *too* well designed. Too predictable.

In less than forty minutes, like the Razor Buzz of old, she was inside, browsing the database, importing a copy of the Nazareth genes file and searching for an exact match of the genetic sequences contained within it.

She reached for the Diet Coke, preparing for a short wait. Even with her powerful 100 terrahertz machine the search through a database this size could take some time.

But the '*Match Found*' message blinked almost instantly.

So fast that she was taken off balance, spilling her drink over her T-shirt and jeans.

'Jeez.'

Her fleeting annoyance swiftly changed to excitement when she saw the screen change and a scanned photograph appear with a body of text beside it. The image looked like a mug shot; a man's dark face framed with long grey hair looking straight at her. She liked the face; it was strong and dignified, even noble. The man looked old, but in excellent condition; his torso was bare and the muscle definition firm. She scrolled half-way down the text beside the picture. He was a Wayuu Indian from Carisal in Colombia. His surname was Puyiana, but his first name was only given as Al. Her heart jumped when she read the lines near the bottom of the screen.

'*Credited with powers of healing*,' read the text.

Al was a medicine man. Jasmine read how Al Puyiana, unlike other healers in the area, didn't use his knowledge of local herbs and plants to tend the sick, but the *'laying on of hands'*. The scientists who compiled the record claimed not to understand how he did this, but stated that there was *'strong evidence'* he possessed a *'genuine gift'*.

On the top of the screen she saw option icons offering more information on the man. The one she paid most heed to was the 'genetic data' icon which would confirm the match with the Nazareth genes – genes which the scientists before her no doubt missed because of their different stop-and-start codons. She was about to click on the icon when she noticed there were two dates under Al's name, not just his birth date. The second was a little over three months ago.

She went back to the body copy and scrolled down to the bottom of the text.

'On no,' she whispered. She felt a twinge of real sadness for this man she'd just met. Al Puyiana, with the strong face and healing hands, had died three months ago at the ripe old age of ninety-two.

She checked the genetic sequence match again. It was perfect. The dead man had the three Nazareth genes hidden within his genome, each one identical to the sequence found in the Christ sample. She copied his file and gene scan and exported it to the back-up disk next to her PC. Even in death he might offer up other secrets.

'Shit.' To learn they'd missed him by three months just wasn't fair. She considered calling Tom to tell him what had happened, but dismissed that when she looked at the time again. Almost one-thirty in the morning. She knew he was staying late tonight, but doubted he was still here. Perhaps she should go home and get some sleep too, but she felt too restless. She read the text on the Wayuu Indian from Carisal one more time. The words *'Credited with the powers of healing'* seemed to project off the screen and taunt her.

With a deep sigh she double-checked that there were no more matches in the system, then methodically exited ensuring she left no trace of her intrusion. Like all those times many years ago she had once again stolen invisibly into a dark, seemingly impenetrable fortress and then crept back out, leaving the guards sleeping, unaware that their defences had even been breached.

Perhaps it was frustration at having got so close that made her do what she did next. Or the fact that she was too revved up to sleep. Or possibly she was simply enjoying being the rebellious, anti-establishment Razor Buzz again. Whatever the reason, Dr Jasmine Washington ignored the long list of DNA databases painstakingly compiled in order of ascending risk, and went straight to the final entry. It was time to see whether Razor Buzz really could still hack it. Whether the cyberlord could steal into the darkest fortress of them all – the 'Black Hole'.

HALF AN HOUR LATER, THE GENIUS SECURITY GUARDS WERE changing shifts in the main gatehouse. The two new guards clattered through the door and exchanged a few obscene pleasantries with their outgoing colleagues.

Gus Stransky had been with SHIELD, the private security firm who oversaw the GENIUS campus, for almost seven years. He was in his fifties and had been one of Boston's finest before being pensioned off early with a bullet-damaged right ankle. Despite the hours he liked security work. It gave him a breather from his nag of a wife, Doris.

The GENIUS contract was a dream. The place had money and was equipped with the best technology. All he had to do was sit in the gatehouse and watch the CCTV screens for anything weird. And ever since Sweden, when Mrs Carter had been shot, security had been doubled, so he even had company too. His partner tonight was a new guy, a young dark-haired guy called Bart Johnson, tallish with a strong build. Bart had only been drafted onto the GENIUS contract a couple of days ago. Still, he seemed OK and Gus was used to being paired off with the rookies. His supervisor always said that he had a way with them.

In the gatehouse there were two banks of CCTV monitors. One showed views outside the main pyramid, covering most of the campus including the protein production sheds across to the right. The other bank looked inside the pyramid, including one screen that perma-nently displayed the atrium and the other two guards sitting there. One man could sit between both banks and cover them all, but tonight Gus took the external set and let the rookie have the interior shots.

Gus quickly checked all his CCTV screens and saw that everything appeared to be in order. He turned to his partner. 'You married Bart? Or are you happy?'

Bart smiled. 'Happy I guess.'

Gus watched the younger guy scanning the screens in front of him. All showed empty offices. Only the ward and the Crick Laboratory appeared to be occupied. Dr Carter was still at work in the Crick Lab. It was impossible to make out exactly what he was doing, but he seemed engrossed at his bench.

Bart punched a button, opening up the intercom to the guards in the atrium of the pyramid.

'How's it going in there?'

One of the guards on screen put up his right hand and raised a thumb. 'OK so far. That you Bart?'

'Sure is Georgie boy.'

'Is old Gus there?'

Bart looked across and grinned at his frown. 'Yeah, *old* Gus is here. How you both doing?'

'It's very quiet,' crackled back the voice on the intercom. 'So quiet that I could do with some excitement.'

Gus took out a stick of Doublemint gum and began chewing it. He offered some to Bart, but the younger man just shook his head. Gus put the gum away in his top breast pocket, sat back in his chair and methodically flicked through his screens. The protein sheds were deserted inside and out, as were all the grounds. Nothing stirred.

Suddenly he felt his young partner stiffen beside him. Gus turned to see Bart staring at the screen that displayed the Crick Lab, where Dr Carter was working.

'Anything wrong?' he asked wearily. Why were these young guys always so uptight; always seeing danger lurking in every shadow?

Bart's eyebrow creased. 'Not sure.' He stood up and vacated his seat. 'Gus, come and take a closer look at this, and tell me what you see.'

Gus sighed, but stood up. 'OK,' he said unenthusiastically. If he had a dollar for every time a rookie asked him to pass his experienced eye over some stupid shadow or dirty smudge on the screen, he wouldn't need to work. That was for sure.

The younger guard made way for him as he bent to check the monitor. 'What's the problem?' Gus asked, 'I don't see anything.'

'Bottom right. It's small. Real small.'

Gus leaned further forward. But he saw nothing. Only Dr Carter scratching his head over a row of glass dishes. What the hell was Bart playing at? Then there was a quiet metallic click behind him. At first it didn't register, then like a note from a long-forgotten song he remembered what the sound was.

A gun being primed.

He turned, more angry than frightened. 'What the fu—?'

He said no more as two hissed reports sent a searing heat into his chest. It was a strange feeling. Not so much pain as total breathlessness. Stunned, he reached down and touched his tunic. It was damp and sticky, and there were red splatters on the monitors ahead of him. Blood, he realized, with bemused calm; *his* blood. Shit, he'd been shot. He felt weak and giddy, so he sat down on the chair and tried to get his breath back, but it was gone, gone for good. He looked round and saw Bart watching him closely. It didn't make sense; his young partner was holding a gun, with a silencer attached to it. He felt a deep tiredness and lay back in the chair, trying to get more comfortable. All the time Bart kept staring at him.

As everything began to fade, only two thoughts remained to trouble his consciousness. One was the realization that he would never see his wife Doris again, which made him surprisingly sad. The other was why he'd never noticed before that one of Bart's eyes was blue, and the other brown.

MARIA BENARIAC MADE SURE GUS'S LIFELESS BODY WOULDN'T FALL from the chair, before opening her bag. She put the gun inside it and checked the other tools she had brought along for tonight. It had taken her a whole day to find the nails. None of the hardware stores seemed to stock any which were long or strong enough. But she was confident the five she had eventually found in Charlestown would suffice. She only needed four but a spare might come in handy. The mallet she found in Johnson's apartment was heavy enough to drive in the nails.

Shooting Gus hadn't counted as a kill in the true sense of the word. Nor had killing Bart Johnson, the rookie guard from SHIELD security from whom she had borrowed the uniform, job and identity. They had merely been irritating obstacles that stood in the way of completing her sacred mission.

For a fleeting moment she thought with sadness of the Father, and their recent argument. She hoped that once Dr Carter and his project were finished the Father would see the wisdom of her actions, and welcome her back into the fold. But even if he didn't, she was convinced that she was following the Second Imperative correctly. Her God would tell her where to strike next, and she would have to do without the guiding intervention of the Father, or the comforting bosom of the Brotherhood.

So be it, she thought. She had been reborn once before. She would be again.

She flicked on the intercom switch and kept her trained voice low in tone. 'Hey guys. I'm coming over to deliver something. OK?'

On the screen one of the guards in the atrium of the pyramid gave a small nod. 'No problem. We'll open the door for you.'

'Much obliged,' she said, clicking off the switch. Then without even a backwards glance at Gus's slumped body she left the gate-house.

She adjusted her cap as she crunched down the gravel driveway. Ahead of her the glass pyramid seemed to soar into the night sky like some futuristic temple. It would be right to kill the scientist in his lair. She had waited for this moment and allowed herself a whole week, but it had finally arrived. With every step she could feel her excitement build, and with every step she whispered a line of her creed:

'I am Nemesis. May my sword of justice be keen . . .
May my armour of righteousness be unblemished . . .
And may my shield of faith be strong.'

With every crunch of her shoes on gravel she repeated the lines like an incantation into the cool night air.

The walk took less than five minutes and the main door opened for her just before she reached the DNA scanner. In the lit atrium beyond she could see the guards sitting behind their consoles grinning at her. Her eyes fell on the junction box behind the second guard; the box that controlled all the phone lines coming into and out of the building.

'Hey, buddy, welcome to our humble abode,' greeted George, the man who had spoken to her on the intercom. 'What have you got for us then?'

She walked inside and with a smile, patted her bag. 'Just what you were looking for.'

The guard's grin widened. 'Oh yeah? And what's that?'

She reached her hand into the bag and closed her fingers over the trusty Glock. 'A little excitement.'

21

IT SECTION, GENIUS HEADQUARTERS, BOSTON.

NO MORE THAN FORTY YARDS AWAY IN THE IT SECTION, RAZOR Buzz was in a trance as she worked on breaching the ramparts protecting the 'Black Hole'. Her fingers moved with precise speed over the keyboard, whilst her eyes stayed locked on the virtual world beyond the screen.

The official database title at the top of the monitor acted as a permanent reminder of the seriousness of her task – and the consequences of getting caught. As did the warning message flashing red across the middle of the screen: PREDATOR V. 3 PROTECTION ENABLED. She'd already disabled the first three password gates of probably the most secure DNA database in existence, and was on the verge of turning the fourth and final red light to green – breaching the last barrier to the files.

Once she entered the database proper, the PREDATOR system would immediately detect her, and could within one minute trace the origin of her computer. She would have just sixty seconds to search for a match and then exit cleanly, leaving no files of her own behind. If she delayed for one instant longer she would be trapped, unable to log off, whilst the system owners tracked her down. And they definitely weren't people either Jasmine or Razor Buzz wanted to mess with. Not at all.

Suddenly the screen flickered as if there'd been a power surge. Then the final red light on the bottom of the screen turned green. She had disabled the fourth password gate.

So far so good. And to come this far had felt good, *very* good. Going deep into the complex program language behind the database, she had rewritten extensive stretches of it without alerting the system itself.

She paused for a moment, calming herself down as she placed the cursor over the on-screen icon that acted as an electronic 'open sesame' giving her access to the data. Once this was pressed the PREDATOR countdown would commence and there would be no other chances.

She extended her left hand and took off her watch. She tested the digitized voice alarm. '*5 seconds*,' said the toneless voice of the watch. With a satisfied nod she set the alarm on the watch and laid it beside the keyboard. Her hand went back to the mouse and moved the cursor over the file icon containing the Nazareth genes. This compressed electronic file held only the genetic sequence of the three hybrid genes. Jasmine had created it to expedite the search for a match. By inserting the icon into the database and activating 'search' the files could seek out the matching sequence in any of the genomes residing on the database. She moved the icon to the centre of the screen, allowing her quickly to insert it into the database.

Razor Buzz took a deep breath, pushed a button on the side of the watch, then clicked the mouse cursor on the entry icon.

She was now inside the database.

With lightning finger movements she embedded the Nazareth genes icon in the search box, and selected, 'Topline Quick-Search.'

Then the PREDATOR system kicked in. A red 'WARNING' message flashed in red at the top of the screen and an electronic voice barked from the speakers, '*Trace enabled. You have 60 seconds to give personal identification code and access authorization symbol.*'

Suddenly a large 60 appeared at the top right hand corner of the screen and instantly started ticking down. 59, 58, 57 . . . .

Razor Buzz was aware of the perspiration threatening to break out on her forehead, but she remained calm. Ignoring the distraction of the declining numbers she kept her eyes on the search window in the centre of the screen. A horizontal strip of white ran across it, which was gradually filling from left to right with black. Beneath it a percentage figure was displayed, which increased in steps of five, indicating how much of the database had been checked.

The black fill was now a tenth of the way along the strip with the message '*10% of database searched*' displayed below it. Then after what seemed an eternity the black fill moved along another notch and the 10 per cent changed to 15 per cent.

The clock on the top righthand corner continued to count down. 42, 41, 40 . . . .

The progress of the white strip was erratic. The black raced from 15 per cent to 20 per cent and 25 per cent. But then took an age to reach 30 per cent.

32, 31, 30 ticked the clock.

'*Thirty seconds*,' warned the digitized voice of the watch beside Razor.

She could hardly bear to keep her eyes on the screen. The 'Topline Quick-Search' facility would give only the barest details of any match, but at least it *should* allow a 100 per cent search of the database in the time. It was getting tight though, very tight.

Seventeen seconds.

The fill was now 78 per cent.

Then, suddenly and simply, a match was found.

'Hallelujah,' she whispered, springing swiftly into action. She didn't bother to open the found file and examine it. She just selected it, copied it and exported it to her back-up disk. Then with speedy clicks of the mouse and sweeps of the cursor she moved the Nazareth genes icon out of the search box and exited.

As the clock on the screen ticked to 3.

'*Sixty seconds*,' bleated her watch.

Only now did Razor Buzz wipe off the perspiration that had gathered on her brow, and let out a long sigh of relief. She had her prize. The cyberlord had been into the heart of the 'Black Hole' and escaped undetected to tell the tale. She was safe.

Suddenly the screen fizzed and the main menu came up. With a frown she realized that the modem line must have gone down, or been disconnected.

She reached for her phone and punched out the internal number for the atrium reception desk. Nothing. Dead silent. What the hell was going on?

She rose and walked out of her office to the computer room, and looked through the tinted glass to the atrium. Where were the guards? Both desks were empty. Since the scare over Carter, Jack had made it a sackable offence for both stations in the atrium or the gate-house to be left unmanned at any time. She walked over to the nearest desk.

Then she saw the black, perfectly polished shoe.

It looked odd, sticking out from the other side of the desk at a weird angle. It took her tired brain a second to realize that the shoe possessed a foot. With mounting horror she walked round the desk, watching the ankle come into view, then the trousered leg and its twin splayed out to the left; and finally the whole body of George, the security guard. She liked him; she'd met his wife and two sons at the company barbecue last summer. He was staring at her, but his eyes were like a blank computer screen. Three neat bullet holes punctured his chest and neck, and a slick of blood had leaked across the marble towards her, nudging her toes.

Jasmine felt nauseous as she stepped across the sticky puddle of spreading red to check the pulse on George's still warm wrist. But his eyes had told the truth; George's wife was now a widow, his two sons fatherless. Just as the nausea hit her she saw the second body lying behind the other desk.

Holding her hand over her mouth and trying to quell the rising panic she instinctively grabbed for the phone. She numbly put it to her ear and cursed her own stupidity when she once again heard the silence. Think! damn you! Think!

Run! Get out of here! Now! The orders came coldly and unbidden from deep within her. With them came the fear. No longer was she simply shocked by what had happened to the two men; she was suddenly terrified that it might happen to *her*. She turned from the bloody bodies, and the desks, barely registering the CCTV monitors as she focused on the stairs to the underground garage.

The TV monitors.

The white coat on the screen, only seen for a micro-second, burned

229

into her retina. Hoping her eyes had been mistaken she forced herself to delay her flight, and look again at the monitors in front of the desk. The figure in the white coat was moving now; on the screen marked *Crick Laboratory.*

Tom was still here.

And in that instant she knew that the Preacher had come to kill him.

There were two voices in her head now. One still shouted *Run!*, but only louder, and more persuasively. *Get to your car!* it said, *Call for help! No one could ask you to do more than that.* The other voice, a whisper she could almost ignore, told her that help wouldn't come in time. That it was up to *her* to help her friend, to warn him.

'But what can I do?' she said aloud, looking down at her feet, watching them lead her to the garage stairs and safety. Then the thought came to her and she stopped. She turned and walked back to George's body. Trying not to look in his eyes, she rolled his body over in the sticky blood.

The holster was clipped down, but the ugly, black gun was still there.

With trembling fingers she unbuckled the leather, checked the gun's chamber, just as her brother had taught her to. Fully loaded. She took off the safety and held it in her hands, feeling its weight, reminding herself of her dead brother's macho words — *only pull a gun if you're prepared to use it.*

Was she prepared to use it? To do what she had vowed never to do; to aim a gun at someone and shoot? Her mouth felt dry and her legs jelly-weak as she walked to the elevator.

No! commanded the voice in her head. *Don't take the elevator! The killer will know you're coming. She mustn't even know you're here. Take the stairs!*

She turned and ran for the stairwell. And as she pushed open the doors she tried to imagine she wasn't Jasmine anymore, but the Razor Buzz of old — a cyberlord freed from the virtual world to roam the real one. She had a gun, and she had motivation.

What more could she ask for?

Courage, she thought, *I could do with a hell of a lot more courage.*

Then she took a deep breath, steadied her trembling legs and began to climb the dark stairs.

*　*　*

ON THE FLOOR ABOVE, TOM SIGHED AND LOOKED DEEP INTO THE man's eyes.

'Tell me about the third gene!' he commanded. 'Tell me what it does!' He raised a glass phial of the serum loaded with the new genes, and thrust it in the man's face. 'And tell me what this does?' he demanded. 'How the hell do the three genes work together? Dammit, tell me!'

The man said nothing; just stared back at him. Tom took a frustrated swing at his head, but gained little satisfaction when his hand passed through it. That was the problem with holograms; they didn't make great talkers, or punch bags.

Tom shook his head in disgust and yawned. He walked back over to DAN, still running countless iterations in its 'virtual mind', trying to unravel the Gordian knot of the third gene. He bent and punched two keys on the keyboard and the hologram of Christ vanished. Tom had been reviewing all the findings since half past eight in the morning – yesterday morning – and was still no wiser.

He picked up one culture dish bearing the title '*Naz 3 – E coli*' written in Nora's tidy script. He held it up to the light and just stared at it for a while. No proteins. Nothing. He did the same with '*Trinity – E coli*', containing all three hybrid genes together. An entirely new protein had been produced. Lots of it too. But what the hell did it do?

Perhaps the genes do nothing, his tired mind taunted him. *Perhaps there is nothing to know*. Tom checked his watch and walked to the phone. He wondered whether Jasmine was still downstairs working on finding a match. It wouldn't be the first time she'd worked all night. He picked up the hand set and put it to his ear. Then he shook it and listened again. This was all he needed. It was completely dead.

He slammed the phone down and turned to walk to the elevator. The shadowy uniformed figure in the doorway took him by surprise.

'George, is that you? What the hell's gone wrong with the phones?'

'I've closed them down, Dr Carter. We're alone. Just you and me.'

The deep female voice shocked him, raising the hairs on the back of his neck. 'What the hell's going on? Who the hell are you?'

The shadowy figure stepped into the full light of the lab. 'You know who I am.'

231

Tom froze by his workbench, an icy band of fear squeezing his chest. The man was shorter than he was but still above average height. His build was athletic with powerful shoulders. The face conventionally handsome to the point of being bland, with a firm jaw, fine nose and sculptured cheekbones. It was only the eerie voice and striking cat-shaped eyes – one blue and one brown – that told Tom he wasn't looking at a man at all, but a woman. He remembered seeing those eyes before. On the hologram of the Preacher. And he knew without a shadow of doubt that he was looking at Olivia's killer.

At that moment, even as he watched the woman pull a gun out of her bag, his fear left him. And in its place came a rage he had never known before.

Keeping his eyes locked on hers, Tom edged his right hand along the workbench, trying to locate the keyboard behind him.

MARIA BENARIAC WALKED TOWARDS CARTER AND WEIGHED THE Glock in her hand. It was lighter now she'd used eight of the slugs in the magazine, but there were still nine left. The guards in the atrium had been too easy to kill. And sealing the door to the hospital suite so the night nurse couldn't come snooping around meant she had Carter all to herself.

Up close his eyes were Arctic blue. When she looked into them she was annoyed to find them unrepentant and devoid of fear. But that would change when she used the nails. And when he was dead she would leave her message in his blood – *He that increaseth knowledge increaseth sorrow. Ecclesiastes ch.1, v.18.*

She levelled the silenced gun at his head and smiled. This was truly a righteous moment. 'Dr Carter,' she said, 'the wages of sin is death.'

'What is my sin?' came the immediate response, his voice betraying only one emotion – anger.

With her left hand she put the bag on the large table next to her, while her right kept the pistol pointed at him. 'What is your sin? I have been watching you, Dr Carter. Very closely. Your sin is wanting to become God. Not only have you meddled with God's creation, you have meddled with God's own Son.'

'My meddling *saves* lives. How many lives has the Preacher *taken*?'

She smiled, recognizing the foolish sobriquet the papers had given her. She liked the fact that he knew she was responsible for killing the others. 'Only those that needed cleansing.'

'Cleansing? You mean *murdering*? Who decided they should die?'

She swept all the other debris off the table. Bottles, flasks and beakers smashed to the floor. A strange white instrument with a round rubber pad sticking out the top, and *Omnigene* written down one side, almost fell on her foot. She sized up the scientist and reckoned the table would be just about big enough if his arms weren't extended full stretch. One by one she took the nails out of the bag, laying them in a neat row. 'God decided they should die, of course.'

'What God?' scoffed the scientist. 'You can't pass the responsibility on to him. He doesn't exist. We only created Him to explain what we couldn't understand, and now science has given us knowledge we don't need Him any more. Is that why you need to kill me? Or do you enjoy killing, using God as an excuse?'

She laid the rope and mallet next to the nails and tried to keep her anger in check. She knew how important control was, but this angry, arrogant man in front of her wasn't like the others. He had no sense of his guilt, or any fear of his executioner. He clung on to the stubborn, twisted belief that he was *right*. If she still maintained some vestige of righteous detachment towards him, then it vanished at that moment. No longer could she see him coldly as a threat that needed to be removed; he was someone she hated; the very personification of everything she feared and despised.

'I will give you a choice,' she said. 'Which hand?'

His angry eyes looked puzzled for a second. 'What do you mean?' He was looking at the nails now, wondering what they were for. Or trying hard not to.

'As I said, I have been watching you. I know what you are doing. Since you want to possess the power of Jesus, then you will die like him.' She trained the gun on his left hand hanging by his side. 'I am going to tie you to this table and drive a nail through each hand and foot.' She couldn't help a smile. 'I need to make a hole for the first nail. A bullet will make it easier for both of us. Which hand?'

Fear at last. Genuine fear flickered in those fierce eyes. Good. Not so arrogant now, are we, Dr Carter? Then, before he could react further she fired.

'Shit!' he screamed in agony.

233

It was comical the way he jerked and spun round, nursing his injured left hand with his right.

She felt a rush of satisfaction when she saw the neat hole in his palm and the blood dripping to the floor. The scientist looked pale as he examined the wound. She thought he was going to be sick. But when he raised his head she saw no trace of fear in his eyes – only an icy glare. 'You sick bitch.'

He was incredible. 'Do you still not repent?' she demanded. She wanted him to yield before she executed him, to acknowledge her righteous truth.

He laughed then, '*Repent*? For what? For wanting to save lives?'

She stepped forward to push the gun into his temple. They stood now between his workbench and the table. 'Those lives aren't *yours* to save. You don't change what God ordained just because you can. People have to earn salvation. The Lord decides who should be saved by his miracles, not men like you.'

Dr Carter's jaw muscles tensed as he tried to control the pain in his hand. And when he spoke his words were spat out through clenched teeth. 'But they're not *His* goddamned miracles, you witch,' he hissed, 'they're *ours*. Like fire and being able to fly. Anyway, what gives *you* the right to decide what He wants done . . . to *know* His will?'

'He has chosen me.'

Carter laughed at that, a loud manic laugh. 'How do you know? Have you asked him face to face?'

She was tiring of this conversation. The insufferable scientist wouldn't concede on any point. It was time to make him see reason. She ground the gun into his temple. 'Place your left hand on the table.' She was prepared for a struggle but to her surprise he grimaced and laid his damaged hand palm upwards on the table beside the nails. All the time his blue eyes stared defiantly into hers.

He had courage. She had to give him that. She shifted the gun to her left hand and reached for the first nail.

'Have you ever met Christ?' he asked, his tone now surprisingly calm. He sounded genuinely interested in her response.

She ignored him and concentrated on the nail. She only had one free hand. So she had to plunge the nail hard through his bullet hole to get some purchase on the wood, then use the mallet to drive it in deeper and anchor his hand to the table. But if she missed the hole, the nail would not pierce the wood sufficiently to stop him from pulling his hand away.

As she focused on this problem she didn't see his other hand move to the keyboard on the workstation behind him. She only registered a sudden movement to her left. A figure in her peripheral vision. Instinctively she turned and fired at it, but the shadowy person didn't even flinch. Mesmerized, she watched the ghostly form take shape, until a 'man' stood not two feet away.

'Go on,' she heard Carter say from some distant place. 'Now you've met Christ, ask him what he really wants us to do with his genes!'

She froze, transfixed by the apparition beside her. The naked man was clean-shaven with long brown hair, and for a long moment she just stared at him.

Then, even as she took in the lights coming from the circular black pad beneath the figure, and realized it must be some kind of projection, she felt the glass flask smash over her head, and a strong hand push her dazed to the ground. Before she fell she lunged out and fired off three rounds.

It took her a second or two to sit up and wipe the blood from her cut forehead. Furious, she turned back to her prey. She would finish this now, crucifixion or no crucifixion.

But he was gone.

She turned to the main door just in time to see him limping out. She stood and lurched after him. At the doorway she looked left, through the wide expanse of the main laboratory, to the elevators beyond. And there he was, his tall frame standing out above the low workbenches and humming apparatus. The knee she had damaged in Stockholm slowed him down, and there was something comical about his awkward run. Through her anger she smiled at the spectacle and the justice of it all. Then she raised her gun and aimed at the back of his head. Now this foolishness would cease.

MOVE, DAMN YOU! MOVE! HISSED TOM, WILLING HIMSELF TO REACH the bank of elevators and ignore the volts of agony pulsing from his hand. If he could get to Jack's office at the top of the pyramid, he might stand a chance. It had a cellular phone and Jack kept a gun in the lower right drawer of the desk.

It didn't matter what he told himself, because in the dark glass wall ahead he could see her reflection. She wasn't coming after him any more; just raising her arm, pointing the gun at him. Shit, the flask he'd smashed over her skull hadn't even slowed the bitch down, let alone knocked her out.

He considered ducking behind one of the benches to his left, but that would only delay the inevitable. If he was going to be shot at, then he'd rather be moving, not cowering behind some piece of furniture. At least this way there was a chance, however small, that she might miss. He bent his head, trying to make himself as small a target as possible, and forced his stiff knee to propel him the last ten yards to the nearest elevator.

At that moment he saw the flash reflected in the glass, and heard the gunshot.

And he fell.

IT WAS A LUCKY SHOT. AND WHEN JASMINE OPENED HER EYES, SHE realized how lucky.

Coming up the stairs she'd felt OK. Scared out her skin, but in control. But when she'd squeezed open the door to the main lab and seen the figure chasing Tom she'd frozen, suddenly realizing the stark reality of what she had to overcome: the Preacher.

If she'd ever experienced such terror before, she couldn't remember it. It rushed through her in great gusts that seemed to petrify every muscle in her body.

Then the figure chasing Tom had stopped, standing with her back to Jasmine, calmly aiming the gun.

Not allowing herself time to think, Jazz snapped out of her paralysis, eased opened the door to the stairwell and crept out behind the killer. Her mouth was so dry she couldn't have shouted 'Freeze' if she'd wanted to. She took the gun in both her shaking hands and aimed at the middle of the Preacher's broad back. Then as her brother had told her to, she'd slowly squeezed the trigger, and like he'd told her *never* to do, she'd squeezed both her eyes shut.

The shot had deafened her. The recoil wrenched her shoulder, almost pushing her hands back into her face. And the sharp smell of cordite had caught in her throat, making her retch.

Way to go, Razor Buzz.

When she opened her eyes and looked through the smoke the

Preacher was down, lying motionless on the ground. But where was Tom? Then she saw her friend get up from the floor by the elevators, and brush himself off. He must have fallen, but seemed unhurt.

'Get her gun, Jazz!' he shouted, limping towards his would-be killer.

Still surfing her wave of adrenalin Jasmine rushed over to the still figure and kicked the dropped gun towards Tom, who picked it up in his right hand. When Jasmine looked down at the killer she saw a red gash on the back of her head where the bullet must have creased her skull, knocking her unconscious. Another millimetre higher and Jasmine would have missed entirely. A few millimetres lower and the Preacher's brains would now be decorating the floor below her feet. Both possibilities made Jasmine feel sick.

The woman's dark hairline looked odd as she stared down at her — sort of crooked and crinkly, like a hurriedly donned cheap shower-cap. It took a second to realize that the close-cropped, utterly natural hair was actually a wig. Her bullet must have dislodged it, and where the hairpiece had slipped Jasmine could see that the killer's scalp was completely shaved. She felt a shiver travel up the back of her neck. *Creepy*.

'Good shot, Jazz!' said Tom levelling the gun at the killer with enviably steady hands.

'Not really,' she said, trying to control her own jelly-legs. 'Considering I was aiming between her shoulder blades.'

Tom smiled and hugged her, his eyes bright. 'Well, in my book you're a marksman, a real Annie Oakley. If you hadn't hit her, she would have hit me *exactly* where she was aiming.'

Jasmine's left leg began to twitch as she relaxed in his arms, coming down from the adrenalin rush. As he let go of her she noticed the bloody hole in his left palm. 'What happened to your hand?'

He shrugged. 'I'm OK. Let's just say the Preacher didn't plan on me having an easy death.'

'So it is definitely the Preacher?'

'Yeah. You've just brought down one of America's most wanted criminals.' A note of concern entered his voice. 'You OK?'

'Yeah. Just a bit shaken.' She looked down at the figure on the ground. As she studied the masculine profile she thought of the beautiful hologram of the woman she had seen with Special Agent

Karen Tanner. This was no longer creepy, it went way beyond that. She looked back to Tom. 'I thought he . . . *she* had got you for a moment.'

'You're not the only one. But I'm—'

The Preacher stirred, and blinked open one eye. In that instant Jasmine recognized her from the hologram; the shape and colour of that eye were unmistakable.

'Jazz, go to Jack's office and use a cellular to call for help,' said Tom. 'I'll look after our guest.'

She nodded and made her way to the elevator, then heard Tom ask: 'What happened to George, and the other guards?'

She turned, not sure how to tell him. 'I don't know about the gate-house'.

'But the atrium . . .?'

She just shook her head. Tom stared at the waking killer. And for the first time since she'd known him, she saw something in those blue eyes that frightened her. At that moment the man who had dedicated himself to saving lives looked capable of taking one.

'Tom? You OK?'

He didn't look at her, just muttered, 'Someone once said that revenge was a wild kind of justice resorted to by animals. But that isn't true. Animals feel no need for revenge. Only we do. Now I can see why.' He turned and she saw his full pain and rage, and was glad to be on the same side as he was.

IT WASN'T THE PAIN IN HER HEAD THAT FIRST INTRUDED ON MARIA'S consciousness, but anger. She had failed, and when she saw the scientist standing over her with her own gun she realized the extent of her failure. Someone must have been behind her when she was aiming at Dr Carter. Why hadn't she checked the building after killing the guards, and not just relied on the monitors before rushing off to confront the scientist? Her desire to kill him had made her an amateur.

For a moment she considered trying to overcome him, but could see from the look in his eyes that if she so much as moved he would gladly shoot her. She thought about risking it anyway, so great was her shame. She had failed twice – Stockholm and now this. She had failed the Father, the Brotherhood and worst of all, herself. But then

238

she figured that the longer she survived the more chance she had of putting everything right.

'You're a lucky man, Dr Carter.'

'Yeah, perhaps you weren't meant to kill me after all,' he said with no humour.

She smiled. It did appear that the Devil was looking out for the scientist, and for reasons she didn't yet understand God was letting him. 'God tests us all,' she replied, not taking her eyes off his.

'Looks like you failed yours big time. Last chance too. The next time you get a message from your maker, he should be able to give it to you personally.'

'It's not over yet,' she said.

He laughed at that. A bitter laugh. 'It is for you.'

22

CAVE OF THE SACRED LIGHT, SOUTHERN JORDAN.

EZEKIEL LOOKED INTO THE YOUNG GIRL'S BEAUTIFUL EYES. SHE smiled nervously at him and he returned her smile. 'Relax my child,' he whispered as he picked up the ancient dagger with its razor-sharp blade. 'It will be over soon.'

He pulled her right arm towards him, so it lay above the pewter bowl on the altar. With a gentle movement he smoothed the sleeve of her ritual robe up over her elbow, revealing her forearm. Then with great care he traced the tip of the ceremonial blade up and down her flesh, allowing her skin to become sensitized to the steel. He felt her arm stiffen as the cold edge tickled her. He paused for a moment, then with one practised movement cut into the arm. Her eyes now showed pain, but she bit her lip and gave no other sign of her discomfort. When the thread-like crimson incision was three inches long, he removed the blade and bisected the wound with a horizontal cut, forming a cross. When the second incision was complete he replaced the dagger on the table by the pewter bowl. Then he twisted her forearm pointing the cut downwards. Gently he kneaded the flesh of her arm until the blood dripped into the bowl. He counted eight precious claret-red drops before the blood began to clot. It was enough.

He dipped the forefinger of his left hand in the ruby liquid, then painted a red cross on her smooth forehead.

'Your blood is his blood,' he said solemnly. 'Your body is his body.'

Her voice trembled with passion. 'I give him my flesh, so he may save my soul.'

He nodded encouragement. 'May he be saved.'

More relaxed now, she smiled back at him. 'So he may save the righteous.' Brother Haddad, the initiate's regional Head of the Holy Lands, wiped her cruciform cut with the scarring ointment, and the newest member of the Brotherhood turned away to resume her seat.

The cavern reverberated with a collective sigh of relief, both from the other nineteen initiates around the vast table, and those at the back of the cavern who had come to witness the ceremony. The first of the bloodings was always the most nerve racking.

Ezekiel greeted the next initiate into the Brotherhood, a young man from Jerusalem, asking him to extend his arm over the bowl. As Ezekiel blooded him, he thought how fine the collection of twelve men and eight women looked in their white robes. Good stock to take the Brotherhood into the future. Most were children of current Brothers, or close friends monitored from childhood. About twenty of these relations and guardians stood at the back of the cavern, witnessing the ceremony and no doubt remembering the day when they themselves had been initiated.

As the third initiate rose from the table, stepped forward and extended her arm, Ezekiel De La Croix recalled how at eighteen his father had taken him here from their home in Damascus. He remembered the burden of expectation his father, a member of the Inner Circle, had placed on his shoulders. Even then Ezekiel was being groomed for the day when he would one day become Leader.

At that time only men could fully join the Brotherhood, but the blooding ceremonies had still been larger affairs, with sixty or more initiates attending. The young today had lost their dedication and discipline. Fewer and fewer could be trusted to devote themselves completely to the Brotherhood.

Still, he had just spent the last two hours explaining the laws of the Brotherhood, reminding the initiates of the sect's history and its Primary Imperative. They had also been told of their individual responsibilities; how each one of them would be expected to reach a suitable level of attainment in their chosen field to best serve the organization. They knew that there were Brothers and Sisters already placed at senior levels in the world's major churches, banks, hospitals, armed and police forces and media organizations. All watching and waiting; ready to answer the call from the Brotherhood and ultimately their Messiah at a moment's notice.

The one practice Ezekiel and the others of the Inner Circle had not shared with them was the Second Imperative. That was only ever revealed to the six members of the Inner Circle and the two operatives.

The girl who now stood in front of Ezekiel reminded him of the young Maria Benariac, the daughter he had never had. He had known that Maria was special from the very first time he'd seen those bewitching eyes. Even when the vindictive Mother Clemenza had told him about Maria's childhood lies, he had become more convinced that Maria was in some way chosen. These claims of hers, made when she wasn't yet eight, may have been the fantasies of a lonely child. Even the older Maria had dismissed them as such, saying she couldn't remember them. But at least these 'lies', incredible for one so young, had shown her vision and imagination.

Ezekiel cut the flesh of the girl in front of him and watched dispassionately as she squeezed back tears. Maria hadn't even blinked at her blooding; just beamed at him with unrestrained pride as the blade sliced across her arm. He regretted their argument now. He'd known she would overreact when she heard about the deal with Carter. But he was surprised that Maria had ignored Brother Bernard's subsequent messages. That was unlike her.

Ezekiel reassured himself that despite her passionate views she was ultimately loyal to him and the Brotherhood. He felt sure she would contact him soon, and then he and Bernard would decide what to do with her.

Ezekiel turned his mind to Dr Carter as he prepared the next initiate, a young man from Beirut. All the Inner Circle had been excited when the scientist had returned the samples and told them about the three rare genes. Now they just had to wait until Carter contacted them again with progress on finding the match. According to Helix if it existed on any of the DNA databases they should know within weeks, perhaps even days. Ezekiel felt a surge of excitement so strong that he had to steady his hand as he cut into the young man's arm.

The rest of the bloodings took the best part of an hour. And throughout the ceremony he allowed himself to bask in the warm possibility, even probability, that they were close now; close to the realization of the prophecy and the fulfilment of all his obligations and responsibilities.

It wasn't until he delivered his concluding speech that he noticed Bernard gesturing from the back. He saw Helix beckoning him also and his excitement bubbled over. They must have news. He quickly finished the address and handed over to Brother Haddad.

Next door, in one of the adjoining caves, he huddled in a quiet corner with the two senior Brothers.

'So, have we news from Carter?' he asked. 'Has he found the Messiah?'

Bernard cast a worried look at Helix, then looked down at his shoes. 'No, Father. Not exactly. The news relates more to Nemesis.'

'Maria? You have found her? Where is she?'

'We didn't find her,' said Bernard quietly. 'The FBI did.'

'What?' Ezekiel's warm glow left him.

Helix said, 'According to our sources, it appears she tried to kill the scientist. But one of his colleagues stopped her. Maria is now under arrest.'

'Under arrest?'

'She has been unmasked as the Preacher,' continued Helix, 'and because of the overwhelming evidence against her, she will go on fast-track trial within weeks, even days. If she's found guilty, which she undoubtedly will be, she'll be executed shortly after.'

'The question is, what do we do about her?' said Bernard.

Helix paused. 'Can she be trusted not to betray us? Or do we need to silence her?'

'Of course she won't betray us,' retorted Bernard. 'We trained her. Whatever her failings, betrayal isn't one of them.'

'I agree,' said Ezekiel.

An embarrassed cough from Helix. 'With all due respect, Father, you were wrong about her defying you and going after the scientist.'

Ezekiel De La Croix turned to his Champion of the Primary

Imperative. 'Brother Helix, you do not know Maria. She defied us because she believed in what she had to do. She is perhaps too zealous, even dogmatic. But the last thing she will do is betray us to the authorities. She will stay loyal to us and take her punishment.'

Helix shrugged. 'So we can forget about Maria? And concentrate on Dr Carter?'

Ezekiel didn't like the way the two imperatives had now clashed. He felt personal regret about Maria but more importantly the Brotherhood had lost their most effective operative. At least Carter hadn't been killed, because then both Imperatives would have been compromised. He nodded at Helix. 'Yes, we shall have to leave Maria to the US justice system, and concentrate on Carter. But if he doesn't deliver us a match, then I will personally see to it that Gomorrah finishes him. And everyone else involved in this Project Cana.'

FOUR DAYS LATER. GENIUS HOSPITAL SUITE, BOSTON

TOM FELT GOOD AS HE STOOD IN THE GENIUS SUITE WITH THE patient's file notes open in front of him. Even the pain in his bandaged hand seemed bearable. According to what Karen Tanner had told him yesterday, with the evidence the FBI had on the Preacher she would be making her last sermon in a matter of months – to the state executioner.

Events finally seemed to be going his way. His wife's killer brought to justice. A match on the database. Just reading the file on Al Puyiana, the Indian who shared Christ's genes, had given him a boost. The dead man's DNA might be no more use than the original Nazareth genes, but at least the evidence suggested he could heal. All this added weight and reason to his wild goose chase. And on top of everything, Hank Polanski looked like he was getting better.

'Well Doc?' asked the young man, sitting upright in his bed. 'How am I doing?'

Hank was a completely different person from the pallid, sunken-eyed patient who had started his gene-therapy treatment only a few months ago. Nurse Lawrence stood beside him checking the intravenous drip going into his arm. The drip was coming from a bag of red liquid suspended from a stand next to the bed.

'Looking good, Hank,' said Tom eventually.

'Yeah, I feel a heap better.'

Tom smiled as he read the file. Things *were* going well. He pulled out an X-ray and showed it to Hank. 'The primary tumours in your lungs have stopped growing, and are even beginning to reduce. Your three secondaries have all died.'

'So the fifteen per cent long shot paid off?'

'So far, Hank. But we've still got to monitor you closely. You won't get the all-clear for years. But things are definitely improving.'

Hank laughed. 'No kidding. I'm still alive, aren't I. I'd call that a definite improvement.'

Tom smiled, but said no more. Hank was no longer at death's door, but he wasn't out of the waiting-room yet, even though the odds had shifted significantly in favour of the young man's survival. He said goodbye to Hank and walked back down the ward. As he checked on the other patients he thought of Project Cana and allowed himself a rare, giddying fantasy. If they could get the genes to work, then perhaps they could save every Hank Polanski and Holly in the world. He turned to the other beds and imagined all their occupants well again. He pictured this ward closing down, simply because there were no more patients.

If only Jasmine could identify the name behind the match she had found in the 'Black Hole'. He wished that the match from the Paris database carried an identifying name or title, not just the coded index number: #6699784. He also wished Jasmine had been able to copy the whole genome, and not just the sequence matching the Nazareth genes. They could then have used the Gene Genie to establish the individual's appearance.

Still, at least he knew a living match existed, and on what database. It should now only be a matter of time before Jasmine wheedled her way back into the 'Black Hole', and found the name behind the coded number. The name of the Brotherhood's and Holly's saviour.

'Tom?'

He turned to see Alex walking towards him. Suddenly he wasn't in such a good mood any more. Before his father said another word Tom knew his news. Alex had taken Holly for her brain scan at Massachusetts General today. And it was plain from his drawn look that the scans had been positive. Even though Tom had known

245

DAN's prophecy would come true, its accuracy still shocked him now that it had become a physical reality.

THAT NIGHT HOLLY READ THE NEWSPAPER REPORTS OF THE Preacher's capture, telling Tom how *awesome* it was that her dad and godmother were heroes. It was then, almost in passing, that she mentioned her headaches and dizziness for the first time. She told him how although she'd stopped playing with her computer, they still wouldn't go away. He listened to her, saying nothing, then gave her two painkillers.

Earlier, Tom had examined the shadow on his daughter's brain scans. The scans had told him that Holly's cancer had not only started, but was accelerating at an alarming rate. It had become even more imperative that Jasmine identify the match she'd found. But whatever happened on Cana, and *whenever* it happened, Holly couldn't wait for it. It was important now that she was told what was wrong with her, and what was required to help her. He'd informed patients of serious illness countless times before, he hoped with compassion and humanity. But telling his own precious child was different and once again he wished that Olivia was here to guide him.

After breakfast the next day he walked with his daughter in the garden. It was a clear spring morning in mid April, with dew still on the lawn. The bulbs Olivia had planted the previous autumn were in full flower, a riot of reds and yellows. There was a freshness to the air that spoke of life and rejuvenation.

The gardener was tending the rose bushes at the far end of the lawn. He looked up from his work and smiled from under his faded Boston Red Sox baseball cap.

'Morning.'

'Morning, Ted,' said Holly and Tom in unison.

Long since retired, Ted had helped Olivia in the garden once a week for almost seven years. But ever since Olivia's death he had come round most days to carry out the seeding plans they had discussed together. Tom often tried to pay him for his time but Ted always refused. Taking off his cap and scratching his short grizzled hair he'd give a sad smile and say: 'Thanks all the same Dr Carter, but I ain't got much else to do at my age. And anyway, this is my way of keeping close to Olivia. You understand?'

246

Tom did understand. But he also knew that the widower was not averse to Marcy Kelley's company either.

Tom held Holly's hand as she walked with him to the other end of the garden, the hem of her over-baggy jeans damp from the dew-laden grass.

'Do you know why you get your headaches, Hol?' Tom asked.

She kicked the wet lawn with her day-glo trainers. 'Isn't it the computer?'

'No, Holly, it's not.'

She looked up at him, her forehead creased in thought. It was an expression he'd seen before. 'What is it then?'

Tom stopped walking and crouched down beside her on the grass. Holly's hazel eyes were watching him very closely now.

He smiled at her. 'First of all, Holly, don't be frightened. We are going to stop the headaches, and you're going to be OK. Do you understand that?'

'Yes, Dad', she replied in a quiet voice. Her wide eyes looked at him with such complete trust that it squeezed his heart.

'Do you remember the check-up you had with Grampa yesterday?'

'Uh, huh.'

'You know that it's a scan that checks everything's OK in our heads. Well, on the last scan you were fine as usual. Except for a tiny bump.'

Holly's forehead creased in incomprehension. 'Bump?'

'Yeah, do you remember that time when I knocked my head on the larder door at Grampa's and I got that big lump on my head?'

Small smile. 'And Mom called you cone-head?'

Tom gave a mock frown. 'You *all* called me cone-head.'

The smile broadened. 'No, Grampa called you "rhino skull".'

'Anyway, your bump's special because it's on the inside. My bump hurt because it was like a big bruise. But yours hurts because it puts pressure on your brain. This gives you headaches at times, and makes you feel sick and dizzy.'

Holly frowned, but nodded slowly. 'How did I get it?'

'Well, with my bump it was my fault, because I banged my head into the top of the doorway. But your bump isn't your fault at all. You've been very unlucky. Something has gone wrong with some of the cells inside your head that makes them form a bump.'

'Why?'

'Imagine all the cells in your body are like schoolkids that have to behave in order to keep the body healthy. Occasionally, for no real reason, some of these kids disobey their teacher or parent. When this happens they disrupt all the other kids and cause a disturbance in our body . . .'

'And we get sick?'

'Right.'

'When will the bump go away?'

'Well, Holly, it won't go away by itself. And because it's inside it's difficult to get rid of. But don't worry, we will get rid of it. First of all we're going to give you medicines to reduce the swelling and limit the effect these bad kids are having. And then we might have to take the bump out.'

'Like sending the bad kids out of school?'

'Exactly. But you're going to have to be brave. The treatment isn't easy. And you'll have to stay in the hospital for a while.'

Holly cocked her head to one side. It was exactly the same mannerism Olivia used to adopt whenever she was thinking hard about something. 'Are *you* going to give me all the treatment?' she asked.

'If you like. Others will help, but I'll be your doctor.'

'And I can stay in the special hospital at your work?'

'Of course.'

She seemed to weigh up this information before giving a satisfied nod. Not only did she seem unafraid, but even a little excited. She'd always visited him at work. And had often gone into the ward to meet the patients. Now in a perverse way she seemed to look forward to *being* one of those special patients she'd seen him devote so much time to. This absolute trust made telling her easier, but at the same time the very real possibility of betraying that trust terrified him.

'It's not going to be easy,' he said again. Usually he had to urge patients to be positive after giving them the bad news, but in Holly's case he felt the need to temper her optimism.

She asked, 'Can Jennifer and Megan visit?'

'Sure.'

'And I can still use the computer?'

'Of course you can. As long as you feel up to it. We'll make sure you're fully connected with the best computer stuff Jazz can get hold of.'

Again she thought about this and nodded. 'And I'll see more of you?'

'Sure you will,' he said. 'Whenever you want me. Night or day. I'll be there.'

A WEEK LATER. BOSTON DETENTION CENTRE.

BY 24 APRIL MARIA HAD BEEN IN CUSTODY AT THE BOSTON DETEN-tion Centre for less than two weeks, but already she hated it. It wasn't so much the trial and probable death sentence, and she even found the interrogations by Karen Tanner a welcome diversion. What she hated was the loss of control. In her cell she couldn't keep the light on, exercise properly or shave her head. And because she wasn't allowed access to sharp edges of any kind she couldn't even relieve her stress with her customary blood-letting. So she kept herself together by focusing on her one imperative: getting out and stopping Dr Carter.

Her ankle manacles chafed as she shuffled into the interview room to speak with her expensive lawyer. She took her seat opposite Hugo Myers and stared at his styled silver-grey hair, and matching silver-grey suit. The man was in his forties and looked like an extra from some TV show, but the attorney was supposed to be good at what he did. Even if all he'd done so far was explain how *little* he could do without her co-operation. He had approached her only hours after her arrest, offering his services in exchange for nothing more than the attendant publicity. She hadn't even needed to dip into her Chase Manhattan account, set up for just such emergencies.

The guards manacled her hands to the ring on the table in front of her. She smiled at that. She may have lost control, but they at least still showed her respect.

After greeting her, Hugo Myers hammered away with the same question he'd been asking all week; the same question Special Agent Karen Tanner had been asking her.

'So,' he said, levelling his muddy eyes at her with the best sincerity money could buy, 'have you considered whether you're going to make the deal?'

'How can I? Like I told the FBI, I don't know what they're talking about.'

Hugo Myers raised an immaculate eyebrow, then made a steeple with his hands. 'Look, Maria, in case the Federal Bureau of Investigation wasn't explicit enough at the last meeting, let me clarify a few things. Scotland Yard has taken the Bureau to visit your London apartment. They've seen your unusual collection of weaponry, and the wigs and the make-up. But most importantly, they've read your neatly stacked pile of manila folders, containing detailed files on homicide victims over the last thirteen or so years. They've also got your custom-made pen nib and testimony from the only guy in your files who's still alive. This Dr Carter is a respected scientist who has given a statement outlining how you tried to kill him on two occasions, and how you killed his wife during the first attempt. This statement is corroborated by another eminent scientist, his colleague, Dr Washington. OK, so you weren't actually seen killing the four guards at GENIUS, but the bullets match your gun.

'Tomorrow you're going to have your DNA read at the FBI scanning facility. And if your genetic profile matches the DNA found at the Fontana murder scene, then the Feds can tie you to the Preacher's kills. Are you getting the picture here? I'm your defence lawyer, and even I think things look pretty bad. Basically unless we do a deal, you're gonna fry. From the detailed files the FBI found at your apartment they reckon you must have had some help. In fact they're convinced you were working for someone. And if you tell them who gave you the files, the DA has said he'll cut a deal.'

'But I wasn't working for anybody. Only God.'

Hugo Myers clenched his jaw and nodded slowly, plainly trying to maintain his composure. 'Maria, have you heard the soundbite: "Make the criminal pay, not the taxpayer"? It's the President's tagline for his Crime 2000 initiative. His war on crime was a big votewinner and most State Governors have embraced it. Do you realize that ninety-eight per cent of all murder trials since March 2000 have been completed on fast-track? That means taken less than two weeks. Your trial starts the day after

250

tomorrow, and will be over in ten days or less.

'But what should most concern you is the innovation over death row. The liberals have always branded waiting ten years or more to be killed as inhumane, and the far right have long squealed about the costs of keeping these "dead" people alive. So, now everyone's happy. The longest stay on the row since the new law was passed two years ago is thirty-seven days. This is justice McDonalds style. It's fast, satisfying, the same everywhere, and people love it.' Myers paused and levelled his muddy eyes at her again.

'Unless you co-operate, you could be dead within two months. Just tell them who you were working for, and I can probably do a deal to get you life.'

Maria frowned. She wouldn't betray the Brotherhood to these unbelievers. However weak Ezekiel had been, the Brotherhood was the only family she had known, and it still represented the one hope for protecting the righteous and finding the New Messiah. Betraying them wouldn't help her finish Dr Carter. Silently she called to her God for guidance.

'What if I plead not guilty?' she asked, enjoying the effect her question had on the frustrated counsellor.

The lawyer's eyes rolled and a sigh issued from his thin lips. 'Are you innocent? Despite all the evidence?'

'Innocent? In the eyes of God. Completely.'

'If your DNA scan tomorrow proves positive, then that is *not* how you'll be seen in the eyes of the State of Massachusetts.'

'I thought you were meant to defend me. Not just explain what might happen. Of course, if you don't want this high-profile case I can always find another lawyer.'

A resigned shrug from the silver-padded shoulders. 'Not guilty, huh?'

'I was never the guilty one. Certainly never as guilty as those I'm charged with killing. Anyway, I don't really care what the jury decides.'

'That's all right then,' said Hugo Myers, his voice as dry as tinder. 'Because if you plead not guilty, there's about as much chance of you getting off as there is of your being elected President.'

*   *   *

251

WHY THE HELL WAS NOTHING EVER SIMPLE? THOUGHT JASMINE, AS she reached across her desk for the Diet Coke. She put the ice-cold can to her forehead. She had run out of ideas. Whatever she tried she couldn't get any more data out of the 'Black Hole' in the minute allowed, other than the coded number and a small stretch of genome.

In the three weeks since Maria's arrest she had been busy giving evidence, and avoiding TV cameras. Larry had been great. When it came to handling fame and media interest his film producer contacts came to the fore. He had brought in one of his Hollywood press specialists to be Tom's and her spokesman, fielding all the press interest over her 'saving Dr Tom Carter's life', and the 'heroic capture of the Preacher by Nobel scientists'. Having the media channelled away from her had given her room to breathe, allowing her time to think through what had happened.

The Preacher aside, Jasmine still hadn't come to terms with the fact that she had now scanned every DNA database in existence and found *two* matches, including the recently deceased Al Puyiana. That was two out of five hundred million people. Given that the world population was about five billion, did that mean proportionately there were some twenty people walking the earth carrying Christ's genes? The chosen few were rare in the extreme, a minuscule percentage, but hardly unique. Which one was the *real* Messiah, if any of them was.

Jasmine had been wrestling with her faith. In the end she told herself that Christ had been unique for spiritual reasons, but by coincidence had also possessed these three genes. She knew this conveniently sidestepped the issue, but she'd intentionally distracted herself by working flat out on the search to find the identity of the match on the 'Black Hole' database.

She looked at the computer screen in front of her. So far she'd been able to get back into the 'Black Hole' and access file #6699784, but in the sixty seconds before the PREDATOR system traced her she hadn't had time to pull off the whole genome. She had tried to pull off new sections of the sequence, but each time she had gone back in she had only been able to access the sequence she already possessed. She certainly didn't have enough of the genome to do an appearance analysis and without the sex chromosomes she couldn't even identify the gender.

She opened the can and took a drink. Idly she tapped a few keys and called up IGOR. She hadn't checked the latest entries collected by Big Mother for at least a week. Without thinking she clicked on the icon containing the Nazareth genes and fed them into the IGOR UPDATE window, clicking the on-screen '*Match Sequence*' button. At the last minute she realized she hadn't imported the Nazareth genes icon at all, but the icon containing the incomplete #6699784 sequence she'd taken from the 'Black Hole'.

'Jeez,' she was even more screen-drunk than she thought. She moved the mouse but before she could press the cancel icon, '*Match Found*' suddenly flashed up on the screen.

'What?' That shouldn't have happened. The #6699784 sequence had been scanned weeks, months, even years ago, whereas the IGOR updates were scans done in the last few days. A cold clammy panic descended, as she realized what might have happened. Immediately she clicked on the Nazareth genes icon and inserted it into the IGOR UPDATE window. She crossed her fingers and watched the screen.

And waited.

'*Match Found*' flashed the words again.

Quickly she selected the matched genome and opened it. Seconds later the screen was filled with three pictures of the subject's face; left profile; full frontal; and right profile. Beneath the pictures was a name and personal details. The database title on the top of the screen told her that this was the exact same subject she'd located in the 'Black Hole'. But this barely registered on her brain as she stared at the face in front of her, a face she knew too well.

OVER IN THE HOSPITAL SUITE TOM DIDN'T KNOW WHETHER TO FEEL elated or depressed. This morning Hank Polanski was leaving the ward, to continue his impressive recovery at home. Tom saw how the other six patients took encouragement from his cure. He just wished that one of them – the newest arrival – wasn't Holly.

Hank Polanski went to each patient in turn to say goodbye and wish them well. He seemed painfully aware of how lucky he was to be able to leave this exclusive, close-knit club before he was forced to take out life membership.

'See ya Holly,' said Hank Polanski as he came to Holly's bed. Most of her beautiful blond hair had already fallen out from the first round of chemotherapy and she looked pale. 'You'll be OK.'

'Bye Hank,' smiled Holly bravely, returning his offered high five.

'And when I get stuck with Wrath of Zarg or my old DOOM games, I know who to ask for help,' said the twenty-three-year-old with a grin.

'Yeah right,' said Holly, trying to hold her tired smile.

Finally, Hank came to Tom and there were tears in his eyes. The young man began to say something, then thought better of it. He just reached for Tom's hand and shook it strongly. 'Thanks Doc. Thanks for everything.'

Tom smiled and patted his shoulder. 'Hank, this is what it's all about. It's a joy, a genuine joy to see you well again.' He meant it too. And as Hank and his mother left the ward to continue a life they thought had been lost to them, Tom turned his attention back to Holly.

Karl Lambert, the NIH neurosurgeon based at GENIUS, had advised immediate keyhole laser surgery, but the scan had shown Holly's tumour to be in a particularly inaccessible part of the brain. The risk of paralysis or worse from just one slip of the laser was great. So Tom had elected to try and slow the tumour's growth, buying time till Jasmine identified her match and Project Cana could be used. As well as chemo, this stalling strategy involved radiotherapy and some pro-drug therapy.

Even if these treatments worked they were at best holding measures, and he would have to operate eventually. But at least they bought him time to give Cana a chance of coming to the rescue.

He entered Holly's cubicle and sat on the bed beside her. 'How are you feeling, Holly?'

The brave smile Holly had flashed for Hank suddenly crumpled, and tears welled up in her eyes. 'Why can't I go home like Hank, Dad?'

Tom felt his heart squeeze deep inside him. Holly had reacted particularly badly to the radiotherapy, which had made her nauseous.

There were no other kids on the ward to keep her company, and now even the lively Hank had gone.

'It took time to make Hank well, Holly,' he soothed. 'And we need to keep you here to observe you, and ensure you get the right treatment.'

'But I hate it here,' she said, hurt and frustration flaring in her hazel eyes. As her voice got louder and the pitch higher, large tears rolled down her cheeks. 'If Mom was here, *she'd* let me go home.' Holly turned away from him and pushed her face into the pillow. 'I don't want to be sick,' she shouted into the linen, her small shoulders racked with her sobbing. 'I hate it. I hate it. I hate it.'

He leaned forward and put his hand on the back of her neck, stroking her. He sat there in silence for some moments, until gradually her sobbing calmed and her breathing became regular. Leaning forward, he kissed her. 'Holly, you will feel better soon. The tablets the nurse gave you earlier will start to work any moment now.'

Standing up, he told Holly he'd see her soon and headed for the atrium. Before he reached the door Jasmine came running into the ward, brandishing a printout in one hand and looking flushed.

She grabbed Tom by the arm and steered him through the still-swinging door into the deserted waiting-room. As soon as they were alone she passed him the folded printout and hissed. 'I've found out who our match is.'

'What? That's great!'

'Read it before you say it's great.'

He quickly unfolded the paper, then did a double take when he saw the face.

Jasmine muttered darkly, 'Your Ezekiel fellow's in for a bit of a surprise, isn't he?'

But Tom didn't say anything. He couldn't. He was so shocked he just stared at the paper in disbelieving silence.

23

GENIUS HEADQUARTERS, BOSTON.

AS THE LIMOUSINE TURNED INTO THE GENIUS CAMPUS EZEKIEL DE LA Croix twisted the ruby ring on his finger. He felt an uncomfortable blend of heady excitement and nervous apprehension. Were all his prayers going to be answered at last?

He disliked the pyramid of tinted glass as soon as he saw it. It was everything the Cave of the Sacred Light wasn't; brash, modern, bright and arrogant. There was no attempt to blend into the surrounding natural world. Unlike the Brotherhood's cave, which had been fashioned over centuries out of an existing space, this was overtly imposed on the green lawns of the GENIUS campus – a symbol of the scientist's insecure and vain need to dominate God's world.

De La Croix hadn't wanted to come, and Carter's unusual request that he forward one of his hair follicles in advance had done little to reassure him. However, Dr Carter had refused to give him any details of the match over the phone, so he had been obliged to make the visit. 'It's better we discuss this face to face,' the scientist had told him two days ago. 'You will understand why, when you come.'

Not only did he feel uncomfortable coming to his enemy's pagan temple, but the thought had also crossed his mind that it might be a trap. If Maria had betrayed him and the Brotherhood, then the best way for the authorities to arrest him would be for Dr Carter to invite

256

him here on American soil. He had discussed this with the Inner Circle and decided it was highly unlikely. After all, if they had been betrayed then the authorities would no doubt have already raided the cave. But being cautious he had asked Brother Helix to brief him on the scientific questions and had come alone. If there was a trap only he would be sacrificed. Brother Helix could then take over the Brotherhood's mission with Brother Bernard by his side.

He watched as the limousine, which had picked him up at Logan Airport, pulled up outside the main door. Carter was waiting on the gravel drive. Next to him was a young, black woman with a fine-featured face and a compact afro. He guessed this was Dr Washington.

On leaving the car he was greeted by his hosts and escorted briskly into the building. It was a Saturday and the marble-floored atrium was as quiet as a tomb. Despite his dislike of the exterior he couldn't help but be impressed by its airy grace. He was particularly drawn to the thirty-foot hologram in the middle of the atrium, with its double helix of multicoloured DNA spiralling up to the apex of the crystal pyramid. The beauty of its complex, iridescent hues contrasted starkly with the white purity of the sacred flame. As the glass elevator took them up past the mezzanine level to the next floor he was struck by the light and space of the interior.

Coming out of the lift he came to a glass door bearing the etched legend *'Mendel Laboratory Suite – Authorized Entry Only'*, where Ezekiel was introduced to Bob Cooke and Nora Lutz. 'Both have helped with analysing the Nazareth genes,' explained Carter. 'They wanted to meet you.'

'Is this the whole Cana team?' asked Ezekiel, indicating the four of them.

'Yes, I decided to keep it as discreet as possible.'

'Very wise,' he said with an approving nod. This would make it easier in the future, he thought. 'Very wise indeed.'

The scientist and his people then led him through the door into an alien landscape of glass tubes, spotless white workbenches, humming apparatus, blinking lights and alarming messages:

Warning! Biohazard.

Danger! – 180 degrees – Thermal gloves must be worn at all times.

Ethidium Bromide – avoid contact with skin.

This was a hostile environment, cold and unnatural. A brave new world he wanted no part of. He was relieved when Dr Carter finally ushered him through another door, marked *'Francis Crick Conference Room'*. Here he found a familiar conference table and chairs, a projection screen and a bizarre instrument, which sat like a mechanical swan in one corner. Two black circular pads lay on the floor in front of it.

He took a seat next to Bob Cooke, and accepted the coffee placed in front of him by Dr Washington.

'First of all, Mr De La Croix, thank you for coming,' began Carter. 'You will understand why I asked you to send the hair follicle in a second. But what we want to do now is take you through what we've found.' Jasmine Washington took over then and for the next half-hour explained how the black swan-like Genescope worked.

Ezekiel listened intently. Brother Helix had explained much of the basics already, but it was somehow more powerful hearing it here, in this bright, harsh place under the shadow of the strange swan. He was appalled by the power these people had at their disposal.

He said nothing when Jasmine finished, only opening his mouth in wonder, when the three-dimensional image of a man appeared before his eyes. At first he just marvelled at the magic of creating a seemingly solid image in this air, then to his shock he realized the young man with the small wiry physique was himself sixty years ago. He felt a twinge of sadness as he looked at this ghost of his younger self. A man he had known years ago, but who had long since disappeared.

'The hologram will show the subject at the age the cell came from the body. But DAN can extrapolate the data if we want the hologram to show a different age,' explained Jasmine. 'This is set to just over thirty years.'

'It's incredible,' he said quietly, convinced more than ever that Carter was dangerous. 'Truly incredible.'

Carter explained how the Genescope had found three new genes in the DNA of Christ's tooth. Ezekiel listened whilst the scientist outlined the properties of the so-called *naz 1* and *naz 2* genes, and the apparent inscrutability of the third gene. Carter then went on to explain how, because of the difficulty in understanding the genes, he was now committed to finding a match too. But before Ezekiel could probe on this, a second figure appeared on the other circular pad. This figure was taller than his hologram, with long brown hair and a narrow intelligent face. The brown eyes were wise, with a stare that haunted Ezekiel.

Dr Carter said, 'This is Jesus Christ aged in his early thirties; about the same as your hologram. The age when he was supposed to have been crucified.'

Ezekiel De La Croix stared for a moment in complete silence, unsure what to feel. Disgust that this atheist had recreated Christ's image? Or joy that he was the only Leader of the Brotherhood since the founder, to see the face of the original Messiah? 'You can do this just from the powder in his tooth?' he asked eventually.

'Yes,' said Carter softly. 'As we did with your hair.'

Ezekiel was almost as surprised at *how* he was able to see what he was seeing, as he was at the content. Carter had exceeded Icarus flying too close to the sun. He was manipulating the very essence of God. At that moment, although Carter sounded respectful, almost subdued, Ezekiel hated him. He understood why Maria had been so adamant in her need to stop the man's outrageous over-reaching. Carter hadn't just picked one of the forbidden fruit from the tree of knowledge, he had stripped every apple from its boughs.

Despite these thoughts Ezekiel De La Croix kept his face impassive, and focused on his reason for being here. 'What about the match? You said you had found one.'

A pause as Washington and Carter exchanged a worried look. 'We have found one live match,' said Carter eventually. 'But there's a problem.'

Ezekiel was surprised at the scientist's tone. 'A problem? How do you mean? Can't you find him?'

'No, we know exactly where the person is,' said Carter. 'But it's not quite as simple as that.'

'Let me explain,' volunteered Jasmine Washington, moving her seat nearer a black microphone at the end of table. 'I found the match on Interpol's DNA database. This is a loose relational database situated in Paris. It doesn't contain that much information itself, but it acts as a doorway to affiliated databases around the world. Scotland Yard, the FBI and all the major international police forces are linked to it. It is highly confidential and very well protected, because once inside it, you can access any individual stored on any police file in the world.

'To add a further level of security the genomes on this system are each allocated a code number. I actually found the match over three weeks ago, but I couldn't get to the name behind the coded number. Then last week the subject's DNA was scanned again. This time, because I'd asked our central computer to collect every new scan from our licensed Genescopes, the subject's genome was secretly sent to IGOR, as well as the Paris database.'

Ezekiel frowned. 'So, you've got the match. What's the problem?'

'The problem depends on your expectations.'

'What do you mean?'

'All individuals stored on this database are suspected, or convicted criminals.'

Silence.

Ezekiel felt numb for a moment, but the more he thought about it the more sense it made. Hadn't Christ been jailed? Hadn't the first Messiah been executed, crucified as a criminal?

He said, 'The first Messiah was so branded, and he was a righteous man.'

Jasmine cleared her throat and spoke into the microphone. 'Show the chart!' she ordered the computer.

Ezekiel was now breathing more calmly again, although his stomach ulcer still ached. He sat back and watched as an image slowly came into focus on the screen.

'This is our match,' said Jasmine quietly.

'No!' he heard himself exclaim, when the image finally appeared. All he could think, as he stared at the enlarged newspaper clipping unfurl on the screen, was that there must have been some awful mistake. This wasn't possible. He felt the acid boil in his stomach, making him reach for his white pills.

'I know it's a shock,' said Carter quickly. 'And I'm as horrified about it as you are. But the genes match perfectly, and they offer the only chance we know for developing a cure. We intend to obtain and examine blood samples, and develop viral serums from the subject's genes. We are also going to gain permission to examine the individual thoroughly, to try and determine how the genes work in the body. Naturally, whatever we find out we shall pass on to you. But, I hope you now understand why I felt it necessary to invite you over here, and present the match to you, face to face.'

Ezekiel could only give a weak nod. He understood better than Dr Carter could ever know. He felt the scientist looking at him, but he could not, dared not meet his gaze. Instead his eyes remained locked on the screen, mesmerized by the projected clipping taken from yesterday's *Boston Globe*. The bold headline read: 'THE PREACHER'S LAST SERMON?', with *'Death Sentence Now A Certainty'* printed beneath it. Below the words was a grainy picture of a tall, powerfully built woman being pushed into a police car, her intense eyes looking straight into the camera, her once-shaven head now covered in fine stubble.

Ezekiel was suddenly reminded of his Pontius Pilate nightmare; of him standing by whilst the Messiah he had dedicated his life to saving was executed. And an involuntary shudder rippled through his tired, old body.

THREE DAYS LATER. MASSACHUSETTS SUPREME COURT.

'WILL THE DEFENDANT PLEASE RISE FOR THE VERDICT,' SAID JUSTICE Sancha Hernandez, turning from the jury to Maria Benariac. Maria didn't like the Justice. She reminded her of the toad back at the orphanage in Corsica. Like Mother Clemenza, Justice Hernandez was a big-bosomed, deep-voiced woman with large spectacles. And like the Mother Superior she had hard, flinty eyes that now bored right into hers.

Justice Hernandez had consistently prevented Hugo Myers' attempts to open up the trial, and explore the conspiracy theory of Maria being in the pay of some government agency. The media may have bought, and sold the story of the vigilante in the pay of the CIA, but not Hernandez. And she had made sure that the jury didn't buy it either. She had stuck rigorously to the core issue and not a day had gone by without her bashing out her guidance with self righteous zeal:

'This trial is to determine the defendant's guilt or innocence of the forty-two alleged homicides on US soil. It is *not* to speculate on what may, or may not have motivated those who may, or may not have paid the defendant to perform these said murders. That is a subject for another investigation and another trial. Is that *clear?*'

It had become so crystal-clear that the Justice had not only eased the District Attorney's job, but made it virtually redundant. As Hugo Myers had warned Maria, the evidence was damning. The match from the DNA found on the roses at Fontana's apartment had been irrefutable. The weapons and folders in her apartment, along with her tell-tale biblical messages written in the victims' blood, had linked her to the other deaths in the US. But the real clincher had been the killing of the GENIUS guards, and the testimony from Dr Carter and Dr Washington. The argument from the prosecution was barely required. Keeping the excellent but beleaguered Hugo Myers to the facts had sufficed to condemn Maria.

When Maria saw the small oriental-looking man stand in front of his fellow jurors, nervously brandishing a piece of paper, she already knew what verdict the foreman would give.

'On the count of first-degree murder for the killing of Sly Fontana, the jury finds Maria Benariac . . . *Guilty as charged*,' the foreman said, echoing the words in Maria's own head. Then, one by one, like a rogue's gallery of evil, the names of the other victims were read out: Helmut Kroger the arms dealer; Santino Luca the mobster; Bobby Dooley the corrupt evangelist. And after each one the foreman concluded with the same three words . . . *Guilty as charged*.

When the foreman reached Olivia Carter's name, Maria turned to the gallery and caught the scientist's eye. Carter was sitting between his partner, Jack Nichols and Dr Washington. They had only been in the court once before, to testify. Expecting Dr Carter to gloat she smiled defiantly at him, but was surprised to see his face tired and gaunt, his blue eyes dulled. It was bizarre how now, when she was about to be sentenced to death, he looked defeated. When she had held a gun to his head, he had been strong and unbowed.

As the verdict was given, a brief stirring raced like wildfire round the reporters and spectators, but it soon burned out. This verdict was no surprise. Hugo Myers, professional to the end, put a hand on Maria's shoulder in a show of support, as if there was something he could have done. But Maria ignored him and said loudly to judge and jury, 'I am innocent in the eyes of God.'

There was another excited murmur from the spectators before the Justice gavelled them into silence and proceeded to read out Maria's sentence.

Maria didn't register all Justice Hernandez's long speech, but key phrases: *sadistic killer – menace to society – set an example – Crime 2000 – fast-track death penalty* rang out clearly. The only detail she needed was the timeframe. Myers had explained how the Crime 2000 initiative had put an end to the costly and 'inhumane' appeal procedures which could see a prisoner languishing on death row for ten to twenty years. But she hoped her execution wouldn't be too soon. She still had God's work to do. She still had to stop Carter and his Project Cana.

When the Justice announced the date of execution, it took Maria a second to realize its proximity. And as the two guards stepped forward to return her to her cell, she looked back at Carter.

Flashing her most defiant smile, she raised both manacled arms and pointed at him. 'Those that escaped His vengeance have only delayed the inevitable,' she shouted through the noise of the crowd, 'for they have already been judged in a higher court than this.' She wanted him to know that it wasn't over, that she would still be coming for him. But to her genuine surprise Dr Carter's expression remained impassive; no triumph; no fear; no anger; nothing. She couldn't understand it. He had just heard his wife's killer sentenced to death, with the execution set for less than four weeks' time. But he just stared at her, not a trace of satisfaction showing on his stony face.

At that moment, Maria thought he looked more like the condemned prisoner than she did.

TOM WATCHED MARIA'S STUBBLY HEAD AS SHE WAS LED AWAY. Oblivious to the noise and bustle of everyone around him standing to leave, he sat back on the hard wooden chair, two rows back in the spectators' gallery, and tried to figure it all out.

Over the last week, ever since Jasmine had told him the identity of the match Tom had been trying to understand what it all meant. And as he thought about it again he ended with the same questions: *How the hell am I supposed to understand that my wife's killer might be my daughter's saviour? Where's the sense or meaning in that? Why couldn't it have been the Indian, or some other obviously good person?*

They had searched the world for a person who possessed three of the rarest genes in existence; genes originally found two thousand years ago in a man of unquestionable goodness. Now these genes which promised to save countless lives, hadn't been found in a person of similar vision and greatness, but a ruthless killer.

Tom had always accepted the lottery of Nature, but this was too much even by his standards. This looked more like mischievous intent. No wonder the old man Ezekiel De La Croix had been so shocked. The Messiah he had devoted his life to finding had been unveiled as a mad fanatic who believed she was put on this earth to kill, not to save.

What was it that Maria had said to him when she was captured? 'God tests us all.'

He bent his head and stared at the scuffmarks in the polished wooden floor below him. He failed to think of something positive in all this. He had acquired blood samples from Maria's medical examination, and even read her detailed doctor's report, but no clues had been yielded from her genes. And without her co-operation he wasn't going to find any either.

Of course there was still a chance that IGOR would eventually pick up one of the other nineteen or so people in the world who possessed all three Nazareth genes. But the odds of one of them being scanned and picked up in the next few weeks were infinitesimal. Tom had to face facts. As far as helping Holly was concerned Maria was in effect unique.

'Let's go, Tom,' said Jasmine softly beside him, resting a hand on his shoulder. 'Jack's arranged for us to go out through the chambers to avoid the press.'

He stood and allowed her to lead him to the front of the court-room. He thought again of the mysterious but apparently useless serum developed from the combined Nazareth genes, and the risks of the inevitable brain surgery for Holly. The bitter taste of nausea caught in his throat. Short of begging Maria to try and heal his daughter, these were the only options open to him now.

As they passed the witness chair Jack appeared on his left.

'Tom, it's not over yet.'

He turned to his friend and shook his head. 'Isn't it, Jack?'

Without the distracting glimmer of hope the future seemed clear to him. Project Cana was dead, and soon, surely, Holly would be too.

24

GENIUS HOSPITAL SUITE, BOSTON.

HOLLY LOST ALL FEELING DOWN HER LEFT SIDE ON 12 MAY, FOUR DAYS after Maria was sentenced. The seizure lasted over two hours. Tom could see it frightened her more than all the pain and sickness she had endured till then. The pro-drug and radiotherapy had slowed the tumour's growth but it was still growing at a rate that unnerved him. The pressure it exerted on her brain was now affecting some of her motor functions. Steroids reduced the swelling and seizures, but he knew its effects would only worsen.

The tumour was entering the fourth and final stage of clonal evolution; the key genes on Chromosome 9 had long since been lost, as had a whole copy of Chromosome 10. The pace of growth had been almost three times faster than DAN's most optimistic estimate of one year, and more or less in line with its most pessimistic. Tom had originally ignored the gloomiest prognosis, telling himself he would find a way to buy the maximum time, but now when he considered the breaks he'd been getting it seemed bitterly appropriate that this should have happened.

He was fighting the old enemy, cancer, and it was winning. And this time the battleground was his daughter. He had to consider Holly's comfort above everything, even fighting the disease. The treatment he was giving her now made her feel weak and sick, and it wasn't even going to save her.

The conflict between Tom as her father and as a surgeon had become agonizingly simple. He had to either help her to live, or help her to die, and forget everything in between.

'YUCH. GREAT GRAPHICS.' JASMINE LEANED FROM HER CHAIR NEXT to Holly's bed to look at the computer on her goddaughter's lap. The warrior queen on screen was being eaten by a two-headed troll. 'So you can't get beyond level six, eh?'

Two days had passed since the last seizure and Holly was sitting up in bed, enjoying one of her rare good days. 'I can get into the castle, kill all the orcs and the blue dragon. But when I come out again I always get got by the troll or the huge seasnake in the moat. Every time.'

'Have you picked up all medical creds in the secret compartments?'

'I think so. And the hidden weapons and the extra armour. But what I need is invulnerability. And there's no magic potion in the castle.'

'You've looked everywhere?'

'Everywhere.'

'And you've tried everything?'

'Yup.'

Jasmine smiled. 'How about cheating?'

Holly gave a resigned shrug. 'Impossible. Every one knows that Wrath of Zarg is the one computer game with no cheat codes.'

'You mean no *published* cheat codes.' Jasmine knew that every games programmer put in shortcuts that allowed them to have unlimited firepower, lives, or invulnerability at the press of a particular combination of keys. With most games like Doom or Dark Forces these cheat codes were discovered by hardened gamers and passed around on the Internet. But according to Holly no-one had yet been able to crack the Wrath of Zarg cheat codes. 'Hey, move up, will you. And pass the laptop.'

Holly budged up on the bed and Jasmine sat next to her. Holly smiled when she gave her the computer. 'You think you can find 'em?'

'Uh huh. I might not be a fairy godmother, but I'm the next best thing: a cyber godmother.'

Holly giggled. 'OK, bet you can't find them in an hour.'

Razor Buzz's fingers were already dancing on the keys. 'Hey, don't insult me. We're talking *minutes* here.'

Holly cocked her head to one side for a moment, as if thinking. 'OK. How about ten minutes? Bet you can't find them in ten minutes.'

Jazz's fingers stopped their tapping. 'Right, what do you want?'

Holly looked at her and then at the screen. Her eyes were round with disbelief. 'You've done it *already*?'

Jasmine gave a modest shrug and handed back the laptop. 'Sure, no big deal. For invulnerability you need to press N*PAIN. Try it.'

Holly entered the code and found that her warrior queen was indeed troll-proof. 'Wow. Awesome.' Within three minutes she was looking up with a triumphant grin on her face. 'Level seven. Wait till Jennifer and Megan hear about this.'

Jasmine laughed. 'Just don't use it all the time, otherwise it'll get boring. To toggle it off just press control P. OK?'

'Yeah, thanks, Jazz. This is great. But how did you do it?'

Jasmine put her hand on Holly's shoulder. 'There's always a way, Hol. Like your Dad used to keep telling me. Still does at times. It might not be the obvious, popular or even correct way. But if you want to do something bad enough, there's always a way.'

Nurse Beth Lawrence appeared from the direction of the operating room. 'Dr Washington, could you see Dr Carter for a moment? He's in the examination room.'

'Sure.' She stood and squeezed Holly's arm. 'Good luck with level seven.'

WHEN SHE ENTERED THE EXAMINATION ROOM SHE FOUND TOM standing with Dr Karl Lambert, looking at a series of Computed Tomographic Scans on the computer screen in front of them. Lambert was a neurosurgeon from the National Institutes of Health in Maryland. He had been seconded to GENIUS to facilitate the sharing of ideas, and to ensure that no patients were abused by GENIUS for pure commercial gain. He was a short, round man with a jovial face, curly red hair and intelligent eyes. Jasmine knew Tom liked and respected him, since they had both studied together at Johns Hopkins.

Karl Lambert pointed at the yellow shadow on the colour scan. 'I still say an operation is the best chance.'

Tom shook his head. 'But look where the tumour is, Karl. I wouldn't want to go in there. Would you? The margin of error is too great.'

'I know, but at least it gives her a chance . . .' said Lambert.

'But of what? Delaying the inevitable.'

'It'll make her more comfortable, Tom.'

'Or kill her.' Tom paused, his shoulders seemed to sag. 'But I suppose you're right.'

She cleared her throat and they both looked up from the scan of Holly's brain. Tom looked pale and drawn. He was clearly wrestling with what was best for Holly, and was losing. 'Hi, Jazz, thanks for coming. I just wanted to ask your advice about Holly.'

Lambert checked his watch. 'I've got to go. I'm due in sutgery in ten minutes. I'll leave you two to it.' He walked to the door, then turned back to Tom. 'I still say keyhole laser surgery is mandatory, Tom. And the sooner the better.' He smiled at Jasmine, then left.

'So what do you want to do, Tom?' she asked.

He paced around the room. 'I don't know. You heard Karl. And he's right. Drugs and radiotherapy can only slow the growth and manage her pain. Eventually the tumour will have to be removed, just to relieve the pressure on her skull. But it's in such a goddamned difficult place it's almost inoperable.'

'What about Cana? The serum?'

'Cana's finished, Jasmine. The serum does nothing.'

She took a deep breath. 'What about Maria Benariac then? The Preacher?'

'The Preacher isn't an option,' said Tom stiffly.

Since Jasmine had found that the Preacher possessed the genes, she and Tom hadn't once discussed the killer together. Jasmine still hadn't got her mind round the full implications that there were probably twenty people in the world with Christ's genes, let alone the fact that one of them was a cold-blooded murderer. And since Tom had found it far too painful to talk about, they had just let it hang between them like a death in the family. But it was becoming too important to ignore, and since he'd started the whole damn thing, he might as well face up to it.

'Surely, you've got to at least try?' she said.

'She killed Olivia, Jazz.'

'She could also save Holly.'

He gave a snort. 'Yeah, right.'

'Come on, Tom, you might be able to do some sort of deal with her.'

'Are you being serious?'

'Deadly serious. I don't exactly see you being overburdened with options. Don't you even want to find out if this woman *could* save her?'

He shrugged his shoulders unhappily.

She felt a stab of anger. 'Tom, it's not like you to give up.'

'I'm not giving up. I'm being realistic, trying to find the best way to make Holly comfortable.'

'*Bullshit!* You once told me that being realistic and giving up were the same thing. You've never been realistic in your life. You're *crap* at being realistic. Jack's a realist. Even I am to an extent. But you've always gone off and done the impossible. Don't for God's sake stop now!'

Tom gave her a pained look. 'But you don't understand, Jazz. How can I—'

'Look, you started this Project Cana thing. I wanted no part of it, because I was terrified where it might lead. But I trusted you and let you talk me into it, believing that however much this screwed up what I believed in, at least I was doing everything to help Holly. All through this I've been trying to square circles with my conscience just to keep sane, and now you're chickening out because you've come across something *you* find hard to accept. Well, buster, welcome to the land of confusion and doubt. And don't tell me I don't understand. Go tell your daughter. Tell Holly you feel *uncomfortable* about begging Maria to help her.' She took a deep breath, her tirade had made her dizzy. She pointed her finger and jabbed his chest. 'And another thing, Tom. You better stop feeling sorry for yourself damn soon, because it's not just Holly whose days are numbered. Maria won't be around for too long either.'

With that, she turned and walked out.

MARIA WOKE IN A COLD SWEAT. SHE OPENED HER EYES IN THE CELL on death row but could see nothing. Only blackness. Her fevered, half-awake brain imagined she heard rats scurrying on the floor beneath her bed. She was a six-year-old child again, in the orphanage lock-away for telling lies, or for some other misdemeanour she didn't understand.

The panic pressing down on her chest with the heavy darkness was exactly as she remembered it. She yearned for someone to comfort her and soothe away her terror. But most of all she missed the Father. She felt a sickening doubt deep in her stomach. Not doubt over the killings, because they had been righteous. But doubt for defying Ezekiel and the Brotherhood.

What if Ezekiel really hadn't wanted her to kill Carter? What arrogance had possessed her to believe that she understood his real wishes better than he did himself; the man who had taught and given her everything? Perhaps Ezekiel was right to listen to Helix and use Carter, before finally finishing him. Had she succeeded in halting the scientist her way? And even if she had been right to try, how did she expect to fulfil God's plans in here?

All of the confidence and conviction that had so buoyed her throughout the trial evaporated. Perhaps God *didn't* have plans for her at all? Perhaps this imprisonment and death sentence weren't a test, but a punishment? Perhaps God was working through the Father to find the New Messiah *and* stop Carter? Perhaps Ezekiel and Helix had been completely right, and she completely wrong?

And now she was to be forsaken, forgotten, unforgiven.

As these questions ran around her brain on spiked shoes, her nails picked at her right thigh, at the old scabs and scars until the first warm dampness told her fingers that the blood was flowing. But in this darkness she felt no release. It seemed as if no amount of shed blood could drain the anxiety, guilt and loneliness from her body. Beyond the unseen cell walls, in the light and bustle outside, she had ceased to exist. She had been abandoned in this nine foot by fifteen foot cell on death row; the only marooned inhabitant of a desolate world filled with darkness and despair.

The first tear touched her cheek when she considered that even during her worst moments as a child the dreaded spells in the lock-away would end. But this time she was in a lock-away for ever, alone with her doubts and regrets. Only death in twenty-two days would set her free.

She only wished she could see the Father once again before then.

* * *

ACROSS THE WORLD IN DAMASCUS, EZEKIEL DE LA CROIX SLEPT NO
better. At 5:37 he rose and walked from his bedroom on to the
balcony, savouring the coolness of the smooth tiles under his bare feet.
In the distance the Damascus skyline was grey against the dusty
orange sky of early dawn. The sun would not rise fully for at least an
hour, but the frangipani-scented air was already warm. Stretching his
arms above aching shoulders he yawned twice, thankful for the slight
breeze that ruffled his white cotton nightshirt, and cooled his skin.

Last night he had dreamed again of Pontius Pilate. But this time
it was Maria into whose hands he had hammered the nails. As he did
so the hologram of his younger self had looked on in judgement. The
dream had unsettled him, but not as much as the memories;
memories of stories told to him years ago in Corsica.

Since Dr Carter had unveiled the truth that Maria possessed the
genes, Ezekiel had been struggling to believe that she could be the
one. His first reaction had been to deny it, put it down to the scientist's imperfect technology, or some trick of the Devil. How could
Nemesis be the New Messiah?

When he had told Helix and Bernard back at the cave the next day,
they had both been stunned. Like him, Bernard had scoffed, saying
it must be some kind of trick. Helix had responded differently. He
had stayed silent for a long while before entertaining the possibility,
even probability, that she was indeed chosen. Ezekiel had sent them
away to think through the implications and consider what must be
done. Then he had summoned all of the Inner Circle to a meeting
today, to decide the best course of action.

Ezekiel checked his watch. It would take him some hours to
prepare and reach the Cave of the Sacred Light. At least after his restless night he had finally come to a decision.

He remembered the young woman in Mother Clemenza's office,
no more than a girl really, confused and betrayed by a religion that
had not only failed to protect her, but actually abused her. When
Maria had finally been nominated as the new Nemesis she had done
what no other operative had ever done before. She had changed her
appearance to fit the role of the perfect avenger.

He recalled the day she had demanded the radical surgery; when
she'd sat down and explained how she felt trapped by her looks. Like

271

a butterfly wanting to be a caterpillar she longed to lose her bright wings and gain the freedom of anonymity.

At his first meeting with Mother Clemenza he had berated her for allowing girls in her charge to be preyed upon by Father Angelo, holding her directly responsible for Sister Delphine's suicide. She had told him of Maria's early 'lies' to explain why she had ignored Maria's claims of having been raped. 'She was always lying as a small child,' the Mother Superior had said. 'They were always lying.'

Only now did he realize for the first time that Maria's early 'lies' weren't just the fantasies of a lonely child, but were perhaps true. He could still recall them, small miracles in themselves: the big fall; the bee-stings; the diabetes; and at least six others. The more he thought about them the more bizarre sense everything seemed to make.

He turned and walked through the bedroom to the bathroom, and as he passed the bureau took a white tablet from the silver box beside the photograph of his wife. Deep in his heart he felt sure that the New Messiah had been found. But how was he going to rescue her before she was crucified again? And how was he going to gain the support of the others, to plan how to save her, so she in turn could save the righteous?

AS TOM CARTER TOOK ONE LAST LOOK AT HIS SLEEPING DAUGHTER and left the ward, he remembered Jasmine's words. She was right; he couldn't afford to feel sorry for himself. His scheduled meeting with Karen Tanner was in just over half an hour. Jack had arranged for her to show him the relevant files at her offices in the JFK Building downtown. And after he'd seen them he planned to do some investigating of his own.

Bob Cooke's shout across the atrium took him by surprise as he walked towards the garage stairs. The usually laid-back Californian was running towards him. 'Tom! Wait up!'

He turned, smiling at two rookie GENIUS scientists, who greeted him with a reverential 'Morning, Dr Carter,' as they passed.

'I've been . . . looking for you . . . everywhere,' panted Bob, crouching hands on knees, like a spent sprinter.

'Well, you've found me now. What's up?'

'The mice . . .'

'What about them?'

The winded Bob began to try and speak again, then shook his head and grabbed Tom's elbow. 'Come up!' he said, steering Tom towards the elevator. 'I'll show you.'

Upstairs in the Mouse House Tom found Nora Lutz standing over two cages. She kept looking at the notes on the clipboard in front of her, then looking back at the cages and shaking her head.

'What's happening, Nora?' asked Tom, pointing at Bob behind him. 'Surf boy here can barely talk.'

'It's the mice,' said Nora.

'What about them?'

Nora pointed at the three cages in front of her. 'They're clear.'

Tom did a double-take. 'What? You mean cured?'

Nora shrugged, as if she couldn't believe it herself. 'It seems that the Trinity serum has cured them of all their cancers.'

'All the mice have been cured?' Tom repeated, not trusting his ears.

'No, not all of them. That's the weird thing. You remember how the first tests used single isolated mice, and every time we tried the Trinity serum it showed no benefit?'

Tom nodded impatiently.

'Well, for the most recent trial we used some batches of two and three mice to a cage. And in these batches the treated mice were all cured of their cancers.'

'And the single mice?'

'No better than the control batches. Still diseased.'

'What's the difference between the two batches?'

Again the shrug of incomprehension from Nora. 'None. Except for the fact that the deceased were solus and the cured were in pairs or groups of three.'

'So we don't know why they've been cured?'

Bob said, 'No, not yet. But we do know it's not a fluke. The numbers are too consistent.'

Tom walked over to the cage nearest Nora and stared at the three healthy mice, which only days ago had been visibly ill. 'This is great. But it's only useful if we can understand how it happened.'

Bob smiled and said, 'We're investigating that now.'

Tom checked his watch. For a moment he considered calling Karen Tanner and postponing their meeting. But there wasn't much he could do here, over and above what Nora and Bob would do anyway. He turned to leave. 'I've got to go now, but I'll lend you a hand when I come back.'

'Where are you going?' asked Bob.

'To do some investigating of my own.'

THE INNER CIRCLE WERE ALREADY SEATED ROUND THE VAST TABLE when Ezekiel De La Croix arrived at the Cave of the Sacred Light. He felt the tension as their hushed whispering ceased. All rose as he approached the table. The incandescent flame in front of the altar was at least a foot taller than usual and burned whiter and brighter than before.

He greeted Brother Haddad first, 'May he be saved.'

'So he may save the righteous,' responded the Regional Head of the Holy Lands. His heavy eyelids were darker than usual as his hands clasped Ezekiel's in the ritual crossed handshake.

Next Ezekiel greeted the rest of the circle: the tall, silver-haired Brother Luciano, Head of the Brotherhood in Christendom; the sallow-skinned Brother Olazabal, Head of the Brotherhood in the New World; and finally the Champions of the Primary and Secondary Imperatives. All looked grim, and none, save Brother Helix, would meet his eye.

He began by recapping on the key points. He outlined Project Cana and the deal with Dr Carter; Maria's attempt to kill the scientist; her subsequent capture and sentence. Finally he reminded them of Dr Carter's crucial discovery that Maria Benariac, known to them as Nemesis, possessed the three genes of Christ; in effect implying that she was the New Messiah. Ezekiel stated this last point as a fact. It was at this stage that the objections started.

Not surprisingly Brother Bernard led them.

'It must be a mistake,' the stout Brother said bluntly. 'Or a trick. Nemesis can't be the one. You and I have known her for over twenty years. We would have known.'

'Why?' asked Ezekiel calmly.

'Father, she's a killer, not a saviour. She was an excellent tool of the Secondary Imperative, but certainly not the subject of the Primary.'

'Why not?' Ezekiel probed again.

'She's an assassin.'

'A trained killer,' endorsed Haddad from the other end of the table.

'Trained by *us*,' reminded Ezekiel. 'And all her kills were right-eous, sanctioned by *us*. Who shall say that the New Messiah should be a meek evangelist, and not a scourge of evil sent by God to avenge his Son's death?'

'But she doesn't meet the ancient signs,' objected Brother Olazabal.

Ezekiel scowled at that. It was clear that they had already agreed a policy in his absence, no doubt led by Bernard. 'What signs? Do you mean the three guidelines laid down by our founder?'

The usually quiet Luciano answered, 'Yes. The signs clearly state that the New Messiah will be righteous, of the correct age and *male*.'

'But they were only ever guidelines. She isn't male, but Maria is certainly righteous; so righteous she defied our expedient deal with the scientist. And as for the age, I don't know her precise birth date, but it's very close to the same day the flame changed colour thirty-five years ago. And don't forget she possesses the rare genes of our Lord. Plus I know of abilities she had as a young child.'

'But we have no proof of those abilities,' exclaimed Bernard. 'And I say again, I have known her for twenty years. I cannot believe she's the one. I'd have known.'

Ezekiel sighed. He could order them all to do his bidding, but that would be highly unsatisfactory. This issue was fundamental to the Brotherhood; ultimately they had to *believe* in the need to save Maria.

It was then that the Champion of the Primary Imperative spoke.

'Brother Bernard,' said Helix casually. 'Do you have any proof that Maria *isn't* the chosen one?'

Until now Helix had been silent, his bald head turning from speaker to speaker, his eyes magnified behind the round wire-rimmed spectacles, watching the proceedings. He turned his gaze upon Bernard and Ezekiel could see the countless candles that lit the cavern reflected in his thick lenses.

'Of course not,' replied Bernard.

'But you are convinced that she *can't* be the New Messiah?'

Bernard crossed his arms. 'Yes.'

'You are utterly certain?'

'Yes. As I can be.'

'So, when Maria is executed in three weeks' time you will sleep in

275

peace? No doubt will cross your mind that after a wait of two thousand years we perhaps let the New Messiah die on our watch . . . on *your* watch. You will take that responsibility, because you are sure she can't be the one. Is that right?'

Bernard said nothing, but nodded. Ezekiel could see that the others were now shuffling nervously in their seats.

'I envy your certainty,' said Helix softly.

'I've known Maria for twenty years,' repeated Brother Bernard by way of protest. 'She can't be the one.'

Helix nodded slowly. 'You would have known earlier?'

'Exactly.'

'Even if she didn't know herself? Still doesn't know?'

Silence.

Helix paused to let his point sink in before continuing. 'Don't forget the prophecy. This time the Messiah will not know his or her calling. We, the Brotherhood, have to find them to inform them of their destiny. And then help them fulfil it.'

'Yes, but Maria will be executed.'

'Then perhaps we should try and stop that.'

Bernard laughed and looked to Ezekiel, but the Leader said nothing. He was happy to let Helix argue his case for him. 'But,' protested Bernard looking for support from the others, 'the Brotherhood can't risk its very existence rescuing Maria, just on the chance she might be the one.'

'I disagree,' said Helix evenly. 'The whole point of our existence is to risk everything to save the New Messiah. That's why we're here.'

'I agree,' blurted Brother Luciano, suddenly changing his mind. 'And what is the harm in trying to save her?'

Bernard turned and glared at him.

Haddad blinked his heavy lids. 'The risk of exposure, even if Maria isn't the one, must surely be less than the risk of letting our New Messiah die. So perhaps we should save her? Just to be sure.'

Bernard looked around the table, knowing the argument had turned against him. 'So now you all want to give Maria the benefit of the doubt?'

The others nodded.

Ezekiel chose his words carefully before he spoke. 'Brother

Bernard, are you still adamant that she can't be the New Messiah? It is important that we act as one, and we particularly need your expertise if we are to achieve what we need to. Have you no doubt at all?'

The fat Brother sat back then, milking this face-saving moment, before nodding magnanimously. 'Yes, of course I have doubts. The possibility exists, certainly.'

'I'm glad you share our concerns,' said Ezekiel solemnly. 'But what worries me is how to act.'

'It will be a delicate operation,' said Bernard with a frown.

'Do you think we can do it?' asked Helix respectfully, clearly taking his cue from Ezekiel.

Bernard nodded sagely. 'Through our Brethren within America, I think we can find a way. But, what about Carter?'

Ezekiel reached into his robe and pulled out a slip of paper. On it were four names; the top one was Tom Carter's. 'Now the scientist has done our bidding the Righteous Kill can go ahead as planned. You can tell Gomorrah immediately.' He handed the paper to Brother Bernard. 'According to Dr Carter this is the whole Project Cana team. They have been working in secret, and nobody else has been involved in the technical side of it. Kill them all, and you will kill the blasphemy of Cana. It will be what Maria, our Messiah, wanted.'

Bernard nodded. 'Very well, I will contact Gomorrah today. And I will start planning Maria's rescue as soon as this meeting is over.' He turned then and looked down the table. 'Brother Olazabal, I will need the relevant names of Brethren in the US.'

'You will have them,' replied the Head of the Brotherhood in the New World.

Ezekiel now addressed all the three regional heads. 'If any of you have ideas, speak to Bernard. Otherwise, return to your regions and tell the Brethren that the time for searching and waiting may be over. Prepare them for when they may be called on to anoint the New Messiah. Soon she may be walking the world as the saviour of mankind.'

Wide-eyed, they nodded in assent.

'Good,' said Ezekiel. 'If there is no other business, then I suggest we get to work. I for one need to give our New Messiah the tidings.'

He stood, crossed his arms and said:

'May *she* be saved.'

The others rose in unison, crossed their arms and chorused as one.

'So *she* may save the righteous.'

25

CORSICA.

CARTER CHECKED THE ADDRESS IN THE FBI FILE ON THE PASSENGER seat beside him, then looked back to the winding road ahead. He turned the hired Peugeot convertible into the next bend and was rewarded with his first sight of the single turret dominating the skyline.

Below, to his right, the Mediterranean glowed apricot-pink as a dying, overripe sun bled into the horizon. In the rear-view mirror he could see the medieval citadel of Calvi towering over the terracotta-topped buildings that studded the contours of the large sandy bay.

The day was almost over, but the air was still mild and he was grateful for the convertible. It felt good to drive and enjoy the caress of warm sun on his skin. At that moment he thought of Olivia and he felt the touch of sadness.

Three days ago, Karen Tanner had told him all she knew about the killer, and passed him copies of the more relevant files. He had been disheartened at first, because everything Karen had told him and everything he had read in the files pointed to only one thing: that Maria was highly skilled at *taking* lives. Nothing had even hinted that she had any desire, let alone ability, to *save* them. He had determined to probe further back into her past.

Karen had warned him that the Preacher wasn't interested in

doing deals. But yesterday Tom had visited the state Governor, Lyle Mellish, to see what bargaining chips he could gain. Governor Mellish had been a friend for many years, and was as straight as a politician could ever be. Tom had also cured his grandson of cystic fibrosis, which helped. When Tom had asked how likely it was that Maria's death sentence could be postponed or commuted to life, Mellish had stressed that her death penalty was written in stone, and nothing short of a miracle could change it. 'Look Tom, I'm here on a crime and punishment ticket,' he'd said. 'That's what's sexy. I can't be seen to be being soft on one of the most notorious killers of recent times. Can I?'

'Would your electorate thank you for helping put away even bigger killers?' Tom had asked calmly. 'Such as cancer, heart disease and possibly many more?'

Mellish had pricked up his ears at that. 'Depends. What exactly are you talking about?'

When Tom had explained about the healing genes in general terms, including the fact that Maria Benariac possessed them, Mellish had been flustered.

'What exactly do you need?' he had asked eventually after pacing around his office at least five times.

'I need unrestricted access to her, and if necessary permission to conduct tests.'

'Is that all?'

'I also need to be able to offer her something to co-operate.'

'Like what?'

'Her death sentence commuted to life?'

'You've got to be kidding. Tom, she killed Olivia, for Christ's sake.'

Sharp intake of breath. 'I'm aware of that. I've got to offer her *something*. Or she'll have no reason to help.'

A pause. 'She would have to do something big to justify her death sentence being commuted. *Before* her execution date.'

'How about curing a terminally ill patient?'

A nod. 'That would do it.'

'Good. I'm demanding no less.'

With the Governor's deal in his pocket he had taken the next flight to Paris, and then to here: Calvi, Corsica.

He turned the Peugeot around the next corner and caught his first complete sight of the grey, Gothic building beneath the looming turret. It sent an involuntary shiver down his spine. A cross between Colditz and the Bates Motel. Not an appealing place to spend one's childhood.

The large gates were open but the grounds looked deserted. He turned into the driveway and up to the main house. The tall dark windows were broken and the maquis had run wild, not only invading the gravel drive, but creeping up the walls as well. A yellow earthmover, a stack of bricks and other building equipment were piled outside the large french windows to the right of the imposing front door. A brand new construction sign indicated that L'Hôtel Napoleon was due to open on this site in the summer of 2004.

The orphanage had closed down five or so years ago, but the staff at Europcar, where he'd hired the Peugeot, had told him that an old woman, who once had something to do with the orphanage, still lived there. She had been working the gardens over the last few years and in exchange had been allowed to stay on the grounds. The man at the Europcar desk had tapped his temple a couple of times and warned Tom that Madame Leforget was a little 'confused'.

But confused or not, she didn't appear to be here now. Trying to curb his disappointment, Tom brought the car to a stop and looked around. What did he expect? To just turn up and find her strolling around the grounds? It would be getting dark soon. He should go back to Calvi and come back tomorrow. He drove further down the drive looking for a place to turn. On his left was a gap in the bougainvillea, where a small path snaked round the end of the house. Since he was here, he thought he might as well check it out.

Parking the car, Tom followed the overgrown path on foot. The pungent smell of maquis and bougainvillea accentuated the long shadow of unease cast by the dark house. Behind the main building was a row of children's swings and a small ordered garden surrounded by a white waist-high fence. Something about them seemed unusual, then Tom realized that unlike the surrounding jungle they were beautifully maintained. The fresh, glossy red paint of the swings gleamed in the dying sun, and the white fence, manicured lawns and well-stocked borders of the small garden formed an island of order and care in this sea of neglect.

Madame Leforget was obviously still a very active presence around here.

A sound to Tom's right made him turn. There, standing silently beneath the cluster of trees was a woman of about seventy. Squat, she had an obese body and a sagging round face. Her eyes, behind large glasses, were tiny beads set deep into fleshy sockets; her mouth, a frowning line bracketed between heavy jowls. Wispy grey hair hung down on either side of her face and her dark shapeless dress looked like a habit. The beady, unblinking eyes appeared to be studying him closely.

'Madame Leforget?' he asked.

The woman stood motionless, and said nothing.

Tom walked towards her and introduced himself in his rusty French, hurriedly trying to explain that he hadn't come to trespass on the grounds or damage them, but to visit her.

'*Pourquoi?*' the woman asked eventually.

Tom explained about the orphanage, and how he was trying to find somebody who might remember a girl who had stayed here from about 1968 to 1983.

The old woman appeared to think about the question for a while and then said, 'There were so many children.' Her voice suddenly became sad. 'And now they've all gone – *elles sont disparu.* But when they return the gardens and playground will be ready for them . . . and they will be safe.'

Tom nodded slowly. 'The gardens are indeed beautiful.'

The woman gave him an angry look. 'And *safe.* Nothing will happen to them here,' she said defensively.

Tom's heart sank. He could see from her wild eyes that Madame Leforget was more than just a little confused. It didn't look as if he was going to get any new information.

He turned to go back to the car. 'I'm sorry I troubled you, Madame. I was just trying to find out about someone called Maria Benariac.'

The change was incredible. Her eyes cleared and her posture straightened in an instant. 'Maria?' she asked in a faraway voice. 'It was my fault you know. All my fault.'

'What was your fault?'

She looked suddenly wretched. 'Father Angelo. Sister Delphine. I didn't believe, you see. I thought the girls were all lying. I thought

282

Maria was a liar. So clever, so pretty, and so deceitful.'

'You knew Maria well?'

'All the nuns remember her.'

He looked at her habit-like dress again. 'You were a nun here?'

A short sad laugh. 'I was the Mother Superior once – many years ago. Until the troubles, and my breakdown. They tried to make me leave, but I insisted I stay here and work out my penance.'

'Will you tell me about Maria? What she was like?'

She stared at him with those unnerving eyes for a moment, as her troubled mind came to a decision. 'Come,' she said, eventually. 'You will be my confessor.'

THE LODGE WHERE SHE LIVED WAS HUMBLE BUT SURPRISINGLY COSY, and Tom found himself in the kitchen. In no time a bowl of fish soup, croutons topped with rouille and grated cheese, and a glass of red wine appeared on the table in front of him. Eventually she sat opposite and proceeded to tell him of the young girl called Maria Benariac.

'The nuns never knew whether she was an angel or devil. She looked beautiful and was very clever, but she was a terrible liar – so I thought anyway. The poor girl was punished often.' A sad shake of the head. '*I* punished her often.'

Tom sipped his wine. 'Why did you think she was a liar?'

She shrugged. 'Much of what she said was hard to believe. But many things, good and bad, happened around her.'

'What sort of things?'

'Well, at the end, when she was older, awful things. She claimed Father Angelo, a senior priest, raped her. I thought she was lying until Sister Delphine committed suicide and the priest . . .' She trailed off.

'What happened to the priest?'

'He died badly.'

'Was Maria responsible for his death?'

The ex-nun shrugged, clearly not shocked by the question.

'You said there were some good things that happened around her,' he tried, not holding out much hope.

'Oh yes. They happened when she was very young. There were many stories – so fantastic that at the time I was sure they were lies,

283

devilish lies.' Her eyes glazed over as her mind wandered back to the past. *'La grande tombée,'* she whispered to herself. Her eyes focused on him again. 'It was a clear night in June, and I was woken by a noise outside on the drive. I rushed outside and saw four of the younger girls, the oldest eight, the youngest about seven, screaming outside the front door. The girls were forbidden to go outside their dormitories at night, so they were punished. Maria claimed she shouldn't be punished because she had only gone outside to help the other girls. Did you see the large turret on the roof of the orphanage?'

Tom nodded.

'Well, Maria claimed that the other girls had fallen off the roof balcony. And she had rushed down to help them. Of course the other girls said they weren't even up on the balcony. That was completely out of bounds. And when I checked the girls they had no injuries. If they had fallen from that height they would have been killed.'

'So?' asked Tom, utterly absorbed.

A shake of the head. 'So I punished Maria even more than the others, for lying. It was much later that one of the other girls admitted she had gone up on the balcony for a dare. And the janitor found a gap in the rotten board through which they could have fallen.'

'So you think Maria was telling the truth after all? That she made them better?'

A shrug. 'That wasn't the only incident. There were many others. It was the same with the bees.'

'The bees?'

Clemenza Leforget poured herself some more wine. 'One afternoon the girls went on a trip to Corse. When they got back Maria and Valerie were sent to me for disturbing a nest of wild bees. Apparently they had walked off to a nearby stream and Maria had thrown stones at the nest. The local farmer had been furious because the bees had disturbed his sheep. Maria claimed that Valerie had been attacked by the bees and covered in hundreds of stings. But she had made her better.'

'What did Valerie say?'

'She backed up Maria's story, but I thought that was just to make me feel sorry for her and let her off the punishment. And I was angry with them both for being so stupid. Valerie was allergic to bee stings, you see? According to the doctors just one sting could kill her. I had

Valerie checked of course, and not surprisingly, he couldn't find any evidence of even one sting. The girl had either never been stung, or Maria had somehow neutralized all the poison. You can guess which option I chose to believe. But there was one strange thing which at the time I refused to take any notice of.'

'What was that?'

'The doctor claimed that not only could Valerie not have been stung by a bee, but she no longer had an allergy. She had somehow been cured.'

Tom said nothing for a while. He just looked closely at the woman opposite him. 'Why didn't you believe her?'

'I hated her. Maria was so beautiful, and clever. She lacked humility. She needed to be taught a lesson. And when she began to claim she could heal people it was too much; it was blasphemy.'

'Are there any other stories?'

'Yes, many. And there is one that I definitely know to be genuine, whatever I chose to believe at the time. Maria was often punished by being locked in the cellars. She was terrified of the dark, and once, when she was very young, she held onto the nun who was punishing her and begged not to be sent to the lock-away. Maria said she would do anything if the nun didn't send her away. Of course the nun didn't believe her, but for once felt compassion and sent her off to bed unpunished. Afterwards, perhaps a week later, the nun, who had had diabetes all her life, went for a routine check-up and was told she was cured.'

'And you're sure it was Maria who cured her?'

'Positive.'

'How can you be so sure?'

Clemenza grimaced. '*I* was the nun.'

'And yet you *still* didn't believe her?'

'No. I couldn't. I didn't want to. I just put it down to coincidence.' She wrung her hands. 'But if I had believed her then, I could have protected her from Father Angelo. And perhaps even nurtured her gift.' She suddenly fixed him with a pained stare. 'Do you know where she is now?'

Since Clemenza clearly had no idea of Maria's predicament, he decided not to burden her with the information. 'Yes,' he said.

'One day I will ask for her forgiveness.'

Tom paused and found himself appraising the woman opposite. Even if she was unbalanced, why would she tell a complete stranger these fantastical stories unless they were true? He hadn't even told her he wanted to know whether Maria could heal or not.

'How do you believe Maria did these acts of healing?' he asked.

'I don't know.'

'But what do you *think*?'

A shrug. 'I'm not a doctor, and I'm no longer a nun, but I've been thinking about this for the last twenty years. I have a simple theory. I think Maria had a gift from God. A gift she could pass on to others. It was almost like she had a good disease, that she could make other people catch off her.'

Tom smiled as he looked into the woman's eyes.

'Does that sound foolish?' she asked.

'Not to me it doesn't. Not at all. But why did you use the past tense? You said she *had* this gift.'

Mother Clemenza smiled sadly, and poured him some more wine. 'I think it was because I always punished her for telling "lies" about what she did. But as far as I'm aware she didn't perform one other act of healing after the bee-sting incident, after her eighth birthday. I doubt she even remembers what she once could do.'

THE SAME NIGHT. NORTH BOSTON.

THAT NIGHT BOB COOKE TURNED IN HIS SLEEP. IN HIS DREAMS HE wasn't in his apartment in North Boston, but back in California, and the surf was big. He loved his science, and working with the great Tom Carter, but however exciting or important it was, there were times when he wished he could give it all up and ride the waves again.

The noise woke him just as he was about to paddle out for the last big one. Yeah, he thought, in his groggy half-asleep state, come August he'd go back and catch up with the gang. Maybe do some hot-dogging.

That noise again.

Was someone downstairs? It sounded as if it was coming from the kitchen. Then, just as suddenly as it started the noise stopped.

'Hey Dawn! Did you hear that?' he whispered to the woman next to him.

'What?' she said sleepily, turning into him and pushing that cute butt of hers into his crotch.

'Thought I heard something.'

She moved her soft buttocks against him, and then snaked her hand behind her to grip his hardening penis.

'I didn't hear nothing,' she murmured. 'But I sure as hell felt something.'

'It was probably nothing,' he said, enjoying the feel of her hand on him.

'Don't be so tough on yourself,' she said, gripping him. 'It doesn't feel like nothing to me.'

He laughed in the dark. 'I meant the noise.'

'Noise?' she groaned. 'If you use this thing like you're supposed to, I'll give you noise.'

He closed his eyes whilst she manoeuvred him inside her, and then moved his hips to her rhythm. OK, he admitted, as he allowed her to roll him over on his back, and mount him, brushing her breasts over his face. There were some things better than science and surfing.

Half an hour later both their bodies were entwined and asleep. Perhaps if they had stayed awake just another ten minutes they would have smelled the gas coming from the carefully cut pipe in the kitchen downstairs. And been able to dismantle the simple match, sandpaper and spring contraption expertly rigged up beside it.

THE NEXT MORNING. CHARLESTOWN.

NORA LUTZ PUT THE LAST PIECE OF TOAST ON THE TRAY, NEXT TO the pot of imported Scottish marmalade her mother liked. Then she poured out a cup of tea — milk first, naturally; her mother wouldn't drink it any other way since her trip to England in '78. Finally she placed the bowl of bran-rich cereal with its small jug of cold milk in the remaining corner. Once the breakfast tray was organized to her satisfaction she left the kitchen of her two-storey apartment in Charlestown, and stepping past two of the cats, made her way up the well-trodden stairs to her mother's room.

There was a time when she resented her mother's sickness. But that was years ago, when she was in her thirties, when she still had a life

287

to sacrifice. Now, forty-five, her whole existence outside of Mother revolved around her work at GENIUS. Being put onto Cana had been a godsend, an important project that placed all her gripes into context. And it didn't matter that her mother didn't understand or appreciate what she did. Carter and the others valued her contribution and that's what counted. Cana and all it promised was her escape from the claustrophobic demands and emotional blackmail of the woman she loved dearly, but sometimes wished would quietly pass away.

She was coming to the fifth step, so she paused a second, preparing to mouth the words her mother would usually call out about now. 'Nora, is breakfast ready yet?' Without fail the words would come just after she began her climb.

But she heard nothing. No demands, no pleas, or complaints. Not even any sound of movement. Only silence.

It wasn't till she reached the bend in the stairs that she felt compelled to call out herself, 'Mom, breakfast's coming. I've made the tea, just like you like it. OK?'

Silence.

'Mom?'

Unconsciously she began to quicken her step. She couldn't remember the last time her Mother had overslept. Suddenly she thought the worst, and instantly regretted the times she had thought of her mother's death. On the landing she called again. 'Mom, are you all right? Talk to me and stop fooling.' Still nothing. She was now almost jogging, and the tea had spilled onto the toast and cereal. Her mother wouldn't like that, she thought, as she elbowed the door open.

'Mom, wake up!'

Then she dropped the tray, and put her hands to her mouth. She wanted to scream, but was too terrified.

It wasn't just her mother's twisted body lying motionless, a pillow over her head, that provoked Nora's reaction. It was also the dark-haired man with smoky-green eyes, who suddenly appeared beside her, holding her hands over her mouth, before plunging a syringe into her arm.

*   *   *

288

BACK BAY, BOSTON.

MOMENTS LATER IN THE BACK BAY AREA OF TOWN, JASMINE Washington reached for her car keys, and bent down to where Larry sat drinking orange juice on the sunny terrace. She kissed him and said, 'I'll see you tonight.'

Larry put his copy of *Variety* down on the table, returned her kiss and said, 'Have a good day at the office. And give my love to Holly.'

'I will.'

She kissed him one more time, and then went down to the car port. Above her she heard Larry call: 'When will you be back?'

'Shouldn't be late.'

'What you wanna eat?'

She climbed into her 325i, pulled back the soft top, and started the engine. She backed the car onto the road, into the morning sunshine, then looked up at Larry, leaning over the terrace. She blew him a kiss, gunned the engine and shouted, 'Surprise me!' then screeched off with a whoop.

Perhaps if Larry hadn't called down and diverted her attention she might have noticed the slick pool of liquid in the car port beneath where her BMW had been parked. The liquid that Larry would later discover was brake fluid.

26

DEATH ROW, MASSACHUSETTS STATE PENITENTIARY.

AFTER HER NIGHT OF DESPAIR, MARIA BENARIAC HAD TOLD HERSELF to accept the inevitable. Within a couple of days she had control over her fears again. There would be no reprieve, no divine intervention; no grand plan put in place to allow her to finish the scientist. She knew that now and had forced herself to come to terms with it.

She ate her breakfast slowly from the plain white plate, trying to extract every last pleasurable sensation from the textures and flavours of the eggs and hash browns.

When the approaching click-clack of the guard's heels disturbed her breakfast, she looked up, annoyed. And when the heavy-set woman appeared outside the bars of her cell, Maria frowned at her. 'I haven't finished yet,' she said. 'I haven't even had half my time yet . . .'

The woman eyed her carefully. 'Relax, Preacher woman, your food's going nowhere. Just came to tell you you've got a visitor.'

Maria groaned. Hugo Myers was taking his professionalism too far. She thought he wasn't going to visit any more. After all, if there wasn't any chance of an appeal, then there wasn't much point seeing her lawyer.

'Do you know what my brilliant attorney wants?' she asked, not expecting an answer.

'Attorney?' The guard laughed. 'Your visitor's no lawyer, he's about as different from a lawyer as you can get. Hell, he wants to be your spiritual adviser.'

MARIA BENARIAC FELT A TINY FLOWER OF EXCITEMENT BLOOM IN her stomach as the two guards led her manacled from the cell on Tier B of death row down the white tiled corridor, past the execution chamber to the interview rooms.

When Ezekiel De La Croix stood and smiled at her, she felt so moved she wanted to embrace him. She stared deep into his dark eyes, and said nothing. The guards sat her down, and attached her manacles to the metal ring in the middle of the steel table. When she was secure they walked back to the door. The taller one paused and addressed Ezekiel. 'Sir, this is a secure room for use by attorneys and spiritual advisers. Your conversation cannot be monitored or recorded. But on no account must you touch the prisoner.' He pointed to a large button on the wall. 'When you've finished, or if you want anything, just ring the buzzer.'

'I will,' said Ezekiel, as the guards left the room, locking the door behind them.

Now they were alone, Maria opened her mouth to speak. 'Father, I am sorry. Please forg—' But before she could continue Ezekiel placed a finger over his mouth. Then he walked round the table and stood beside her, looking down at her. For a long while he just stood there saying nothing, staring at her. She wanted to ask him what was wrong, but stilled her tongue, sensing he wanted to say something.

Suddenly she noticed tears on his cheek. He didn't make a sound, but there was no disguising it. The Father was crying.

Before she could say anything he knelt before her and bowed his head. When he did eventually speak it was so quiet that she couldn't hear him, and when he raised his voice and repeated his words she didn't understand them.

'May *you* be saved,' he said more strongly.

She frowned. 'What do you mean?'

Head still bowed, eyes still averted, Ezekiel said, 'Dr Carter found our match on Project Cana . . .'

'And?' she prompted.

'He has identified the person who possesses the genes of the

291

Messiah. The same person who was born when the sacred flame changed. The same person who as a child had Christ's gift of healing.' Ezekiel raised his head then, his black eyes drilling into hers. 'That person is *you*, Maria. You are the New Messiah. *You* are the chosen one.'

For a moment she froze, staring into his eyes, her brain unable to process what she had just heard. It went beyond shock; she was a bystander to the revelation Ezekiel had just made.

Could this be possible? Could this be true?

Despite her disbelief, a small part of her, a part deep in her consciousness had no doubt. *You always knew you were chosen*, it seemed to say. *Now you know what for.*

'May you be saved,' said Ezekiel again.

This time Maria only hesitated a second before replying, 'So I may save the righteous.'

Ezekiel then stood and retook his seat. 'Now you know your destiny, there is much I need to tell you. There is much we need to do.'

Still barely able to believe how everything had suddenly changed, Maria was simply glad to be back in the Father's affection. She coaxed a smile, leaned forward as far as her manacles would allow, and listened to what he had to say.

THAT NIGHT MARIA BARELY SLEPT. GONE WAS HER DESPAIR, AND even her stoic sense of resignation. Instead she couldn't stop thinking about all Ezekiel had told her, particularly the childhood stories she had long forgotten.

Could they have been real? Had they actually happened? All those feelings and memories she had suppressed as the fantasies of an unhappy child now came back. Every story Ezekiel had recounted to her now evoked and corroborated recollections that she had assumed and always been told were figments of her own imagination.

She opened her eyes and looked defiantly into the darkness that filled the cell, willing herself to recall everything she usually tried to forget. What she most remembered was the fear and fatigue as she'd walked around every broken and bloody girl who had fallen from the orphanage tower, trying to make the still bodies move again. On her prison bunk her body re-lived the dull ache and out-flowing of energy every time she'd embraced the girls, and the numbing tiredness afterwards that left her feeling pale and wretched. But most of all she remembered the relief when, one by one, they had brushed themselves off and stood up.

Somehow the patina of the past and her own denial were gradually peeled away by Ezekiel's revelation of her destiny, leaving the preserved images and feelings uncorrupted by time.

Ezekiel had told her all about his visit to Dr Carter's lab and how the scientist had revealed her genetic inheritance. He had also informed her that Gomorrah had been unleashed on Dr Carter and his team. She told him that she wanted to finish Dr Carter herself, but Ezekiel would only give a noncommittal shrug. More importantly, the Inner Circle still hadn't resolved *how* they were going to get her out of here. And she only had twelve days left.

The thought of her imminent execution made her mind wander back to her abilities. They fed her with a feeling of power and control that went beyond any righteous thrill she had experienced executing a kill. The story of the bee stings affected her more than the others not only because could she remember it vividly but because it gave her an idea; an idea that made her tremble with excitement.

She wondered if she could still perform these feats of healing. She tried to think back to the time when she gave up these powers, but couldn't. All she could recollect was the fear and despair of being continually punished for her 'lies'. Still, she felt sure that if she only allowed her powers to return, they somehow would.

She had always felt she was chosen. She now realized that there had been a plan laid down for her after all, and she had been wrong to doubt her faith. A fever took control of her. Man had always been able to effect death; she knew that better than most. But only God had ever wielded true control over life as well. So, if she shared this ability, what did that make her? A true child of God?

She rolled off her bunk and paced the dark cell, willing the dawn. Exhilaration raced through her. It was clear what she had to do now; obvious even. She hoped the Father would return tomorrow so she could tell him her plan. If she was to get out of here, then she would need his help, and that of the Brotherhood; of *her* Brotherhood. She smiled in the now harmless dark.

There was so much to prepare.

EZEKIEL DE LA CROIX DID NOT RETURN THE NEXT DAY. BUT MARIA Benariac did have another visitor later that afternoon.

Tom Carter waited alone in the featureless interview room of the State Penitentiary, unaware that Ezekiel had sat in this very chair the day before. Tom's blue shirt and cotton jacket were crumpled. Dark semicircles of tiredness cast shadows beneath his eyes and his head ached. He looked vacantly round the depressing room, registering the off-white windowless walls, and the harsh fluorescent tube lighting. His mind was elsewhere. He wasn't even sure why he had come any longer.

He had returned from Corsica yesterday feeling both frustrated and excited. Confident that Maria could help Holly, but far from confident that she would, whatever inducement he gave her. At Logan Airport he had sailed through customs and on reaching the main concourse had scanned the waiting faces for the GENIUS driver he'd arranged to meet him, desperate to get back and see Holly.

To his surprise Jack was there instead, with two policemen flanking him. One look at his friend's unsmiling face and his first thought was that Holly's condition had deteriorated, or worse. However his relief on hearing otherwise had been shortlived.

'What? An explosion in Bob Cooke's apartment? How is he?'

A shake of Jack's head. 'He's dead, Tom. Along with his girlfriend, and an old man who lived in the apartment below.'

'Dead?' Tom hadn't been able to take it in. Still couldn't.

And then after the initial shock the question that flashed across his brain was: *'Did he solve the mouse puzzle before he died?'* He had guiltily pushed this query to one side almost as soon as he had thought it, but it was still there, unanswered.

Bob Cooke's death hadn't been the whole news of course. Far from it. It was when he heard how Nora had apparently found her mother dead in bed, and subsequently died of a heart attack that he'd begun to understand the implications.

'Nora, die of a heart attack?' he'd said incredulously, repeating what Jack had told him like some idiot mimic. 'But Nora had the constitution of an ox, and her mother had been ill for years. Her death would have been anything but a shock to Nora . . .'

And finally in the car on the way back to GENIUS Jack had told him about Jazz's crash.

'Oh no! For God's sake, tell me *she's* OK!'

A tired shake of the head from Jack. 'It's too early to tell.'

That was when it had all become clear. Horribly clear.

'My guess is that whoever was behind Maria Benariac is still trying to stop Cana,' Jack had said. 'And that means that Preacher or no Preacher, you are still a target.'

For a long moment he had thought of giving up there and then. Not because his life was in danger – the novelty of that had long since worn off. But because his obsessive quest to save his daughter had cost so many other lives. He was no longer just one in a long list of people some sicko fanatic didn't agree with and wanted dead. This was about someone wanting to stop his project and *everyone* attached to it at all costs. And now they had killed people – *his friends* – because of what *he* was doing. Because of his selfish, single-minded, fuck-what-anybody-else-thinks quest to save his daughter. And come to think of it, was he really just trying to save his daughter? Or was that quest just a cover for his obsessive crusade to teach nature a lesson? To kill cancer and all those other twisted turns of vicious chance that Mother Nature throws out to prove how pathetic we and our technology really are. Wasn't he really just trying to subjugate her and redress the balance, whatever the cost to those around him?

Isn't that what this is all about? he had asked himself as Jack turned the car into the GENIUS campus. It was only after he'd gone to the ward and looked into Holly's trusting eyes and fed off her courage that he'd managed to suppress these demons that fuelled his self-doubt. It was only then that he'd seen the true purity of what he was trying to do, the simple truth that he was using everything in his power to save his daughter. Nothing more. Nothing less.

If he managed to save others, that was all fine. But that mission, that *burden* was already taken care of by the other initiatives underway at GENIUS and countless other places around the world. All Cana was concerned with, all *he* was concerned with, was saving his daughter. If the deaths of those who had been killed helping him on the project were to mean anything, then he had to follow it through to the end. And if anyone else tried to stop him, then *they* were the evil ones tampering with nature; tampering with a father's natural drive to save his child – not him.

Still, as he sat in the interview room in Death Row listening to the approaching footfalls, he knew his situation – a man negotiating with his murdered wife's killer for the salvation of his daughter – was far from natural.

When the two guards brought Maria into the room, Tom was struck by two things. The first was how content she looked. This was no normal inmate on Death Row. No normal person could look this relaxed only days away from death. But then he reminded himself that the Preacher was anything but normal. The second thing that struck him was that she didn't seem particularly surprised to see him. If anything she seemed a little disappointed that he wasn't someone else. For a fleeting instant he wondered who.

He didn't exchange words with her as the guards secured her manacles to the loop on the table. But when they gave him the call-us-if-you-need-anything speech, and pointed out the buzzer near the door, Maria smiled at him. It was a conquering, pitying smile.

After the guards had gone Maria still made no move to say anything. Her hair was growing back and if it wasn't for those eyes and her unnaturally sculpted bone structure, she would have looked almost cute, even vulnerable, like a newly hatched chick. He had prepared a speech before he'd come, but on seeing her sitting there it seemed suddenly irrelevant, so without bothering with any preliminaries he told her about Project Cana and how it had succeeded in finding a match. He was surprised by her lack of reaction. Then he revealed that she *was* the match. Again her calm was shocking.

'What do you think about what I've told you?' he asked eventually, wanting her to say something. But she just shrugged, as if he'd asked her which flavour ice-cream she liked.

'Don't you find what I've told you . . . interesting?' he pushed. 'Not even a little ironic?'

'Sure,' she said in that offhand manner of hers. 'But what I really find interesting is that you've come here to tell me. I told you it wasn't over yet.'

Tom bit his lip. Her attitude made him want to reach across and slap that smug, evil face. What was it Alex would always say after telling him ghost stories as a kid?

'*A witch is the only lady you can hit.*'

'*What about a She Devil?*'

'*Them too. But they're different, son, with them you've got to make sure you hit them so hard they stay down. Because when they come back at you they're as vicious as hell . . .*'

Tom tried to keep himself calm. It was obvious Maria already knew about the genes. Nobody could be this cool. But who could have told her? Then it hit him. Ezekiel must have made contact with her, introducing himself to her to check out his New Messiah. It was the old man who'd told her about the genes. That was how she knew. Tom wondered for a moment what Ezekiel had made of her. The Preacher must have been as big a shock to the Brotherhood's holy plans, as she was to his Holly plans.

He took a deep breath and decided that the only way he was going to get through this was to stick to the facts. If she helped, she helped and if she didn't . . .

'Miss Benariac,' he said, trying to keep his voice as businesslike as possible, 'Of all the genomes we've searched, which is now well over five hundred million, we have only found three which bear these three mutant genes. Two belong to people who are dead; one was an Indian from Colombia, and the other of course was Christ. You are the third. You all have one thing in common apart from the genes. A history of being able to heal at some stage in your life.' He paused, waiting for a reaction. There wasn't any. 'I believe,' he continued, 'that you still have that gift and I want to help you unlock it.'

The unusual eyes were now studying him, the smile still there. 'Why?'

He had lain awake nights thinking of the perfect reply to such a question; the reply that might convince a murderer to save Holly. But when it came down to it he decided that there was only one option – to play it straight. He reached into his inside pocket and pulled out a photo of Holly. It was one he'd taken last summer in Bermuda: Holly waving to the camera in her red one-piece suit on the pink-white sands of Horseshoe Bay. He placed the photo in front of Maria, wanting her to connect with Holly, to go beyond him to helping his daughter. After all, she was still a woman . . .

'I want you to save her,' he said.

'Who is she?'

'My daughter, Holly.'

Maria nodded and looked closely at the picture. She picked it up in her right manacled hand, and seemed to stroke Holly's likeness with her left. 'She's got your jaw,' she said with a smile, as if looking through the family photo album. Maria looked up and for a second he saw something vulnerable in her eyes – a yearning.

Then came the questions.

'Do you love her a great deal?'

He nodded. 'Very much.'

'Does she know how much you love her? Do you tell her?'

'Yes, she knows.'

'Does she know what you're doing to help her? Does she know about you coming here?'

'No, I haven't told her about you.'

'What's wrong with her?'

'She has brain cancer.'

'How long does she have? Longer than me?'

'I don't know. I hope so.'

'And you want me to help her?'

'If you can.'

'Oh, I think I *can*,' she said, sitting back in her chair.

Really? thought Tom. This surprised him. He hadn't expected her to be knowledgeable of her powers and certainly not so confident. He felt the same rush of frustrated excitement he'd experienced yesterday coming off the plane. But he kept his face poker-straight. When he mentioned the deal he tried to make it sound as casual and un-pleading as possible. 'I've spoken with the Governor. I can get your death sentence commuted if you do help her.'

Maria's smug smile broadened. 'Commuted to life? A life for a life. Is that it?'

He shrugged. 'If you like.'

Maria seemed to think about the offer for a moment, looking from the photo of Holly to Tom and back to the photo again. 'Do you think Holly is unlucky?' she asked eventually.

He was somewhat taken aback by her question, but stuck to his policy of answering honestly. 'In getting brain cancer at her age, sure. Very unlucky.'

'I don't,' said Maria quietly, and as she looked at Holly's likeness he fancied he saw a wistfulness in that unnerving face – almost envy. 'I think she's very lucky. She has parents who love her . . .'

'Only one's still alive,' said Tom angrily, before he could stop himself.

Maria gave no sign of having heard. 'She has been cherished and wanted from the day she was born.'

'That is true,' said Tom, willing himself to control his feelings, wanting Maria to connect with Holly. 'But without help she will be dead in a few months, perhaps even weeks. And she is completely innocent.'

Maria smiled at that. 'Dr Carter, no-one is *completely* innocent. But you want me to cure her from her disease? To stop what is ordained, because you regard it as unfair? And because you love her?' Her voice sounded reasonable, even sympathetic.

He nodded.

She went on. 'And in return you will treat my terminal disease, stopping me from dying prematurely in eleven days?'

Again he nodded, keeping his face as deadpan as possible, not wanting to provoke her in any way.

She looked at him, cocking her head on one side like she was listening out for something. 'You are prepared to do this even though you *don't* think I'm innocent?'

'Yes.'

She leaned towards him and he fought the impulse to move away. Instead he inclined his body towards hers until they could have been two lovers whispering intimacies over a candlelit dinner. He could smell coal-tar soap on her skin and mint toothpaste on her breath.

'Even though I shot your wife down in cold blood?' she continued, her lips inches from his, 'and tried to kill you?'

'Yes.'

'You would do all this to save your daughter?'

'Yes, and more. Will you help her?'

Maria paused and her smile returned. Tom tried to read that smile, searching for any signs of magnanimity, but she was unfathomable. Maria looked down at her manacles and seemed to study her hands for a moment, as if they were objects separate from herself. When she looked up again the smile was gone; replaced with a mask of cold dismissal.

'No, Dr Carter, I will not help your daughter. That is the very last thing I would do.'

PART IV

THE MIRACLE STRAIN

27

A WEEK LATER. GENIUS OPERATING ROOM, BOSTON

JASMINE WASHINGTON SAT ON ONE OF THE BLUE UPHOLSTERED chairs in the waiting-room outside the GENIUS operating room. Scratching the skin beneath the cast on her broken left arm, she was sure she'd felt more pain in her life, but couldn't remember when. Her left collar-bone and radius had been broken in the crash. The whole left side of her body was bruised. Of course she'd been driving too fast; that's the whole point of having a sports car. But no-one had ever cut her brake cables before. She was only grateful the grocery van she'd hit outside the Seven Eleven had been stationary, and thank God there'd been no pedestrians around when she'd shunted it onto the sidewalk.

Yeah, all in all, she should count herself lucky. Nora Lutz's funeral had been two days ago in Boston, but Bob Cooke's body had been flown back to California. Just the thought of their deaths, and how close she'd come to joining them, made her shudder. When she considered what was about to happen next door, she realized how *really* lucky she was.

Much had occurred in the last week, since the Preacher had turned down Tom's deal to help Holly. For a start, Holly's condition had considerably deteriorated. If Bob had unravelled the mystery of why some of the mice had been cured and others hadn't, then he'd taken the knowledge with him to the grave. After Holly's last two seizures Tom had no option but to operate on her, just to relieve the pressure of the tumour, which was one of the most aggressive either Tom or Karl Lambert had ever seen.

Jasmine heard the swing-doors open to her right and saw a tired Alex Carter walk into the waiting-room.

Tom's father looked much older and for the first time she thought he looked every one of this sixty-eight years. He appeared lost as he scanned the room and gave a relieved smile when he saw her by the coffee machine. He waved and walked towards her.

'How is she? Have they started yet?' he asked, taking a seat next to her.

She shook her head. 'Holly's still being prepped in the ward.' Jasmine used her good hand to point her thumb over her shoulder at the wall behind her. 'For the last hour Tom and Karl Lambert have been in OR planning the op. It should happen soon.'

'Right, right,' Alex said, clasping and unclasping his hands in his lap. He looked terrified, and Jasmine suddenly remembered that he had been through all this before. Watching his wife suffer from the same disease.

'Karl Lambert's an excellent surgeon,' she said, resting a hand on his shoulder, 'and you know how good Tom is. She couldn't be in better hands.'

The old man turned his head towards her and tried to smile. But in his eyes she could see that he knew this was the end, or at least the beginning of the end. Jasmine blinked back a sudden rush of tears; tears of frustration and anger as much as anything. After all they had been through, after all the lives that had been lost, Cana and the real chance of saving Holly had been stopped by a murderer, the same murderer who had set the whole ball rolling in the first place. She could find no consolation in the knowledge that Maria would be executed in four days. It seemed a sad, stupid waste.

Alex got up and moved to the coffee machine. 'Do you want anything?' he asked, clearly needing to do something.

'Yeah, thanks. Black decaff, no sugar.'

The swing-doors opened again and both their heads snapped

round, expecting to see Holly coming through. But it was Jack Nichols. The big man stroked his scar self-consciously, like he wasn't sure he should be here. 'Just thought I'd see what was happening. Couldn't get much work done and kept on thinking of Tom and Holly . . .' he trailed off.

'Yeah, I know,' said Jasmine.

'Coffee?' asked Alex still standing by the machine.

Jack gave a crooked smile that seemed to say, 'Wouldn't it be great if a cup of coffee could make everything right again.' 'Thanks. Light please. Four sugars.'

Alex was about to comment on his choice when the doors were suddenly swung open again, revealing Holly on a gurney. Two people in green scrubs stood over her. Holly lay on her back with her hairless head held in place by a clamp. *One slip of the laser*, thought Jasmine, remembering what Tom had said about the risks: *Paralysis or worse*. But when she saw her goddaughter's frightened eyes darting from left to right she wondered if death *was* worse. If *anything* was worse than this.

Jasmine and Alex stood and approached the gurney as it stopped outside the doors to the operating room. Jasmine extended her hand and Holly gripped her index finger like a newborn baby. Her other hand did the same with Alex. Jack Nichols walked over and joined them.

'See you soon,' Jack said, making the circular 'A OK' sign with his finger and thumb.

Holly tried to smile, and released Jasmine's finger to return the sign.

'Good luck, Hol,' said Jasmine, keeping her voice bright.

'You'll be fine,' smiled Alex sadly, stroking Holly's cheek. 'Your dad'll see to that.'

The operating doors opened and Tom Carter stepped out. Karl Lambert followed close behind. Both were gowned up in surgical greens. Tom's mask was hanging from his neck, and Jasmine could see the pain in his eyes as he leaned over and kissed his daughter's forehead. When he spoke his voice was unbearably gentle. 'Don't be frightened, Holly, OK. I'll be right beside you all the time. Are you ready?'

'Yes Dad,' Holly whispered, as her face relaxed and the fear dimmed in her eyes.

Tom kissed her once more, then straightened up. 'Well then, let's get started, shall we?'

Jasmine watched as the gurney was wheeled into the brilliant white of the operating room. The last vision she had before the doors swung shut in front of her was of her small goddaughter being flanked by four guardians in green. As she stood there, the lapsed Baptist crossed herself and prayed to her God.

FIFTEEN MILES AWAY, EZEKIEL DE LA CROIX PACED AROUND THE interview room of the Massachusetts State Penitentiary, whilst his Messiah, Maria Benariac, sat manacled to the table in front of her.

'I'm sorry I didn't return sooner. There were things to arrange,' he tried to explain, 'people to put in place to get you out.'

'But I've already told you,' said Maria, drumming the fingers of a manacled hand on the steel table. 'I have a better plan and I need your help with it.'

Ezekiel was still not used to taking orders from the woman who for so long had taken orders from him. His last week had been spent urging the Inner Circle to perfect their escape plan. He even had to contend with the still sceptical Brother Bernard requesting that Maria provide some proof that she really was the chosen one. Now, when he had finally reassured Bernard, and they had pulled together the bare bones of a working scheme, Maria was telling him to abort it. She could at least have listened to it and he doubted if her plan was any better. Still, the Messiah had to feel confident with what was proposed. Once she was free and had been anointed in the flame, then he could stand down, his task done. Just the thought of that moment, when the responsibility would be lifted off his shoulders, made him sigh.

'Very well,' he said, putting his pill box on the table and popping one of the white antacid tablets into his mouth. He hoped her scheme was at least workable. 'Tell me of your plan.'

Maria beckoned him over to sit opposite her. She looked to her left and right, as if others might overhear, then leant towards him. When she spoke it was in a whisper, so low that he had to put his head to within an inch of hers to catch what she was saying. Quelling his impatience he listened while she outlined her idea. At first more out of duty than genuine interest, but as her measured whispers explained her proposal in greater detail he found himself listening more and more intently. When she finally finished his mouth was open in disbelief. Her plan was brilliant. But how could it possibly work? The risks were phenomenal.

He stayed silent for a while, just staring back at her bi-coloured eyes.

'But how do you know it will happen?' he managed at last. 'How can you be so sure?'

Maria smiled at him, her face a beacon of confidence. 'Have faith in me!'

'I do, but . . .'

'Am I not the New Messiah?'

'Yes, but . . .'

Maria shook her manacles and gestured for him to come closer to her. 'Hold my hand.'

He hesitated.

'Don't be afraid.'

Tentatively he did as she asked. He felt her fingers close round his, gripping him tightly. He watched as she closed her eyes and appeared to go pale, as if in pain. Then a strange warmth suffused his hand before travelling up the arm to his torso. It was as if his skin had been rubbed with liniment. Suddenly she released her hold, and a thin smile curled her lips.

'I don't understand,' he said, reaching for the box of pills he'd left on the table near her manacled hands.

'Leave them,' she said quietly.

'What?'

'The tablets. You no longer need them.'

He froze and just looked at her. It wasn't possible. And yet the pain in his stomach had gone – not just lessened as normal, but gone *completely*.

She smiled at his shock, but beneath her smiles he could see she was almost as stunned as he was.

She asked, 'Now do you believe my plan can work?'

He managed a mute nod. He could now give the doubting Brother Bernard his proof.

'Good, then go,' she said. 'You have much to arrange.'

*   *   *

TOM WATCHED KARL LAMBERT'S HANDS DIRECT THE LASER scalpel, trying to remove the black diseased tissue without damaging the rest of the brain – his daughter's brain.

Half of him desperately wanted to be holding the laser, rather than just assisting with the operation. But the more rational half of him knew he would be a liability, even without an injured left hand. He'd always believed that he should be able to perform any surgical procedure with clinical detachment, but he now knew this wasn't true. However much he tried to see Holly as the patient, and nothing else, he couldn't. She was his precious, vulnerable daughter and just the thought of operating on her made his hands shake.

Around the table were four monitors. Three tracked Holly's life signs; the middle one with the insistent, reassuringly regular *Beep-Beep-Beep* was an ECG tracking her heartbeat. The fourth screen showed a close-up of Holly's brain with Karl Lambert's micro-laser cutting away the dark tumour cells. These screens were monitored by Staff Nurse Lawrence and the younger nurse Fran Huckleberry. Tim Fuller, the anaesthetist, stood at the head of the table about four feet away from Karl Lambert and Tom.

Although Tom was technically assisting Karl, there wasn't much he could do except watch. The surgery was so delicate that even one pair of hands seemed too many. He tried to console himself with the knowledge that Karl Lambert was an excellent surgeon, one of the best. Still, he was only too aware that even if Holly did survive the operation, it would only buy her a few more months at most. Once again he wondered whether it was really worth it, just to extend the suffering and sadness.

He still found it hard to accept that Maria Benariac would rather die than save Holly. It was so vindictive, so pointless. What did she hope her execution in four days' time would achieve? He remembered all the stories Mother Clemenza had told him about the young Maria. He also recalled Maria's confident acknowledgement that she could help Holly, if she wanted to. What a terrible waste.

Beep, Beeeep, Beee . . . eep, Bee . . . eeee . . . eeee . . . eep.

He turned to the ECG and felt his heart stop beating. The line was flat. Holly's heart *had* stopped beating.

Suddenly time seemed to pause. He saw Karl Lambert look up from his hands, his normally calm eyes worried. Lambert must have cut into healthy tissue, vital brain tissue which had thrown Holly's system into shock. As Tom charged up the paddles to kickstart Holly's heart, Nurse Lawrence applied the conducting gel. Holly's left leg began to twitch violently and soon her whole left side was in spasm. It took all Tom's strength to press the paddles to her chest and administer the necessary shock to her heart. He tried to forget that this was his daughter beneath him, tried not to think of the trauma going through her small body. He concentrated only on what needed to be done to keep her alive.

The first shock had no effect; the line on her ECG stayed flat.

Tom waited whilst the paddles were re-charged, then again applied them to Holly's chest. Her whole body convulsed and for a second he imagined he saw the line spike, but he was mistaken. It remained flat.

The third shock. Nothing.

Then the fourth.

To Tom, the battle to bring her back seemed to last an epic amount of time, but in reality it was over in ninety-two seconds. At exactly 11:09 a.m. it became clear to everyone around the operating table, that nothing more could be done.

Holly Carter was dead.

Two things happened to Tom then. The first was that he heard an awful wailing cry like that of a wounded animal, and for many seconds didn't realize that the cry was his own. The second was a revelation, so sudden and so obvious that it made him cry out again.

Before anyone could console him, he shouted, 'Don't touch anything!' and ran from the operating room. Ignoring Jasmine, Alex and Jack waiting outside, he sprinted as fast as he could in the direction of the Crick Laboratory.

WHEN A BODY DIES IT DOES SO IN STAGES. NATURALLY WHEN THE heart stops pumping blood, or the lungs stop taking in oxygen or the brain ceases to function, then to all intents and purposes the body is clinically dead. But a body is a collection of cells, and not all cells die at once . . .

TOM CARTER IGNORED THE BUSY ELEVATOR AND RUSHED TO THE stairs. Running up them as fast as his injured leg allowed, he jerked open the door to the second floor, pushed past one of his virologists entering the Mendel Suite, and ran across the expanse of the main lab. Oblivious to the looks from some of the scientists bent over their work, he pushed his palm into the scanner of the secure door leading to the Crick Laboratory, willing it to open.

As soon as it hissed and slid to one side, he raced across the empty lab to the refrigerated cabinet, which contained the thirteen phials of *Trinity* serum. Clawing open the cabinet, he reached in and pulled out one of the glass phials. He opened the drawer below the adjacent workbench, and scrambled around for a syringe. Ripping off the sterile wrapper he thrust the needle into the phial and filled the hypodermic with virtually all the contents. Tapping the syringe he pushed the plunger to release any air bubbles. He pulled up his left sleeve, twisted it like a tourniquet to raise one of the veins in his forearm, then thrust the needle into his arm and depressed the plunger.

WHEN JASMINE LED JACK AND ALEX INTO THE OPERATING ROOM she had no more idea than the rest of them where Tom had gone. She had considered going after him until Alex had held her back, telling her that Tom would want to be alone.

Karl Lambert looked pale, as did the rest of the operating team. He made a half-hearted gesture to keep them out of the theatre, but didn't press it. He tidied up Holly's keyhole incision and covered the top of her head with a green surgical cloth.

When Jasmine looked down at her goddaughter, Holly's eyes were closed as if in sleep and she looked strangely peaceful. Jasmine had a strong urge to touch her and prod her into life.

Jasmine didn't touch her though. She didn't cry either, although she felt the same cold sadness in her heart that visited her when both her brother and Olivia had died. She didn't even cry when she saw the grief in Alex's face. Only when she saw the single tear leak from Jack Nichols' left eye and follow the arc of his scar down to his mouth, did she weep. Seeing the tough ex-FBI man shed that one tear brought home to her the whole tragedy of what had happened.

The sudden noise startled them all. Tom didn't so much push open the swing-doors as slam them open; a gale blowing in from a hurricane. The left sleeve of his green gown was rolled up and his eyes were fever bright. Oblivious to them all he strode to the table and stared down at his daughter. For a moment Jasmine saw the fever leave his eyes and a look of infinite tenderness soften his gaze, then he leant down and put his arms around Holly as if to lift her from her bed. But he didn't lift her, he crouched over the table and hugged his dead daughter close to him.

Jasmine couldn't see Tom's face because he was looking down, but Holly's pale visage was clearly visible over his shoulder. The same shoulder that now began to shake as he clutched his daughter still tighter to him.

Alex Carter placed a consoling hand on his son's back, but as soon as his fingers touched Tom he jerked his hand away, as if he had touched a hot stove. As he turned, his face showed no pain, only puzzled shock.

Then Jasmine saw something that would stay with her for the rest of her life. It happened so fast that at first she wasn't sure she'd really seen it, or if she had, whether it even meant anything.

Holly blinked.

Jasmine looked around at the others to see if they'd witnessed it too. But Jack and the doctors had turned away leaving Tom to his grief. Even Alex was looking down, wrapped up in his own thoughts. No one could see Holly's face except her.

Then Holly's eyes opened.

Jasmine was either going mad or something very weird was going on. She looked around her again, trying to control her breathing and get her disobedient mouth to speak. Still the others stood in silent grief, paying no attention.

Then Holly smiled sleepily at her and said. 'Can I have a glass of water please, Jazz?'

And Jasmine did what she had never done before in her entire life. She fainted.

28

FOUR DAYS LATER. MASSACHUSETTS STATE PENITENTIARY.

MARIA ATE HER LAST BREAKFAST IN GOOD SPIRITS. DESPITE THE FACT that her execution was scheduled for midnight, she couldn't remember feeling more exhilarated or alive. The eggs tasted as if they had been prepared by the finest French chef, and the milk was fresher and colder than any she'd drunk. Her every sense was so heightened that even the most mundane experience gave her the childish joy of fresh discovery. The blue of her prison fatigues suddenly had a cornflower purity to it that made her wish she had worn clothing of this colour before. And the new holding cell she had been put in prior to the execution was a wondrous distraction. She had amused herself most of yesterday afternoon just itemizing every subtle but discernible difference between this cell and her previous one. Still, what brought her the most joy and comfort was the simple but awesome power she knew resided in every cell of her body.

She was the chosen one. She knew that now and accepted it. She had been bathed in the gene pool of God, and now had mastery over life and death. No longer was there anything to fear from anybody or anything. She could still give herself an electric thrill just remembering her meeting with Father Ezekiel. When she'd touched his hand and cured his ulcer she had felt the energy – *the power* – flow from her body into his. The exhaustion that followed was nothing compared to the exhilaration of knowing that her power remained undimmed from those half-remembered childhood days.

She had found her meeting with Dr Carter equally satisfying. She had always gained a righteous thrill from performing the kills. There was something primal and pure about *taking* a life, but none of her executions, not even the most exhilarating face-to-face encounters, had come close to the rush she'd experienced turning down Dr Carter's request. She had discovered that to kill is one thing but to deny life is something else entirely. It was a virtual kill. To have the power to *give* life, and then to choose not to use it, was like nothing she had experienced before. It felt like . . . like . . . like she was a god.

She heard the now familiar click-clack of the guards' heels coming down the corridor. Her spiritual adviser had arrived for his final visit.

NINE MINUTES LATER IN THE INTERVIEW ROOM SHE WAS LOOKING at Father Ezekiel's tired but excited face.

'Is everything arranged?' she asked.

He nodded. 'As your spiritual adviser I will attend your execution along with the witnesses and the Warden. Our contacts in the Brotherhood have ensured that the relevant personnel will be on duty to do what is necessary.' A pause. 'Are you still sure it will work?'

Maria found Ezekiel's concern touching. 'Have faith, my Father.'

'I do have faith in you, my child, but I'm scared that after waiting this long . . .' His voice trailed off. 'It's just that I would have preferred a more . . . *conventional* rescue.'

'But can you think of a better way to ensure no one doubts who I am? This way I will be able to prove I am truly the chosen one.'

Ezekiel gave a reluctant shrug and played with his ruby ring. 'I suppose you are right.'

'I know I am. Will Dr Carter be at the execution?' The less Dr Carter could connect her to the Father the better.

'I don't think so,' said Ezekiel De La Croix. 'Only two relatives of the unrighteous slain have asked to attend, and the scientist is not among them. He is too busy attending to his dying daughter. But if he does come it need not jeopardize the plan. He probably knows that I am your spiritual adviser, but assumes I only met you after discovering you possessed the genes. After all, it is only right that after

313

a wait of two thousand years I should be with the New Messiah during her final days.'

She nodded at this. He was probably right.

The Father rose from his chair. 'I should go now and check all the preparations are in place . . .' He hesitated for a moment, playing nervously with the ring on his finger, suddenly reluctant to leave. 'And I may be too busy to speak to you again before the execution . . .' His usually impassive face was suddenly an open canvas of intense emotions. She saw sorrow, regret, hope, fear and love – yes *love for her* – colour the contours of that ancient face like cloud shadows rolling across a landscape. He walked round the table and stood over her. This time he didn't kneel in front of her, but bent and embraced her. Then he did something which so surprised and touched her that it brought tears to her eyes; he kissed her left cheek.

She wished she could return the tenderness of that embrace, but the manacles denied her. Blinking back disobedient tears she heard him whisper in her ear:

'My child, I am *so* glad I found you in time.' Then before she could say anything in reply he quickly straightened up, his face again void of all emotion. 'I will go now.'

He walked to the door and pressed the buzzer. 'May you be saved,' he said, by way of farewell.

A thin smile creased her stinging eyes. 'So I may save the righteous, and punish the ungodly.'

When the guards opened the door the Father waited whilst they unfastened her manacles from the table and led her to the door. Then he gave her a small smile and walked out.

In the corridor of white tiles she turned to her left; to the door that led to the Death Row visitor reception area, and the already bright sunlight of the world outside. Normally the guards quickly hustled her to the right, back down the long corridor past the execution chamber to her cell. But for some reason today they stopped and let her stand there watching Father Ezekiel's stooped frame walk away from her, down that white tunnel to the light.

She was about to turn away of her own accord when she saw his shoulders stiffen, and his feet halt their busy steps. At first she thought he was going to turn back and say something to her, but instead he looked up through the reinforced glass screen that made

314

up the top half of the door to the visitor reception area. The door opened and a tall figure stood there. She was only fifteen yards away but there was so much light streaming in from outside that she couldn't see who it was. Then the figure stooped and shook the Father's hand. She watched as the Father talked to the person silhouetted against the light. Ezekiel seemed awkward and anxious to leave, but he talked for a good few minutes before eventually nodding his head, shaking the person's hand again and moving past the silhouette to the dazzling sunlight beyond.

The guards made no move to hurry her along. When the door closed on the Father's departing back, blocking out some of the light, she identified the figure. Dr Carter. He had plainly come to visit her and she found this strangely annoying. She wanted to see him when she was out of here, when she could make him pay for all he had done, not now when she wasn't ready. But there was also a part of her that relished the prospect of goading him.

She waited for him to approach her, but he stood there, fifteen yards away, toying with a piece of folded paper in his left hand. He looked radically altered somehow, a different person from the man who had visited her only eleven days ago. He was dressed casually in faded jeans and a blue polo shirt, but it wasn't the clothes that accounted for the change. Then he smiled at her and she knew what it was. The smile wasn't particularly arrogant, just confident. It made him look younger, even boyishly handsome. The difference, she realized now, was that he was happy, and she found this realization oddly unnerving. It certainly wasn't what she was expecting.

She watched him turn back to the door and ask the guard behind to open it. Again the flood of light burst in, and when the door re-closed she saw another shorter figure standing with Dr Carter, shorter even than Father Ezekiel. It was a girl wearing a red baseball cap. The child was holding the scientist's hand, but it was only when the girl waved at her as she had in the photograph that Maria recognized her as his daughter, the terminally ill Holly Carter.

Maria didn't understand. The girl should be near death, dead even. But apart from the absence of hair beneath her cap she looked healthy, *vibrantly* healthy.

What trick was this? What had happened?

Before Maria could re-orientate herself the door opened again, letting in the blinding light, and the girl disappeared. It was only now that Dr Carter began to walk towards her. As if on cue, the guards marched her back into the interview room and fastened her manacles to the table.

WHEN TOM CARTER ENTERED THE ROOM AND SAT OPPOSITE Maria Benariac he felt no hatred. She was doomed to die whereas Holly had been saved. This was more than enough for him. The person he felt most sorry for was old Ezekiel De La Croix, and seeing his stooped frame moments ago had only increased his sympathy for the man. He imagined searching his whole life for someone, only to find them on Death Row, on the brink of being taken away for ever.

Tom had come today because he couldn't bear Maria to die believing that she had succeeded. He needed her to know that ultimately her homicidal fanaticism and vindictive spite had been futile. He also wanted to tell her about the genes, the wonderful genes that had saved his daughter.

He recalled the last time he had sat in this chair, and could still summon up the metallic taste of fear and anger in his mouth. But this time he had nothing to fear from Maria Benariac. He sat back in his chair, toyed with the piece of paper in his hand and waited.

'What happened to your daughter?' she asked moments later.

'She died,' he replied.

'But I saw . . .'

Tom nodded. 'Yes. You saw Holly.'

'But I don't understand. You said she was dead.'

'She *was*. But she isn't any more.'

He could see the shock in Maria's face.

'How?' she asked.

'I used the genes.'

'*You* used the genes? *My* genes?'

'No, I used the original ones. The ones from Christ. But I could have used yours.'

Maria Benariac's guard was down now and her face displayed a strange blend of emotions. He could see anger and outrage that he had succeeded with Cana. But he also saw something else in her eyes: excitement.

'But how did you use them?' she asked.

Tom unfolded the piece of paper he had been toying with. The handwriting was clearly legible. 'Well, there's something about the way they work that I think you'll find interesting.' He leaned across the table with the scrap and Maria automatically turned her manacled hands palm-upwards as if holding a begging bowl. When he laid the piece of paper in her hands he noticed a cross-shaped scar on the pale skin of her right forearm. It was clearly an old scar, but the deep jagged quality of the cut informed his surgeon's eye that it had been made by the blade of a large knife, or dagger, not a precise instrument. His natural curiosity made him want to ask her about it, but when he considered her violent past he thought better of it.

Instead he waited for her to read the message on the paper. 'I didn't write it in blood I'm afraid. But I thought the Preacher might appreciate a little quote from the Bible. Do you know where it's from?'

'Of course,' she scoffed without a moment's hesitation. 'Acts, chapter 20, verse 35.'

He smiled to himself. 'Yes, I thought you would. It's one of the Christian teachings I admire most.'

She shrugged her shoulders in frustration. 'But I still don't understand. What's this got to do with how the genes work?'

Refusing to be hurried, he leaned further back in his chair, trying to find the right words. And at that moment he saw the depth of hatred in her eyes.

'You think you've won. Don't you?' she said, clearly believing he hadn't. Even at this late hour she was trying to pretend she had one last trick up her sleeve.

He shook his head sadly, remembering Olivia, Bob Cooke and Nora Lutz and all the others who had died. 'I don't feel like I've won. Not against you anyway, because I was never really fighting against you. Your war may have been against me and mine, but my war was with other killers; killers far more deadly than you.'

Maria clenched her jaw so hard he could see the muscles tensing on each side of her face.

'Tell me what the message has got to do with the genes,' she demanded again, stabbing the piece of paper with her finger. 'Tell me what it's got to do with *my* genes.'

'Very well,' he said, 'I'll tell you.' And after clearing his throat he proceeded to do just that.

When he finished he was surprised by Maria's reaction. Far from being angry like he expected, she looked stunned. All her arrogance seemed to leave her and for a fleeting moment he thought he detected fear. When he rose and walked over to press the buzzer she didn't even look up. The guards who came to take her away had to lift her physically out of the chair. The whole time she kept on staring at the message he'd left for her: *It is more blessed to give than to receive.*

She now understood what the message meant, but Tom still couldn't understand why his revelation had so affected her. How could what he had told her change anything? She was going to be executed in a few hours. It wasn't as if she expected to live beyond today.

29

EXECUTION CHAMBER, MASSACHUSETTS STATE PENITENTIARY.

AS THE HOUR OF MIDNIGHT APPROACHED MARIA BENARIAC KEPT replaying Dr Carter's words in her head.

Carter must have been lying, she told herself, as the prison doctor injected her with antihistamine. She was so engrossed in her thoughts that she didn't register the irony of a doctor worrying about her adverse reaction to poisons he would later help inject.

But I saw Holly alive, she thought, *and the scientist couldn't have known about the plan, therefore it must be true.* When she'd first realized Holly had been brought back from the dead she had been as excited as she was confused, because it proved her plan would work. But after the scientist had explained, her excitement had evaporated. The more she obsessed about what he'd told her, the more worried she became that perhaps the plan *wouldn't* work.

As the female guards made her put on the diapers for when she voided herself at death, she tried to look for other possibilities. Dr Carter had admitted that he didn't know *exactly* how the genes worked, so he could be mistaken. That meant her plan wasn't *necessarily* affected. If only the Father were here to advise her.

Yes, but how could he help? If the scientist was right, then it was too late to put another plan in place. She had to face facts; the die had been

319

cast and all she could do now was hope Dr Carter had been mistaken.

It was on these thoughts that her mind frantically ruminated as the guards led her down the white corridor towards the execution chamber. But when the door opened and she saw the room in which she was to die, her mind went momentarily blank.

The white chamber, no larger than ten feet by fifteen, was dominated by a black upholstered table in the shape of a drooped cross. Both arms and the main body of the table were fitted with thick leather straps for restraining the condemned prisoner. Beside each arm was an intravenous tube linked to a free-standing chrome box the size of a large TV. On the top of the box was a battery of plunge syringes used for administering an anaesthetic and two separate poisons through tubes into the prisoner's arms. Two intravenous drips were used to safeguard against the unlikely event that one should fail.

She had been told earlier that the poisons would be released from behind the Plexiglas that divided the witnesses from the condemned prisoner. In this area there were two telephones, one of which was connected straight to the State Governor's office, allowing for reprieves to be received right up to the last minute. It was tradition for the Prison Warden to stand by this phone and wait for three minutes after the designated execution hour of midnight before giving the order. However, with the US President's Crime 2000 initiative this had become little more than a meaningless ritual. Since 8 February 2000, not one last-minute reprieve had been given to any condemned prisoner on any death row across the United States of America.

Scanning the witnesses standing behind the Plexiglas barrier, Maria's eyes alighted on the short, wizened figure of Father Ezekiel. He was dressed in a simple black suit that hung loose on his bony frame and owed no fealty to the fashions of the day. She had never really noticed before how old he looked, but tonight his wrinkled face reflected his ninety-six years. To her he was still timeless. He was simply the Father; the man who had given her support and direction when the world had turned its back on her. How she wanted to talk to him now, to share her doubts with him − her fears. She felt sure that he could reassure her.

But she couldn't speak to the Father. She had to have faith and face her Golgotha alone.

As the guards guided her to the table she looked through the Plexiglas, trying to catch Ezekiel's eye, suddenly desperate to warn him that something might be wrong. He just smiled at her, a smile of encouragement and complicity that stopped just short of a wink.

But you don't understand, she wanted to shout at him. *It might not work.* She began to struggle when the guards angled the table vertical and tried to strap her to it.

'Something's wrong,' she shouted. She tried to push one of the guards away and lunge for the glass. 'Make them stop,' she shouted. 'I'm not ready.'

Ezekiel's eyes clouded with concern, not understanding. But the warden and other witnesses looked on impassively as the four experienced guards wrestled her to the table, each man responsible for strapping a particular limb. First her right and then her left leg were strapped to the table, then each of her arms. Next her torso and head, until her whole body was secured. Finally the table was returned to the horizontal. The prison doctor then inserted the intravenous drips into the vein on each of her outstretched arms, and attached the monitoring device to her heart that would tell him when she was clinically dead.

It was when she saw the simple white clock above the Plexiglas screen showing 11:58 that the full implications of what Carter had told her came into focus. There was no more time for self-delusion. If his theory was correct, then not only was she doomed, but her life had been wasted. Not only had she failed to stop Carter, but she had squandered her gift of healing, devoting her life to killing in God's name instead of saving.

She was left now with only one truth, the lesson of forgiveness and redemption taught by the first Messiah – the one who had died so all might repent and find eternal life.

As she lay there on her cross, waiting for the poisons to flow into her veins, she took a deep breath and mouthed a silent prayer.

'Forgive me Father, for I have sinned.'

EZEKIEL DE LA CROIX TRIED NOT TO PICK AT HIS RUBY RING, BUT his mutinous fingers obeyed their own instructions. Have faith, Maria had said, but he was still nervous. He had been shocked by Maria's obvious consternation when the guards had first brought her into the execution chamber. She had been confident this morning, dismissing all his concerns. Yet from his position behind the glass she had suddenly appeared frightened and full of doubt. He could only understand her struggle when he considered the fear that must strike even the most confident soul when faced with death. Had not Christ himself experienced a moment of despair on the cross when he thought he had been forsaken?

Ezekiel looked at the New Messiah stretched out on the cruciform table and turned to the clock above him. 11:59. Now was not the time to be weak. The doubt and fear would end soon and a brave new beginning would dawn.

The other witnesses and the doctor watched the warden. The next few minutes seemed to take forever, but at exactly 12:03 he moved away from the silent phones and nodded to the doctor.

Without hesitation the button was pressed, starting the process of ending Maria Benariac's life. First sodium thiopental, a barbiturate used to put patients to sleep, was released into the intravenous tube. Then a heavy dose of Pavulon was added, a muscle relaxant that stops the lungs functioning. Finally an equal dose of potassium chloride was released, stopping the heart.

Ezekiel watched Maria's body intently for any signs of the poisons' invasion. But all he saw was her close her eyes, then after a few seconds, take a deep, final breath.

At 12:04 the doctor checked his monitors and pronounced the prisoner dead.

Maria Benariac was gone.

Ezekiel lowered his head and mouthed a brief but heartfelt prayer for her soul, and her safe return. The next hours would be critical. The Brotherhood were now committed and couldn't afford one mistake. He was so preoccupied with these thoughts that he didn't notice the official photographer step in to record the witnesses present at the execution. As Ezekiel abruptly turned to leave the room he only just raised his hand in time to stop the flash from blinding him. Waving away the photographer's apologies and blinking back the dazzle in his eyes he quickly strode towards the exit. He had to hurry. There was so much to do.

*　　　*　　　*

CELLS FROM DIFFERENT PARTS OF THE BODY DIE AT DIFFERENT TIMES. There have even been accounts of corpses, dead for many hours or even days, whose hair or fingernails have continued to grow. Like those fanatic Japanese soldiers on isolated Pacific islands after the Second World War, the genes in these outlying cells don't always realize that the main battle is lost and that they should surrender. Instead they keep on fighting for as long as they can, until of course eventually they die too.

PRISON MORGUE.

IN THE TILED BASEMENT MORGUE THE YOUNGER OF THE TWO orderlies kept rubbing his sweaty palms down the front of his overalls as he waited for the elevator to arrive, bearing the corpse of the latest executed prisoner. Lenny Blaggs had been working down here for almost a month now, but the stiffs still gave him the creeps. Working with dead bodies was OK, even in the middle of the night. He'd done that before when he worked at the hospital. But dead murderers and rapists were something else. This was unreal, like something out of a Stephen King novel.

A rumbling of gears started abruptly above him. The elevator was coming down with its cargo.

His boss, Calvin Jetson wheezed noisily on one of his cigarettes. 'Here it comes, man. The death express.'

'You keep smokin' those you're going to catch it yerself,' said Lenny, waving the smoke away, although he secretly preferred the smell of Marlboro tobacco to formaldehyde and death, even if there were some who thought they were the same thing.

'I don't mind dying,' said Calvin, his grey, sun-starved face wrinkling into a grin. 'Death and me are old buddies.'

There was a clank and then the lights on the elevator lit up and the door opened.

Calvin gave him a wink. 'Tonight we are truly honoured, my young protegé. Because tonight we are dealing with one seriously famous badass; none other than the Preacher.'

'Yeah, great,' said Lenny, helping roll the gurney from the elevator into the front section of the morgue, by the door. If killers gave him the creeps then the Queen of the killers gave him the King of the creeps.

'You know what the Preacher did to her victims, after she killed them?' said Calvin, his cigarette sticking to his lower lip as if by magic. 'She got a pen with a special extra long nib and stuck it into—'

'I don't want to know. Just leave it alone. OK!'

Calvin laughed. 'Sure thing, Lenny my boy. No need to get so uptight. Hey, could you go next door and get the stuff, and we'll clean the body up here in the light, so you don't get too scared.'

'I'm not scared,' Lenny protested as he walked to the back of the morgue to get the wipes and chemicals, and the bin to put the soiled diapers in.

'Sure you're not Lenny, my boy,' he heard Calvin say soothingly behind him. 'Sure you're not.'

Lenny pulled up a small trolley and wheeled it over to the supply cupboard. As he busied himself getting the wipes, which he noticed were running low, he thought he felt a subtle breeze, a change in the room temperature, like when a door is opened. Putting it down to his imagination he collected the chemicals and other stuff on the trolley and wheeled it back to the archway that led to the front section of the morgue. As he approached he listened for one of Calvin's 'little jokes', but for once he was silent.

'We'll need to order some more wipes,' Lenny said as he went through the archway. 'I'll get some—'

The sight of Calvin cut him short. His boss just stood there, directly in front of him, staring, his face even whiter than usual. His mouth was moving but no sound came out. A dead cigarette stub dangled from his lower lip, and his eyes bulged. This acting was pretty good, even for the great prankster Calvin Jetson. The man was freakin' terrified.

'Calvin? What the hell's going on, Calvin?'

Calvin's face suddenly changed and he gave Lenny a sly look. 'It was you, right?' Calvin appeared to regain some of his composure, but when he spoke his voice was still so panicky it set Lenny's teeth on edge. 'That was a good one. Shit, how'd you do it? I just turned round for a second, man. Two at the very most.'

'So? What freakin' happened?'

With trembling fingers Calvin lit a new Marlboro and took a deep drag. 'Stop foolin' man. You got me OK. But how? I just turned for a second. Just one lousy second.'

'I don't know what you're freakin' talking about,' said Lenny, his nuts starting to shrivel with fear.

Then Calvin stepped to one side and Lenny understood what all the fuss was about.

Maria Benariac's body was gone.

The freakin' Preacher had disappeared.

30

BEACON HILL, BOSTON.

THE MORNING AFTER THE EXECUTION, MARIA BENARIAC COULDN'T have been further from Tom Carter's mind as he woke from a deep, restful sleep. The kind he hadn't enjoyed since before Stockholm. Eyes closed, he reached across the bed and was about to pull his hand back – *Will you never learn? Olivia's gone* – when he felt her shoulder. He half opened his left eye and smiled at the small figure curled up in a baggy red T-shirt next to him. Holly.

His joy at the memory of how she had crawled into his bed last night was some compensation for the everyday ache of Olivia's absence. Holly was here and she was well.

For a while he lay there in the half-light afforded by the sunshine streaming in between the curtains, and stared at her. Her eyes were closed, and her lips slightly parted as her chest rose and fell with every regular breath she took. Her hair still had to grow back, but it was already returning faster than he thought possible, and even the neat scar on her head was fading at a rate that left Karl Lambert bemused.

He reached across and gently stroked her forehead. Only two days ago she had undergone a CAT scan which could find no trace of her tumour. Her genome now appeared normal, all defects miraculously corrected.

He jumped out of bed and pulled back the curtains of the large windows overlooking the garden. The June sunshine streamed through the mullioned glass, covering his pyjamas with squares of light. The warmth felt good through the cotton, soothing away the chill of the last few nightmare months.

He took a deep breath from the open top window and reached his arms above his head, like a cat stretching in front of a fire. Below him, the garden looked beautiful; the emerald of the lawn; the red of the roses; the yellow of the marigolds; the colours more brilliant than he could ever recall.

'Dad, what time is it?'

He swivelled round to see Holly sitting up in bed yawning, rubbing her eyes. 'Almost eight. Don't forget, Jazz is coming round for breakfast at nine.'

'Larry too?'

'Nope. He's still busy in LA making his movie. When are Jennifer and Megan coming?'

Holly crawled out of the covers, till she was sitting on the edge of the bed, and began scratching the scar on her head. 'They said they'd be here about ten-thirty.'

'Anything planned?'

'No, just hanging out.'

Tom laughed and shook his head. Here was a kid who should be dead, the last five days already a bonus. But today on one of the most fantastic mornings in creation, with her two best friends about to visit, all she wanted to do was 'hang out'. Talk about living life to the full.

'What happened, Dad?' Holly asked, her voice suddenly serious.

He walked over and sat on the bed next to her. 'What do you mean?'

'During the operation.'

He paused. This was the first time she had mentioned the operation in the five days since it had happened. He had purposely not probed before, waiting for her to talk about it in her own time. 'We made you better,' he said simply.

'Mom told me *you* made me better.'

'Mom? When?'

Holly leaned her head against his shoulder, making herself comfortable. 'In my dream. When I was sleeping in the operation. It was weird. I seemed to wake up whilst I was still asleep. I was on a platform and you were putting me on a train. And as the train pulled away you and all these people were waving goodbye to me. There was Alex, Jazz, Jack, Jennifer, Megan – everybody.'

'Where was the train going, Holly?'

'To see Mom. You said that you would be coming along later.'

'Really? So what happened?'

'Well, I was kind of sad to be saying goodbye to you, but happy to be seeing Mom. Then suddenly Mom was there on the train next to me. She explained that she was there to make sure I got to where I was going. It was fantastic seeing her again; she was exactly like she used to be, the way she smiled and laughed – everything. She asked how you were, and whether you were worried about us both. I said you were OK and would come along soon, then just as the train slowed down she began to smile and cry at the same time.

'She said I wasn't getting off with her. That you'd made me better and were taking me back. I didn't feel too sad, because I knew I would see her again one day, and I wanted to come back and see you. The next thing I knew I was waking up looking at Jazz, feeling real thirsty.'

'Some dream,' said Tom.

Holly shifted her head and looked up at him. 'So how did you make me better?' she asked quietly, her intelligent eyes looking into his.

He sighed. This wasn't going to be easy to explain. He still wasn't exactly sure how it had happened himself.

He said, 'I made you better with a special medicine.'

'What kind of medicine?'

'A medicine so special that it doesn't work on the person who's sick. I had to take it instead, so I could make you better.'

'*You* had to take medicine to make *me* better?'

Tom nodded. He remembered his revelation during the operation; the connection he'd made at the point of crisis: why mice injected with the serum had been cured when kept in cages of two or three, whereas injected individual mice had not. The flash of insight had inspired him to inject himself with the Nazareth genes, when he realized that the mice had made each other well; that the Nazareth genes didn't work on the host - but *through* the host.

'You see, Holly, the medicine only works by giving a person the power to help someone else. You can't use it to make yourself well, only others.'

Holly thought about this for a while, then gave a matter-of-fact nod. 'I get it,' she said, standing up from the bed, apparently unfazed by what he'd just told her.

'You do?'

She shrugged diffidently like she was discussing a movie. 'Yeah, I guess it's kind of like a cool software program that doesn't affect the computer it's installed on – but can do awesome things on other ones it's connected to.'

Tom gave a nod and said, 'Yeah, it's sort of like that.'

'Sounds simple,' said Holly as she walked out of his bedroom towards her bathroom. Then just as she was going out the door she casually asked, 'So why didn't you use this medicine before?'

Tom groaned and threw his pillow at her. 'Because, smartass, it wasn't that easy.'

OUTSIDE, THE TWO POLICEMEN WATCHING OVER THE HOUSE SAT slumped in their squad car. It had been another long, boring night and both were looking at their watches. Their relief should be along in half an hour. On and off they had both been staking out the house for the last six months, ever since Mrs Carter's funeral in December. In all that time nothing had happened, and although neither ever said it, both thought their presence was more to reassure Dr Carter, than to really keep him safe.

Bill, the taller cop, was rubbing his eyes as he tried to convince his partner.

'Lou, it's no contest, Ali was the best. Easy.'

Lou shrugged and took another bite of his pastrami and rye. 'Best talker, sure. But boxer, no way. Tyson at his peak would have creamed him.'

A laugh. 'Tyson? Tyson wouldn't have even got close. Ali would have danced all around him.'

The two cops from the Boston Police Department paid little heed to the broad figure in the Boston Red Sox baseball cap, now walking up the drive to the Carter home. It wasn't unusual for Ted to tend the garden so early on a Saturday.

'We're not talking dancing here,' scoffed Lou. 'We're talking boxing. For a faggy pirouette Ali might be the man. But in a *fight* Tyson would have killed him.'

Both cops were so involved in their discussion that if either man noticed that Ted walked a little taller and straighter than usual, they didn't mention it.

JASMINE WASHINGTON PUT DOWN HER COFFEE CUP IN THE conservatory and frowned at Tom across the breakfast debris.

She asked, 'So the genes release chemicals that can be passed on by touch? But the chemicals don't work on the host?'

Tom shrugged. 'It seems that way.'

Jasmine shook her head and watched Holly excuse herself from the table. As Holly passed her the little girl raised her right hand in a high five and Jasmine slapped it.

'Way to go, Holly.'

'You're sure she's completely OK?' Jasmine asked Tom again, watching the young girl leave.

'She's fine. According to all the tests she's never been better.'

'And all because of the Nazareth genes,' she said. *Just because you touched her*, she thought.

Tom reached across the table to pour them both more coffee. As he did so Jasmine caught herself staring at his hands – *one of the hands that had brought Holly back to life*. The hairs rose on the back of her neck. If she had found it difficult to accept that the killer, Maria, had been born with Christ's healing genes, then she found it equally confusing that Tom Carter now possessed them. What was evident, though, was that these genes didn't define or determine who the Messiah was, or even whether the possessor was good. The Nazareth genes were simply a rare God-given talent that stretched the Christian tenet of free will to the ultimate. Just because you were blessed with the power to do amazing good, you didn't have to use it. Like Maria Benariac, you could still choose to kill, rather than save. Jasmine had to smile at the irony of Tom Carter, an atheist, unlocking their benign power, using his science to cheat the lottery of Nature and possess the genes himself.

'So what do you think the mysterious third gene does?' she asked, sipping her coffee.

'I'm not sure,' Tom paused, collecting his thoughts. 'But guessing from DAN's early findings, *naz 3* is a control gene that activates and modifies the other two Nazareth genes. And from the data I think the gene obviously interacts with a host of other genes too. It seems to perform as many as *three* key functions.' Tom put down the coffee flask and began to count on his fingers. 'The first is a trigger function, probably linking up with genes that control emotion and thought, so the host can *decide* when the Nazareth genes should or shouldn't kick in. The second function is that of a control, *activating* and *customizing* the *naz 1* and *naz 2* genes, which repair and regulate DNA respectively, so they give the most benefit to the recipient's damaged cells. The third function is as a vehicle – *delivering* the optimized genetic instruction from the host to the recipient and then spreading that benefit throughout their body. My guess is that it's a pheromone type agent that's secreted through the skin – transmitting the healing program through touch.'

'But you don't know exactly how they work yet?'

'Nope. And we probably won't understand precisely how the genes function for years. But I do know the host has got to want it to happen and *believe* it can happen at either a conscious or emotional level.'

Jasmine smiled and drank her coffee. 'Sounds a lot like good ol' fashioned faith to me. A real gift from God.'

Tom shrugged at that. 'Perhaps you're right. And as gifts go it's got to be the ultimate one. It's the only one I know that has to be given away to be enjoyed.'

Jasmine raised her cup in a 'cheers' gesture. 'Well, it is more blessed to give than receive.'

Tom laughed. 'I couldn't have put it better myself.'

Holly walked back into the room, holding a copy of the *Boston Globe*. 'Paper's come,' she said, dropping it on the table between them, before walking over to the garden door.

'Aren't your friends here yet?' asked Tom, idly picking up the newspaper. He glanced at the front page, his eyes skimming the news.

'About half an hour,' said Holly, opening the door. 'I'm going to wait in the garden.' She looked outside and shrugged her small shoulders. 'I didn't know Ted was here this weekend. I thought he was going to Martha's Vineyard with Marcy.'

'OK, Hol,' Tom mumbled as his daughter walked out into the garden. But Jasmine could see he was barely listening, his face frowning at whatever was in the paper. Suddenly his face turned pale. 'Shit!'

'What? What is it, Tom?'

TOM CARTER FELT SOMETHING COLD UNCOIL IN HIS STOMACH AS HE read the type before his eyes. The main story was about the President's trade visit to China, but beneath it under the title *Latest News* was the headline: '*Hunt the Preacher*' and two pictures – one showed a side profile of Maria Benariac taken shortly after she was sentenced, the other was the official photograph of witnesses to her execution. He could just make out Ezekiel De La Croix, but that wasn't what surprised him or filled him with dread.

The article stated that although Maria had been executed and certified dead, her body had disappeared from the morgue. And when he read about the method of execution – lethal injection – his unease deepened.

What was that story Mother Clemenza had told him about in Corsica?

Maria neutralized the poison in the bee stings. Isn't that what the nun had said? *Neutralized the poison.*

He remembered how shocked Maria had been when he'd told her how the genes worked.

Shit, she was *planning* on being resurrected.

'What is it, Tom?' Jasmine asked again, leaning forward.

He passed her the paper. 'The witch has apparently got on her broomstick and flown away.'

Jasmine read the article open-mouthed. 'What does this mean?'

'Don't you see? She planned on being executed by lethal injection – poison. Then use her genetic ability to neutralize the poison in her body, and bring herself back. She *knew* she could neutralize poison, she'd done it once before on someone else.'

'I don't believe it. Anyway it wouldn't work on herself, would it? And who did she expect to help her get out?'

'I don't know,' said Tom, turning to look out the conservatory. Holly was bending over the rose bed, smelling the flowers. Beyond her he could see Ted walk across the lawn to the shed at the bottom of the garden. He wore his Boston Red Sox cap but something about his gait was different. He wasn't stooping as he usually did. He looked taller too. Tom watched him open the shed door and step inside.

What had Holly said? – 'I didn't know Ted was here this weekend. I thought he was going to Martha's Vineyard with Marcy.'

He was.

A sudden coldness rushed through him, more rage than fear. Tom reached across the table and grabbed Jasmine by the arm. She looked up from the newspaper, surprised.

'Jazz, don't ask any questions,' he said. 'Just go out the front door and get the police watching over the house. Tell them Holly and I are in danger. Do it now!'

'Why? What . . .?'

'That's not Ted out there. Just go!'

Holly was now ten yards away from the house, walking to the shed. A spade rested against the side by the door.

Tom didn't dare call out to her, in case it alerted whoever was inside. Instead he rushed out of the conservatory and raced across the lawn towards her. She was close to the shed now.

Tom ran as fast as he could, ignoring his injured leg.

The shed door began to open towards him. Tom was ten feet away, six feet from Holly. A hand holding a gun reached from behind the door.

'Holly!' he screamed. 'Get back!'

Holly turned frightened, puzzled eyes towards him. Good, if she was scared she'd run faster.

'Go back into the house!' he shouted. 'Run! Run as fast as you can!'

As she ran past him, Tom threw all his weight against the shed door. He heard the crunching of bone as the door crushed the man's arm, forcing him to drop his gun. Frantically Tom reached for the spade resting against the shed, jumped around the door and hit out as hard as he could. As he fell the man tried to roll away and reach for the fallen gun, but Tom rained blows down on his body, forcing him to shield himself with his arms. Tom kept hitting him and hitting him. Only when the man lay still did Tom finally stop, panting from adrenalin and exertion. Now that he was calmer he recognized the man from Tel Aviv Airport and his helicopter trip to meet the Brotherhood. What was Gomorrah doing here?

Shaking, Tom threw the spade to the ground and reached for the gun. Why was this man who worked for Ezekiel De La Croix's Brotherhood here with a gun?

Then he saw the scar on the man's forearm. The same cross-shaped scar he had seen on Maria Benariac's forearm. Finally he understood. Tom's spent rage returned when he remembered Karen Tanner's words, '*We may never know who was behind the Preacher.*'

Maria had been a member of the Brotherhood all the time. Ezekiel's Brotherhood were responsible for killing Olivia and trying to stop Cana, after they had got what they wanted from him. He realized now that Holly and he would never be safe so long as the Brotherhood continued to exist.

'Tom, are you OK?' shouted Jasmine running up behind him. She was flanked by two cops.

Too angry to speak, he gave an abrupt nod as he walked past her, towards the house and Holly. He remembered the tracker Jack had made him swallow on his first visit to the Brotherhood's cave. He now knew who had moved Maria's body from the penitentiary and where they had taken her.

'Tom,' said Jasmine. 'Where are you going?'

He didn't turn back when he eventually spoke.

'To finish this.'

31

CAVE OF THE SACRED LIGHT, SOUTHERN JORDAN.

AND ON THE THIRD DAY THE INNER CIRCLE KNELT IN CEREMONIAL robes before the Sacred Flame, which now burnt stronger and whiter than ever. Ahead of him Ezekiel De La Croix could see the open door leading to the Vault of Remembrance. On the altar before it lay the New Messiah. Maria Benariac's corpse was wrapped in a white shroud with only her pale face showing. The pungent oils, herbs and spices that anointed her body vied with the cavern's usual aroma of incense and burnt wax.

Ezekiel felt exhausted but exhilarated. Gomorrah should have despatched Carter and Washington by now, so he could concentrate on Maria. He hadn't slept more than a few minutes since the day she died, and could barely keep his eyes open. He desperately wanted to rest, but couldn't risk missing the moment when Maria awoke. When that happened and she passed her hand through the flame, his part in fulfilling prophecy would be over, and he could rest for an eternity.

The plan had worked better than he'd hoped. Brother Bernard had arranged for the guards to be paid off with relative ease. After all, where was the harm in keeping silent and turning a blind eye when a *dead* prisoner was taken from the prison? It wasn't as if she was actually escaping. By all accounts the body had been spirited away so quickly that rumours were already circulating in the prison that Maria Benariac had risen from the dead and walked out. If only they knew, thought Ezekiel with a tired smile.

Brother Olazabal's brethren in the New World had arranged the ambulance from the prison, and the plane to fly the body from the private hangar at Logan Airport. Brother Haddad and his Brothers in the Holy Land had arranged for the necessary papers to bring the 'deceased son' of one of the brethren 'home' for burial on Jordanian soil.

On arrival in Amman the body had been transported to *Asbaa el-Lah* by the Brotherhood's helicopter. Once she was safely ensconced in the Cave of the Sacred Light, Brother Helix had prepared the ritual oils, herbs and spices with which they had anointed her body. Finally, almost a whole day after the execution, Bernard and Luciano had taken the ritual shroud from the Vault of Remembrance and wrapped her body from head to toe, leaving only the New Messiah's face exposed.

Now there was no more to do. Except to watch and pray.

The third day had already arrived and they still waited.

Ezekiel shifted his weight on the prayer mat, stifling a groan when the movement reawakened the ache in his numbed muscles. He glanced at the others keeping the silent vigil alongside him, checking their faces for any signs of fatigue, trying to gauge their commitment to this endeavour. All knelt, motionless, their heads bowed, as if in deep prayer. All except Brother Bernard. Since Ezekiel had explained how Maria had cured his ulcer, even the sceptical Bernard seemed to believe. But from the furtive looks the stout Brother was casting at Maria's inert body, Ezekiel could tell his doubts were returning.

Bernard suddenly turned and caught his eye. 'Leader De La Croix, how long must we wait?' he hissed, fracturing the quiet of the cave.

'She didn't say. She only said that we should be patient and have faith.'

'It's been almost three days.'

'It took as long before,' chided Helix from Ezekiel's right.

Now all the Brothers looked up.

'But . . .' started Bernard, scratching his goatee beard. 'What if . . .?'

Ezekiel cut him off, guessing the fear he was going to express. 'She *will*. Have faith!' He shrugged off the icy fingers of doubt that threatened to walk down his own spine. He couldn't even countenance the possibility that Maria wouldn't return. He had stood by and watched the New Messiah die; *let* her be executed without doing anything to intervene. Maria had to come back. She'd promised him she would. Any other outcome at this stage was unthinkable.

'All I'm saying, my Leader,' wheedled Bernard, 'is that perhaps we should consider a fallback—'

Ezekiel turned his black eyes on the Brother's round face and fixed him with his most baleful stare. 'Have faith, Brother Bernard! She will return!'

'ACCORDING TO THE CO-ORDINATES WE MUST BE HERE,' SHOUTED Karen Tanner above the noise of the helicopter's rotors, pointing to the map on her lap.

Tom Carter felt a rush of nervous exhilaration as he looked through the glass at the five pillars of rock marooned in the desert below. On the sand near the tallest rock, a helicopter and two vehicles were visible. In the air to his right he could see three helicopters crammed with a joint task force of Delta Force, FBI and Royal Jordanian Army personnel.

'Won't they know we're here?' Tom asked.

Karen adjusted her shades and gave a grim smile. 'Oh, they'll know we're here soon enough. But they won't have enough time to do anything about it.'

Tom believed her. It impressed him how quickly Karen Tanner had acted after he'd told her about Gomorrah and the Brotherhood. The FBI had easily pinpointed the location of the cave once Jack Nichol's anonymous friend had given them the tracker co-ordinates from Tom's first visit here. Then after a few hurried phone calls from the Director of the FBI and the US State Department to the Jordanian authorities, the Task Force had been despatched within hours. Karen had tried to leave Tom behind, but nothing was going to stop him seeing this through to the end. And, as he'd told her, he was the only person outside the Brotherhood who had ever been to the place before.

'Dave, what do they have?' Karen Tanner asked the man to her right. Wearing shades and desert fatigues, Dave was studying an array of data on his laptop. Like all the men from the Delta Force team he hadn't supplied his surname, and Tom wasn't even sure whether Dave was really his first name.

'Sensor readings give us three men on the surface, but as for underground, that's anybody's guess. Given the data and what Tom's told us from the last time he came here, I reckon the place relies more on secrecy than force for protection.'

'Well, they've lost their protection.' Karen reached for her walkie-talkie and patted the pilot on the shoulder. 'Chuck, get us down as close to the tallest rock as you can. Fast and low, OK?'

Karen shouted orders into the walkie-talkie and all four helicopters immediately dropped in altitude, closing on their target. Tom felt his stomach contract as he looked down and saw two antlike figures running between the vehicles and the cave. His nervous excitement must have shown on his face because Karen gave him a tight grin. 'You wanted to come along for the ride. Well, the ride starts now.'

BROTHER BERNARD HAD ONLY JUST STOPPED VOICING HIS DOUBTS when Ezekiel De La Croix heard the sound of running feet from the stairs. It annoyed rather than concerned him at first. He had expressly told the three men above and the guard outside the cavern to leave them undisturbed. The noise grew louder and he could hear shouts now. Then two sharp reports. Gunshots? What was going on? The other members of the Inner Circle were now exchanging worried looks.

Brother Bernard stood. 'I'd better investigate.'

Suddenly the doors burst open and a group of men in uniform flooded into the chamber.

This couldn't be happening. Not here. Not now.

Surprising himself with his own agility, Ezekiel leaped up and ran behind the altar, putting himself between Maria and the open door to the Vault of Remembrance. Reaching under the altar cloth he felt for the ceremonial dagger and slipped it into the waist-cord of his ceremonial robe. The others still hadn't moved; *couldn't* move. Only Brother Bernard was standing.

'Everyone, stay where you are!' ordered the auburn-haired woman in a blue coat with FBI emblazoned on the back. At least eight uniformed men stood on either side of her. 'My name is Special Agent

338

Karen Tanner of the United States Federal Bureau of Investigation. And in co-operation with the Jordanian Authorities we are arresting you on suspicion of abduction, multiple homicide and conspiracy to murder.' Behind the Americans, Ezekiel could see a squad of what looked like Royal Jordanian troops.

His quick scan took in the Inner Circle: Bernard standing motionless, his eyes staring at the gun in the nearest FBI man's hand; Helix calmly shaking his head in disbelief; Luciano reaching for the sky like an outlaw in a John Wayne film; Haddad and Olazabal frozen, staring like rabbits into the headlights of a speeding truck.

Blood pounded in Ezekiel's temples. This was a nightmare. It couldn't end like this. *How did they find this place?*

Crouching behind the altar he began to pull the New Messiah towards him from the table, until her corpse fell with a dull thud at his feet. He had only one objective now, to protect the body. Nothing else mattered.

'Don't move sir!' shouted a tall blond soldier, raising his pistol and walking towards him.

Then *he* stepped out of the shadows. And at that moment Ezekiel hated *him* more than any living thing. The atheist must have betrayed them on his last visit. The scientist had eluded Gomorrah and led these people here. He was going to ruin everything.

Ezekiel watched Carter gesture to the soldier to back off, and then saw him walk towards him. *Don't waste time on the blasphemer*, he admonished himself. *Concentrate on protecting the New Messiah, keeping her safe.* He quickly checked behind him to see how far away he was from the open door to the Vault of Remembrance. Less than a metre. And next to the door he could see the rope pull hanging from the heavy wooden stake that jutted waist-high out of the stone wall. Maintained but unused since it had been first installed in the early years, the drastic precaution should only be used in moments of extreme emergency. But surely this qualified.

He forced his racing mind to remember the instructions he'd been given on his inauguration to the Leadership.

He glared at the unarmed Dr Carter coming closer and closer, seeing his own anger at betrayal reflected in the man's blue eyes.

'Be careful, Tom!' he heard Tanner shout when the blasphemer reached the front of the altar, less than four feet away. The scientist was directly between Ezekiel and the crescent of armed men, almost on the white flame, momentarily shielding him from their guns.

Now was the ideal time to make his move.

SEEING EZEKIEL DE LA CROIX STANDING OVER MARIA BENARIAC'S elaborately shrouded corpse brought a cauldron of emotions to the boil in Tom. To think that he had eaten with this man, dealt with him, even felt sympathy for him, when all the time he had been biding his time, waiting to finish what his bloody Brotherhood had started in Stockholm. This wizened, black-eyed dwarf had killed his wife as certainly as Maria had. In many ways he was worse than Maria; if she was the foot-soldier obeying orders, then he was the General who had given them.

Tom could guess why they wanted him dead, but he wanted to hear this man tell him. He needed to understand what warped rationale the Brotherhood used to order a man's death simply because he had dedicated himself to saving lives. No doubt it had something to do with that fanatical bullshit Maria had spewed at him in the GENIUS laboratory; tampering with God's work; undermining the divine order or some such crap. But he needed to understand why a whole organization committed to finding and protecting a Messiah they believed would save mankind, also saw fit to kill people, to kill *him*. He needed to know this to make sense of Olivia's assassination.

He stepped closer to Ezekiel and sensed, rather than saw, the agents train their guns more intently on the Leader of the Brotherhood. He had been impressed by how speedily they had despatched the guards. Two on the surface had tried to fight back with handguns, giving the third time to close the concealed door to the Great Stairs. But the attack had been too fast and too fierce. The helicopters hadn't even landed before agents were streaming across the ground. The three men had been incapacitated in minutes, all wounded but none killed. The guard below had taken more time, because Karen's team hadn't known he was alone. But the man hadn't even known they were under attack and he was soon overpowered. Carter had only been a bystander but he'd shared the adrenalin rush as he'd followed the team into the Brotherhood's lair.

Now he was face to face with the man who had changed his life irrevocably.

'So you think Maria's coming back, do you?' he asked as he walked past the sacred flame, his hands within reach of the altar cloth.

Ezekiel didn't answer him, just crouched behind the altar like a cornered rat, black eyes staring with unconcealed hatred.

'This was *her* idea, wasn't it?' Tom probed. 'She thought that because she'd saved an allergic girl from bee-sting poison she could save herself. Didn't she?' He could see Ezekiel's eyes narrow and knew he was right.

'Don't get too close!' warned Karen behind him.

'It's OK. I just want to ask the man a few things.'

'Let it wait! You'll have all the time in the world to ask him later.'

But then Ezekiel moved, and Tom knew he wouldn't have any time later. With unexpected speed the old man suddenly leaped back and reached for the stake jutting out of the wall that Tom had asked about on his first visit, and began to turn it clockwise.

'*What you might call a final precaution*' – isn't that what he'd called it? *What kind of precaution?* Tom asked himself as he clambered over the high altar, not realizing he was obstructing the line of fire. All he knew was that he must stop Ezekiel.

In the seconds it took for him to climb over the altar, he became vaguely aware of a commotion behind him; Karen shouting at him to get out of the way; Ezekiel pulling the stake out of the wall, throwing it defiantly on the floor, grabbing Maria's corpse under the arms, and dragging her through the opening to the Vault of Remembrance.

Tom moved towards him, but suddenly his ears were filled with the terrible grinding of mighty levers and cogs, and the groan of heavy rock moving high above him.

He didn't see Brother Bernard use the distraction afforded by Ezekiel's sudden move to wrest away the gun from the FBI agent standing over him, and lumber to his leader's aid. Tom only had eyes for Ezekiel. He had to get to the old man before he could drag Maria beyond the stone door and close it behind him. Tom remembered the old rope ladder in the ancient vault. He wasn't about to let the old man wriggle out that way.

The din of moving rock above him was rolling thunder, but as Tom threw himself at Ezekiel he could just hear Karen's yell: 'Look out, Tom! Behind you!' And at the same time he saw Ezekiel glance up from Maria's body shouting: '*Kill* him, Brother Bernard! *Shoot* him!'

Then he heard two gunshots and felt an impact in his back, winding him, slamming him into Ezekiel. Then he, the Leader of the Brotherhood and whatever or whoever was on his back were rolling through the stone doorway with Maria's corpse; a writhing scrum of bodies and flailing limbs. Tom panicked. He thrashed out wildly with his arms and legs, desperate to get away from the beady eyes and pouting mouth only inches away from his face. It took him a good five seconds to register the blood on his hands and realize he was fighting a dead man; Brother Bernard had a gaping bullet-hole in his back.

He eased the dead man's bulk off him, and rolled onto the cold, stiff body of Maria. The cloying reek of death, oils and herbs invaded his nostrils. Recoiling in revulsion he pushed himself away and rose to a crouch. Gasping to catch his breath he looked up to find he was in the small room between the Sacred Cavern and the Vault of Remembrance. Ezekiel stood four yards away by the second door lever that opened the door to the Vault. In his right hand he held a dagger, his forearm bloody, obviously wounded by the second bullet. Tom considered rushing him, but could barely find the breath to speak, let alone fight. Instead he kept his distance whilst he struggled to regain his breath. They both stared at each other for a moment, Maria's inert body marking the no-man's-land between them.

Tom wondered where Karen and the other agents were, and why - they hadn't come in after him. Then he felt the vibration as a boulder came crashing down to the cavern floor outside the antechamber. Edging to the doorway, he looked back to the altar and beyond. The FBI men, Jordanian troops and the rest of the Inner Circle were all looking up at the now-quaking pillars, backing away towards the far doorway that led to the Great Stairs. Only Karen was standing her ground, but even she had her eyes locked on the shifting rock above. The myriad of candles and torches that illuminated the cave were falling from the walls along the cavern like shooting stars, throwing the golden glow into a murky gloom, making the white fire of the Sacred Flame appear to burn even more brightly. When Ezekiel had pulled the stake from the wall he must have released tons of loose rock and boulders penned up in the granite above; no doubt positioned there by the Brotherhood's early engineers, to ensure that the secrets of their cave had the ultimate protection – total destruction.

'Karen!' he shouted across the fiery gloom, beckoning frantically with his arms. 'Get out of here before the whole goddamned place comes crashing down. Hurry!'

'What about you?' Karen yelled back.

Tom was torn. Ezekiel had now opened the door to the blackness of the vault, and was dragging the inert Maria into it. He guessed the vault with all its precious treasures would have been designed by the engineers to be safe from their rigged Armageddon. But he couldn't be sure. The idea of Ezekiel escaping made him sick with anger.

'Come on Tom!' Karen shouted, moving back towards the Great Stairs.

Tom waved her away, yelling as loudly as his empty lungs and bruised ribs would allow. 'Don't worry! I'm coming.'

Then the first pillar fell in front of him, crashing down onto the altar. He couldn't see Karen any more, or any of the others. They were lost in the dust and flying splinters of rock. Tom just stood for a moment, miraculously untouched by the debris, seeing his only route to Karen and the Great Stairs closed to him. He saw a section of pillar slide off the shattered altar and roll onto the stone on the other side, sealing the hole through which the Sacred Flame burned, denying the subterranean gas its escape. Concealing its fire.

Retreating into the relative safety of the antechamber, Tom stepped over Brother Bernard's inert body and moved towards Ezekiel, just as he disappeared into the blackness of the Vault with Maria. Then the door to the Vault began to close.

Tom's ribs ached, and it hurt to run. But he forced himself into the stale darkness before the door closed on him, wishing he could remember where the light switch was, his only bearings the sound of Maria's body being dragged on the stone floor.

He strained his ears but the only sound he could hear was his own ragged breathing and the hellish destruction being wrought beyond the thick walls in the Sacred Cavern. Feeling to his left and right, he tried to make out shapes he could recall from his last visit. If he remembered correctly then the concealed niche holding the relics of Christ should be at the other end of the vault, directly in front of him, and the huge sword he'd so admired should be on his left. If he could reach that, then despite its weight he would at least have a weapon. Hugging the left-hand shelves he edged his way along the side of the vault as quietly as possible, his hands blindly feeling parchment, boxes and metal objects as he went. When he came to the break in the shelves he reached to his left, to the wall against which the sword should be leaning. His searching fingers found nothing but rough, dry stone. Shit! Where was it?

At that moment he felt the first tremor beneath his feet. It wasn't the same vibrating shockwave he'd felt from the falling boulders. More like the rumblings of something beneath the rock floor trying to escape. Dust and debris fell around him, and the objects on the shelves rattled like loose teeth. He fell forward against the wall and banged his knee against steel. The sword.

He reached down and touched its hilt, just as the second tremor rippled its muscles beneath him. Of course, he thought, *the gas*; it must be the gas that fed the Sacred Flame. Denied its escape valve, it was seeking out a new opening, some weakness in the rock through which to vent its mounting pressure. With all the rock crashing down in the cavern outside, he was sure the gas should find a weak point soon. But he wondered if the Brotherhood's ancient engineers had factored gas pressure into their calculations for keeping their precious Vault of Remembrance safe.

He hefted the sword off the ground and turned his back to the wall, trying to keep his breathing as silent as possible. He had a weapon now. So assuming the engineers did know what they were doing, then he should be relatively safe in this black womb.

Suddenly he felt a hand on his shoulder, and foul breath on his face. For one terrifying, irrational moment he thought it might be Maria, come back from the dead.

He whirled round, bringing the sword's huge blade level with his waist and felt it hit something; he heard a grunt of pain. He leant back against the wall to support the sword's weight better, holding its blade against whoever still had their hand on his shoulder.

Suddenly he felt the stale breath on his face again, only this time it was accompanied by a cold blade against his neck. Angling the sword, he pushed its point against his invisible attacker just as a third tremor, quickly followed by a fourth and fifth, rocked the foundations of the vault.

'I think this is stalemate, Dr Carter,' Ezekiel spat out of the darkness, his unseen face only inches away. 'I wonder if your friends got away. I doubt it.'

'If they did, they'll be back, and you can say goodbye to your secret Brotherhood. What about your precious Inner Circle? What if you killed them too?'

A small laugh in the dark. 'They are expendable. *We* are all expendable. As for the Brotherhood, once Maria awakes, its purpose will have been served. The Final Judgement will come and everything will end. The Brethren will be saved, because we found the New Messiah in time.'

'But she's dead,' said Tom. 'You missed the boat again.'

The dagger bit into the flesh of his neck, warm blood trickled down his neck. 'She will be resurrected,' said Ezekiel, his voice thick with hatred. 'She has the power.'

'No, she hasn't. That's not how the genes work.'

A contemptuous laugh. 'Liar. As a child she could perform miracles. She cured my ulcer. She has the power.'

'Not on herself, she hasn't. I told Maria that on the day of her execution. And from her reaction I reckon she believed me.'

The dagger cut deeper into Tom's flesh and he was powerless to defend himself. He tried to push Ezekiel away with the sword, but it was too heavy. He had to distract him. Allowing the pressure of Ezekiel's own body to hold the sword's weight Tom moved his right hand off the hilt. Then he reached for the old man's injured left arm, where the second gunshot had hit him.

'I know how the genes work,' Tom said softly into the dark, 'because I used them to save my daughter.' He gently placed his hand on Ezekiel's arm, feeling for the wound. 'I injected myself with Christ's genes. So I now possess them too.'

Ezekiel tried to pull away as soon as he touched him, but Tom held his arm in a vice-like grip. Tom's legs almost buckled with the outflowing of energy and his muscles ached as if they were stretched on the rack, but he could feel Ezekiel's dagger hand shaking against his neck. He knew that Ezekiel could feel the healing power flowing into him.

When Tom finished he slumped back further against the wall, and as he relaxed his grip Ezekiel pulled away. The heavy sword drooped in Tom's hand, its tip sparking on the stone floor. Seconds later he heard a switch being clicked and the vault was bathed in dazzling light. He turned with squinting eyes and saw Ezekiel by the door to the vault. He stood, legs apart, straddling Maria's body. His ancient face looked pale and now his dark eyes showed fear as well as hatred.

'Maria was right,' Ezekiel said. 'You are evil, and I should never have negotiated with you. I should have let her kill you.'

God, he was tired of this. 'She tried to kill me. Remember! Twice. But I'm not the evil one. I've only ever tried to save lives.'

Ezekiel scoffed. 'By going against the natural order. By defying God!'

'There is no God. There is no natural order. If there was, then these genes wouldn't be so rare.'

Ezekiel laughed then, a loud, manic laugh that had no humour in it. 'You still don't understand, do you?' the old man shouted. 'You still don't know why we needed to kill you even more than the obvious peddlers of evil we eradicated: the arms dealers, the drugs dealers and the porn merchants. They were weak and only poisoned the world we live in. Whereas your evil genetics threatens to *change it completely*. Even now that you have somehow used your diabolical technology to give yourself the genes of God, you *still* don't understand how dangerous you are.'

Another tremor, even more violent than the others, shook the ground, and there was the sound of stone rending below. But Ezekiel ignored it, and carried on.

'You have great knowledge, Dr Carter, some say genius. But it takes more than knowledge to be God. You need *wisdom*. You said that if God existed then these genes wouldn't be so scarce. But that isn't true. Just think about a world in which *everyone* possessed them. A world in which anybody could heal everybody, and no-one ever died of natural diseases. Imagine a world where there would be no consequences for any actions we took. A world with such an enormous population that instead of a heaven on earth we would create a living hell. No space. No food. No respect for life, or death, and certainly not God. Just a crowded desert of lost souls assured of only one certainty – a long life of suffering.'

Still wielding his dagger, Ezekiel slumped to the stone floor beside Maria, and pulled her body onto his lap. He remained oblivious to the now incessant rumblings underfoot. Tom looked to his left and saw the rope and wood ladder hanging from the fissure in the rough rock ceiling. He began to move towards it.

'Tell me, Dr Carter!' continued Ezekiel, 'does wanting to save your daughter – one insignificant human in a sea of humanity – give you the right to play God? Does it give you the right to risk creating a hell on earth? She was destined to die, and *should* have died. You had no right to use your intelligence and resources to change that. And that applies to the others you saved with your meddling genetics before Project Cana.' Ezekiel paused then, as if weary.

Tom didn't bother to answer him. There was no time. He dropped the heavy sword, grasped the swaying ladder and pulled himself up. His anger had evaporated. He felt nothing when he looked back at the stooped figure cradling the corpse on his lap in a grotesque parody of the *pietà*. Except some pity for a misguided, broken, old man.

He reached the fifth rung of the ladder, halfway inside the fissure, when he heard the first cracking hiss of gas rip through the stone floor beneath him.

He looked up but could see only blackness above. There wasn't much time. He gritted his teeth and carried on climbing. The hand Maria had pierced was aching now, as was his old leg wound from Stockholm. With every rung he climbed, his elbows hit the rough side of the fissure, bruising and cutting his flesh. But the real pain came from his stretched muscles and joints. Every muscle burned with effort as he inched his way higher and higher.

Rather than abating, the rumbling below him grew louder the further he climbed.

At last. A glimmer of light above. If he could only keep going.

The sudden explosion beneath him was deafening. Seconds later a rush of hot air rose up, hitting him with such force that it tore him from the ladder, pushing him upwards, crashing his head against the walls of rock on either side. Excruciating pain flowed through his whole body, every nerve ending on fire.

Then mercifully the pain stopped, and there was nothing.

MOMENTS BEFORE, EZEKIEL DE LA CROIX SAT AND WATCHED DR Carter disappear up the ladder. Despite the urgent tearing of rock beneath him, Ezekiel felt a tired calm. The scientist may escape, but once the New Messiah awoke none of this nightmare would matter any more. Once Maria passed her hands through the Sacred Flame, then the Day of Judgement would come and all the ungodly, not just Dr Carter, would be punished. But he as leader of the righteous would be saved.

He shifted Maria's weight on his lap, making his exhausted, aching frame as comfortable as possible. He looked down at her pale, peaceful features, willing those unusual eyes to open. As he caressed her cold forehead, he remembered the first time he saw her. She had been so vulnerable then, so bruised by life, so unaware of the greatness of her destiny.

He examined his wounded arm and marvelled at the fading injury. Dr Carter might have been able to unnaturally steal the genes of Christ, but he had been lying about Maria. Maria had been *born* with the genes – they were her birthright. Despite what the atheist said, Maria would wake. He was convinced of it.

The sudden cracking of rock to his left, followed by a roaring hiss, made him turn his head in fear. Before his eyes he saw a fissure open up in the floor. The crack started by the wall where the tooth and nail of Christ were kept, and moved across the stone floor as if following some preordained route towards him.

'Not yet!' he screamed, watching the fissure lengthen like the shadow of a giant accusing finger.

He shook Maria's body, shouting: 'Wake up! Wake up!' Then he threw her off him, and staggered to his feet.

'I can't die yet,' he screamed, his body racked with mortal terror. 'I'm not ready, we are not ready.'

Just as the tip of the shadowy finger reached between his feet he heard an explosion beneath him, an incendiary of rage from the earth's core. Then a ridge of searing flame rushed from the fissure in a vertical sheet of pure white, that seemed to reach for heaven itself. Even in his agony and terror, Ezekiel thought the white flame that now consumed him was the most beautiful thing he had seen in his whole life.

32

GENIUS HEADQUARTERS, BOSTON.

FOUR WEEKS LATER THE VINTAGE RED MERCEDES PULLED INTO THE deserted car park beneath GENIUS, and turned towards the first parking slot. It braked suddenly when the surprised driver realized the space was already taken by a metallic green BMW convertible.

Tom Carter checked his face in the mirror. The superficial burns had now all flaked away, and the tender skin underneath had lost most of its pink complexion. 'Cosmetic companies would charge a fortune for a peel like that,' Jasmine had joked on his last day in hospital three weeks ago. He knew he had been unnaturally lucky. According to Karen's people, if the flue had been fractionally more crooked, then the gas explosion would have splattered him against the walls 'like a roadkill on the freeway'. Instead he had been coughed up beside the smallest of the five rocks, landing unconscious but intact on a ridge of mercifully soft sand. The short burst of white flame that accompanied him had even helped alert Karen's team, who had only just crawled to safety themselves. Miraculously only one FBI agent and two Jordanian troops had been injured in the escape. Apart from Ezekiel and Bernard the only death had been Brother Helix. He had been lost in the confusion and was now buried in the rock.

Not surprisingly, the other members of the Brotherhood hadn't told the FBI anything. But at least they had Gomorrah and Tom had been able to tell Karen about Ezekiel's confession. It was still unclear what could or couldn't be proven against the surviving members of the Inner Circle, but according to Karen they wouldn't pose a threat to him any longer. As for the rest of the Brotherhood, its assets and members were impossible to identify, let alone locate. But there was no indication that they were even aware of the killings. As far as Tom was concerned, he didn't care what happened to the rest of the Brotherhood as long as they left him alone.

He climbed out of the car and locked the door behind him. In the last three weeks, after having had the opportunity to think everything through in hospital, he must have flown around the world at least four times. But it had been worth it. Almost everyone he had spoken to had eventually agreed to the principle of his scheme. What's more, their response had reassured him that he had made the right decision. But after tonight's meeting he would definitely take a holiday. Just Holly, him and some sunshine.

He walked across the quiet atrium and greeted the two new guards. The sun had barely risen but he still revelled in the pyramid's space and light. He felt a sense of freedom here, a sense of no frontiers or walls to hold him back. He walked through the hologram of DNA that issued from the centre of the atrium, and headed for the hospital ward. He hoped he would find confirmation there of the choice he had made.

He crept into the silent ward and waved at the duty nurse smiling behind her desk. The small bulb above her head was the sole light in the slumbering darkness. In the gloom Tom could just make out the dormant shapes of patients in the seven occupied beds. With the stealth of a ghost he went from bed to bed staring down at their sleeping faces, registering the humanity behind each pair of closed eyes. Tom knew that at best the experimental therapy available at GENIUS would save three of them, perhaps significantly lengthen the life of one other. But even with the best odds, three would almost certainly die.

Unless *he* cured them.

In the semi-darkness he looked down at his hands, and at that moment Ezekiel's words came back to haunt him.

'. . . A *world in which anybody could heal everybody, and no-one ever died of natural diseases. Imagine a world where there would be no consequences*

350

for any actions we took. A world with such an enormous population that instead of a heaven on earth we would create a living hell. No space. No food. No respect for life – or death – and certainly not God. Just a crowded desert of lost souls assured of only one certainty – a long life of suffering.'

Perhaps the old man was right? he thought. Perhaps three of these unfortunate people *should* die? Who was he to interfere? He couldn't play God deciding who should live and who should die. But then the doctor in him spoke, telling him that if he could save patients then he must save them.

He imagined for a moment that each of these sleeping forms was Holly, and that he was their father, husband or son. He knew then that he had no choice when it came to these seven patients. But as he walked past their beds again, touching a hand here or a forehead there, feeling them draw the energy out of his body, he still felt a sense of disquiet. This was easy. Thinking again of the meeting tonight, he hoped that he'd correctly answered the *bigger* question; made the right *overall* decision.

He left the last patient and waved back at the nurse, wondering what her reaction would be in a few hours when her sleeping charges awoke refreshed and well.

Leaving the ward he made his way to the elevator and went straight to the second floor. Passing through the main body of the Mendel Suite he opened the door to the Crick Laboratory. Jasmine was sitting, Diet Coke in hand, poring over a pile of documents.

She looked up at him, her face lit up with pleasure. 'Hello stranger. How are you? How was your mysterious trip?'

'It was good. What are you doing in so early?'

Jasmine flashed an excited smile and patted the papers on her desk. 'Well, since your success with Holly, Jack and I have been busy filling in the first draft patent applications for the serum. Plus of course this.' She picked up a typed form from her desk, brandishing it like a trophy. 'The FDA application so we can go into trials. Jack's already signed it. We just need your approval and signature.'

Tom found her enthusiasm unsettling. He took off his jacket and hung it on the coat rack by the door. He walked over to the glass-fronted refrigerated cabinet at the end of the lab. Looking through the locked door he counted the phials left in the tray marked *Trinity Serum - Nazareth Genes*. Good, he thought, they didn't appear to have

351

been touched in the month he'd been away. There had originally been thirteen after the mice trials, one of which had been used on himself. This left these twelve phials; the only twelve in existence.

'What happened to your healthy scepticism, Jazz?' he asked, moving over to the drawer where the labels were kept. He opened them and checked there were enough. 'And what about your religious concerns? Now that Holly's safe I thought you'd be happy to put Cana behind you and get back to more conventional stuff.'

Jasmine paused. 'I've thought about this a lot, and believe that these genes aren't what made Christ the Son of God. How he used them, what he taught us and how he died for us were what made him divine. These Nazareth genes are the greatest discovery in medical history, a true gift from God, and as such should be used. Just think how much good we could do once we gain FDA approval and market the genes. After we mass-produce them—'

'Whoa, Jazz. We haven't even decided whether we *should* develop the Nazareth genes for wider distribution. You're making the assumption that it's a good thing.'

'Of course it's a good thing. How can it not be?'

Tom moved to the cupboard where the back-up hypodermics were stored. He quickly counted them and gave a small nod when he realized there were enough of them too. He'd be able to gather everything together discreetly, with no fuss or requisitions. 'All I'm saying, Jazz, is I think we should consider it very carefully.'

JASMINE COULDN'T BELIEVE HER EARS. HERE WAS THE MAN WHO HAD always said that the only constraint to what you can do, should be what you *can* do. Nothing more, nothing less. This was the man who had inspired her to help him invent a fantastic super-computer that could read DNA as effectively as a check-out scanner reads the barcode on a can of beans. The same man who had convinced her to trust him, and put aside her religious fears, to seek out and exploit the genes of her Christ in order to save her goddaughter. And now all of a sudden, after succeeding beyond his wildest dreams, he was saying 'Whoa, Jazz!' and getting nervous about *overreaching* himself.

'What's going on, Tom?' she asked, folding her arms across her chest. 'You have amazing power literally at your fingertips. But all we've got is a lousy twelve phials. We've got to make more of it, clone the genes and give them to others. We've *got* to spread the healing power. It's only right.'

'But who do we give it to?' asked Tom quietly. 'Or as Jack would have it, who do we *sell* it to? Just those who could afford it?'

'This isn't about money,' said Jasmine, horrified.

'I agree, it *shouldn't* be. But even if we ignore the greed factor, you must realize the economic implications. For a start, making the serum universally available would bankrupt every major pharmaceutical company in the world, causing shockwaves that could cripple whole industries, perhaps whole economies. But assuming we *could* control the financial repercussions, then who would you give the genes to?'

'Well, eventually everybody, I hope.'

'Everybody? So we can create a world in which anybody can heal everybody, and no one need die of natural diseases?'

Jasmine frowned, not sure where he was heading with this. 'Yeah, why not?'

'So we can create a world with such an enormous population that instead of becoming a heaven on earth it becomes a living hell? With no space. No food. No respect for life – or death.'

Jasmine's frown deepened as she listened to Tom. His eyes seemed far away as he spoke, as if he was reciting lines he'd read or heard from someone else. 'Well, perhaps we shouldn't give them to everybody,' she conceded, seeing some of the obvious dangers. 'Just some people.'

'Who?'

'I don't know.' And she didn't. She hadn't even considered the negative consequences. 'People who could do the most good, I guess. Like those in third-world countries.'

'Why? Because they could save the most lives there? Thousands, perhaps millions of people?'

'Yeah, I guess.'

'The same people who currently don't have enough food to feed the population they already have? Did you know that accidents, murder and suicide only account for five per cent of all deaths? This serum could eradicate all other causes, including ageing itself. Do you know how long that would make the average human lifespan?'

'No, not off the top of my head.'

'Well, I'll tell you. Given our current population, the *average* age we would have an accident, be murdered or commit suicide would be about six hundred years. Some of us might be run over by a bus on the day we were born, but others could live for ever. Just think about it. An average lifespan of six hundred years.'

She shook her head in frustration, trying to absorb the staggering implications. He was right of course. It wasn't as simple as she'd thought. She looked down at her FDA and patent application forms; the forms that would unleash this powerful secret gift of healing on an unsuspecting public. Twice she thought she had the answer and turned to voice them, but each time she thought of an obstacle and swallowed her words.

Eventually she turned, deflated, and looked at Tom standing quietly by the cabinet, staring at the phials of serum. He'd obviously gone through all these questions in his own mind already, and had reached some kind of answer himself. An answer that probably explained why three weeks ago, still far from recovered, he had leaped out of his hospital bed and jumped on a plane to God knows where; returning only a couple of days ago. There were times when Tom's genius could really tee her off. And this was one of them.

'Well?' she said eventually. 'I assume you think we should do something about the genes, right?'

He nodded coolly. 'Obviously.'

'But you don't think we should flood the world with them?'

He shook his head. 'Not until we know the ramifications. It could do more harm than good in the longer term.'

'It's not like you to worry about disrupting the natural order.'

A humble shrug. 'Perhaps I was wrong. Perhaps there is some method in the madness out there.'

She couldn't believe this was Tom Carter speaking. 'You mean God?'

A dry chuckle. 'Hardly, but perhaps old Mother Nature isn't quite as arbitrary as I thought.'

Jasmine drummed her fingers on the desk in front of her. 'So, maestro, what the hell *should* we do with the genes? Destroy them? Pretend we never even found them?'

Tom shrugged again. 'That's one option.'

'Tom, I was kidding. You can't seriously believe we shouldn't use the genes *at all*?'

Tom smiled at her then, and in his blue eyes she saw a spark of excitement. 'Do you really want to know what I think we should do with them?'

'Yeah.'

'Well, come here at midnight tonight, and I'll show you.'

AT 23:56 ALL WAS DARK WHEN JASMINE PULLED HER CAR UP OUTSIDE the closed gates to the GENIUS campus. She peered into the darkened gatehouse, but it was completely deserted. She was just about to get out of the car and open the gate using the DNA sensor when it suddenly opened for her.

She gunned the BMW into motion and drove under the full moon to the pyramid ahead. Pulling up outside the main door, she caught herself shiver in the warm night air. There were no visible lights on in the dark, glass pyramid, save for the dull glow in the atrium and a light on the first floor above her – where the Crick Laboratory and conference room were.

'This is too weird,' she whispered to herself, as if someone might overhear her. She had left work early after she'd realized she wasn't going to get any more out of Tom. Trying to fill the time, she'd immersed herself in mundane chores. But she'd kept on thinking of the genes, and Tom's response to her sarcastic challenge about destroying them by saying: 'That's one option.'

What the hell was he going to show her tonight? The only thing she could think of was Tom destroying the twelve remaining phials of serum in the sterilizing autoclave. Just the idea incensed her, and she had racked her brains all day and all evening trying to work out how best to use the genes, without abusing them. But the problem was proving far harder than any cyber-challenge she'd faced, and so far she'd come up with a big round zero.

She opened the car door and heard her feet crunch on the gravel. The main door was open when she reached it, so she walked straight into the dimly lit, deserted atrium. The DNA hologram writhed in the gloom like ghostly serpents. Beyond it she noticed that the doors to the Hospital Suite were open. Hearing only the clicking of her heels on marble she walked towards the open door. There was no light inside, so she pressed the switch beside the door, instantly bathing the waiting-room in light. Walking onward she came to the ward.

Again darkness. Not even a glow from the duty nurse's reading light. Nothing.

As her eyes became accustomed to the gloom she searched for the shapes of the patients lying in the beds. But there were none. Every bed was stripped. A neat pile of blankets and two pillows sat atop each bare mattress. Jasmine felt her heart beat a little faster as she turned round and walked back to the atrium. When she'd left this afternoon, she'd noticed some excitement outside the ward, but had thought nothing of it. Still, she knew that at least seven of these beds had been occupied with seriously ill patients.

When she walked back into the atrium she was so tense that the gentle whoosh of the elevator door opening five feet away made her jump. And when she saw Tom step out she was so relieved she wanted to hug him.

'Thanks for coming,' he said warmly, as if he was hosting nothing more unusual than a barbecue.

'What's going on, Tom? Where are the guards?'

A shrug. 'I wanted to keep this strictly between us.'

'What about the patients?'

Tom smiled and ushered her into the elevator with him. He pushed the button for the Mendel Suite and said. 'The official line is that they all responded extremely well to their treatments. And I for one am not going to deny it. Two have already gone home, and the others are now in Massachusetts General undergoing observation and tests. But I'm pretty sure that soon they'll be allowed to go home as well.'

'*You* made them well?'

He smiled and nodded. 'But I'll never admit it. It's vital that no-one knows I have the gift. I got a bit carried away this morning, but in future I'll be less dramatic.'

'Is that what you wanted to show me?'

The elevator stopped and the door opened.

Tom shook his head. 'No. That's just how I could personally deal with the genes. Hide the cures under the guise of conventional treatments.'

'What about the genes in general? What about the other phials?'

Tom led the way out of the elevator and turned towards the door to the Mendel Suite. 'Follow me.'

As Tom put his hand into the DNA scanner and Jasmine watched the door to the Mendel Suite open he began to talk about the genes:

'Just think how the serum works for a moment. The viral vector is designed to insert the Nazareth genes into an individual's stem cells. That means the person will have the ability to heal for their natural life. But they can't give their gift to anybody else, only the benefits. And since the genes aren't inserted into their germ cells they can't hand them down to their children. The gift therefore dies with them.'

Jasmine followed Tom through the door and blinked as the sensors triggered the tungsten bulbs to come on, revealing the large cryopreserve bank on the left, and the gleaming expanse of white and glass that made up the main lab ahead of them.

Jasmine frowned and said, 'But the gift wouldn't die with them if they had the technology to clone their Nazareth genes, or if somebody else with the know-how cloned the genes from them, with or without their permission.'

Tom nodded. He had clearly thought of this already. 'Yes, you're right. To control the spread of the miracle strain we'd need to ensure anybody who carried the Christ genes was trustworthy, and that their possession of the gift was kept secret.'

As Jasmine followed Tom through the eerily deserted main lab, she tried to think where he was leading her; both in terms of what he was saying and where they were going. 'Carriers of the gene would also need to be extremely responsible,' she said, 'or else they might abuse their power. They could only use the gift when it was absolutely necessary, and they could never tell anyone about it.'

'Or charge for it,' added Tom. 'That would be the worst abuse of all.'

'Tell Jack that.'

Tom chuckled. 'Oh, Jack's OK. He'd understand.'

She followed him round the corner to enter the first security door, and walked into the Crick Laboratory. The lights were on and when she glanced at the refrigerated cabinet she could see that the tray containing the twelve serums was missing. Jeez, she thought, he's already destroyed them.

As they approached the glass wall of the Crick conference room she thought she heard voices. She turned to Tom and opened her mouth to ask him what was going on, but he just smiled and put his finger to his lips.

'Don't worry,' he said, 'It'll all become clear soon.'

The voices were more audible now; the volume low but their tone excited. Most spoke English but in an array of accents; from Indian to Australian to Russian to African to Japanese to French. What the hell was Tom up to?

Then she saw them through the tinted glass of the conference room. There must have been over ten men and women milling around the large table. They were helping themselves to coffee and snacks from a trolley at the far end of the room, by the brooding Genescope.

'Who are they?' she asked.

'Look,' he said, pointing through the glass, 'surely you recognize some of them.' He singled out a short dark-haired man with large hangdog eyes, who was talking energetically with a tall Indian woman in a sari. 'That's Jean Luc Petit, the doctor who first gave me the idea for Cana. He's a good man, an extremely responsible man, to use your expression. The woman he's speaking to is Dr Mitra Mukerjee from Calcutta. You met her last year at the cancer seminar we held here. You remember! You liked her. You said she had integrity.'

Jasmine nodded slowly, still not fully realizing what she was seeing, but yes, she could recognize most of them now. Indeed, many of them were famous; Dr Joshua Matwatwe, the AIDS pioneer from Nairobi, Dr Frank Hollins, the radical heart specialist from Sydney, and Professor Sergei Pasternak, the Russian virologist. Plus there were others who were simply good doctors and nurses whom Jasmine knew Carter rated highly, as much for their compassion and commitment as their skill.

Jasmine was about to ask Tom why they were all here, when she suddenly registered the thirteen places set round the table. The place at the head of the table had just a pad and pen laid out in front of it, but the other twelve had a pad, a pen and two other items that made Jasmine finally understand Tom's plan. She gasped and felt a rush of blood to her head when she took in the single syringe and glass phial of serum laid out neatly by each place setting. If she looked closely at the phials she could just make out the handwritten labels bearing what appeared to be the name of each intended recipient.

'So,' she said eventually, trying to keep her voice steady, not sure how she felt, 'this is what you've been doing for the last three weeks? Flying round the world recruiting your twelve apostles.'

Tom smiled at that. 'I prefer to see them more as a jury, than apostles. A jury to help decide what we should do with this so-called miracle strain. The twelve are spread around the world. Most are doctors or nurses. But not all of them. The only common bond they all share is that I respect and trust each and every one of them, and their motives.'

Tom paused and took Jasmine by the arm, leading her towards the doorway. 'The way I see it is that the twelve should meet at regular intervals to keep track of how much good, or harm, we think we're doing. Then, if it's appropriate, we either make more serum and recruit more like-minded members, or keep the number to only twelve, replacing members as they die. And of course if it proves a disaster, we can simply abandon the whole scheme. This way we can at least control the effect the genes might have. Do good without tempting evil, if you like.'

They were now by the doorway and Jasmine felt dazed, not sure why she was here. As they entered, all the people looked towards them and smiled, then quickly made their way to stand near the place with their named phial.

Jasmine tugged on his sleeve and whispered, 'Tom, you've shown me your plan. I don't need to be here any more.'

His big blue eyes opened wide in surprise, then they creased into an incredulous smile.

'I thought it was understood,' he said. 'The Nazareth genes are as much yours as anybody's.' Then he gestured to the one remaining free place on the right-hand side of his own.

Jasmine turned, and there by the hypodermic was a small glass phial. On the label she could read a name written in Tom's scrawl; it was her name: Dr Jasmine Washington.

But before she could register the implications of possessing the genes herself, she saw Tom turn to address the others, all still standing by their places.

'Welcome,' he said, 'and thank you for coming. Before I continue I suggest you all sit down. There's something rather important I want to ask you . . .'

Epilogue

THREE MONTHS LATER.

THE TALL MAN DISMOUNTED STIFFLY FROM HIS HORSE. HE WAS NOT a natural rider, but a horse was useful to get to this remote place. He could have used a helicopter; he had access to almost limitless funds. The numbered accounts in the Geneva banks had shown him that. But he needed to search the area discreetly, and a horse offered him the required flexibility and anonymity.

He checked the ancient map – something he had also found in the bank vaults, just as his Leader had told him – and studied the five rocks rising steeply out of the desert sand. The place was deserted in the merciless sun except for the four men digging into the face of the middle rock, their pickaxes falling in rhythm on the hard surface. They had been working there under his instruction for the last two hours, but had so far found nothing.

He had studied the map intensely from every angle, riding around the rocks, comparing their configuration in reality with their counterparts on parchment. The symbol on the map was in exactly the same spot, relative to the real rocks, as the place the men were now digging. It had to be the right place. Admittedly it had been unused for over a thousand years, but it should still be there and it should still be serviceable, if the ancient engineers had been correct in their calculations.

He lifted the broad-rimmed Panama from his head and wiped the sweat from his bald head, before replacing it. Blinking through his thick round spectacles he walked towards the men.

Suddenly one of them stood and shouted something he couldn't quite hear. The man, naked to the waist, lifted his pickaxe high in the air and beckoned to him.

He broke into a run and hurried across the baking sand. 'What have you found?' he asked when he eventually reached them.

The stocky man who had wielded the pickaxe pointed into the hole they had dug. 'Father Helix, look!'

Helix looked into the hole and his heart beat faster. There was the unmistakable square shape of a stone lintel; a small doorway. Grabbing one of the men's pickaxes, he stepped into the hole and began to chip away at the rock covering the lintel. But it wasn't rock, only clay, designed to disguise the opening. After a few feverish blows he revealed the four foot tall doorway to the tunnel.

'A torch! A torch!' he demanded. The Brother with a curly, dust-covered black beard stood by an ill-tempered camel, laden down with panniers of equipment. He pulled out three large Maglites. Helix grabbed one of the torches and started into the opening.

Ahead, in the beam of the Maglite, he could see what was effectively a steep ramp. It dropped at a forty-five degree angle, with large ridges of rock carved into the floor like vicious, tooth-shaped steps. There was no handrail to steady himself, but every ten yards or so the ramp turned back on itself so if he did fall he would be stopped by the turn. But he had no intention of falling onto the jagged rocks underfoot.

'Be careful!' he called back to the two men following. 'I don't want any of you falling on me.'

The air was stale and the incline made his thighs ache, but he was so focused on his descent that he ignored the discomfort.

Ten steps. Turn. Ten steps. Turn.

He tried to count the number of turns to temper his mounting excitement, but lost track after forty. Just as he was beginning to despair of ever reaching the bottom, he saw something below him. He felt a tightness in his throat and turned off the torch. He could still see it, even this deep down in the rock. The light that twinkled like a beacon in the stygian darkness was unmistakable through the crack in the wall, and its white brilliance told him he wasn't too late.

With new energy rushing to his tired muscles he switched on his flashlight and hurried down the last ten-yard ramp till he was in a small space, four foot by four. Straight ahead was a stone door, beside it a heavy wooden lever. The lever was unnecessary, because the door had been riven from top to bottom, leaving a gap though which he could just squeeze. Through the gap beyond the door he could see the pure white flame burning even more fiercely than he remembered it.

Helix paused then, waiting for the two men to arrive gasping with wonder and exertion behind him. 'Stay here!' he said. 'When I've checked inside, I'll call you.' Then ignoring the disappointment on their faces, he pushed through the gap. As he entered the Vault of Remembrance he almost stepped into an ugly crack, six inches wide, that ran across the entire floor. The Sacred Flame issued from the other end of this fissure, illuminating a pile of charred remains in the doorway between the vault and the far antechamber. Helix knew that beyond that antechamber lay the remains of the Sacred Cavern where it had originally burned. He again thanked God for his deliverance when he remembered how he had escaped in the confusion of the cavern's destruction.

To his right was the covered recess containing the golden tabernacle and relics of Christ. The secret door he had just come through had looked indistinguishable from the wall when he had last been in the vault. Was it only four months ago that he had been here to collect the ritual oils and herbs with which to anoint Maria's body?

He looked around the vault. The rope-ladder was gone, only a charred trail of black marked where it had been. But aside from the blackened ceiling and the remains in the far doorway there was remarkably little damage. None of the artefacts on either side of the fissure had been harmed. Only the mighty sword appeared to have been touched by what had happened here. For some reason it was lying on the floor in the middle of the vault, its blade severed at the very point it crossed the fissure.

With hesitant steps he moved towards the burnt remains by the far door. He soon realized it was a man, and when he saw the

362

ruby ring on one of the clenched black fingers he knew who it must be.

Grimacing, he bent down and removed the ring of leadership, rubbing it on his shirt. After removing most of the soot he stared with wonder at the blood-red gemstone, its inner fire glowing like embers. The cross-shaped mounting of white gold had been superficially blackened, but was otherwise undamaged. With trembling hands he placed the ring on his own finger and was gratified when it fit perfectly. A rush of emotion suddenly welled up inside him.

When he had become Champion of the Primary Imperative he had been briefed on succeeding Ezekiel De La Croix. He had been shown all the mechanisms of Leadership; the Brotherhood's numbered accounts; the security boxes containing the ancient maps, the rollcall of members and the original documentation of the rules and objectives of the Brotherhood. But with the chaos four months ago he hadn't really *felt* that his succession had been legitimized, not until this simple act of placing the ruby ring on his finger. This digital coronation symbolized the passing of the mantle of leadership to him, and brought home the full impact of the duty and honour that now rested with him. He removed his thick glasses and rubbed the dusty sleeve of his cotton robe across his eyes before he realized they were filled with tears.

Composing himself, he pulled himself up, preparing to usher in the two Brothers waiting patiently beyond the fractured door. Then he noticed the smaller pile of ash next to Ezekiel's charred body, and an inch square of white cloth beside it.

His mouth went dry.

He had been so engrossed in the ring and his Leadership of the Brotherhood of the Second Coming, that he had momentarily forgotten the very purpose of that high office. Kneeling on the stone floor, he studied the pile of ash. Composed of black plains and contours, it looked like unravelled folds of charred fabric. He touched it and the pile collapsed into dust, all semblance of structure lost. Then he picked up the inch square of white cloth, one edge browned by flame. With exaggerated calmness he slowly brought the fabric to his nose. It smelt predominantly of smoke, but he immediately recognized another smell; the cloying aroma of the ritual herbs and oils.

This square of cloth was all that remained of the shroud he himself had helped prepare four months ago.

But as for the body that had been wrapped in it. There was no sign.

THE END

AUTHOR'S NOTE

ALTHOUGH THIS NOVEL IS SET IN THE NEAR FUTURE, MUCH OF THE technology is already possible.

Gene therapy has been around for years, as has the Human Genome Project, which is due for completion within the next half-decade, mapping each and every gene that specifies a human being.

Tom Carter's Genescope is a product of my imagination, but on 25 August 1996 the *Sunday Times* in London ran an article outlining the development of a 'gene machine capable of predicting people's lifespan and their susceptibility to serious disease'. This machine developed in America for pharmaceutical research is called 'Genechip'. It cannot yet read the entire human genome but is to all intents and purposes an early Genescope.

Similarly, Jasmine Washington's Gene Genie software is an extension of what is already being developed in the US by law enforcement agencies – the physical depiction of subjects from their DNA.

Science is moving ahead at such a pace that throughout my research I found the questions that most taxed the credibility rarely related to the future at all, but to the past.

Two questions in particular still keep me wondering:

Could a genuine biological relic of Christ be found today? And if so, what might it reveal?

Michael Cordy
London, December 1996